BEARS MAUL

July 20/17

BEARS MAUL

BEARS AND EAGLES FIVE

———

R.P. Wollbaum

First Published in Canada by Midar and Associates Ltd. 2016
Copyright © R.P. Wollbaum 2017
While some of the events and characters are based on historical incidents and figures, this novel is entirely a work of fiction.

ISBN: 1539484335
ISBN 13: 9781539484332

All rights reserved. No part of this publication may be reproduced, stored in a retrieval system, or transmitted, in any form or by any means, electric, mechanical, photocopying, recording or otherwise, without the prior permission of the publisher.
www.bearsandeagles.ca

Contents

Chapter 1 · 1
Chapter 2 · 12
Chapter 3 · 20
Chapter 4 · 26
Chapter 5 · 33
Chapter 6 · 38
Chapter 7 · 47
Chapter 8 · 73
Chapter 9 · 95
Chapter 10 · 130
Chapter 11 · 157
Chapter 12 · 163
Chapter 13 · 200
Chapter 14 · 236
Chapter 15 · 256
Chapter 16 · 263
Chapter 17 · 284
Chapter 18 · 291

Author's Notes · 319
Also by R.P. Wollbaum · 325

CHAPTER 1

ONE HUNDRED FIFTY OF THE regiment's cadets, in fatigues and well-worn combat boots, lounged about in small groups around the train platform. Their packed rucksacks had sleeping bags across the tops and M1 rifles leaning against them. Each trooper had a weapons belt with a 1911 CAP holstered on one side—with two extra clips—and an ammo pouch on the other side. Across one shoulder, each had another belt with ammo pouches carrying spare clips for the M1s.

Two men were seated in the front of a jeep parked to the side, both dressed in green army fatigues. The only decorations showing were a brass eagle on one shirt collar and the word *Canada* in an arc on one shoulder. Their shirtsleeves were neatly rolled up to just below the elbow, and dark-blue, almost black berets bore their unit's crest in brass. Both men appeared to be fit. The driver slouched behind the wheel with his head resting on the seat back. He was in his late thirties and well tanned. The man in the passenger seat was about the same age and, like the driver, slouched down but with his beret down over his eyes. He was a very big man with broad shoulders and the dark skin of a Native American.

The train from Calgary chugged into the station, and the cadets started forming up but were not yet shouldering packs. The regular daily train had two extra coaches today, and as it steamed to a stop at the station, Nicolas, the jeep's driver, used his toe to nudge the man in the passenger seat. "Right, Sleeping Beauty," Nicolas said. "It's time to say hello to the new boys."

Two distinct groups, each with fifty soldiers, came off the first coach. The first fifty were definitely British; twenty-five of those were army—one of whom was female—and the other twenty-five were split between the navy and the air force. The second group was Indian, some of whom wore turbans and some who did not. Both groups were dressed in fatigues and combat boots and ready to go, like their Canadian counterparts. The two contingents lined up in formations in the "at ease" stance.

Nicolas and Charley Red Cloud, the jeep's passenger, walked down the ranks, noticing most of these people had the looks of veterans handling their equipment with practiced ease.

"Getting a little long in the tooth for this, no, Colonel?" Nicolas said, standing in front of the lone woman, who was retying her boots.

"Up your arse, cousin," she growled back at him, grinning ear to ear. No one else was close enough to hear the conversation.

Nicolas kept strolling down the line as if nothing were amiss. The Americans piled out of their coaches, chatting noisily, lighting cigarettes, hanging around the platform or just milling about, and tossing their duffel bags to the ground in front of them. All were in class A uniforms and had unfastened tunic buttons, loose ties, and overseas caps slung through their belts. Instead of boots, they all wore shoes. The only exceptions were ten Marine Corps sergeants, who were lined up and at ease, their uniforms squared away. All the Americans had their ranks, badges, unit designations, and fruit salads.

"Fall in!" Charley growled just above normal conversation level.

The marines caught it and hollered, "Officer on deck," which got the Americans scrambling, buttoning tunics, tossing cigarette butts, and lining up at attention. An army major marched up to Charley, saluted, and started to speak.

"If God wanted candidates to speak," Charley growled, "he would have told me, and I would have told you. Back in line, candidate!"

Charley trooped the line, keeping the soldiers at attention with their duffel bags close by their legs. "Army Rangers and Force Recon," Charley sneered at the Americans, coming to a halt in the center of their group. "And whatever the hell a SEAL is. All big hotshots, eh? Right then." He used his parade-ground voice now. "You have two and a half hours to get yourselves and your gear to tonight's bivouac area. You will do it on foot and on your own. If you show up late or missing gear, you're gone. Now get!"

The Canadian cadets had shouldered their packs and rifles the minute Charley talked, and they were off in columns of four at a mile-eating jog as soon as he finished the order. The British closely followed, and the Indians went right after the British. The Americans, except for the marines, were a mass of bodies, flying into coaches and tossing equipment out windows. The marines stripped off their shoes. Three went into the coach and came out with armfuls of gear, and then another three replaced them. In short order, packs were packed, and even though the marines were still wearing class A uniforms, they had discarded their shoes and now had on combat boots. Slinging on their packs and rifles, the marines were on the road ten minutes behind the Canadians, Indians, and Brits. The army and the navy took almost a half hour to join the rest of the training class on the road.

Five miles down the road, in the center of the barrack's parade ground, Nicolas and Charley were once again slouched in the front seats of an almost-brand-new jeep. With the top and windshield down, they enjoyed the sunshine and ignored the tramp of two hundred pairs of boots entering the parade grounds. Charley waited until the last sounds stopped before cracking an eye open to slowly gaze at the gathered cadets, who were all at attention. Hearing more boots approaching, he waited until they stopped. "At ease!" he growled. "Smoke 'em if ya got 'em. Nobody leaves until the last cadet is in line." He put his cap back down over his eyes, leaned his head against the top of the seat, and went back to enjoying the June morning. "Ours, the Brits, the Indians, and the marines," Charley said under his breath to Nicolas.

In groups of ten or twenty, the other Americans arrived, some still with shoes on but all with their packs and personal weapons. With ten minutes left, twelve Americans were still missing. Charley nudged Nicolas, and the two came out of the jeep, stretched, and casually walked over to where all the trainees stood or sat on packs as they smoked or talked.

Ten of the missing twelve trainees pounded into the parade ground. Six were carrying a comrade on a rigged impromptu stretcher, while the other three carted all their gear. Five minutes to spare, they not so gently laid the prone member on the ground and stood with hands on their knees, breathing hard. "I'm afraid he overindulged on the train, sir," a sailor said in response to Charley's raised eyebrow. "We were expecting the next couple of days off. Nobody told us any different, sir."

Nicolas casually walked down the American line, making jokes and asking the odd man to see his weapon. He asked questions, like, "Where are you from?" and then gave the weapon back. He also made the same casual survey with some Indians and Brits, ignoring the Canadian cadets.

Ten minutes after the allotted time, an American major and captain appeared. Leisurely strolling into the parade ground, they walked up to Charley. "Good of you to join us, gentlemen," Charley said. "If you would be so kind as to proceed to that building there with the flags, some refreshments are waiting, and we will join you shortly." The two men smiled their thanks, strolled over to the headquarters office, and disappeared into its interior.

"Ten-hut!" Charley bellowed. He and Nicolas waited in the center of the group until all the other cadets were lined up and at attention. "The regiment will unload and clear weapons by fire!" Charley bellowed. The Canadian, British, and Indian troopers fired their rifles into the air, grounded them, and stuck the loaded clips into their pockets.

Nicolas marched up to the American trainees. "One demerit for being out of uniform, and one demerit for not having weapons and ammunition ready. You, last group, five demerits for not arriving in combat condition. The carried man gets two demerits for not being able to complete the mission on his own. You accumulate ten demerits, and you're out of here."

Nicolas continued. "You will have two demerits forgiven at the end of each week. Not completing a task means an automatic expulsion. You need to be mission ready at all times. In the real world, we get called out and are expected to be ready to perform no matter the time of day, the season, or the weather. That man," Nicolas said, pointing at the drunken SEAL, who was now standing, "could have jeopardised the whole mission and should have been left behind. None of you were in any condition to complete anything, except to die when you arrived here. The mission comes first, always."

Nicolas pointed first at the Americans and then at the British and Indian troopers. "The one hundred of you and you, all of you have your ranks and achievements; those you will not lose." He now pointed at the Canadian cadets. "Those cadets over there are fighting for a rank and even a position in our regiment. They are guaranteed nothing, and I assure the rest of you that they take this all very seriously and will not be happy if, because of something one of you does, they are awarded demerits. Is that clear, people?

"There will be some weekends, such as this one, when you will have no duties, but you are allowed only to go as far as town and must be back by twenty hundred each night until morning muster. I recommend being good little trainees, as most of the townsfolk have been through this training. You will definitely bite off more than you can chew if you cause trouble among the locals. Once a month, you will have from Friday dismissal until Monday muster to do what you will. Be one second late, and you'll receive eight demerits. Being over an hour late means dismissal from the program. Causing any trouble with the locals or being arrested is grounds for instant dismissal." He ordered, "Female candidates, front and center."

Twenty-five Canadians and one British candidate came forward. The Americans had not even realised any women were in the group. "Major Andrea," a woman's voice growled, "have you ever seen such a precious gaggle in your life?" She was tiny, just over five feet tall. Like Nicolas and Charley, she was dressed in green fatigues with trousers tucked into combat boots and shirtsleeves rolled up to just below her elbows. The same dark-blue beret covered her blond hair, the brass unit crest centered over the right eye. Unlike Nicolas and Charley, she had major's crowns on her epaulettes.

"Indeed, Major Ingrid," Andrea said. "I think if Grandmother were to see this group of princesses, she may well lose her breakfast in disgust." Andrea was dressed the same as Ingrid. She was just under six feet tall, her dark-blond hair also pulled tight to the rear of her head. A small scar ran downward from her right eyebrow, and from her similar facial features, she appeared to be related to Nicolas.

"Look at the pretty sailor boys grinning and smirking over there," Ingrid said. "Major Andrea, you know how I just adore sailor boys, especially after Sicily. I think we will add the sailor boys to our little group, do you think?"

"I completely agree, Major Ingrid," Andrea said. Her eyes narrowing, she walked up to a navy officer and stood with her nose a half inch from the man's mouth. "In Sicily, the American navy landed us ten miles away from our landing zone, and we had to fight our way back every inch of the way." She took two steps back and pointed at a barracks. "The left side is yours, squids. The right is the girls. You have ten minutes to get squared away and back here with full combat packs and weapons," Andrea ordered. "Ladies, you have the same ten minutes but require only running gear and water bottles to complete the ten-mile run."

"You can thank the squids for the nice run this afternoon, ladies," Ingrid said. "Now move! I have a hair appointment at four." The group exploded into action, disappearing into the barracks, and now no one was smiling or smirking.

"Captain Red Cloud here is in overall day-to-day charge of your training," Nicolas told the rest of the candidates. "He graduated at the very top of his group in the First Special Service Brigade. We do not own the skies or the water, people; we rely on others to provide us with that. But we do own the night You may perhaps have heard of us. The Devil's Brigade, the Germans called us. Captain, carry on while I dispense with some deadwood."

"The regiment has physical training for an hour, from five until six every morning. Everyone is invited to join in, but it is not mandatory," Charley said as Nicolas walked to the headquarters building. "At six thirty every morning, we do a five-mile run. That is mandatory. After the run, we have breakfast. Your names are posted on the board in front of HQ. Grab your gear, find out where your billet is, and remuster in the mess hall in an hour with your squads and fire teams."

As all the trainees moved to the bulletin board to find their billets, Charley turned to Ingrid and Andrea. "Majors, can I have a word? If we wanted the drunk one out, we would have cut him with the officers," Charley explained. "He should have known better, but the officers did not tell him what was expected. Have him clean the floor or something. I don't want him dying from dehydration. Maybe have Windsor watch over him. She'd give it a good try, but I don't think she's ready for that long of a hike yet."

"Oh jeez," Ingrid said, "I forgot about her. Thanks, Charley."

The cadets were returning. The sailors squared away their rifles and packs, and the women tied their hair out of the way. Andrea walked up to the drunken sailor, who was sobering up fast, but not fast enough. "Jesus, trainee!" she yelled into his face. "Did you leave any rum for anyone else? Christ but you stink! You, there." She pointed at the British trainee. "Take this rum sot, and hose him and his equipment down for ten minutes. He is then to dry the equipment out, and if he smells like a distillery when I get back here, you will join him under the hose."

"I can hear the queen now," Ingrid said in a whisper only Andrea could hear. "Laughing her bloody head off while the princess royal gets a soaking-wet T-shirt."

"May I see your orders please, Major?" Nicolas asked the American officer inside the headquarters building.

"I am only to hand these to the commander," the major said with a smirk, holding his hand out to stop the captain from giving his orders to Nicolas.

Nicolas said, "Let me introduce myself, Major. I am General Sir Nicolas Bekenbaum, VC, DSO, DSC, and, oh yes, Congressional Medal of Honor. Now your orders please, Major. Now!"

Nicolas grabbed them out of the major's hand and rifled through until he came to the appropriate section. The orders on dress and what to expect on arrival were clearly written, not missing as Nicolas had half suspected. He tossed the orders on the desk and held his hand out for the captain's, which stated the same thing. "Captain, were you aware of what is written here?" Nicolas showed the captain the page.

"Sir, yes, sir!" the captain barked.

"Yet you did nothing to warn your men?" Nicolas asked.

"The major forbade it, sir," the captain answered.

"Did you, now, Major?" Nicolas asked.

"Well, not really forbade it," the major answered. "More like I said to ignore it."

"You are in the habit of ignoring orders, are you?" Nicolas noticed a West Point ring on the major's finger.

"Well, Sir Nicolas, we all know some orders are just not that important, and besides, the captain could have informed his men if he really wanted to," the major said, smiling. "After all, I did not order him to ignore the orders. I merely suggested that he do so."

"Yes, I see now," Nicolas said, nodding sternly at the captain, who saw his career disappearing before his eyes. "Captain, would you indulge me and step outside for a moment? Please have Captain Red Cloud escort you back in here in two minutes."

After the captain stepped out, Nicolas turned to the major, not trying to hide his contempt. "I have met assholes like you everywhere I have served with Americans. You make your own rules to suit yourself, and when the shit hits the fan, there is always a fall guy close by to take the heat. Not this time, jerk off. I don't care who you are or who your daddy or uncle or whoever is—you're gone!"

Nicolas tossed another packet of papers at the major. "Those are your new orders and a train ticket to Great Falls. Someone from your army will meet you at the station. You can explain to them why you were sent home early. Oh, yes, the train leaves in an hour and a half, and the ticket is one way and nonrefundable. You miss the train, and you will be classified as AWOL. Now get out of my sight."

The two captains passed the major on their way into the building. Nicolas was reading the personal part of the captain's orders now. "I expected more from you, Captain," Nicolas said. "Your grandfather was a member of my grandfather's inner circle, and his advice was sought after and held in great respect. You graduated in the top ten of your class at Texas A&M and have shown a good grasp of light armour and scouting tactics. That you chose to become a professional soldier when you could have easily been a reserve soldier and made a good living with your engineering degree in civvy street also speaks highly of you. Explain?"

"No, sir. No excuses, sir," the captain said. "I should have found a way to warn my sergeants."

"Yes, well, we will be speaking with them and the other junior officers shortly. OK, eight demerits for being an idiot. The major had it in his mind for you to be his fall guy all along. I cannot punish you for missing the formation deadline, as you were following his orders. You have two demerits left," Nicolas warned. "You lose only a maximum of two per week. That is all the chance I will give you. Go to the bulletin board, and find out where you bunk. Dismissed."

"He won't last three days," Charley said.

"He's a Cossack," Nicolas said. "He'll make it or die trying."

CHAPTER 2

NOT ONLY DID HE MAKE it, but he and the drunken sailor, a petty officer, had not accumulated one more demerit point and were competing for the top American trainees' honours along with most of the marines. About half the rangers had left on their own, but all the sailors and marines were still there, as were the Indians and the British. By the start of November, the regiment's people had shaken themselves out, with five women and twenty men pushing to obtain their eagles. The rest were content with the service-battalion bear.

All the Brits, marines, and sailors wanted to try the final optional training exercise, along with about fifty Canadians. The Indian troopers, unused to the subzero weather, declined and had already left for home. The weather had, in its usual fashion, turned nasty around the middle of November and, not in typical fashion, stayed that way. It was going on the third week of minus-twenty-degree temperatures, and a major blow and snowfall seemed imminent. "They'll hunker down and let this blow over," Charley said. "It's too hard to move in this weather."

"If I was commanding that group," Nicolas said, "I'd hit this base in the middle of the blizzard." This final task for the candidates was an assault on the regiment's main barracks. No one had as yet succeeded in taking the barracks—but not for lack of trying. An assault in blizzard conditions might succeed. Visibility and hearing would be severely hampered during a blizzard, and both troops and weapons would need to stay warm.

"The only difference between a dust storm in Libya and a blizzard here is the temperature and snow," Nicolas said. "Sand would clog the engines and stop them and us because we couldn't breathe. Snow won't do that. The troops are acclimatised to the cold now and have enough clothing to protect them for the most part. They will only be in the open for the last two hundred yards or so anyway."

A number of high-ranking military officers from Britain and America were on hand to observe the final exercise. The British supplied a battalion of infantry who had been in Canada for other training. This battalion was to man the barrack's defences and defend against the candidates' assault.

Nicolas was up on the central guard tower at daybreak, glassing the area. The snow had started about two that morning, and now the wind picked up. Scanning slowly past the tree line, Nicolas saw something out of the ordinary and scanned back to his left until he saw it again.

"Charley," Nicolas said quietly, so the British defender could not hear, "your three o'clock about two hundred metres back in the trees."

"Just steam from a brook over there is all," said Charley.

"Make a note, Charley," Nicolas said. "Somebody left an engine running over there. Now scan down to fifty metres."

"Nothing there, Naj," Charley said.

"Beside the big tree, they forgot to camo the mortar," Nicolas said. "You can see the gunners, too."

"Whoa, shit!" Charley exclaimed. "You've got good eyes."

"Not really," Nicolas said. "Just know what to look for. They'll be moving to final positions. I doubt we'll see the troopers until they are ready to hit us."

"That exhaust cloud is moving, Naj," Charley said.

Nicolas could barely see the tree line now, as the snow and wind intensified. But something moved slowly across the open kill zone. Several small groups approached the camp's wire perimeter and the bottoms of the guard towers. All the figures were dressed head to toe in white. It was hard to see them, even from up high and looking right at them. From ground level or if they were not already being tracked, they would be invisible.

"You boys are dead, dead, dead," a voice said from the guardtower platform ladder just minutes later. Four troopers took up positions around the platform, aiming their weapons at the barrack's buildings. One trooper had a Browning .30-calibre machine gun, and another had a Bren. The trooper who had spoken held a portable radio to his ear, listened, and then reported his position taken.

Suddenly, smoke rounds from the mortars impacted around the fence's perimeter, and the machine guns and the Brens in all the guard towers opened fire. Just as surprised soldiers pelted out of barracks, armoured cars smashed through the gates to the camp and scattered with fire belching from mounted machine guns. A few of the cars set up a perimeter, keeping the machine guns firing, while the other cars swung sideways behind them and disgorged their troopers, who added to the rifle fire. It was all over quickly.

"Nice job, Candidate Windsor," Nicolas said. "I just might have to buy you a beer for this."

"You can bloody well buy me a hot rum toddy, you cheapskate," she said, laughing. "It's too bloody cold for beer."

"A proper introduction to George might be nice," the woman behind the Browning said.

"Oh, come on," the woman with the Bren said. "You were in the same class all the way through school."

"Captured by women," Charley said, shaking his head and pointing his finger at the British sentry. "And you better believe I am going to tell everyone, too."

"Come on, ladies," Nicolas said. "Let's get down from here before my old legs get too frozen to move."

Nicolas made sure he sat with the five women who had captured the guard tower and bought them a round of drinks to go with their heaping plates of hot food. Colonel Windsor was right at home with the younger women, laughing and sharing jokes. Her upper-crust British dialect had softened somewhat with exposure to the Canadian accent, and at times, she incorporated some German or Russian slang words members of the regiment used instead of English. Most of the British contingent still gave her a wide berth, treating her with more respect than a colonel would normally receive. The Americans generally stayed away from the Brits as much as they could but readily made friends with the Canadians.

Nicolas was enjoying the informal gathering with the young troopers when movement at the front door caught his eye. John and Tatiana, Nicolas's parents, stood there with a young woman in their midst.

Nicolas turned to Colonel Windsor. "Hey, cousin, you expressed an interest in seeing our communications center. Why don't we tear ourselves away from these youngsters, and I will show it to you."

The colonel had seen where Nicolas's eyes had gone and rapidly stood up, placing her back to the door. "Yes," she said, "let's go." He took her arm in his elbow, and the two cousins left the mess hall, fielding a few robust remarks, which they gave back with just as much relish. Walking back out into the blizzard, they buttoned up their jackets and headed over to Nicolas's office instead of the communications building. He held the door open for Colonel Windsor, and she removed her heavy jacket. She sat down, and he poured them both large glasses of vodka as she lit a cigarette.

"She really is pushing her luck, leaving home this close to Christmas," Princess Margaret, the British colonel, said.

"You'll be back home in twelve hours by air," Nicolas said. "It's not like the old days with trains and boats."

"I suppose so," the princess said. "Liz really wanted to come here and do this training herself, but that can't be allowed, so I came and had some fun instead."

"There are times when I feel sorry for both of you," Nicolas said. "You are always in the public eye."

"Having good friends like you is a big help," Margaret said. "You treat us like normal people and don't judge us. Having a place to come and be normal is a treat."

The door to the office banged open, and Tatiana (Nicolas's mother) and the Queen of England ran in with Katherine (Nicolas's wife) at their heels. They slammed the door behind them. "Bloody hell!" the queen exclaimed. She grabbed Margaret's glass and took a deep swig. "You were out in that?" she asked her sister.

"Gives one an appreciation for the weather back home, Liz," Margaret said.

"And you!" Tatiana said to Nicolas, pointing her finger at him. "You have no manners to leave our guest in such a manner."

"Come on, Mamma," Nicolas said. "If Liz wanted a state affair, she would have made arrangements a year ago, and we would be inundated by diplomats. Am I wrong?"

"Yes, that is true, Naj," the queen said, Nicolas was known as Naj to friends. "We would have to address each other as *Your Majesty*, *Your Highness*, and *ma'am*, and *sir*, and whatnot."

"How did you make out, sister?" the queen asked.

"Oh, the girls and I got along just famously," Princess Margaret answered. "The regular regimental lads were all right, and some of the Yanks. I stayed away from our lads as much as possible so as not to influence their training."

"And Naj?" the queen asked.

"She did all right," Nicolas said. "Of course some of our people figured out who she was, but out in the bush, it doesn't matter. You put out, or you die. It's that simple. She pulled her own weight, better than some."

"Not good enough for an eagle?" Margaret asked.

"Sorry," Nicolas said. "If you had served under fire with us, maybe then. That is one thing we will not just grant to anybody, no matter who you are. It has to be earned. You are good enough to plan and take part in Special Forces operations; even your own people say that. Not that you will ever be allowed to go out on any."

"Yes, can't have a member of the royal family in harm's way, especially a female," Margaret said.

"Perhaps we could make her colonel-in-chief?" the queen said. "Or myself? To honour the regiment's achievements?"

"We enjoy our anonymity," Katherine said, "but I believe we can accomplish a few things even at that. Margaret shares our interest in telecommunications. She could perhaps be the colonel-in-chief to the Signal Corps. That would make the Canadian government happy, and we are affiliated with the Signal Corps. As for you, Your Majesty, a group of our people used to be called the King's Loyal Legion. It was a cavalry regiment from your old German lands. They came to Canada with us and have kept the same traditions. They have just become an armoured reserve regiment, based in the next town over, Olds. We train and usually deploy together."

"I remember reading about them and their campaigns against Napoleon and in the Crimea," the queen said. "Yes, that sounds very good. I will rename them the King's Own Calgary Regiment, which will honour their past. I think the Calgary Highlanders should also be included. They contributed a battalion to the First Special Services Force, I believe, so I would be honouring them as well as your regiment. We will be coming to Canada on a state visit next year." The queen was now in formal mode. "We will make the formal presentations of the colonels-in-chief at that time. A special ceremony here will be also appropriate to honour your Korean adventures."

"On behalf of the regiment," said Nicolas, "I thank Your Majesty for all your kind wishes."

"Can we go back to the mess hall now?" the queen asked. "I want to try some of that hot wine you people make, and that beef smelled fantastic. I'm bloody hungry. All they serve us are small sandwiches and tea."

Two days later, all the graduates of the training program were heading out. The British were going back to Britain, the Americans were heading to their bases, and the Canadians were going to Fort Benning, Georgia, to complete parachute training. The queen and her sister were driven the following day in a Ford sedan to the Calgary airport, where a chartered private plane was waiting to take them home. Enough American oil executives and their families came and went on a constant basis to and from Calgary that little notice was given to two young British girls traveling on a charter plane.

CHAPTER 3

It was the end of June, and the regimental headquarters buzzed with more than normal activity.

"Have the boys join us!" John, Nicolas's father, ordered. Tatiana left to get them from the family house as all the regiment's officers gathered in the main mess hall. Earlier that day John had sent out the order to report, and now was the time to make preparations. All the regiment's active officer corps were in attendance. Some were in uniform, but most were not. Nicolas's two boys entered with their grandmother and stood against the back wall while she went to the dais to be with the senior officers.

"*Achtung!*" John called. He would be speaking German for this assembly. "We have intercepted some disturbing Soviet messages," John began. "The information on these messages has been backed up by other sources, and we have sent our information up the channels. The Russians are planning on installing nuclear-tipped missiles on Cuba. The Americans will never stand for this, and I fear a war is imminent.

"The Americans are discounting our intelligence"—this was greeted with the usual raspberries—"as well as our own government. The queen has requested a full mobilisation of all our

Alberta regiments. The supposed reason is to honour her regiments with a full parade. The reality is very different. A train from Red Deer will have two batteries on it. It will stop long enough to couple up the King's Own, and then it will go to Calgary to pick up the rest of the tankers and the Highlanders.

"We will load all three battalions and all our equipment at Medicine Hat, and we will pick up the rest of the batteries of the South Alberta Field Artillery and go to Halifax. There the Royal Navy, with some Royal Canadian Navy ships, will be waiting for us. Our final destination is the Canadian sector in West Germany, and we are to prepare for invasion by the Soviets. We go loaded for bear, brothers and sisters. Once again, we will be the sharp end of the stick."

The regiment off-loaded at Antwerp and then loaded onto trains to Bavaria. The cover story was that the regiment was there to take part in a joint training exercise with the German military. In reality, they were preparing for a Soviet invasion. The artillery batteries had come with them, but the tanks and infantry had first gone to England to participate in a parade to honour them, and then gone to Germany. John and Nicolas were part of the headquarters company that had been set up in England, and Paul, Nicolas's youngest son, being underage, was serving in the communications section attached to headquarters.

It was the first time Paul had been away from home for an extended period of time, and he was enjoying the sights and sounds of England. The regiment was billeted in an old fortress near the Dover cliffs and could hear the surf smashing the shore below. There were so many people in such a small area, and their English was hard to understand, as were a lot of the words they used. The people were nice for the most part and very patient with the young Canadians, who were trying to figure out how to make change to purchase things. Paul would turn eighteen next week and then be able to enjoy the pubs and other sites.

He wasn't worried about being sent to Germany. He didn't have an eagle, and since the regiment had more than enough communications techs, he wouldn't be needed over there. When he pondered it at all, he thought of his brother, George, who was commanding a company and would be one of the first involved if the Soviets decided to come across the border.

Most of the time, Paul copied code he heard over frequencies the regiment knew the Soviets used and then sent the messages to the crypto guys to decode. Some of the messages were sent in clear Russian, and he found those interesting as they normally concerned personal matters. Lately he was assigned as nursemaid to an RAF ensign, Charles Windsor, who was a year or so younger than he was. His family and Paul's were involved together somehow, and Paul was showing him around and answering any questions the young officer had. The ensign was training as a helicopter pilot and had a number of things to say about deploying troops by chopper. The two soon struck up a friendship, and the ensign arranged for Paul to go on a demonstration deployment of troops from a helicopter. While it was exciting, Paul saw a number of problems that could have arisen if the exercise had been a real deployment.

The second week of October, the visits from Charles Windsor stopped. Paul was on radio duty for twelve hours on and twelve off. The Americans finally discovered the missiles in Cuba, and shit had hit the fan. All the armed forces in Europe were on high alert, with airplanes continually taking off and landing, ships being deployed to patrol the sea lanes, and infantry troops all being mobilised. The world was on the brink of another major war, this time with nuclear weapons. The death toll would make previous wars seem trivial.

All NATO nations were on high alert, and there were constant air-raid, chemical, and radiation drills and raider-rappelling drills. In between the drills, which came at all hours of the day and night, produced never-ending copying of code to be done. After a week, Paul sensed an easing of tension among the brass. Drills within the regiment stopped, and joint drills with other regiments were ignored. "What does all this mean?" Paul asked Nicolas when they finally had a moment alone together.

"The Americans put some nuclear weapons in Turkey and Italy that could hit Russia directly," Nicolas said. "Then the Americans funded and supported a failed counterrevolution in Cuba, so the Soviets used that to pressure Castro into putting nuclear weapons on Cuba to threaten the United States. The Americans, rightly so, didn't like that too much and demanded the nukes be removed. I think the Soviets were thinking to make a deal about Berlin, but the Americans wouldn't budge. We came very close to another world war, and the Americans would have not had a problem with sending nukes to the USSR. The Soviets would have retaliated and invaded Europe through Germany. I think we would have beaten them, but it would have been messy. President Kennedy kept his head, and finally, the Soviets took theirs out of their asses and backed off. They got away with Hungary, Czechoslovakia, and the rest of Eastern Europe, so they felt they could start further expansion, but the Americans have drawn a line in the sand and said no more."

"What now?" Paul asked.

"I think the Americans are going to get involved in Vietnam and then probably some South and Central American countries," Nicolas said. "It is not in the regiment's or the family's best interests to become involved in those areas. The UN has asked Canada to send a battalion to Cyprus for peacekeeping duties, and the Department of National Defence has agreed to send our regiment, so that's our next move. What did you think of the helicopter idea?"

"It's better than using paratroopers," Paul said. "There's more precision in landing zones. The aircraft are vulnerable, though, and they are like aerial trucks. On their own, the troopers would have many of the same limitations as paratroops, but extraction of the troopers would be easier. They would be ideal for the special operations we conduct at times. We would need to develop new techniques and training."

"Yes, and more cash outlay for machines and pilots," Nicolas said. "The regiment will have to think about this for a while. We have stayed away from the military aviation side of things."

"When we get back home," Paul said, "maybe I can contact some helicopter manufacturers for information."

"Wouldn't hurt," Nicolas said. "Don't forget you still have your advanced training tour to finish and your mandatory service."

"Not a problem, Pop," Paul said. "I like being a signals tech and have a few ideas I'd like to explore in that area. The helicopter research will be part of my service time. I don't plan on pursuing an eagle anyway. If I get one, I get one, but it is more important to the regiment that I find out as much as I can about how we can utilise the helicopters to our advantage and to obtain better communications." Paul looked at his watch and excused himself, as his shift in the code room was about to start.

"He's pretty mature for eighteen," John said. "I caught only the last bit of that."

"That's what you get for sleeping in," Nicolas said. "I won't push him about the eagle. He is right. At the moment, he is more valuable to us doing what he is doing. I was also thinking we could use the helicopters in our pipeline and oil-patch operations."

"Yes, that is much the same dilemma I faced—becoming mechanised versus using horses," John said, "It's not quite the same though. I think we will still need the ground vehicles for most activities. But the idea of an aerial troop deployment is a good one, as long as we can support it quickly. Look what happened at Arnhem. That proved airborne troops have limitations."

"Our commitment to Fabrique Nationale is paying off," Nicolas said. "They are looking into purchasing Browning, so it's a win for us both ways. Most NATO countries and Commonwealth countries are adopting the FN FAL as their battle rifle, so our investment will pay off shortly."

"Good, we need to pay for our own rifles, you know," John said. "What about the decision to convert to the M111? I am not sure about using tracked vehicles."

"We need about two hundred of them," Nicolas said. "Maybe make it three hundred. Leasing them is the way to go. DND, the Department of National Defence, is already unhappy about tracked vehicles and is looking into wheeled versions—a Swedish and a German design. We should hedge our bets and invest in both companies."

"OK," John agreed. "We should look outside the United States more now in any case. Speaking of that, the Saudis have requested a meeting with us—something about Yemen."

CHAPTER 4

"SIR JOHN, SIR NICOLAS," SAID the Saudi ambassador, "I am so glad you could join us."
They were meeting in the main dining room of one of the best hotels in London. It was well known that the Bekenbaums had pipeline and refinery operations in Saudi Arabia, and business meetings between the family and the Saudis were generally held informally. Today two members of the ruling family joined the ambassador, and this normally meant something of import was going to be proposed.
"Mr. Ambassador," John said, "it is always a pleasure. Our mutual agreements have been profitable for both our countries. May I introduce my two grandsons, George and Paul?"
"Ah, they are much the same age as you and I were back in the day," the ambassador said. "It is always good to start the family in the right direction."
The next hour was spent asking after one another's family members and talking about how things were going in their various joint ventures. Pleasantries were exchanged during the meal, and the atmosphere was in line with two friendly families out for a social dinner. Once the meal was concluded, the ambassador got down to business. "The Soviets have been interfering

in Yemen," he began. "We have intervened, but the UN is not pleased and has ordered a cessation of hostilities. We asked for a buffer zone to be established between our two countries and to be patrolled by the UN. We would like you to be the initial UN force."

The Canadians glanced at each other but did not respond.

"You have done service for us in the past," one of the princes said. "We trust you. We also know from our business dealings that you are tough but fair. We have already asked the UN and the Canadian government, and they gave us permission to approach you."

"We are flattered, gentlemen," John said. "We have already committed a battalion to Cyprus for similar duties. I am not sure we can afford to place another battalion in the field, because of both cost and labor."

"The Canadian government has told us of your agreement with them," the second prince said. "We have agreed to pay the Canadian government all the fees they would normally pay you while you are in the field. In addition, we will pay you directly and supply you with whatever you require."

"We will have to verify with our government and the United Nations first," John said. "Then we have to get permission from our people."

"We understand that," the first prince said.

"You also should understand this," Nicolas said. "We will be working under the UN mandate. That means if your people screw up, they will suffer the consequences—not only the Yemenis. If that is going to be a problem, we had best not get involved."

"We understand that," said the second prince. "We really do not wish to be the region's policeman. It was a mistake to get involved in the first place. You will not have problems from our side."

"If we can keep our commitment to no longer than a year," John said, "you probably have a deal. We will arrange transport of the second battalion from Germany and coordinate with the UN."

"Very well then," said the first prince. "We will send the draft agreements for your approval this afternoon."

"Thank you for your consideration," John said. "Perhaps some more coffee or tea?" Now that the business at hand was complete, the men sat back in their chairs and relaxed, enjoying their coffee.

"I see that, like our father," the second prince said, "you keep your family involved in your affairs. What are your sons training for, if I may ask, Sir Nicolas?"

Nicolas nodded at George, who spoke. "At this time," he said, "I wish to pursue a career with the military side of the family. Things may change at a later date, but this is the path I wish to follow."

"The path of the warrior," the second prince said. "Not many of you westerners follow that path. What of you, young Paul? Have you chosen a path yet?"

"Everyone must serve five years in the military, sir," Paul said. "I will follow the supply and services end of things. The regiment tends to follow new trends in communications and transportation, and I will be involved in both those areas. We are researching some new transportation options that may be helpful in our commercial areas, which have always been a focus for us. In addition, along with my brother George, we will evaluate some weapons upgrades. Again, we are focusing on what will be best for the regiment as well as the companies the regiment encompasses."

"Sir Nicolas," said the ambassador, "we have noticed you are switching from the Garand to the FN FAL and not the M14. We are also debating what to replace our outdated weapons with. Is this a personal preference or—"

"A little of both, Mr. Ambassador," Nicolas said. "Springfield will not licence us to build the M14, and it is actually not quite the weapon the FN is. Fabrique Nationale has taken control of whatever stock the regiment did not control of Browning, and they allow us to keep producing the firearms under licence for our own needs and for export."

"Perhaps an evaluation by our procurement people can be arranged?" the first prince asked.

"We will send Paul and a few helpers over for your tests," John said. "If I may make a suggestion, perhaps representatives from Springfield can be present as well. Then you can put both weapon systems through their paces side by side."

"Ah, the Americans will not be pleased," said the first prince with a smile. "They feel we must take all of their offerings sight unseen. Yes, that suggestion is acceptable. I also understand that you are developing some all-wheel-drive armoured vehicles with a Swedish firm?"

"Yes," said Nicolas. "We are not happy using M111 tracked vehicles. They are noisy and costly to maintain, and they cause more damage to roads than is offset by the advantage the tracks give them. Our regiment's role is scouting and mounted infantry. We feel this can be better accomplished with wheeled, not tracked, vehicles."

"If you would not mind sharing your findings with us," the first prince asked, "we have learned that our dealings with you have always been profitable for both parties. Perhaps a joint venture?"

"We will have to discuss that with our government," John said, casually cupping his left ear with a hand and rubbing an eye with the other. "We must follow their export rules."

"Yes, we understand," said the ambassador. "That is as it should be. We will have our diplomats contact your government and find out whether this would be possible."

"Again, Mr. Ambassador," Nicolas said. "We advise that you invite all other major players to compete for this tender. This way you are sure to obtain the best equipment for your requirements."

"This is why we like to do business with your people, Sir John," the ambassador said. "You are honest and honourable. Again, we will follow your advice in this matter." Business now over, the men talked about other shared interests—horses were at the top of the list.

It was late when the four Bekenbaums returned to the barracks allotted to them, and the elders invited the younger men in for a drink. John poured liberal portions of vodka. "George," John said. "You will be assigned with your battalion to Cyprus. It is a peacekeeping mission, but we feel a combat-ready battalion will have more of an impression on the belligerents. The Turks already respect us, and I am sure you will gain a rapport with the Greeks in short order. This will be a six-month deployment. After a month-long leave, you will then be sent to train with the Seventh Cavalry in airborne deployment. You'll possibly be deployed to Vietnam after that, but we are not sure at this point."

"Paul," Nicolas said, "you and your battalion will deploy to Saudi Arabia from right here in Britain, most likely by the end of the week. Orders will be issued tomorrow to your officers. You have earned a commission, if you want it."

"I would rather not, Father," Paul said. "There are others who, like George, want to make the military their careers. They should have the commissions, not me."

"All of us respect you for that, Paul," George said, "but understand that sometimes in order to be heard and have your findings taken seriously, you need to be an officer."

"Look, George," Paul said, "I can do the studies and make the reports. The officers in charge can review the reports and studies and submit them. I don't care for recognition. I just want to get the job accomplished."

"Well, even an enlisted man needs a little rank," John said. "You already have enough time in grade to become a junior warrant officer, so that's what it will be. You will still be a noncommissioned officer, but you'll have enough rank to be taken seriously."

"The family does a lot of business with the Saudis," Nicolas said to Paul. "The Brits are also sending some people to Yemen, and we want you to link up with them as well. You probably already know some of them. They will be an SAS, Special Air Service, squadron. We will send you three of the vehicles we want. You are to treat them hard, and we will do the same back home. This way we can evaluate the vehicles in most of the climates we will face if we need to deploy."

"Once we have selected a vehicle," John said, "we will augment the electronics package with one of our own. That is not to be divulged to anyone else. We may make some of it available to the DND later but not all of it, so keep that quiet."

"A great deal of not only the family's but also the colony's funding comes from projects like these," Nicolas said. "Our companies may do the research in some cases, but in others we will do the testing for another company's research. Then we will fund a joint venture with a private or public firm to produce the product we have developed. So these projects are important, boys.

Your training and deployment with other countries are designed not only to improve or develop our skills but also to explore new avenues for revenue for the colony."

"Are we not worried that we may lose our special status with the Canadian government?" George asked.

"Not really, son," Nicolas answered. "First of all we have a royal charter, which is recognised and signed by the Canadian government. Essentially we are a country within a country. As long as we comply with our end of the charter, no one can do anything about it. We do not ask the Albertan or the Canadian government for anything. We supply our own funding for hospitals and schools. We have our own telephone system and our own natural gas and power supplies, and in fact, we export a lot of the gas and oil. If our companies operate outside the colony, we pay business and property taxes, like other citizens, for the portion of profit made in that particular venture. We supply, at a minimum, one active battalion and one reserve battalion of troops for use by the DND. We train and equip the battalions ourselves and receive compensation only when we are actively deployed. The money we save the DND outweighs what the government would receive in taxes if they chose to renege on the charter."

"Once in a while, a new government may try and challenge us," John said. "We expect the new Liberal government to do so anytime now. Once again we will have to flex a little muscle, and then they will leave us alone again."

CHAPTER 5

PAUL LOUNGED IN THE PASSENGER seat of his assigned jeep. His soft cap was pulled down over his eyes and his feet propped up on the windshield, which was folded down on the jeep's hood. A CAP was holstered on his left hip, butt forward; an FN with a double clip was in a mount on the dash next to his left leg; and an FN modified as a crew light machine gun was mounted on a stand in the backseat, with a two-hundred-round ammo box fed into the receiver. He watched three RCAF Hercules transport planes taxi over to the area where he and an American-built Dodge deuce-and-a-half cargo truck were waiting. The six men in the back of the truck stirred themselves up, and the lieutenant in charge of the detachment came out of the cab, stretching and yawning.

As usual when dealing with peacetime armed forces, arriving at the given ETA had resulted in a four-hour wait at the airport. *At least it's been a cool day,* Paul thought. *Sitting out in the open in forty-degree Celsius temperatures would have been brutal.*

He had only three months left of his last deployment to the desert bordering Yemen and Saudi Arabia, and it would be spent doing the last desert evaluations of the regiment's planned upgrade vehicles. As the transport planes reached the unloading area, they began their shutdown sequences, and one by one, their rear hatches opened up. Out of the first two airplanes came similar armoured vehicles. One was slightly larger and had six wheels to the other's four. Both had turrets; one mounted a 20.00-millimetre cannon with a 7.65-millimetre machine gun beside it, and the other had a .50-calibre machine gun instead of the twenty-millimetre cannon. Each vehicle had a new type of machine gun mounted on a pylon next to the crew commander's hatch.

Out of the third airplane rolled a Volkswagen-made jeep replacement in desert camo, and it had the same new machine gun mounted in the rear. Just as Paul and his driver stood to take possession of the jeep, another vehicle was pushed out of the aircraft. This one was a helicopter; its rotor blades had been removed, and a group of twenty-four people pushed it out. Sixteen of them had eagles on their collars, and eight had bears. As soon as the helicopter reached the ground, the eight bears headed over to another Hercules plane, collected rotors out of it, and installed them on the helicopter.

Instead of walking over, Paul and his driver sat on the hood of their jeep, watching the group around the helicopter. A voice came from behind them. "Well, what do you think of our new toy?"

"Overpriced, underarmoured, and expensive to maintain, Dad," Paul answered. "I thought we discussed this already. Good to see you, by the way. How are Mom and the gang?"

Paul and his driver came to attention and saluted Nicolas before he shook hands with both of them.

A tall lanky female civilian in jungle fatigues was standing beside Paul's father. Her long dark hair was pinned up inside a soft military cap, and her jacket had Seventh Cavalry and US Army patches on its shoulders and breast pocket. "This is Emily

Hershmire," Nicolas said. "She is a reporter for the *American Press Association*, doing a story on us peacekeepers."

"Ma'am," Paul and the driver said, nodding at her.

"Why don't you take the lady over and look at the Huey, Bob?" Nicolas asked the driver. After she left, he said, "Bloody politicians. Damn Liberal Party is always trying to get on the news. They are trying to get us to go into Quebec, but we are refusing."

"Nasty business that," Paul agreed. "That's all the country would need—one of us westerners shooting a Quebec nationalist. I suppose the government is still trying to renege on our charter and our rights?"

"All they see are the taxes they think they are losing," Nicolas said. "Our tax people are meeting with them right now to show them the facts of life. We have determined need for the helicopters, Paul—not in a traditional role like what the Americans are doing in Vietnam but more of an urban or antiterrorist role. Rapidly deploy, hit a target, and get out. We'll still keep our original role. We just want to augment it."

"OK," Paul said. "Before your hotshot airborne troopers get too cocky, I want to show them something. I assume most of them are new guys?"

"Yes, most of them are," Nicolas said. "They had to qualify to get into the program and bypassed everything else. They are exclusively training in this role."

"OK," Paul said. "Have my equally new lieutenant distribute the men who are not flying to camp among the vehicles. You and I are commandeering the new jeep."

After waiting for crews to unload all the mail and other supplies and then secure the airplanes, the aircrews jumped into the trucks, and the group—minus the helicopter crew, troopers, and the reporter who was going to fly into the base—headed out toward the camp.

Early the next morning before breakfast, the helicopter crew and the reporter went to the firing range, where a Lynx scout car sat. Two hundred metres down range from the Lynx was an old Mercedes car.

Nicolas and Bob, his driver, were sitting on the front fenders of the Lynx when three trucks carrying the helicopter people came into the range. The new jeep came with them. Nicolas was driving, and the reporter sat beside him.

Paul waited until all the helicopter people had jumped to the ground and were standing around, smoking and talking. Nicolas and the reporter walked over to the Lynx. Paul nodded to Bob, who climbed into the commander's turret of the Lynx and cocked the .30-calibre machine gun mounted there. This got everyone's attention.

"That Mercedes down there," Paul said, "is about the same size as your Huey. It has a sheet-metal body instead of an aluminum body like your Huey has, and the metal is thicker than on the Huey."

Paul waved his arm, and Bob stitched up and down the Mercedes's side, with a wild grin on his face. He stopped after the two-hundred-round belt was empty. "That was only a thirty-calibre machine gun," Paul said. "Go ahead. Have a look."

The men, accompanied by the reporter, went down to look at the destroyed Mercedes, laughing and whistling at the level of devastation. Paul gave them ten minutes and then honked the jeep's horn and waved them back. Bob climbed back into the Lynx, disappearing into its interior.

As soon as the group joined Paul beside the Lynx, the twenty-millimetre automatic cannon mounted in the turret opened up, hitting the Mercedes with every shot. Pieces of the car flew off in all directions, and the vehicle caught fire.

"Before you hotshots get too big for your pants," Paul said, "that is what will happen to you and your fancy Huey if you are caught in the open." Then he climbed into the Lynx and fired it up. Bob reloaded the .30 calibre. Paul let out the clutch and sped off, and Bob emptied another belt into the burning car as they passed it.

CHAPTER 6

"You are not an officer or a combat trooper, but all of your family members are and always have been," Emily said. She sat beside Paul in the cramped interior of the six-wheel vehicle they were testing. She had been with the regiment for over a month now, spending most of her time with the helicopter eagles. This was her first time coming along on a ground patrol.

"My brother is the soldier," Paul said. "My five years are up after this tour, and I'll go back to being a part-time soldier and full-time civilian."

"You don't agree with the family tradition?" she asked.

"Not at all, miss," Paul said. "I will still serve if required, but the family and I agree that my real talents are required elsewhere."

"What would those talents be?" she asked.

"Oh, we are just poor farmers at heart," Paul said. "I want to try my hand at improving our cattle herd and possibly spend some time out in the oil fields. I'm not much different than most people my age."

"Yet your family history, as well as the regiment's history and your community's involvement in the regiment, suggest otherwise." Emily kept pushing.

"When members of our community are called, we all will serve," Paul said with a sigh. "But some of us would like to have a somewhat normal life. That does not mean we do not appreciate the members who wish to remain in the service. It's quite the opposite, in fact. Not all of us are cut out to be frontline soldiers, and unlike other people in Canada, we know it."

Before she could ask more, Paul raised his hand and put it on his headphone. He keyed in his mic to acknowledge the transmission and keyed the intercom to the driver, giving her instructions. She swung the wheel to a new heading and floored the accelerator. "Seems to be a disturbance about ten miles east of us," Paul said. "HQ wants us to check it out." Along with the other six people in the crew compartment, Paul put on his web belt. He made sure he had a full clip in his assault rifle and that reloads were close at hand on his webbing.

"I thought you Bears were not combat troops," Emily said.

"There are no noncombatants in the regiment," Paul answered. "All of us have to achieve minimum standards to stay in the regiment."

The lieutenant in the commander's position slid down, slamming the hatch after her, and a sound like hail hitting the side of the vehicles could be heard. "Shit! Contact front, contact right, contact left!" she yelled as she pulled the turret around to the right. After getting a sight picture, she fired a three-second burst from the cannon and then traversed left.

"Driver, lower the ramp. Dismounts, MG to the front, rifles to the front, left, and right. Flank left," she ordered. The ramp in the rear of the vehicle crashed down, and all the troopers but Paul erupted from the back of the vehicle.

Paul put his hand on the reporter's shoulder and pushed her back into her seat. "You stay right here," he ordered. "This is no exercise, and it's not playtime."

Scrambling out, he cleared the rear of the vehicle and squatted down, getting his bearings. The section had followed their training—half of them were laying down a base of fire to the left of the vehicle, while the other half advanced on the enemy. The cannon and machine gun mounted on their vehicle hammered away now at the front of the vehicle. Paul touched two men on the shoulder and had them join him to watch the right side. Soon enough fire from the right slacked off, and Paul saw figures run away. He shot two, and the rest threw down their weapons and went to their knees with their hands behind their heads. The shooting was soon over. Troopers rounded up living enemies and herded them to an open area, where members of the section and the vehicle's machine guns covered them. Paul directed remaining members of the section to help the wounded or collect the dead, while he plugged into the command broadcast net to make his report.

Paul heard a helicopter approach, and by the time it landed and the troops inside jumped out, the enemy had been subdued and the wounded treated. Paul had the worst of the wounded placed in the helicopter, and it took off in the direction of the field hospital. Its troops were left on the ground, looking for something to do. The next two helicopters to arrive were white with UN markings. They landed, their passengers disembarked, and the rest of the wounded were loaded into those copters.

"These insurgents raided a village about five miles from here," said the Indian major who had come in a UN helicopter. "A Yemeni village, not a Saudi one."

"You'll probably find they are communist freedom fighters," Paul said. "They all have Soviet weapons and uniforms. Ten are dead, twenty wounded, and we have sixty prisoners."

"Did your people sustain any casualties?" the Indian major asked.

"Some chipped paint, and it looks like we have a flat tire. I have a few burn marks from the expended shells," Paul said.

"Jesus," Emily said. "You said your people are not combat troops. What would have happened if you were?"

"There'd be ten wounded and ninety dead," Paul said. "Yo, somebody get this bloody tire changed. I want to be home for supper."

"He's not boasting," the Indian major said to Emily. "Paul shows a remarkable amount of self-restraint. His troopers could have quite easily killed all these men, especially after what they just did to that village. This regiment is very well trained. They go from a firefight back to being policemen in a heartbeat. The Canadians are the best at this, and this regiment is the best of the Canadians."

Back at camp Emily asked the test vehicle's commander, "You don't mind taking orders from a noncommissioned officer? Or is it just that you are a woman?"

"Not at all," the lieutenant said. "We don't operate like that in the regiment. Paul was the most qualified, and we automatically deferred to him. Rank doesn't matter in a firefight, and honestly, Paul should at least be a major. He has the knowledge, training, and mind for it."

"This man is such an enigma," Emily said. "In America he would be in high demand as an officer. Yet, here, he is happy not to be. I will have to look into this more deeply."

"Not to mention he's about as cute as a guy can get," the lieutenant said. "Most of us would give our eyeteeth to catch him. He's got a brain as well as a bod. You better watch you don't fall under his spell and get your heart broken."

"He's not taken?" Emily asked.

"Nope," the lieutenant said. "Not for a lack of trying, I can tell you. We've all had a go at him."

"He's not, um...a little—"

"Who—Paul? Likes men? Not!" the lieutenant said. "He's left his fair share of broken hearts behind him, believe me. Not that we women didn't know better. No, he's looking for Mrs. Right is all, and he hasn't found her yet. Maybe you should give it a try. You could do worse out here in the middle of nowhere." The reporter turned beet red and walked away, but she didn't take her eyes off Paul.

"Mind if I join you?" Emily asked, holding her tray of eggs and ham. She was standing beside Paul's table.

"Suit yourself. There's lots of room," Paul said. He was sitting with his driver Bob and two other corporals, having breakfast in the junior ranks' mess. Unlike the officers' mess, which had individual tables and waiters or waitresses, the junior ranks' mess was buffet style. Long tables could seat twenty, with benches ranging down both sides.

The corporals resumed their conversation as she sat down. "I'm telling you that new Mustang is going to blow anything GM has out of the water," one said.

"No way," said another. "The Pontiac GTO is the fastest thing on two wheels. That puny 289 in the Mustang is a joke. What do you think, Miss Hershmire?"

"I think the Mustang is cute. I am buying one when I get back to the States," she answered.

"Well, I think that will be the end of the Mustang for us, eh, boys?" Bob said to the nods of the two corporals. "Cute doesn't cut it. Well, boys, we have some work to do before the sarge there comes out to have a look at the beasties. Nice to see you again, Miss Hershmire."

Paul sipped his coffee and watched Emily tuck into her pancakes, eggs, and ham. *She's kind of cute herself,* he thought. *Too bad she's so stuck up, hanging out with the officers all the time.* "The OC's not open yet?" Paul asked.

"Actually the food here is better," she answered. "By the time the food gets from here to the OC, it's generally getting cool. No, I wanted to spend some time with the regular people. Sometimes officers get a little high on themselves."

"Just the rookies fresh out of the RMC, Royal Military College," Paul said. "It takes them a few months to get back to normal when they first rejoin the regiment. Thankfully not many choose that route."

"You have your own training regime, I hear," Emily said. "You allow women not only to serve but also to serve in combat roles. That is not the norm in the Canadian military."

"Far as I know, outside of Israel, it is not the norm anywhere," Paul said. "This is the way it has always been in the regiment, since it was first formed."

"The Canadian government has no say?" she asked.

"Not really," Paul answered. "We have to supply a certain amount of bodies up to a maximum. The agreement does not specify gender or age."

"How many people can you supply?" she asked.

"In a full-out emergency, around ten thousand," Paul answered. "They would have firearms, ammunition, uniforms, and rations for one month. Transportation and armoured vehicles would be another issue. We have enough only for two battalions with modern weaponry and another two with out-of-date equipment. When we mobilise, we come fully equipped with our own medical and logistics teams. It is up to the Canadian government, or in this case, the UN, to make good on our expenditures in fuel, food, and so on."

"Why doesn't your regiment have a name or designation?" she asked.

"We call ourselves *the regiment*. We usually assume the name of the regiment we are attached to, in this case the fourth battalion of the PPCLI. Our battalion in Cyprus is the fourth battalion of the Lord Strathcona Horse. Some of the people we are attached to call us the EBBs."

"EBBs?"

"Eagles, bears, and beavers," Paul explained, pointing at his shoulder flash, "like on our crest."

"I know Eagles are your combat arm and Bears are your service arm, but what are beavers?" she asked.

"So many questions," Paul said, draining his cup. "We added the beavers and maple leaf after our people came to Canada. If you will excuse me, I have to make sure Bob and the gang have not ruined my new toys."

"I was hoping that reporter would be long gone by now," Paul said, climbing into a German jeep. "She's beginning to be a pest."

"American journalists," Bob said. "They're always a pain in the ass."

"Take me to our airborne brothers, if you please, Smithers," Paul said in a put-on British accent. As they took off in a cloud of dust, Emily ran up, just a little late.

Paul and Bob pulled onto the helicopter pad just as the morning patrol was climbing aboard the Huey. The pilot started the engine, and the rotors picked up speed. The Huey took off in a roar of noise and was soon over the horizon.

Paul and Bob walked over to the tent that served as the group's office and went in.

"Could I have a moment of the captain's time?" Paul asked an officer, who sat behind a desk with his feet propped up on it.

"Sure, Paul, what's up?" the captain asked. "Have a seat." He pointed to some empty stools and dropped his feet to the ground.

"I've been thinking about how long it takes for you to deploy," Paul said. "You are vulnerable coming in, flaring, and dismounting the troops, and that process takes a lot of time. I think I have found a way to halve the amount of time it takes to dismount. If you were to stay in a hover, perhaps at about twenty feet and rappel down ropes, it would take about half the amount of time to deploy."

"Rappel, like when we rappel down the side of a mountain or a building?" the captain asked. "I never thought of that." The captain picked up the telephone. "Karl, can you come over here?" In a short time, a mechanic with sergeant stripes came in, and the captain asked him, "Is there any place on a Huey to mount some ropes so we can rappel out of the chopper?"

"Should be possible," Karl answered. "You'll have to be careful of the center of balance, but I am sure the pilots can figure it out."

"OK," Paul said. "I'll send over some climbing rope and carabineers and the like. How soon can you get started?"

"This afternoon," the captain said. "I'll brief my copilot and crew chiefs on what we want to do, and we'll start simulations.

When the grunts get back, I'll have them start a refresher on rappelling. There is a tower not far from here we can use. I'll let you know when we are going to try it out of the chopper, Paul."

"Outstanding," Paul said. "Thank you, Captain. Come, Smithers, back to camp. I believe it is teatime."

CHAPTER 7

THE SUN WAS GOING DOWN, and Paul was sitting in front of his tent, a beer in his hand and his feet up on a stool. "Got another one of those beers?" Emily said, walking up to him.

"Yeah, sure, help yourself," Paul flipped open the lid of the cooler at his feet.

"Why didn't you tell me your regiment is a hundred years old and that your great-grandfather started it?"

"You didn't ask," Paul answered, "and it's personal anyway."

"Your people were one of the first groups to settle not only in Western Canada but also in western North America," Emily said. "I would think you would want everyone to know that."

"Look, Miss Hershmire...it is miss, isn't it?" Paul said. "We do what we do for a reason. This military stuff is just a job. Once the job is done, we go home and resume our lives. It is a way of life that is hundreds of years old, and I do not expect you or anyone else outside our community to understand."

"Yes, it is miss, and my name is Emily," she said. "I am trying to understand. That is why I ask all these questions."

"Well, Miss Hershmire," Paul said, "from where I sit, we are just a story that will get you a paycheck. It won't be the first time, and probably not the last, a reporter has done that—although your predecessors were not as pretty. Members of the American press have been following us since our inception. Grab your beer, and come with me."

Paul stood and walked toward the edge of camp, not stopping until the only sounds were of the wind and their feet scrunching the ground. The moon was full, no clouds, and the stars shone brightly.

"Where are you from, Miss Hershmire? New York?" Paul asked.

"My office is in New York, but I am from Sacramento, California," she said.

"Big city girl, eh?" Paul stopped walking and looked out at the landscape around them.

"This is where I am from," he said, reaching his arms out and sweeping the horizon with them. "Out here we must all rely on each other, or we may very well die. Mother Nature does not care what language you speak or what religion you follow. You follow her rules, or you die. It is that simple. You think about that for a minute."

Paul sat down on the ground and took a swig of his beer. The silence was complete. He could almost hear her heartbeat, and he did hear her breathing change as she looked around and took in the sights nature provided.

"Out there somewhere," Paul said after a while, "a doe is feeding her fawn, hoping it will see another day. A jackal is stalking the fawn, hoping to provide food for its young. The circle of life, Miss Hershmire—the prey and the predator. Who will live, and who will die? Only the most skilled and fit will survive and breed to produce the next generation. In your world you also follow those rules, but out here you will actually die if you don't follow the rules, not just lose your job. Come on. I'll take you back to camp." Paul escorted her back to her tent.

"Tomorrow, we have a special patrol. You are welcome to join us, Miss Hershmire. If you are interested, be at the laager by oh six hundred."

She watched him walk back to his tent area, not quite swaggering but not slouching either. "You have made an impact on him, Emily," her tent mate said, coming out of the tent. "He took you to see the stars, and tomorrow he is taking you somewhere special. You play your cards right and don't push him, and you might get lucky."

"You would help me, Katia?" Emily asked.

"All our boys are a little like him," Katia said. "But his branch of the Bekenbaums has always been a little special. The men are always more sensitive to others and the environment around them. He will turn on you in a second if you do something wrong, but if you don't, he will be yours forever as a friend or something more. They don't make friends easily, but once they do, they are your friends forever. They are hard on those around them, but they're harder on themselves. That is why they have always been our leaders. I will help you with my cousin, if I can. But know this—if you hurt him or use him, you will wish you were dead."

The first of the five APCs headed out of the camp in a swirl of dust, a roar of engine noise, and a clanking of tracks when Emily came to the vehicle park. Katia waved her over to the APC she was commanding and helped her get in with her cameras and equipment bags. Emily found a spot in the cramped quarters of the vehicle's interior with the five other people, their weapons, ammunition, and curiously two western saddles and bridles. The driver fired up the engine, and soon the tracked vehicle was on the move, adding dust and diesel fumes to the smells of the interior. It soon bounced and swayed down the track that served as a road. The troopers were in a good mood and joked with one another, but they were still watchful. The area was peaceful, but recent events had reminded them not to take anything for granted. Half the troopers had the older FN rifles, and the other half had what the Canadians were calling the C7—a modified American M16. The battalion was field testing the new rifles, and the results would determine whether the regiment followed the rest of the Canadian Army in adopting smaller cartridges.

Emily thought about the young sergeant who refused to be an officer but to whom everyone in the battalion deferred anyway. So many of the battalion's future plans were based on his decisions, and not for the first time, she thought about how different this group of military people was compared to the others she had covered. She had caught them talking in German and Russian among themselves, but as soon as she walked closer, they always switched to English. They were an enigma—one minute serious and deadly, the next carefree and joyful. She needed to find out more about these people and their young leader.

About an hour later, the tracked armoured personnel carrier slowed down and veered left. After a couple rough spots, it came to a rocking halt, and the rear hatch banged down. Emily grabbed her gear and followed the first troopers out of the vehicle. Looking around, she found they were parked on the edge of an oasis. Several large tents were set up, as well as horse corrals. Horse-transport vehicles and personal automobiles were parked outside the area. A number of Arabs in traditional dress were in attendance, along with more than a few in Saudi military uniforms. The members of the regiment greeted and were greeted by the Saudis—military and nonmilitary alike. Emily was shepherded to an area where a viewing stand was set up under awnings. The atmosphere was festive, and the troopers of Katia's APC—but not Katia herself—soon joined Emily. Several other troopers, including Paul, were missing. Saudis filled up the stands.

"We do this once a year," Bob, Paul's driver, said as he sat beside Emily. "We have to qualify once each year. For most of us, it is a formality just to achieve minimum standard. But some try to advance to eagle status every year. Three already have, but another four opted for the more traditional method to advance. It is much harder, and once they have opted for it, they can't renege and try the normal method. It is one or the other. Fail either, and you fail period."

The Saudis burst into cheers, and two riders in traditional clothing came out mounted on magnificent Arabian horses and lined up on what appeared to be a course of some sort. At a command, both took off at a gallop, spurring their mounts for more speed. Emily got her cameras ready, making sure the speed winders functioned and that she had full batteries and rolls of film. The two riders dwindled in the distance and, after about a mile, turned around and came back, racing down to the stands. In front of the stands, a group of targets were set up, one at twenty-five yards and the other at two hundred. The two riders, their horses foaming and visibly slowing, pulled to a stop in front of the targets, dismounted, and drew rifles from scabbards attached to their saddles. The rifles were M14s, and both men lay on the ground and fired five shots at the farther targets. Then they rose, withdrew revolvers from holsters on their waists, and fired five more shots each at the closer targets. The horses scattered at the sounds of the first shots, and the two men walked out of the target area to the hoots and jeers of mates in the stands.

Another two Arabs took off as soon as the range was clear.

"The rules are they have to ride a mile up and back," Bob explained. "Then they have to hit the bull's-eye area with three out of five shots with the rifle and the pistol and also try to hit a couple targets over there with their swords while on horseback. They are also timed. Sometimes they have to use lances first, but we didn't think to bring any this time."

The second pair kept control of their animals but were unable to hit any targets with the swords on their one allowed pass. One of the third pair managed to hit a target with his sword.

The next pair were both members of the regiment, mounted on taller and stronger horses. The saddles were more like western cattle saddles. The stirrups were long, and the saddles were double cinched and had breast collars attached. The bridles and saddles were plain, unlike those of the Arabs, whose saddles and tack were highly ornamental. Swords and rifles were slung on the men's backs, the hilts over their left shoulders and rifle barrels over their right. At the signal each rider set off at a canter instead of a gallop. On their return, the horses were sweating but not foaming. Both riders jumped off their horses, leaving the reins dangling on the ground. They took a few steps forward and almost in unison drew their Colt automatic pistols and fired five rounds into the pistol targets. They holstered the weapons, pulled their FNs from their backs, and rapidly fired five rounds into the rifle targets while still standing. They slung the rifles onto their backs as they gathered up their reins and jumped back into their saddles. They drew odd-looking swords and spurred at the sword targets. One rider hit two, and the other hit one.

"We had six horses shipped over here," Bob said. "They are from Paul's personal herd. It's a bloodline started by his great-grandfather back in the old country. This game is sort of a tradition with us. Those two got their eagles. They were well under the time limit, and their shooting scores were good."

The next two riders were a bit faster but not as accurate with their shooting, but both still passed.

"You're going to want to make sure you have a full roll of film now," Bob said, as the Arabs got excited. "What you are about to see is one of the reasons Napoleon called us the best light cavalry in the world. This regiment does this better than anyone else, now or in the past."

The next two riders came out. One was Katia, her long blond hair pulled into a ponytail. She wore an old-style Stetson campaign hat, with the strap done up tightly under her chin. The other rider was Paul. Instead of the FN, a C7 was strapped across his back, and he had a soft baseball cap jammed down around his eyes. At the signal, both riders took off at a fast trot that turned into a canter halfway back.

"Take pictures when they get halfway down the line," Bob said. "And keep that power winder going."

The riders were side by side as they hit the start of the sword targets and spurred into a gallop. As Bob suggested, Emily hit the power winder as both riders hit the halfway mark and simultaneously slid down the sides of their horses. Each gripping their horns with one knee, they fired their Colt pistols at the targets under their horses' bouncing heads. After five rounds, they holstered the pistols and jumped back up into their saddles, pulling the rifles from their backs. Katia stopped and blasted away at her targets. Paul carried on, spinning his horse around and coming back at the gallop. Standing in the stirrups, he fired three groups of three shots at his rifle target. He let the rifle fall to hang from the ring it was attached to, withdrew his sword, and hit all three targets with it before Katia had hit her first. The Arabs yelled and stomped their feet, punching their fists into the air.

"That was really something," Emily said. "I take it they both passed."

"Katia was a bit slower than she normally is," Bob said, "but she already has her eagle. This was just a show for the Arabs. Paul failed, as he does every year."

"What do you mean he failed? That was the most amazing thing I have ever seen," Emily said in shock. "He hit the target with all those shots."

"Yes, he did," Bob agreed. "He does every year, but he needs to get three in the bull's-eye. He will only have two, one above the other, and the third will be two inches above and in line but just out of the bull's-eye. As for the other six, one group of three will be in the left corner, and the other will be in the right. He does not want to pass."

"I still do not understand why," Emily said.

"You will have to ask him," Bob said.

"That is one heck of a skill," she said. "Most soldiers I know have trouble hitting a moving target. Paul and Katia hit them at a full gallop."

"It takes a lot of practice," Bob said. "Most of us don't want to spend the time. Back in the day, it was a requirement. Paul's great-grandfather was the best in Russia, and his great-grandmother was not far behind. Only the most hard core Cossack families follow the tradition now."

"Cossacks?" Emily asked. "Are you people all Cossacks? But most of you have German last names."

"It's a long story," Bob said. "Most of us come from Cossack blood stock. Our settlement is set up under the old rules, and the rules are close enough to the Canadian constitutional monarchy system that the Canadian government leaves us alone. Again that is something you will have to bring up with Paul or his father or grandfather."

"Shit!" Katia exclaimed, retrieving her targets. She walked up to Bob and Emily. "I have to buy Paul another two beers. He put all five pistol shots in the bull's-eye and hit all three sword targets. I hit only two and put four in the bull's-eye."

"Ah, poor baby," Bob said. "I bet you'll cry all the way to the bank. How much did you bet with the Arabs?"

"I got the mare from their second group and about a hundred thousand US dollars," Katia answered.

"I got fifty off you, but only twenty off Paul," Bob said. "They have seen him in action before."

"You bet on this competition?" Emily asked. "I can't believe the Saudis let a woman compete. That is out of the norm for them."

"Not really," Katia said. "They had warrior women in their history, and they respect us for it. You will find the regiment is highly thought of here. But we still have to keep our heads covered, just not to the same degree as other females."

"I still have problems with that and how they treat their women," Emily said.

"For followers of Islam," Katia said, "the royal family is very progressive. Because of Mecca and all the religious furor around the holy site, they cannot show it. We respect their religion and culture as much as we can and still operate, and they appreciate that."

"Can you tell me how your people are able to have this close relationship when so many other Western countries have problems?" Emily asked.

"The Saudis are a warrior race," Paul said, walking up, "as are our people. We defeated them in a decisive battle in the past and then helped them twice against the Germans. We treated them with respect when we defeated them, as we did with the Germans, Turks, and Italians. They asked us to help them exploit their natural resources, and we dealt with them fairly and still do. They trust us, and we trust them."

"But you are Christians, for all intents," Emily said. "That is sure to cause tension."

"We believe in the same God," Paul said. "We acknowledge the teachings of Muhammad and do not force our beliefs on them. They understand us and respect us, as we respect them. Even the most radical of them do not have a problem with us. Now enough of this. Put the cameras and notebooks away. We have been asked to celebrate with the Saudis, and afterward when we return to our camp, they will celebrate with us. You may come along, but please don't take pictures of the Saudis unless they allow it, and don't pester them with questions."

"Once again Allah smiles on you and your troopers," the Saudi prince said. "One day we hope Allah will change his mind and smile on us."

"God works in mysterious ways, Prince," Paul said. "He also helps those who help themselves, it is written."

"Yes, so it is written," the prince agreed. "It is also written, 'No pain, no gain,' as the Americans say."

"Ah, that is so," Paul agreed, "but that which does not kill you makes you stronger."

"That lesson is hard for my people to grasp," the prince said. "They prefer to blame Allah for their failures."

One by one, the six Saudis presented their horses to their opposing Canadian competitors, and one by one, the Canadians accepted the horses and then returned them as gifts back to the Arabs. Paul waved, and all six of the regiment's horses were brought forward. Paul presented them to the prince as gifts. "Horses are one thing," Paul said. "They are mine to give, but money is something different. Now pay up, you bandit."

"Oh, you Canadians," the prince said. "You will make us poor with your constant demands for more money."

"Yeah, sure," Paul replied. "You spend more than what you owe us for coffee every day."

"Yes, but now I will have to go for a whole day with no coffee," the prince said, laughing.

The two groups spent most of the day together at the oasis, and as evening fell, the Canadians made ready to depart. The horses were loaded onto transport trucks under the prince's supervision, and Paul walked with him to his luxury SUV. "Thank you for the horses, Paul," the prince said. "Our bloodlines are getting a little thin. Yours have been beating ours for years."

"Your horses are pretty and fast," Paul said. "Ours are handsome, fast, and tough. Like I said, the horses were mine to give. I would never ask my troopers to part with theirs. They are too expensive for them to do that."

"It would be the same with me, Paul," the prince replied, "but my foolish men thought they could beat you with their own horses. Thank you for your generosity in giving their horses back to them."

"We have horses back home," Paul said. "Horses are not such a big thing anymore."

"This is why we respect you," the prince said. "You are gracious winners, as well as losers. But you don't lose much."

"Take a man's money, and he will try harder next time," Paul said. "Take his pride or his livelihood, and you make an enemy."

"So true," the prince agreed. "Can we trust this reporter?"

"I am not sure yet," Paul answered, "but as with all reporters, we keep personal things personal, if you know what I mean."

"Yes," the prince agreed. "Give her a story but not the whole story. I will see you back at your camp."

"Everyone is waiting for you," Paul said. He walked back to his troopers and circled a hand over his head. Immediately engines started, and troopers loaded into APCs.

"Care to join me?" Paul asked Emily. "Or would you rather go back with Katia?"

"Sure, I'll tag along if you don't mind," she answered.

"I am feeling generous today," Paul said. "I will even let you ride shotgun, and I'll jump in the back. Here, pile your stuff in the back beside the saddles. I have plenty of room." His assault rifle was placed in a specially designed rack on the dash of the German-made jeep. Paul carefully placed the scabbarded sword under his saddle in the rear of the jeep.

"That is my grandmother's sword," Paul said. "She'll have my head if I so much as scratch it."

"She'll have your balls and more if you lose it," Bob said, laughing. "She'll worry about heirs later."

"Yes, there can always be more heirs," Paul agreed, laughing. "But you can't get these swords anymore."

"That is just nasty!" Emily said. "No grandmother would do that."

"Yes, she would," said Bob. "That sword is from Imperial Russia and irreplaceable. Nicolas can always father another son."

"But you have a brother," Emily said.

"Ah, yes, that is true," Paul agreed. "Technically, George is my half brother. We have different fathers. He is definitely a part of the family and will inherit much, but he won't inherit the family traditions. They can only be inherited by blood."

"What kind of a family do you have?" Emily asked. "You are modern but old fashioned. It is all very confusing."

"Welcome to the Cossack world," Bob said, and both men laughed.

"*Devie, devie; chekie, chekie,*" Paul said, laughing. "It means, 'Hurry up, hurry up; take it easy, take it easy.' It's a common phrase among our people. It kind of explains the contrasts we face. Once you understand that phrase, you understand us. So how does a girl from California get to a big-time job in New York?" Paul asked.

"I graduated from UCLA at the top of my class in journalism," Emily answered. "My father owns a number of small-town daily and weekly papers around Sacramento, and he hired me for my first job. I was on my own from there. *American Press* saw some of my work and hired me as a freelancer."

"Now you are a foreign correspondent," Paul said. "Impressive."

"To be honest," Emily said, "nobody wants to cover these small out-of-the-way UN affairs. I get published sometimes, but mostly *American Press* just covers my expenses and minimum pay, which is all right. I get to see a lot of interesting places."

"And meet a lot of weird people like us," Paul said. He and Bob laughed.

"That's not fair," Emily said. "I never said or thought that."

"Only because you don't know us yet," Paul said. "We are definitely weird."

"No doubt about it," Bob agreed. "Only a weirdo would come out to this godforsaken part of the world, leaving all the comforts of home behind."

"You would rather be back home shoveling three feet of snow in minus-thirty-degree temperatures?" Paul asked.

"You had to bring that up, didn't you?" Bob said, smacking his forehead with his palm. "November in the old igloo is not nice. I do hope my wife remembered to feed the dogs. I need them for the dogsled to run the trap lines when I get home."

Paul saw Emily furiously writing that down and elbowed Bob, who looked over and laughed. "Typical Yank," he said between chuckles.

"Emily dear," Paul said, "Bob owns a Ford dealership back home and lives in a twenty-five-hundred-square-foot house that sits on five acres of garden. He has four bathrooms, forced-air central heating, and electric lights."

"Unlike my friend here, who lives in a one-room shack with an outdoor toilet and no electricity," Bob said.

Frustrated, Emily tore the page from her notebook and tossed it out into the wind. The two men laughed heartily. "Uh-oh," Paul said between laughs. "Methinks we have pissed off the journalist."

"Dunno about pissing off the journalist," Bob said, "but take it from an old married man—we have definitely pissed off the lady."

"Now what would a lady be doing out here, I ask you?" Paul said. "A lady would surely have more brains than to bounce around in the middle of nowhere in a jeep with two Neanderthals who are armed."

"Ah, yes," said Bob, "you have a point there, my friend. I admit that on rare occasions, you are very insightful. Now I must ask you, oh almighty one, would a lady be a journalist?"

"I am thinking, my dear student," Paul said, "that perhaps the journalist has forgotten she is a lady and instead has become only a journalist and not a real person."

"After much thought, wise one," Bob said as they came into camp, "I am thinking you may be correct that the lady has now become the story instead of reporting the story." Bob stopped in front of the tent Emily shared with Katia. Emily grabbed her equipment and stomped off into the tent without a word. The two men's laughter followed her until they took off in the direction of their quarters. A few minutes later, Katia found Emily lying face down on her cot and crying.

"It did not go well then?" Katia asked.

"They made fun of me!" Emily said. "I am trying to find out more about you people, and they made up things and then made fun of me."

Katia saw that now Emily was getting angry. She took a deep breath and sighed. "Today was supposed to be a fun day, Emily," she said. "You were asking a lot of questions again instead of just observing. Now I'll ask the questions. Did both make fun of you or only one of them?"

"First it was just Bob, but then Paul joined him. Then they both talked as if I were not there." Emily started to tear up again.

"Well, that's different then," Katia said. "If only one of them had been doing it, or if they were not talking to you at all or were being very polite, you would be on the shit list. The fact that they both made fun of you means they like you."

"That's a funny way to let someone know you like them," Emily said.

"One of us would have slammed them right back," Katia replied. "Look, Paul took you out to the desert, right? Then he asked us and the Saudis if it was all right for you to come today. This thing you witnessed today—outsiders are normally barred from seeing it. Lastly, Paul asked you to come back with him. Making fun of you says a few things. You were being too serious for one, and you are asking some personal questions now. We normally don't do that unless we know people very well. So they are asking you to lighten up and not get so personal, but they're also letting you know they like you. Understand?"

"Not really," Emily said.

"Tonight leave the notebook at home," Katia said. "Observe, and take part if you want, but most of all, have some fun. We are all about the same age and far from home. Let your hair down a little."

Katia changed into a fresh uniform and brushed her hair out, leaving it long and unbound before putting her beret on. Her long blond hair flowed down around her shoulders, and she left the first two buttons of her blouse undone and its tail hanging out untucked.

Emily, taking her cue from Katia, dressed in a blue blouse, which she left hanging outside her black jeans. She brushed out her long black tresses and let them fall to the middle of her back just above her butt. She pulled on some high-top boots and surveyed her face in a hand mirror.

"Wow, I wish I could grow my hair that long," Katia said. "Mine is too curly for that. The boys will be all over you tonight. Raven-black hair is rare among our people. You have such lovely green eyes as well."

"They come from my mother," Emily said. "She's Irish. My father is from German stock, I think."

"Your last name sounds German, true enough," Katia said. "Now my raven-haired, green-eyed beauty, it's time to see whether a Yank can party as well as a Canuck. In my experience, Yanks have trouble keeping up."

"Not you, too?" Emily said. "Are you all sarcastic like that?"

"Sarcastic?" Katia said. "Whatever do you mean, my dear? Why, I was only commenting that blue-eyed blondes have more fun than black-haired green-eyes any day."

"Oh, you Canadians," Emily said. "What pains in the ass you are. No wonder everyone leaves you alone."

"That's the spirit," Katia said. "There is some faint hope for you at least."

A hush came over the crowd as the colonel called the battalion to attention just as Katia and Emily entered the mess hall. There was no sense of urgency as the battalion lined up in their sections and companies, and the RSM called six troopers to the front. The colonel shook each trooper's hand and pinned an eagle to each one's right collar. Then he had them stand up front and accept the salutes of the rest of the battalion.

"Well, those six will be good for nothing for the next couple days," Bob said to Paul after the ceremony was complete.

"They deserve it," Paul said. "They worked hard for it."

"I know," Bob agreed. "Just making a comment. You think she will show up?"

"We'll see," Paul said. "Katia was bound to clue her in, if she can be clued in."

A chorus of wolf whistles from the younger troopers alerted Paul, who took a look at the door to see Katia smacking a cousin on the back of the head.

"Holy shit," Bob said. "Emily cleans up good."

Paul said nothing as he watched his cousin escort the dark-haired beauty up to where he and Bob were standing. Emily's blue blouse was just open enough and just tight enough to give a hint at what was underneath, and the black jeans tucked into the high-top riding boots gave an impression of legs that did not stop. Her black shiny hair cascaded down her back and emphasised her thin waist and white skin. Her red lips were only slightly enhanced by lipstick.

"Holy shit indeed," Paul acknowledged as the two women walked up to them.

"What was that you were saying, cousin?" Katia said. "Am I going to have to discipline you, like I did Cousin Karl?"

"No, Captain," Paul said, "as noncommissioned officers, the corporal and I would never make rude whistling noises to acknowledge a beautiful woman's entrance into the mess hall. I would say though that the competition has definitely helped the captain to enhance the way she looks, ma'am."

"Oh, yes, Sergeant," Bob said. "I fully agree that the good captain needed a reminder. She has been taking her position as the leading beauty of the battalion for granted lately."

"Do you see, Emily?" Katia said. "This is how they respect officers around here. I told you as much. Bob, you'd better hope I don't write home to Greta and tell her how you act over here."

"Oh, you're in shit now, Bob," Paul said. "I, on the other hand, have nothing to worry about. You know, you should get just a slightly tighter pair of pants, cousin. I am sure you can still get out of those without too much trouble. They do enhance your bottom a good deal though."

"You think so?" Katia said, running her hands down her legs and then patting Paul on the cheek. "I will be sure to let Omma know you think so and tell her how nice you have been to our guest as well."

"I will have you know I have been nothing but courteous to our guest, as to be expected, and Omma will tell you so," Paul said.

"You have been making fun of her, her profession, and her country, Sergeant," Katia said. "This is not how we treat our guests in this regiment."

Paul immediately took the grin off his face and came to attention, looking directly at Emily. "Miss Hershmire, I apologise for my behaviour and the behaviour of my corporal," he said in all sincerity. "Please do not take our actions as typical of how the regiment's members conduct themselves. Captain, the fault is mine. The corporal took his lead from me, and I let him continue without saying anything. No excuses, Captain. I apologise for my behaviour, ma'am."

"You see how easy it is, Emily?" Katia said. "Just use their ranks and threaten to tell their grandmothers, and everything changes. Now as a punishment, cousin, you will escort our guest for the rest of the evening. Corporal, I need a drink. *Devie, devie.*"

"Yeah, yeah," Bob said. "*Chekie, chekie.*"

"Would you care for a refreshment, Miss Hershmire?" Paul asked.

"A bottle of that wonderful beer of yours would be nice, Paul," Emily said. "And my name is Emily."

"Right away, Emily," Paul said, the grin back on his face.

"Oh, Emily!" Katia said in exasperation, taking her beret off and hitting Emily on the shoulder with it. "We had him right where we wanted him, and now you let him wriggle off the hook."

"But he was so cute, with those baby blues almost ready to cry," Emily said. "I felt so sorry for him. He looked like a poor little puppy dog."

"He did, didn't he?" Katia agreed.

"How could I stay upset at that?" Emily said. "He is kind of cute, you know, and his butt looks nice and tight." The two women laughed at the obvious discomfort they were causing Paul.

"Now you know what it feels like to be laughed at," Emily said to him. "If you bring my beer in a hurry, I will forgive you."

"Yes, Lady" Paul said with a put-on heavy German accent. "At once, Lady."

"Can you ever get one up on him?" Emily asked as Paul hurried away to the bar.

"Very rarely," Katia said. "The whole family is like that. Tatiana would have wrenched his ear if she heard he made you cry, and that is not a lie."

"Who's Tatiana?" Emily asked.

"We all call her *Omma*, which means *grandmother* in English," Katia said. "But she really is Paul's grandmother. She came from the old country right at the end of the first war and stayed with the regiment, serving as Paul's grandfather's aide. When he was shot at the end of the war, she killed the German officers that shot him and then used her very good medical knowledge to save his life. Some people say she is from an old Russian aristocratic family, but no one knows for sure. She showed up in my grandmother's village in Russia one day—alone, cold, and hungry—and they took her in. Paul's grandfather stood up to the Bolsheviks who wanted to arrest her, and so here she is. She is one tough lady."

"I noticed you people don't have much use for socialists," Emily said.

"Oh no," Katia said. "We are socialists ourselves. We hate communists and in particular the Russian version. They killed a lot of our people during and after the revolution."

"The more I learn about your people, the more confused I get," Emily said. "You seem to be capitalists, and yet you say you are socialists."

"A person can be both at the same time," Paul said, handing Emily a beer and Katia a glass of vodka. "A capitalist who shares a large portion of his wealth for the well-being of others is also a socialist."

"Let's not talk politics," Emily said. "Bob told me you bred those horses you gave the Saudis."

"Yes, my great-grandfather started the breed in the old country," Paul said. "They were much in demand even back then. A good Cossack horse was like having another well-trained trooper in those days. You fought the horse as well as the man. Our horses are almost as intelligent as we are and as loyal to its rider as a man and his wife are to each other. Now we just breed them as a hobby, which is sad really. Do you ride?"

"No, not really," Emily said. "Just at the stables during a high-school program."

"Well, when you come back to Canada with us, I will take you on a nice scenic ride," Paul said.

"Come back to Canada with you?" Emily said.

"You will want to get some background for your story, no?" Paul asked. "What better way than to go home with us to see how we live and to talk to some of the old-timers?"

"Katia," Paul said, "do you think you could put Emily up at your place if she goes with us when we leave to go home?"

"Sure, I have lots of room. If Jimmy doesn't like it, too bad," Katia said. "He should have come with me then."

"Jimmy?" Emily asked.

"Yes, my husband," Katia said. "Paul's father has him doing something with pipelines and wouldn't let him come along this time."

"You have pipelines?" Emily asked.

"Pipelines, pumping stations, facilities for tanker ship loading and unloading of crude oil, and a couple gas plants," Paul said. "That beer you are drinking is made from barley and hops grown on our farms, and my grandmother runs the brewery. Our company has fingers in a lot of pies. We don't usually own the whole pie though."

"What's it like in California?" Paul asked. "We hear a lot about it."

Katia listened for a while and then quietly drifted away, letting the two young people get to know each other while she joined the rest of her section and their celebrations. The afternoon turned to night, and as the sun went down, so too did some of the spirit of the party. Inevitably, someone sang, and slowly the group joined in, making the mess hall hum with strains of "Lily Marlene" in its original German.

"That is such a pretty melody," Emily said. "It is from the last war, is it not?"

"It was actually written after the first war," Paul said. "All the sides during the second sang it, as the meaning is as poignant in any language. Do you know the words?"

Emily shook her head. Paul sang in English and was soon joined by more of the crowd.

"My father told me that in Libya," Paul said, "he could hear the English, French, Italian, and German versions of this song on almost any night. And at Christmastime in France, 'Silent Night' was sung in German and English."

Just as Emily was about to say something, a male voice sang slowly in Russian. Paul and most of the regiment let their heads sink, many with tears already forming in their eyes. Not understanding, Emily looked around and saw that almost the whole mess hall was silently looking at their hands or beer glasses. All conversation had stopped. At the end of the verse, Paul sang it in English, and Emily began to understand. The song was not about their home in Canada, but it may as well have been. It was about a soldier away from home for a long time and dreaming of returning. As good as it sounded in English, nothing matched the soul-wrenching sound of a male Russian voice. Paul and the original singer started the next verse in harmonised Russian, and they were slowly joined by more male voices, then some female voices, and then the massed voices picked up the beat of a walking horse. People thumped tables and thighs to keep time. The beat quickened, and the voices picked up speed along with it. Faster and faster they went, until the beat was as fast as a horse at a full gallop. The words blended into yells and cries.

Paul let out a whoop and jumped onto the table, holding his hands out to his sides and doing a jig. Another trooper did the same on another table, and both men took turns dancing almost as if in a competition. People pulled the tables away to the sides of the room, leaving the center open. Paul and the other man jumped down and danced toward each other. Others joined them, and a long line of men jigged and gestured gracefully when one let out a whoop. Simultaneously all the men squatted down and bounced—one leg up and the other down, and then both legs out while their arms braced them against the floor, with one leg and one arm in the air at a time. The rest of the group formed a circle around them, singing quickly and furiously with a lot of whooping. A group of female troopers formed an inner circle and danced intricate moves around the men while also singing and whooping. The whole time, nobody—singers or dancers—lost the beat or rhythm, voices in perfect harmony. And then suddenly, it was over. Dancers stood, heaving for breath. With their hands on hips or knees, they tried to refill their lungs after the long exertion. Laughter erupted as they regained their breath and gravitated to the bar to replenish their drinks.

"Oh my God," Emily said, "what was that?"

"Come on." Paul handed her a fresh beer and took her by the arm. "Let's get out of here before they get homesick. That, my dear Emily, was our regimental song. It is about a trooper far away from home, dreaming of family. He must fight one more battle before he can go home, and he reluctantly joins the line, and they attack their enemies. There are enemies to the right, to the left, and all around. He flings himself into the fray, swinging his sword until there are no more enemies, and then he gallops his horse day and night to get home. He doesn't sleep or stop, almost falling from the saddle with fatigue. The love of his life can hear him coming and waits impatiently for his return until, finally, he is there, and they are reunited at long last. A lot of our songs are like that. We start slowly and sorrowfully and then end joyously and happily."

As they walked, another song started. This one stayed slow and heart wrenching.

"Like our forefathers," Paul said, "we are a long way from home for a long time."

"You all seem to have kept in touch with your heritage," Emily said. "That is rare these days."

"If we don't remember what happened before, we are doomed to repeat it," Paul said. "Much of our history was unpleasant, especially until we came to Canada. Even with the wars we fought for Canada, life has never been as bad as it was for us back in the old country—never, not even when we first established ourselves and crops and money were tight. It was not as bad as the old country was even in its best years."

"My mother's family followed the railroad," Emily said. "They were blue-collar people and had it rough during the thirties. My father's people came to California from Texas. They were merchants and still are. Newspapers are sort of a hobby for my father. We are Americans though. I don't remember my father ever talking about when his family came over to the States. It was a very long time ago. We live in a nice house, something like Bob's house, on two acres of land. We have a pool and tennis court and lots of trees and grass. I do miss that—relaxing by the pool and getting a suntan without all the dust and grit we get here. I miss the smell of freshly cut grass and the feel of it between my toes. What do you miss about your home?"

"Fried eggs, pancakes, and good ham," Paul said. "My mother is a world-class cook. That's how she hooked my dad. She owned a restaurant in Billings, Montana, during the war, and my father went there for supper once in a while before he got shipped out to Italy."

"Your mother is American?" Emily asked.

"I guess so," Paul said. "She was born in Billings. Her folks came from Germany before the first war. They had it pretty rough."

"What are you going to do after this is over?" Emily asked. "You said your term of service is finished after this tour."

"I am going on a long holiday, probably just a ways down the road from the farm," Paul said. "Then I have to make up my mind which college I want to enroll in."

"College? What do you want to study?" Emily asked.

"I see now why you are a reporter," Paul said. "Always so many questions. I have some choices. I can go to Magill in Montreal or Oxford in England. What do you know about Caltech?"

"It's in Pasadena, just up the road from LA, an engineering-based school. Why?" Emily responded.

"I am leaning toward Caltech or MIT," Paul said. "If you are going to be back in California, I will probably go to Caltech."

"What?" Emily said. "You have a choice between MIT and Caltech? Do you know how exclusive those two schools are?"

"They asked for me, not the other way around," Paul said. "I was just going to go to the University of Calgary, which has a fairly decent electronics program. I think I will go to Caltech. The weather in Boston is almost as bad as ours in the winter, so that's a strike against MIT. Are you going back to New York after this or back home?"

"My home office is in New York," Emily said. "But I can wire my stories in from anywhere. I thought I might go home with you for a while and see how you live first."

"Do you want to see how I live," Paul said, "or how my people live?"

"Um...both," Emily stammered, turning red.

"I don't know how close Pasadena is to Sacramento," Paul said, "but it is a hell of a lot closer than Boston or Calgary, and I want to be close to you."

"You don't even know me," she said.

"I have the next two months to get to know you," he said. He took her chin in his right hand and kissed her on the lips.

CHAPTER 8

THE MISSION WAS OVER, AND most of the regiment was already gone, having flown back to Canada. Paul, Bob, Katia, and her crew were the only ones left, and they were supervising the loading of the last wheeled evaluation vehicle. They would accompany it in the Hercules for the very long trip back home.

"Don't worry, lover boy," Katia said. "She'll be home long before we are. Emily has first-class jet tickets, while we get the slow transport treatment."

"That's what I'm worried about," Paul said. "Mother and Omma have her to themselves for a week."

Emily had left on a commercial jet aircraft two days earlier. Her first stop was Frankfurt, Germany, and then she had a direct flight to Calgary, where someone from the regiment would pick her up and take her to their Didsbury headquarters. Paul and the gang, however, would stop at the Canadian air-force base in Lahr, Germany. They would spend the night there and refuel before going to Iceland. From there they would go to Gander, Newfoundland, and spend the night there and then to Red Deer, where they would deplane and all jam into the Bison APC for an uncomfortable hour-long drive to the barracks. They would have to service and park the vehicle and check in with the regiment before finally being allowed to go home.

"Oh well," said Bob, "home in time for Christmas anyway. My wife and kids will like that. Are you sure Emily is going to Calgary? American girls like to be home with family for Thanksgiving and Christmas, and she will miss both."

"Shit, I didn't think of that," Paul said. "Well, if she goes home, she goes home. It's not like we are married or anything. Hell, we are not even boyfriend and girlfriend, as far as I know."

"I think you are," Katia said. "Unless she told you differently, she'll be with us after New Year's, Paul. She might be infatuated with you, maybe, but her family comes first right now. She hasn't seen them for almost a year—just like we haven't seen our families."

"Yeah, I understand that," Paul said. "I'm going to be busy for a while anyway, completing these evil reports and getting ready to go to Caltech."

They took their places on the plane's uncomfortable temporary seats, which were jammed in with the Bison and remaining gear of the regiment. It was going to be a long, noisy, uncomfortable trip. Paul had a large briefcase with him. He intended to take advantage of the flight to finish up as much paperwork as possible before they reached home.

"So you've made up your mind on Caltech then?" Katia asked.

"Yeah, it's a good school," Paul said. "Their electronic-engineering department is one of the best worldwide. They are going to credit me two years of course work because of my background and experience, allowing me to fast-track my graduate degree. They want me to teach a couple ROTC courses on electronic integration in the battlefield."

"I hope you keep your head screwed on, Paul," Katia said. "Emily could turn into a distraction."

"She probably will," Paul said, smiling. "I hope so anyway. No fear, cousin—I know what I want and how to get it. The faster I am done with school, the faster I can spend the rest of my life with her."

"The world has changed, Paul," Katia said. "She may not want to give up her job."

"Correction," Paul said. "The rest of the world has caught up to us. I am sure we can come up with a compromise. If not, then it is not meant to be. My life is with the regiment and the family. That's just the way it is." He pulled out his portable typewriter and hammered out evaluations of the vehicles and weapons platforms they had tested over the last year. Katia wrote out some reports she needed to file, while the rest of the troopers played cards or slept.

It was downright cold when they landed in Red Deer three days later. The thermometer was at minus thirty degrees, and fresh snow was everywhere. When they left Yemen, it had been over eighty, so the troopers rummaged through duffel bags for more jackets. The Bison started up readily, and Bob drove it backward out of the Hercules. The exhaust spewed white smoke into the atmosphere, joining clouds of visible breath the rest of the troopers were creating.

They all hurriedly tossed equipment into the Bison, and the troopers piled in. Paul, Bob, and Katia walked around the vehicle, making sure all the tires were OK and the road lights were working. Finally Bob sat in the driver's compartment, Katia took the commander's compartment, and Paul jammed into the rear with the other troopers and their gear. Bob raised the rear door and cautiously left the airbase just outside Red Deer and headed to the four-lane highway that would take them home.

The vehicle was still painted white with the large *UN* logo on the front, rear, and both sides; the C9 automatic rifle was still on its pedestal outside the commander's turret; and the main twenty-millimetre gun was still mounted in the forward-facing turret. Looking out the viewing port as they roared down the highway at the maximum ninety kilometres per hour the vehicle could maintain, Paul noticed the looks they got from passing cars. Seeing a military vehicle in Canada was rare, and one with mounted weapons and *UN* markings was even rarer.

"I'm going to add to the report that we need to upgrade the heating system in the crew compartment," Paul said. "It's bloody freezing back here." Suddenly hot air blew around their feet.

"Oops," Bob said, "forgot to turn on the heat. Just remembered it."

"Nice going, Bob," Paul said. "Now it's raining in here from the frost melting."

"Hey, at least you're warm," Bob said. "I'm having problems seeing where I'm going. I have to keep the hatch closed to keep warm, and now the periscope is frosting up, and I didn't have very good visibility anyway."

Paul dug out a notebook and scribbled quickly into it. "Is there a defrost setting up there? I don't think it's any warmer in Sweden in the winter than it is here," Paul said. "There should be some provision for defrost."

"Whatever you hit is making clear lines on my vision ports," Katia said. "I can relay directions to you if you need them."

"Just give me the normal clearance instructions when we turn, Katia," Bob said. "It looks like an electric grid is built into the glass. I'm almost clear now."

Forty minutes later, they pulled off the four-lane highway onto a secondary paved highway that led to Didsbury, and the whine of the transmission changed. "Must have snowed last night or earlier today," Bob said. "Just engaged all-wheel drive."

"Great, and we are painted white," Katia said. "At least we won't get hurt if someone hits us, but I'd hate to be in the car that does."

The vehicle slowed down to turn right onto the road that bypassed the town of Didsbury, then negotiated a series of easy left-hand turns, and finally crossed the railroad tracks that ran through the center of town with a bump. After a final right-hand curve, Bob sped up again, and in another half hour, he slowed to a stop before crossing another highway. Now the road was gravel. "Snow is up to the hubs, Bob," Katia said.

"It's not even slowing us down yet," Bob said. "I can feel a bit of drive slip, though, so it must be icy."

"We're the first ones on the road," Katia said. "Whoever follows us is going to be pissed." The wheels on the Bison were set wider than those of a normal vehicle, so anyone trying to follow them would be able to put only one wheel in the tracks they were making.

Sometime later, the Bison slowed and turned left, bumping over a series of pipes laid over a shallow ditch and known as a Texas gate and carrying on in second gear. It climbed a small hill and then came to a gradual stop. A blast of cold air flooded into the interior when Katia opened the commander's hatch to climb up to the observation post.

"Open the damn gate," she yelled to someone outside. "Look, Private, if I wanted to, I would have blown your ass away with this twenty-millimeter canon before you even woke up in that chair you were sleeping in. Are you blind as well as stupid? Can't you see the big *UN* painted all over this thing? Open the bloody gate before I tell my driver to run over it and make you spend the rest of the day and night marching back and forth in front of it until it gets fixed."

"Wonder whose dunce of a kid that is?" Katia said, plopping back down and slamming the hatch shut. "He demanded to see my papers. Are you kidding me? Like we are invading or something." She pulled a sweater out of her duffel bag and wrapped it around her beret, and in a few moments, she popped out of the hatch again and gave Bob directions to park the vehicle.

The vehicle came to a stop, and the rear hatch banged down, letting even more cold air in. The troopers grabbed their gear as the vehicle shut down, and Paul made sure all the troopers had disembarked before he yelled to Bob to close it up. He waited for Bob and Katia to join him outside after they had exited and dogged down their respective hatches. If the three had been anywhere but on their base, they would have drawn a lot of looks. With automatic rifles hanging from slings across their backs, pistols in holsters strapped to their waists, and duffel bags on their shoulders, the troopers walked the short distance to the camp's office. Paul and Katia also carried briefcases.

The other eight troopers from the Bison finished signing in by the time Paul, Bob, and Katia entered the office, and they were lining up to use the one telephone to arrange their families to pick them up. Katia signed in and asked to see the officer of the day, and she was escorted to another part of the building.

"You in charge of the guard post, Corporal?" Paul asked the clerk at the check-in desk.

"No, Sergeant," the corporal answered. "The guard corporal is in the coffee room."

"Thank you, Corporal," Paul said, unbuttoning his jacket. "Care to join me, Master Corporal?"

"Wouldn't miss this for the world," Bob said with a grin. He followed Paul out of the office and down the corridor to the coffee room. There they found a sleeping corporal with his jacket and cold-weather gear slung over empty chairs and his feet up on the table.

Paul withdrew his pistol from his holster and walked over to the corporal. He slid the cocking mechanism right next to the sleeping man's ear before jamming the barrel hard into his ribs. "One move or sound out of you, and I'll blow your heart out of your chest!" he yelled. The corporal woke up to see an enraged Paul right in his face. "What's your fucking name, trooper?" Paul demanded. "You know what? Never fucking mind. I don't want to know your fucking name. Master Corporal, is there any good reason I shouldn't shoot this son of a bitch right here and now?"

"I believe, Sergeant, you would have to explain the mess to the captain, sir," Bob said. "She might be pissed that she would have to make a report explaining that the sergeant shot a sleeping corporal of the guard who abandoned his post and left a raw rookie in charge."

"Get your fucking ass out of that chair and back to the gate, you slack ass," Paul growled. "I'll deal with you later. Where the hell is your sergeant?"

"Other side of the camp, sir," the shaken corporal said.

"Not anymore." A female voice came from the doorway. "Who the hell are you to talk to one of my men like that?"

"I'm the son of a bitch who's going to cost you your stripes!" Paul said. "This asshole left a rookie in charge of the main gate, while he came in here and slept. If you were a half-decent sergeant, this would never happen. I can't even hide it. My captain saw it, and now we are all in the shit."

"OK, Corporal, get back to the gate. I'll handle this," his sergeant said. "Look, just let this lie. You don't know who that kid is or how much pull he has. If you know what's good for you, you'll let it go. I'm sure your captain will be told the same thing."

"Yeah, so who is he?" Paul asked.

"His great uncle is the general, and his great-grandpa started the regiment," she said.

"Well, dear," Paul said with an evil grin, "my cousin is in for a big shock. He'll be busted back to private in about ten minutes, and I expect he will be on punishment duty for some time after that. Since when is a Bekenbaum given preferential treatment in the regiment?"

"Um...well," the other sergeant stammered.

"Sergeant, my name is Warrant Officer Bekenbaum. My father and grandfather are the commanding generals of this regiment," Paul said. "I assure you the corporal will be severely reprimanded for his actions. If you want to save your ass, have a report on how this happened on my desk in two hours."

Two hours later, Paul made the sergeant stand the whole time he read her report. He looked up at her as he slammed the report shut and threw it on the desk. "All right, Sergeant, have a seat," Paul said. "Bob, get me my whiskey and some glasses." The three noncommissioned officers saluted one another and took a drink. "I take it from your report's wording that there has been some undue interference with respect to the sleeping corporal. Tell me what's going on, and I'll see about putting an end to it," Paul said.

"The corporal wants to be in full-time service," she said. "He was able to use his influence to get his eagle but not a commission. His father uses intimidation to get his way, sir. He threatens to lay off our relatives or us if we don't go along with what he wants. Fortunately your father is still the one who awards officer candidacy, but that is being challenged, too."

"OK, Sergeant," Paul said. "Don't worry about it. I'll have the corporal taken out of your section. Bob, can you meet me by the qualification range in two days? It shouldn't take long to strip him of his eagle."

"Always a pleasure to rip some smart-ass a new one," Bob said. "You might want to come along, Sergeant Heinz. This is going to be fun."

"Right, Corporal," Paul said a couple days later. "You have twenty minutes to get back here and fire your qualification shots. Get moving!"

Paul and Bob watched the corporal and his private from the guard post take off in the snow. It was slightly warmer than it had been when Paul arrived home but was still very cold. Paul took the cold and deep snow into consideration as he designed the test. The two troopers would have to run only two miles today instead of the normal five.

A staff car pulled up, and a lieutenant colonel in a dark-green formal uniform stepped out and approached Paul and Bob, who came to attention and saluted. "Who gave you authorization to conduct this test?" the colonel asked.

"I am entitled to test any new members of my company as to their qualifications, sir, as per regulations, sir," Paul said firmly.

"I'll be damned if a bloody bear will qualify my son," the colonel said.

"Really?" Nicolas said behind them. "Good thing I am here to make sure it's all fair then. By the way, Colonel, when was the last time you qualified?"

"You know very well I don't need to," the colonel said indignantly.

"You will address me as *sir* or *General* when we are in uniform, Colonel," Nicolas said. "Now answer the question."

"Three years ago, sir," the colonel answered, now looking concerned.

"Report to my office after this is over, and we will discuss the findings of this test as well as regulations concerning this and other things," Nicolas said. "Dismissed, Colonel."

"I had no idea this was going on, Paul," Nicolas said. "Thank you for bringing it to my attention. A family meeting is scheduled for this afternoon, and you will be there. Will you be fair in your evaluation?"

"Sir, the evaluation will be impartial and to regulation, sir," Paul said.

"Very well, Warrant," Nicolas said, nodding to both men. "Carry on." Both men saluted, and Nicolas left in the jeep he had driven up in.

The troopers arrived back at the target range, the private ahead of the corporal, and banged away at the targets. They were breathing heavily from the exertion of running through the snow. After their five shots were fired, they opened the bolts, removed the clips from the FNs, and laid them on a table provided for that purpose.

Bob walked down and collected both targets. "All right, Private," Bob said. "Three out of five in the bull's-eye. You can go now. Corporal, you hit the target with only two, and none was a bull's-eye. You will be given another chance to qualify in three days. Dismissed." Bob turned to Paul. "The family meeting tonight is not going to be pleasant, I am thinking. Good luck, and let me know how it works out."

The only place big enough to hold the extended Bekenbaum family was the officers' mess, and they commandeered it, telling everyone working there to go home. By five o'clock that evening, family members were arriving. John and Nicolas dragged two tables to the front and center of the room and placed them end to end. They and their wives sat down behind it, leaving three empty places. Other members of the extended family group came in, pushing tables to the side and lining chairs up in rows in front of the head table.

The father and son, at the center of the reason for the meeting, arrived. The father was still in his impeccable colonel's uniform, and the son was in civilian attire. The father dragged a table to one side at the front and pushed his son into a chair behind it, while he dumped out a briefcase full of papers and organised them. No one else was in uniform. Paul took a chair and went to the rear of the assembly and sat down against the right wall. Almost a hundred people were gathered together for this meeting. It was the biggest family gathering in many years.

The door to the mess hall opened, and those at the head table stood. A man and woman about Paul's grandparents' age walked in, pushing a wheelchair with an elderly woman in it. She was over ninety, the last of the original founding family members. She was John's older cousin, Susan, the offending father and son's grandmother and great-grandmother. She was wheeled to the center of the head table, her bear and eagle broaches shining brightly from the reflection of the overhead lighting system.

"Let the proceedings begin," Susan said, her voice strong. "Who speaks for the accused?"

"I do," her grandson, the colonel said.

"Who for the accusers?"

"I do, ma'am," Katia said.

"And who are you?" Susan asked. "I already know who those two are."

"Captain Katia Chimilovitch, third battalion, second company," she answered.

"I had an aunt named Katia Chimilovitch," Susan said. "She was also an eagle, like her sister, Elizabeth."

"Yes, ma'am," Katia said. "She was my great-grandmother, ma'am."

"Very well. You may start, Katia," Susan ordered.

"Yes, ma'am. My section and I had just returned from deployment with the last Bison, and we were stopped at the gate by a very junior private. He was so junior in fact that later investigation found he had only been processed in the day before. He was clearly unqualified for the duty he was performing. Upon arrival at the base proper, I reported in to the officer of the day and reported my findings. He assured me it must have been a mix-up and said he would rectify it immediately. When we came back to the outer office, we heard a lot of yelling coming from the coffee room. After investigating, we found Warrant Officer Bekenbaum vigorously reprimanding the corporal of the guard. Not wanting to circumvent the chain of command, the OD and I left, and he called his sergeant to have a chat with Warrant Bekenbaum."

"Right," said Susan. "Warrant Bekenbaum, front and center." Paul walked up and stood beside Katia, putting himself at parade rest and nodding his respect to the older woman. "Tat, he has your eyes," Susan said, "but he still looks like Uncle Andy. OK, Paul, spill it."

"Ma'am, when I arrived at the post office, I asked the corporal in charge of the orderly room where the corporal of the guard was, and I was told he was in the coffee room. When my master corporal and I walked into the coffee room, we found the corporal of the guard asleep with his feet up on the table, ma'am. His rifle was lying on the table, and all his outdoor clothing was strewn about the room. I proceeded to wake the corporal, and after a verbal castigation, I ordered him to return to his post."

"Did you not wake him by cocking your pistol and jamming it into his side, threatening to kill him if he did not return to his post?" the colonel interrupted.

"Oh, very good, Paul." Susan clapped her hands. "You showed a lot of restraint. In the old days, we would have just shot him and asked questions afterward. Sit down, Willy, and shut up," she said to the shocked colonel.

"James, is that what happened?" she asked her great-grandson.

"Yes, ma'am, I was asleep and abandoned my post, ma'am," James admitted. "No excuses, ma'am."

"Right then," Susan said. "Go out in the hallway. We will speak with you again later."

"Who was in overall charge at the time?" Susan asked.

"I was," the colonel answered.

"Why were only two troopers assigned to each gate? That is against policy," Susan asked.

"We are at peace," the colonel said. "The guard is merely symbolic, so as a cost-saving measure, I decided only four troopers were required."

"We have millions of dollars' worth of equipment, arms, and munitions on this base, and you wanted to save money, so you had only four troopers on guard duty for the whole base?" Susan was miffed.

"If the council takes my recommendations, we will get out of the military and save even more money," the colonel said. "I have all the figures right here and have shown the leaders these reports several times, but they refuse to act on them. I intend to bring it up at the next general council meeting, and I will petition to have the Bekenbaum family removed as leaders of this host."

"I see," said Susan. "Replaced, no doubt, by you?"

"If the host requests it, yes," he said.

"I have received complaints about your behaviour, Willy," Susan said. "You are threatening people with loan foreclosures and layoffs to get what you want. You used those methods to obtain your colonelcy and to stay in the ranks. What have you found out, John?"

"Willy has not completed any qualification tests in ten years or any physical examinations for the last five," John said. "He never completed his five-year full-time commitment and is definitely not entitled to the eagle or his rank."

"I have every legal right to hold this rank," Willy said. "Under Canadian law—"

"This regiment is *not* governed by Canadian law," Susan shouted, slamming her hand down hard on the table, "nor is this colony! You have been told this repeatedly, but you choose to ignore our charter and bow down to Trudeau and his liberals."

"It's a little worse than that, Susan," Nicolas said. "Our sources tell us he made a deal with the Trudeau cabinet to disband the regiment and colony, making the charter null and void."

The mess hall went completely silent as shocked family members digested that news.

"Well then, it is a good thing the charter has certain protections in place to prevent just that type of thing," Susan said. "Dumb-ass Willy would have known this, if he had actually read it. So what do we do with you, eh, Willy?"

"According to the charter and our bylaws, we have penalties for such occurrences," John said.

"To be a member of the regiment, a candidate must maintain certain minimum standards," Nicolas said. "To be a member of the colony and enjoy all the rights and privileges of membership, a candidate must have completed or be in the process of completing minimum requirements in the regiment. Willy has not performed his minimum requirements, and in addition, he has been masquerading as a colonel for the last three years. That offence alone requires he be dismissed from the regiment."

"So be it," Susan said. "Make it so."

"I will sue your asses," Willy said. "What you are doing is against Canadian law. By the time I am done with you, no one in this family will have a dime."

"How are you planning to do that?" Susan asked. "You are no longer a member of the regiment or the colony, and you have no job or money of your own. Oh, by the way, my will has already been changed—you get nothing, Willy. Good luck, and now get out of here."

"What do we do with James?" Susan asked.

"He has been reassigned to my section," Paul said. "He has been given another opportunity to qualify in two days, ma'am. I believe with the proper motivation, he will make a fine trooper, ma'am."

"If he does not qualify?" Susan asked.

"He joins his father," Nicolas said.

"Brothers and sisters," John said, "we have for many years enjoyed the benefits of the heritage our forefathers left us. Our families have profited from this relationship with our people. It is a relationship based on trust. We trust them to work hard and follow the rules. They trust us to do the same. We have grown lax in our vigilance, and the result is what just occurred here today.

"Things have been too good for too long, and we have forgotten that people look up to us for guidance and support, even though we have stepped back from exercising our leadership rights as outlined in our charter. We still have the responsibility to ensure our people are well looked after and allowed to prosper. We are not entitled, as Willy expected, to be treated differently or be granted special privileges just because of our last names or who our relatives are. I need only look to my lovely Tatiana to see what can and will happen when those in power forget the reason they were placed in that position.

"Every generation must—I repeat, *must*—ensure that the following generations understand why and how we came to be here. They must understand the sacrifices made then and now to ensure we enjoy lives of freedom and prosperity. Do not wait for the government or schools to teach these things. It is up to us. It is our legacy and duty to pass on these traditions to the next generations."

Somebody went into the kitchen for a coffee urn, and another person got some cups, and family members socialised over a huge pot of coffee. Susan was very popular, for she had seldom been seen in recent years due to her advanced years and health issues.

James returned to the mess hall and stood awkwardly at the doorway. Finally he approached Paul, who had retreated to the rear. "Warrant, I am sorry for what my father has done, sir," he said. "I just want you to know that."

"I had a talk with your sergeant and lieutenant, James," Paul said. "They seem to think you are savable. Do you want to be saved? That is the question."

"I would like to try, sir," James answered. "I'm not sure how successful a career I will have after what just happened."

"Most of us do not care about familial connections or lineage. We take you for what you are and do," Paul said. "The fact that you were asleep while on duty will be hard to live down. In a war zone, you could have caused a lot of deaths. I would have shot you—make no bones about it. But like I said, I talked to your superiors, and they told me you were on continuous duty for almost two days. I guess some leniency is called for. You do not have enough time in and are too young to be a corporal, however, so you will be busted back to private."

"I don't have a problem with that, sir," James said. "I didn't want all that responsibility anyway. I started training only this year."

"Big for your age," Paul said. "OK, it's not a total disaster then. We will have you run a qualification again tomorrow and see how well you do. If you fail, due to the short amount of time in and your age, you will have until June to qualify. You want to at least get minimum standard tomorrow, though. It takes a lot of pressure off, and you will not have to qualify again for eighteen months."

"I thought we did that every year," James asked.

"Normally, yes," Paul answered. "But if you qualify now, your year will not be up yet by June. So you won't have to do it again until next June, like everyone else."

"Ah, the way the professional soldier can manipulate the system," Susan said behind them. "I am glad to see you two talking."

"Great-grandma, I am sorry for what I did," James said, giving her a hug. "I really want to do better."

"Come by to see me every evening for the next little while, James," Susan said. "I have some things to tell you and some things for you to read."

"Auntie," Paul asked, "what was Oppa talking about when he referred to Omma's family's past?"

"That is not for me to say," Susan said. "I was not there, but I have been a part of most of the story. If your grandmother and father wish to tell you, they will. Meantime I hear a black-haired beauty has ensnared you?"

"I am not so sure about that, Auntie," Paul said, smiling. "I would like it to be so, but she is a modern career girl, so it may not come to pass."

"Word has it we have received requests for background information on you from some big shots in California," Susan said.

"That is probably about my enrollment at Caltech and teaching an ROTC class," Paul replied.

"Nope," said Susan. "We already went through all that with the US State Department and California governor's office. No, this was a personal favor, both from private and from public people. The girl must be well connected. Well connected and a looker is a good combination. I think I like her already."

"That's a change," Tatiana said. "You usually hate all the young women courting our boys."

"Never yours, Tat," Susan said, "only my own. Can't have any competition, now can I?"

"Come, James," Susan said. "Take me back home before I have to defend myself from all the lies they will be saying about me—how I was such a fine lady and the like."

"She really was a fine lady in her day," Tatiana said to Paul after Susan left, "in her own rough sort of way. She was never one for coddling. No, I cannot say anything about what your grandfather said earlier. He and I have agreed to never speak of it again. All I will say is that my family were of noble but flawed blood, and a lot of people, including them, suffered for it and still suffer for it."

"I have you and Mother," Paul said, hugging his grandmother. "You make up for all the sins of the past."

"I try, Paul. I try," Tatiana's eyes teared as she remembered another young boy in a far-off land—her brother who never had the chance to be what he could have been.

"Paul, you're making your omma cry," Nicolas said as he walked up to them.

"No," Tatiana said. "No, he is not. I am doing a fine job of it myself. Now about this woman—what's her name?"

"Emily," Katherine, Paul's mother, said. She was draped on John, Paul's grandfather's arm as they walked up. "Emily Hershmire of the California Hershmires, as opposed to the Texas Hershmires, who are 'only ranchers.'"

"Oh my," Paul said. "Somebody is full of themselves."

"Yes," Katherine said. "A certain high-society lady called to inquire into the suitability of her niece dating a common trooper and farmer. I am afraid I may have damaged your chances, my son, when I told her where to get off."

"She is supposed to come out here for the New Year," Paul said. "We'll see if she does. I hope so, but if she doesn't, I will look her up when I go to college in April. She is awfully busy, and I fear I will be as well for the next little while."

"Who cares about her stupid family? What is she like?" Tatiana asked.

"She has a journalism degree from UCLA," Paul said. "She writes as a freelancer for the *American Press*. She has been doing foreign-affairs stuff, which is how she ended up with us in Yemen. She is smart, funny, and very, very cute."

"Yes, and cute is the important part for a Bekenbaum," Tatiana said. "I will talk with Katia. Didn't they bunk together in Yemen? Come, Katherine, we'll go to Katia." The two older women walked off in search of Katia, and their interrogation into Emily's suitability for Paul would be ruthless.

"Bad enough to have your mother looking into your girlfriend," Nicolas said. "Now you have your grandmother as well. That old bat in California stirred up a hornets' nest, my boy. I think she is a nice girl, but your mother and grandmother may have decided her family is not suitable for us. If so, they'll do everything they can to sabotage the relationship."

"Like you have told me in the past, Papa," Paul said, "if it is meant to be, it is meant to be. Tatiana was not exactly thrilled with Mamma when she first heard about you and her."

"No, she most certainly was not," John said. "But she changed her mind after she met her. Tat has a good heart, but her upbringing gets in the way sometimes. She means well though. If Katia and Kat can't calm her down, I will. My only concern is about the journalist part. We have very sensitive business and military dealings going on all the time. It would not do for them to be made public."

"I understand," Paul said, "and I fully agree. Just as you keep things from me unless I need to know, I think I can do that with Emily."

"It's a little different with wives, Paul," Nicolas said. He and John both wore knowing grins. "They have ways of ferreting out information, especially if they are as smart as our wives are...and as I am sure Emily is."

"I will cross that bridge when I come to it," Paul said. "It's going to be a long day tomorrow, so I'm off to bed."

The sun was barely over the horizon and the temperature well below zero when Paul and James set up the rifle targets on the practice range. Paul showed James how to work the C7 assault rifle and let him fire two clips of ammunition for practice. They changed to fresh targets, and they both then shouldered their rifles and started off at a trot on the qualification trial. Paul kept them at a steady pace, and they were back at the rifle range well within the time limit.

"Now, James," Paul said, "just like we practiced, go down on one knee, wrap the sling around your left arm, get your sight picture, and gently squeeze the trigger." James went down on one knee and followed the directions, and five single rapid-fire shots rang out. Paul put his binoculars to his eyes and looked at the target. "OK," he said, "you passed. Three are in the bull's-eye, and the other two are close. That will do, since you need only minimum standard right now. You can work on it for the next year if you really want an eagle."

Paul pulled his rifle from his back, put the stock up to his shoulder, flipped the safety off, set the selector lever to auto, and fired three-round bursts at his target until the clip was empty.

"Works just as well in the cold as the heat," Paul said. "Good. OK, James, pick up the shell casings and targets. I will go write up the report and put it in your file. I'll see you after New Year's."

"Thank you for the extra training and a second chance, Warrant Bekenbaum," James said.

"Not a problem, Private," Paul said. "You need proper training in order to succeed."

James picked as many of the spent cartridges out of the snow as he could find and put them into a fifty-gallon drum placed at the side of the firing positions for that purpose. He walked down to the two targets and looked with pride at his. As Paul had said, three holes were dead in the center, and the other two were just outside the bull's-eye area. He looked at Paul's target. All twenty holes were in the bull's-eye area, in the shape of a happy face.

CHAPTER 9

It was the second work day after New Year's, so most of the base was on leave. "Phone call for you, Warrant," James said, peeking his head into Paul's office. "Line one."

"Funny guy," Paul said, as they had only one phone line. *This kid is turning out to be all right,* he thought. *He's got a sense of humor at least.* "Warrant Officer Bekenbaum speaking. How may I help you today, sir?" he said into the telephone's handset.

"By coming to the train station at eleven o'clock this morning to pick me up," Emily said from the other end. "I am taking a cab from the Calgary airport to the train station, and I will be at Didsbury by eleven they tell me."

"Shit," Paul said. "Why didn't you say something earlier? I am on duty until five and can't get out of it. I could have met you at the airport. It's only a forty-five minute drive from there."

"I wanted to surprise you, silly, but the cab driver has never heard of your regiment and doesn't know how to get there," Emily said.

"Yeah, we like it that way," Paul said. "Look, does he know how to get to Didsbury?"

"Yes, he says he goes fishing around there," Emily said.

"OK, ask him to drop you off at the train station there," Paul said. "Somebody will be waiting to pick you up and pay him. Can you do that?"

"He says no problem, Paul," Emily said. "Oh, I can't wait to see you. I've missed you so much and have some big news to tell you."

"I missed you too, Em," Paul said. "OK, one of my guys will pick you up. He will have a sign with your name on it, not that you will miss him. What cab company is it? See you in about an hour then," Paul said, writing down the information and hanging up.

"Private Anderson, get your ass in here!" he yelled. "You will drive my brand-new jeep to the train station in town." He tossed the keys at James. "Have the top up and the heater working. At the train station, you will pick up the love of my life and bring her and her luggage to my parents' house, where they will be waiting for you. She is arriving in less than forty-five minutes in the back of a yellow cab from Calgary." Paul tossed a roll of twenty-dollar bills at James. "Give the cabby a hundred. That should cover the fare. Oh yeah, my girl's name is Emily Hershmire. If you are late or get stuck on the way back, I'll kick your ass so hard you won't sit down for a month."

Paul picked up the phone and dialed his parents' home number. "Hey, Pop, Emily just landed in Calgary. She should be at the house in an hour or so. James is picking her up. Sorry, Pop, she just called. She wanted to surprise us. Thanks, I'll see you about five thirty."

Paul attacked his paperwork with a passion. He wanted to finish it by the end of the day so he could start his one-month leave the next day. All the rest of the battalion was already on leave, and he had just been waiting for Emily to arrive so he could take his.

James stuck his head in to let Paul know he had returned. He ducked back out after seeing Paul furiously attacking paperwork with his typewriter and a mass of it already in the outgoing basket. Occasionally James brought a fresh cup of coffee and left with the old cup. He took the contents of the outgoing basket and put it on the clerk's desk for when he came back from Christmas break.

That girl Emily is a looker, James thought. *Just the right amount of everything.* Even though she wore expensive clothing, she had no problem hoisting her skirt up and jumping into the passenger seat of the jeep after helping him pile her luggage into the back. She seemed excited to be there and was all smiles. "Do you always have this much snow?" she had asked. "We hardly ever have any back home, and it never stays long. My, it is cold. It doesn't get this cold back home either." She chattered away most of the fifteen minutes it had taken to get to the Bekenbaums' farmhouse, where John and Nicolas were on hand to help unload luggage and introduce her to the female members of the clan.

"Warrant, it's quitting time," James said. "Do you want me to stay, or can I go?"

"Holy shit!" Paul said. "I lost track of time. Let's get the hell out of here. Did Emily make it OK?"

"Yeah," James said, "when I left her, the Valkyries were in attack mode, so I beat a fast retreat."

"Don't blame you," Paul said. "I, on the other hand, do not have that luxury. I think I have a white flag around here someplace."

"Your girl looks like she can hold her own, Warrant," James said. "How did she end up here?"

"What you mean, cousin," Paul said, "is how could a beauty like her end up with a putz like me?"

"OK, you got me," James said. "She is definitely good looking, and you are definitely one ugly mother, cousin."

"Oh, the jealousy of the young," Paul said. "When you grow up, perhaps you will find the woman of your dreams." Paul put his right arm around his cousin's back and thumped it a couple times before driving off to his parents' house.

"Paul Bekenbaum, get right back out to the porch and brush that snow off your pants," Katherine yelled. "My God, you're tracking snow all over my kitchen floor."

"Not to mention getting it all over Emily's beautiful dress," Tatiana said, pointing her finger at him. "Put her down, you oaf, and go change into decent clothing. Or do I have to come over there and pull your ear?"

"Oh, Mrs. Bekenbaum," Emily said, "it's OK. I don't mind." Tatiana and Katherine looked at Emily in surprise, as she had spoken to them in American-accented German.

"No grandson of mine is going to act like a swine herd," Tatiana said in the same language. "He has better manners than that."

"What do you mean by not telling us she is German?" Katherine demanded. "You have embarrassed us now."

"Yes, Mamma, Omma," Paul said, his hands up with palms forward. "I go. I go. I'll be right back. Valkyries is right," he muttered under his breath.

"I heard that, young man," Tatiana said. "I'll show you Valkyries."

Paul ran out of the kitchen to howls of laughter from his mother and Emily, as Tatiana picked up a wooden spoon and threatened him with it. "Now that's the way to handle a man," Emily said.

"We have to," Katherine said. "Otherwise, they would run all over us."

"Yes, get after them while they are young," Tatiana said, tossing the spoon back on the counter. "When they get big, they will still be scared of you."

"Oh, I don't want Paul scared of me," Emily said. "I just got him, so he's not scared."

"Oh no," Tatiana said, shaking her finger. "Scared sons and grandsons, yes. Lovers and husbands, no."

"There are better ways to keep them in line," Katherine said, smiling. "We will teach you those later. These men are different from what you are used to."

"Paul said something about Valkyries as he ran past me," Nicolas said. "What are you three up to in here?"

"Why, nothing, dear." Katherine put her arm around his waist and kissed him on the cheek. "Just making Emily comfortable and getting dinner ready."

"Oh, Jesus," John said. "A Russian Imperialist and two American capitalists working together. We poor Canucks don't stand a chance."

"You love every second of it," Tatiana said, kissing her man on the cheek. "Sit down before this food gets cold."

"Did you speak German at home?" Katherine asked Emily.

"No, my mother forbade it," she answered. "Father spoke German with his brothers when they came over but never in the house. I learned it in college. If my mother found out, she would be very upset."

"The more languages one knows, the better, we always say," Tatiana said. "Paul speaks French and Russian as well. Almost everyone in this family does."

"Mother feels only the lower classes and immigrants speak other languages," Emily said. "I have found she is mistaken about those types of things."

"Don't be too harsh on your mother, dear," Tatiana said. "She was brought up that way and does not know better. I was the same way until I met these wonderful people."

"I, on the other hand," said Katherine, "am from the other side of the tracks. My parents were poor immigrant farmers who barely kept their heads above water. This family welcomed me with open arms."

"I have something to show all of you," Emily said. "Will you excuse me for a moment?"

She returned with a portfolio, laid it on the kitchen table, and opened it. Looking up at them was an eight-by-ten colour photograph of Paul, who was squatting down and hugging a young girl with a candy bar in her hand. The next one was of him in the commander's turret of a Bison, with headphones over his blue beret and a microphone to his lips. The dark green of his uniform contrasted with the white interior of the Bison. Other pictures were of the action against the Yemenis; Katia with a C9 in both hands, firing from the turret of the Bison; Paul jumping off the Bison, holding a C7 rifle; and fire coming out of the C7's barrel as he fired from the shoulder. One photo was of Paul directing troopers with prisoners and wounded. In another a helicopter was landing, and troopers with the regiment's flashes and blue berets were jumping out with weapons at the ready. The Huey was hovering two or three feet off the ground, as door gunners scanned the area with their weapons.

The next series of pictures depicted life in camp. Troopers threw baseballs or footballs, played cards, or just sat and read books. Troopers did vehicle maintenance, and others were on guard duty. One was of a trooper with tears in his eyes as he held a child having his broken arm set by a female doctor in uniform. Another series of pictures showed troopers hamming it up in front of a construction site as well as the same troopers hard at work building it. In the last picture of that series, a group of Arab men and women shook hands with the troopers and handed them food. "That was Paul's idea," Nicolas said. "The locals wanted a multipurpose building to house a school, mosque, and medical facility. They provided the land and half the labor. We provided the materials and the other half of the labor."

"The locals are very happy about it," Paul said. "I don't know why the Saudis were not involved."

The next group of pictures included one of Paul standing in the jeep, motioning forward. There was one of Katia with her ponytail flying behind her and hands clutching the .30-calibre rifle in the turret of her M111 as she stood halfway out the hatch. The next was of Paul and Katia, her hair now covered by her campaign hat, shaking hands with the prince in his native ceremonial robes. Then there was a picture of the Saudis shooting on horseback and on the ground. There were more of the regiment's troopers doing the same, but they were down on one knee rather than prone.

The next picture was of two riders hanging under their horses' necks side by side and firing pistols. The horses were at full speed, manes and tails streaming behind them. Next the two riders were going the other way, standing in their stirrups, their rifles against their shoulders. Flames were coming out of barrels, and used shell casings were flying up over their heads. The final series of shots in this series were of the same two riders with their swords extended as they rode by their targets and decapitated them. Katia's hair flew free as her campaign hat bounced on her back.

"Paul, you still can't get your eagle," Tatiana said, "even with all that."

"He likes happy faces," Nicolas said. "It's cute but unfortunately not enough shots are in the bull's-eye area."

The next picture was of Paul on the mess table, his legs splayed in the Cossack dance. There was one of him and Katia. Her hair was long, and she had her hands on her hips, while his arm was around her waist. In the last picture, Paul's hand was under Emily's chin and hers was behind his head as they kissed. Nicolas looked up and saw Emily with her head down and her cheeks red as the Valkyries looked at her. "I forgot that was there," she said. "All the pictures but that one will be published in *Life* magazine's April edition. America and the world need to know what Canada is doing and that the work you are performing is bringing peace to the world. ▪

"It is also a piece about the Old World meeting the New," she continued. "*Life* has found archived pictures of your regiment from Korea, both world wars, and the Boer conflict. They also have paintings and drawings by Fredrick Remington of your trek to this land and your life in Russia before."

"John, perhaps a call to the publisher?" Tatiana asked.

"Thank you, Emily," John said, "but we need to approve the text and photographs before publication."

"But why?" Emily asked. "It is an important story, and the world needs to hear it."

"Our enemies—both foreign and domestic—don't need to see certain things," Nicolas said. "We like to fly under the radar, Emily. It is easier for us that way. We are not saying no to the publication, but we want editorial privileges. It would be like publishing details of your president's security arrangements."

"The magazine will publish whatever I write," Emily said. "You can edit what is written and submitted from my end. I have no control over the archival elements."

"Thank you, my dear," Tatiana said. "The family appreciates it. Someone will contact *Life* with our concerns. You will not be involved. Let's eat, and then you two get out of here for a while, yes?"

The two could see their breath as they walked through the snow-covered farmyard. "It has been a long day for you," Paul said to Emily. The sun had long since gone down. At this time of year, it went down just after five in the afternoon and did not rise until eight in the morning. Unlike most farmyards, the Bekenbaums had a streetlight that, reflecting the snowpack, gave more than enough light to see in the yard. It was quiet, the only sounds coming from their winter boots crunching through snow. It was just below zero, warmer than it had been for days but not warm enough to melt any snow or ice.

Emily took in her surroundings. "Yes, I was on the eight o'clock flight to Denver," Emily said. "I had to wait two hours for the flight to Calgary."

"I wish you had called," Paul said. "I would have met you at the airport."

"It was a last-minute thing, Paul," Emily said.

"We weren't expecting you until late January or early February," Paul said.

Emily put her arm through his and laid her head on his shoulder, snuggling close. She had not realised how much she missed his smell and the sound of his voice. "I don't want to talk about it," she said. "I'm here now, and that's all that matters. God, it is so quiet and dark here."

"Ha!" Paul laughed. "There is too much light here, and it is noisy compared to my place."

"You have your own place?" Emily asked.

"Actually it's my father's old place," Paul said. "When my great-grandfather died, Great-uncle Stephan and his family took over the estate right in Didsbury, and they run the family-held businesses. My grandfather and Tatiana took over this place from him, and my father took over my grandfather's place. So I now have my father's. It's not much. The barn I built before I left for Yemen is three times the size of the house, which is just a one-room shack my father built before the war."

"But what of your brother George?" Emily asked. "Shouldn't that be his place?"

"George has decided to be a professional soldier," Paul replied. "When he marries he will have quarters for married officers. Until then, he lives in a barracks. When he retires he will move to his grandfather's ranch in Montana."

"His grandfather has a ranch?" Emily asked.

"Yes, he will inherit it after he retires," Paul said. "Mother is holding it in trust for him until then."

"You inherit your father's property, and George gets your mother's?" Emily asked.

"We have different biological fathers, Em," Paul said. "My father is the only father George has ever known. He has been adopted by my father and is loved by us all, but he is not a Bekenbaum. He is a Cossack by merit and by acclaim, but not by blood. It is complicated, but he is OK with it. He has full shares in everything but the land."

"Oh," Emily said.

"The Valkyries were not too rough on you, I hope," Paul said. "They can be a bit overwhelming. I hoped to be a buffer for you when you arrived."

"It is only to be expected, Paul," Emily said. "They love you very much and want to protect you from this evil American journalist gold digger."

"Hey, that's not fair," Paul said. "They are decent people."

"Oh, I didn't say that to be mean, Paul," Emily said hastily. "It is only natural for mothers to protect their young. My mother did much the same when I was home, trying to protect her oldest daughter from the gold-digging exotic foreigner, who is after my money and American citizenship."

"Well, I thank her for calling me *exotic*," Paul said, smiling, "but you can also tell her I have my own money and land. And if I want it, I have American citizenship through my mother and stepbrother."

"I forgot about that." Emily sighed. "Now she will be even more upset. She has no more excuses to keep me from you. Why do you call them the Valkyries?" Emily asked.

"It's a family thing," Paul said. "We and the whole community love them dearly, but you never want to get on their bad sides. During the first war, Grandfather was accepting the surrender of a German general and his staff when the general shot him. Grandmother shot the general and half his staff. While a firefight erupted all round them, she dragged Grandfather behind their armoured car and performed field surgery on him right there."

"Oh my God," Emily said, "no wonder they are so close."

"Six months before that," Paul continued, "Grandfather pulled her out of Russia along with the rest of our families. The Communists had pulled her out of the line and were not going to let her go with the rest, so Grandfather put an end to it."

"Your people were involved in that, too?" Emily said. "Rumor says one of the czar's daughters escaped and came to America."

"Don't know about that, Em," Paul said. "Stalin wanted the Cossacks gone, one way or the other. We were fighting in Afghanistan for the British at the time against the Turks, and the British asked us to help evacuate some noble families from the Odesa region. We said we would, on the condition we could evacuate all our family members and other Cossack families that wanted to come. We pulled out around three thousand people, mostly widows and children. Grandmother smuggled her way into the midst of them, and Grandfather took her under his wing."

"Come on," Paul said. "It's cold out here. I'll take you back to the house. We have a lot of time to be together, and I have to feed my horses before bed."

Paul stuck his head out the door of his cabin at the sound of the horn to see his grandmother's four-wheel-drive Ford truck come to a stop in his yard. Emily was in the passenger seat, today dressed in more sensible blue jeans, high-top insulated boots, a toque, and enough layers to totally disguise her womanhood. Tatiana, as was normal for her, had on insulated riding boots over woolen breeches, a rabbit-fur hat, and a down-filled vest under an open insulated blue-jean jacket.

"Welcome, ladies," Paul said. "I have a couple clean mugs here and some fresh coffee."

"Emily wants to see your famous horses," Tatiana said, "so here we are. Since I am here, there will be no hanky-panky."

"Ah, come on, Grandma," Paul said. Emily turned an enchanting shade of deep red.

"Not on first day," Tatiana said, affecting the cute Russian accent she often did when being mischievous. "Maybe next week, I allow hanky-panky. I see." She giggled.

Paul poured two cups of hot coffee for the ladies and found some sugar. He apologised for not having cream or milk on hand. He didn't use it, or sugar, in his coffee and so had none. Emily looked around the clean but Spartan shack. Everything was neat and tidy, unlike most men's apartments she had seen. It had a bedroom, living room, and kitchen, all in about fifteen feet by ten feet, and bookshelves and a number of pictures adorned the wall. One photo was of a fierce-looking, clean-shaven Cossack with a woolen winter hat on his head. He wore a fleece-lined sheepskin jacket, and his sheepskin-gloved right hand held a lance with a long wicked-looking point on the end. Six cartridge loops on each side of his jacket held bullets, and slung on his back was a rifle with the barrel visible over his right shoulder. A sword was fastened to his saddle, and his belt held a brace of pistols. A coiled whip hung from his right hip, and his left hand secured the reins of the horse he was mounted on. The horse and the man were broadside to the camera, both looking into its lens. The horse had one ear forward and the other back. The man scowled, looking as if he had been on the road for some time, as did the horse, which was covered in dust.

"Somebody was unhappy." Emily pointed at the picture.

"If you look closer," Paul said, "you will see the lance's point and top half of its shaft are darker than the rest. What you can't see is the breech of the Winchester, which is dark and discoloured, or the pistol, which has also been fired. Frederic Remington took that picture after my great-grandfather rescued my soon-to-be great-grandmother and her sister from road bandits. This was before Remington became the world-renowned painter. He was just a reporter for a New York paper at the time and had a habit of getting under Andreas's skin sometimes. Andreas is mounted on Bartholomew, the start of our horse's bloodline—he and Elizabeth's, my great-grandmother's, mare. My aunt Andrea is named after him."

The next picture was of a striking woman standing in her stirrups, her hat bouncing on her back and her ponytail flying. She was turned sideways, holding a Winchester with fire coming out of its barrel and an expended cartridge still flying in the air behind her. "That is Great-grandmother Elizabeth on her mare the day she qualified for her eagle. She, her sister, and three others were the first women to do so. The next picture is of Grandfather in South Africa," Paul continued.

There was a picture of a much younger Tatiana in the turret of an armoured car. Her hands were on a Lewis gun, which was obviously firing—brass was flying out from the breech and flames were coming from the barrel. "My small contribution in France in 1918," Tatiana said. "I was on active duty for only a couple of months before the war ended."

"Don't let her kid you," Paul said. "She has a chestful of medals for her dress uniform, and they are not the 'I was there' type."

Next was a photo of Nicolas, who was shirtless and wore a campaign hat, long riding boots, and British campaign shorts. He stood beside an armoured car, with field glasses to his eyes, and an American general was beside him. "Is that Patton?" Emily asked.

"Yes, we served under him in North Africa and Sicily and then again after the closing of the Falaise Gap and at the Battle of the Bulge," Tatiana said.

Another picture was of Nicolas and a Russian officer saluting each other with glasses of booze. Nicolas's crisp American uniform was complete with a shiny helmet with a star on the front of it. "You made the linkup with the Russians. Why am I not surprised?" Emily asked. "That's a lot of history there. Why has no one heard of you people?"

"Because we do not wish it," Tatiana said. "Come and see the other Bekenbaum legacy—Bartholomew's offspring." Paul, Emily, and Tatiana walked into the nearby barn and were greeted by snorts and whinnies from the horses inside.

"Would you care to go for a ride?" Paul asked. "Their exercise routine has gone all to hell, ever since I left for Yemen."

"Isn't it too cold for them?" Emily asked.

"No." Paul laughed. "I have to force them to come in at night. They like being outside."

It was short work for Tatiana and Paul to saddle and bridle two horses and to set up Emily's saddle. "We ride Western style," Paul said, "so the stirrups are a little longer than you are used to. Keep the reins loose, unless you want to stop or back up. These horses are trained to neck or knee rein, so don't jerk the reins to go left or right, or you might find yourself on your ass. Cody is fairly calm, but she is still a trained Cossack horse, so don't fall asleep on her. OK, Grandma, you can get back to the ranch. We should be there by lunchtime."

Tatiana patted Emily on the knee. "I like this girl," Tatiana said. She pulled Paul down by his shoulders and tapped him on the cheek with her hand. "You behave yourself, young man. If you are not at the ranch by lunchtime, or if she complains you were bothering her, I will take Andreas's whip to you." Tatiana jumped into her Ford pickup and roared down the road to the main house.

"She is quite the lady," Emily said.

"So is my mother, in a calmer way," Paul said.

"I'm not sure I can match what they do," Emily said.

"Who says you have to?" Paul asked. "You do with your camera and typewriter what Tatiana and Katia do with a rifle. You get in harm's way the same way they do. You just do it with a pen and a lens. So, you have been on a horse a time or two, I see."

"I told you I had equestrian studies in school," Emily said.

"Well, we won't push the ponies too hard today," Paul said. "It's too cold, and there is too much snow and ice for that. Besides, it is nice to just walk and take in the scenery."

"It is beautiful here," Emily said. "I could do without the cold though."

"Do you see that line of clouds behind us?" Paul asked. "That means the wind will shift to come from the south west and the temperature is about to change. We call them *chinooks*. By the end of the day, the snow will be melting. But I am sure it is still colder than you are used to."

"Yes, it was seventy degrees when I boarded the airplane in LA," Emily said. "It's, what, ten degrees here?"

"More like close to zero." Paul smiled and reined his horse to a stop. "Look to your right, just under the trees there. That's a moose and her calf."

"My Lord!" Emily exclaimed. "They are huge!" She immediately had her camera to her eye, snapping away.

"The bulls are bigger, with impressive sets of antlers," Paul said.

"She is bigger than this horse," Emily said.

"One moose will feed your family for a month or so," Paul said. "We have two types of deer—white-tailed deer keep mostly to the plains areas, and mule deer hang around the wooded areas and the fringes of the plains. Occasionally elk come down here but not too often. They like to hang out in the high-mountain park areas. Up higher are mountain sheep."

"You have your rifle with you," Emily said. "Are you hunting?"

"No," Paul replied. "A grizzly bear is hanging about this year. It might den up and go to sleep, or it might not. Usually grizzlies don't hibernate, and they are always hungry. Anything, including us, is food for them. We should be OK on the horses, but it's better to be safe."

"Are you pulling my leg?" Emily said.

"No, really." Paul stopped his horse once again. "Look down. That griz walked on top of Grandmother's tire tracks. It is headed for the bush, probably after the moose calf." In the snow was a set of very large bear tracks. The claws were extended, and one set pointed inward. "Large male," Paul said. "You can tell from how big the pads are, how deep the prints are in the snow, and the way the front feet are pointed in. If he starts in on the cattle, we will have to do something about him."

"I thought all bears hibernated in winter," Emily said.

"The black bears are hibernating," Paul replied, "but unless it is really cold for an extended period of time or game is scarce, grizzly bears don't. If they do, a chinook will bring them back out."

A short time later, Paul and Emily came to a cleared area, where cattle grazed. The cattle were wary, watching them until they proved not to be a threat, and then went back to grazing. Dotted here and there in the fields and pastures, seemingly haphazardly, were oil pumps. Most were silent and unmoving. "What are those?" Emily asked.

"We call them *duck heads*," Paul explained. "Those particular ones pump oil, but we also have gas wells."

"Why aren't they pumping?" she asked.

"We limit what we pump to a certain amount per month," Paul said. "Once the oil is gone, it is gone, and so will be the money we receive for it. I suppose we could be like Rockefeller and Standard Oil, which put in wells side by side and pump twenty-four hours a day, but we are here for a long time. Our grandchildren will need the money."

"Oh, is Standard Oil up here too?" Emily asked.

"Not that I know of," Paul answered, "but they may have a Canadian subsidiary. We have a deal with BP for the oil and Shell for the gas. We work with both companies in North Africa and the Middle East, so it is a good fit. Now how is California, besides being warm and sunny?"

"Mother is harping on me to stay home and start a family," Emily said, sighing, "but what else is new? American young people are getting restless about the Vietnam War and being drafted and all that. Racial conflicts are starting up again. It is not so bad in California, but Southern states are becoming battlegrounds."

"Our generation wants to be heard," Paul said. "Some of the same things are happening in Canada. Here in the colony, we are a little outside the norm. We are still taught the old ways of putting country first and then our neighbors. The city people tend to forget those things."

"You made fun of me for believing your jokes about igloos and cold," Emily said, "but the reality is somewhat true."

"It's colder now than normal. It is also a lot colder than you are used to, but it is nowhere near as cold as it is way up north or, for that matter, to the east of us. In the summer it is probably as warm or warmer than it is where you live. You are so good at asking questions," he said with a smile, "but not so good at answering them."

"My father's family runs a line of general merchandising and hardware stores throughout the Southwestern United States," she said. "When he went to California to expand the business there, he bought a small newspaper and found he liked it, so that part of his business began. He has pieces of other businesses, and although we're not super rich, we do all right. My sister and I went to private primary and secondary schools, and while she chose the University of California, Berkeley, the normal route for the daughters of the rich and famous—I chose to take business and journalism classes. My sister is married to a very successful litigation lawyer, has a son and a daughter, belongs to all the right clubs, and is the apple of my mother's eye. Those who don't know me well have called me *pushy*, *bossy*, and *bitchy*, and those who do call me a *workaholic perfectionist*. I am on the road ten months a year. I have no kids, no husband, and until recently no full-time boyfriend. My mother is very disappointed in me."

Paul caught the "boyfriend" comment and smiled to himself. "What does your mother expect from a prospective son-in-law?" Paul asked. "As you can see, I am but the younger son of a poor Canadian farmer from the back of beyond."

"I imagine she will put up with you in the short term, my love." Emily leaned over in the saddle and gave him a squeeze. "A good-looking young hunk with all your muscles will not be displeasing to her, but she will expect me to dump you and settle down with a nice doctor, lawyer, or stockbroker from our class. My father will just love you. He loves hunting, fishing, and outdoorsy things, like you do. He, unlike my mother, remembers what it was like to have nothing and scramble for every nickel."

"So do I," Paul said. "I make half-decent money as a warrant officer, but it's not enough to buy a house and car—one or the other, maybe, but not both. When I go to university, it will be even worse."

"But your parents and grandparents—" Emily said.

"We must all make it on our own," Paul said. "That is what brought down the old regimes. They felt entitled and did not have to work for anything. I will never starve or want for anything, but if I want to better myself, I must do it on my own."

"I see that sense of entitlement in my sister and her children already," Emily agreed. "A lot of my contemporaries at school and college were the same. I never felt comfortable around them. I guess, being the oldest, I tend to see things differently. Your people seem so laid-back and relaxed. Your family accepts me as one of their own, and they hardly know me yet. This is so different than what I am used to in New York and even in California. With my people, it is all about monetary status."

"America—the land of opportunity," Paul said, smiling, "as long as you have money and don't make the rich people uncomfortable. Don't give me that look. It's the truth, and you know it. It's the same here, but add the rich Anglo-Saxon and Quebecois original settlers to the statement."

"I suppose you're right. Don't make a habit of it." Emily poked him in the ribs. "This is nice," she continued, looking around at the snow-covered trees. "Stop for a second." She opened her jacket, pulled out her ever-present thirty-five-millimetre camera, and rode away a few steps. She photographed the clearing below them and the farm, where the fresh snow in the yard contrasted with the red of the barn and outbuildings and smoke from the furnaces rose straight up in the cold, still air.

She turned and took a few shots of Paul and his horse, with the farm below in the background. *What a man of contrasts,* she thought. *When last I saw him, he was roaring around the desert in a modern vehicle, ready to kill anyone who had a gun, and now he sits on a horse like someone out of the history books, quietly making jokes and laughing.* "How do you do it?"

"Do what?" Paul asked.

"You went from being a nice but hell-bent-for-leather, hard-charging career soldier to being a mild-mannered, laid-back farmer," she answered. "Back home, our boys have problems coming to terms with being back in civilian life."

"Must be our training," Paul said, after thinking for a minute. "We have our share of people who have problems reintegrating after some hard duty. It might be easier for us because we all—no matter who we are or what our physical conditions are—have to serve five years. At the end of the day, it is a job and not who I am. Come on. Grandma will be upset if her lunch gets cold, and it looks like we have visitors."

More vehicles than usual were in front of the main house. Paul noticed four strange men—two wandering around the yard seemingly aimlessly and the other two stationed to watch the doors and sides of the house. As Paul and Emily rode into the yard and toward the barn's corral, two of the families' ranch hands walked out of the outbuilding attached to the barn and waited for the couple to dismount. Both men had bulges under their left armpits, telling Paul they were armed. He nodded his head toward the four newcomers and raised his eyebrows. "SAS," was all the ranch hand said, taking Paul's reins and leading the horse away.

Paul and Emily walked toward the covered back porch of the house under the watchful eyes of the four new men. Emily happily chatted away about how rare it was to have snow in California, not noticing the men's earphones or the shotguns they were putting back under their greatcoats. Paul held the door open for Emily and nodded at the guard by the door.

"Long time no see, Corporal," Paul said. "It was a hell of a lot warmer the last time."

"Yes, Mr. Bekenbaum," the SAS man said. "Damn near boiled my blood out of my veins that day. Now my balls are freezing off."

"If you couldn't take a joke…" Paul said.

"You shouldn't have joined," the corporal finished. Both laughed at the old standard enlisted man's joke.

Paul slapped the man on the shoulder. He unzipped his jacket as he walked onto the porch. "Very nice," he said, seeing Emily bent over to remove her boots. She looked over her shoulder and stuck her tongue out at him.

"Paul, you beast," Katia said from her vantage point at the kitchen table. "Look at him, Auntie, ogling that poor girl's rear end."

"You are just jealous," Tatiana said. "I never minded when John ogled my butt in the old days. Not much to see there now though."

"Having kids tends to do that," Katherine agreed. "Paul, be nice and show her how to use a boot jack before all the males in this house get distracted."

Paul pulled a boot jack over with a toe and deftly placed the heel of one boot in its V-shaped elevated front and stood on the back end of it with the other foot, pulling the right boot off. He switched feet and did the left. "It's a lot easier than bending over," Paul said, shooting the boot jack over the floor to Emily. "Must have been invented by a woman."

"Probably," Emily said. "We are much more practically minded than you men are." She struggled somewhat to get the right balance but managed to successfully remove her footgear.

"No, dear," Tatiana said, giving Emily a hug when she entered the kitchen proper. "If a woman invented that, she would never let a man near it. Men have such nice bottoms to look at."

"Cousin, behave," said a female with an upper-class English accent. "The matriarch is never to say such things."

"Oh, poo, poo," Tatiana said. "Why not? I heard your mother say the same things when she was younger and your sister, too, come to think of it. My, how things change the older one gets."

"Inside the family is one thing." Margaret switched to speak in German. "Outside is a different matter."

"I think Emily understands that people are people, no matter their status," Tatiana replied, also in German. "Emily, this is my cousin Margaret Windsor from Britain. Margaret, this is Emily Hershmire from America. She is a freelance reporter for the *AP* and has latched onto poor Paul. She will hopefully make an honest man of him. Emily, Margaret's grandfather and my father were cousins."

"Pleased to meet you, Ms. Windsor," Emily replied in accented German. "Are you Charles's mother? I met him when he was in Yemen training with Paul for a short while."

"No, I am his aunt," Margaret said, switching back to English.

"Where is your hubby?" Paul asked. "He and Emily could compare notes and maybe photographs. Margaret's husband is a freelance photographer in Britain, mostly in the fashion industry."

"He and your father went out to Horseshoe Canyon today," Margaret informed Paul. "He wants some shots of the badlands in winter to go with the ones I took in the summer. Tomorrow they are headed into the bush for a couple of days."

"Well, maybe Emily and I will tag along," Paul said. "We are going to see whether Emily's Californian blood will freeze up here. Then I am off to boil to death in California for a few years."

"Do dress warmly tomorrow, dear," Margaret said. "I spent three months up there in this weather with Paul's brother George a few years back. It gave a new meaning to the term *ice queen*. Did you say you are off to California for a few years, Paul?"

"Yes, Caltech has offered me some good terms to attend their university," Paul said. "In addition the US Army wants me to do some training for their reserve officer program at Caltech, so I will get paid while going to school. Works well for me."

"We need to do something like that back in the UK," Margaret said. "I fear we will fall behind in the electronics game. I try to help but to no avail."

"You can always keep buying our stuff," Paul said. "We can use the foreign exchange."

"What do you do in England, Margaret?" Emily asked.

"Oh, not much," Margaret said. "A little of this and a little of that. It is all quite boring actually. Class structure has limits both ways, dear, up and down the scale. There are things I would like to pursue, such as electronics and radios, like Paul here, but I am prohibited from them because of my gender and status in society. I do envy you people sometimes for that."

"Don't kid yourself," Emily said. "I fight hard almost every day to keep doing what I am doing. I receive a lot of negative feedback, on the job and from my family and friends. But it is helpful when women, like both Mrs. Bekenbaums, break the mould so successfully."

"Tut, tut" Tatiana said. "Back home, we had no choice. The men were gone for most of every year, fighting in some stupid war or other. We had to run the farms and the businesses, or we would have all starved. Our men are used to women working, and in fact, they outright encourage us."

"Paul's great-grandmother was very instrumental in granting women the right to vote in the British Commonwealth," Margaret said. "Before she got involved, women were not even classed as people."

Emily looked at Tatiana and Katherine, who nodded their heads. "Elizabeth would never admit to it," Tatiana said, "nor will you see her name anywhere, but she funded and sponsored both women who went to England to address the House of Lords on the issue."

"Of course Andreas and his friend Rudy were wealthy peers, with a lot of prestige and influence at court," Margaret said.

"My God," Emily said. "Women in the States used their arguments in our move to get recognised. Those ideas came from here?"

"Be careful what you say," Tatiana said to Margaret in Russian before switching back to English. "Like I said, Emily," she continued, "we do not seek out the limelight. We funded the research of the ladies who did all the work, that's all."

"How long are you here for?" Paul asked Margaret.

"Just a few days," she answered. "It is always a pleasant break to come here and have your grandmother connect me back into reality."

Having successfully changed the subject, Paul joined the group of females for lunch, and they chatted about mundane and normal topics. "Omma," Paul asked, waiting for a break in the conversation, "can I borrow your truck to take Emily shopping in Calgary for some more appropriate clothing?"

"But of course," Tatiana said. "Her clothing would be really nice, if you were at the beach."

"Would it be all right if I tag along?" Margaret asked. "I can help Emily out a bit, and I really need to pick up some casual things."

"Um…" Paul nodded his head toward the SAS men outside the door.

"Oh, not to worry," Margaret said. "We are not in Mumbai, for God's sake. They can stay here and relax for a couple days." The two women hurried about to get ready for the trip.

Paul walked out to break the news to the princess's security team. "I suppose she is right," the SAS commander said. "No one really knows we are here to begin with, and she will be with you, so it should be all right. The boys and I can use a break. We're off to the Caribbean after this, and it won't be half as casual."

"Just to let you know," Paul said, "it might be casual here, but it's possibly more deadly. I spotted signs of a grizzly bear about a mile west of here, and he's a big one. If he comes by here, your shotguns will only upset him but not kill him. Check in with the ranch hands. They're members of the regiment and will let you know what you need to do."

"Right, thanks," the SAS man said.

Paul walked over to the barn and let the ranch hands know he would be gone until later in the day and warned about the bear. They told him they would keep an eye out and let everyone else know about it as they came in.

Emily and Margaret bustled out of the house, looking for Paul. He waved them over to Tatiana's Ford pickup. Paul was driving, and Emily jumped in beside him. Margaret slammed the door shut as she took her position next to the passenger door. Paul fired up the big V-8 engine and started for the road, which led first to town and then to the highway toward the much larger city an hour away. With three adults jammed in the cab of the pickup, the windows were frosting over. Paul turned the heater up high and directed it onto the windshield. "It will take a few minutes to warm up," he said. "When it's this cold out, the truck's heater can only do so much." Soon they were unbuttoning their jackets as the cab warmed up.

The two women chatted about clothes and the latest fashions, while Paul navigated his way down the snow- and ice-covered highway. As they drove through the center of Calgary, Paul found a place to park in one of the lots. The trio walked a short distance to the Hudson's Bay department store, and Paul, like countless boyfriends and husbands before him, spent several hours sitting around while the two women tried on clothing and asked his opinions. After their purchases were completed, Paul was loaded down with packages. He headed to the truck, after giving the ladies directions to an upscale steak house just down the street. Paul dumped the packages on the truck's seat and then joined them at the restaurant.

He was ushered to a table in the back, away from the high-powered oil executives having their dinners. The two women were sipping red-colour drinks. Margaret's signature cigarette holder was out, with a cigarette burning in it. "Just a bottle of Molson's Canadian," Paul said to the waiter as he sat down, placing his wide-brimmed Stetson on the empty chair at the table. The waiter wrinkled his nose as he walked away, clearly not impressed at having to serve some ranch hand, his girl, and her mother. "The steak here is excellent," Paul said. "All of the cuts are good, and I see you are already trying the famous Caesar cocktail. The bartender here invented it—Clamato juice, lime, and vodka."

"Yes, very nice indeed," Margaret said. "Much better than the vodka and soda I normally indulge in."

"Excuse me," a woman said, coming up to them. She was from one of the executives' tables and looked like the typical overdressed and overly jeweled new-money wife. "You look just like Princess Margaret."

"I get that a lot," Margaret said, affecting a Midwestern American accent. "Why, back home, they even have me wear a crown and fancy gown on special occasions."

"You really must give my husband your number," the woman said, dropping a business card on the table. "We could have you come and perform at one of our parties."

"Certainly," Margaret said. "I will have my cousin here make the arrangements."

Paul took a look at the card and then at the table the woman had come from as she excitedly hurried back to it. As she pointed back at the table, the husband looked over and saw Paul, who nodded. The man pulled his wife down to her seat and spoke quietly to her. She turned white and looked back at their table, and Paul waved.

"Do you know them?" Emily asked.

"Yes," Paul answered. "Her husband manages one of our pipeline companies. Cousin, do you think you could forgo the cigarette holder just this once?"

"Yes, I believe so." Margaret kept the American accent. "We are having such a nice time. It would be a shame to ruin it with too much attention."

Their waiter returned with Paul's beer and a glass, plunking them on the table. The trio ordered their meals, and the unimpressed waiter hurried away. *The faster I get these people their meals, the faster I can get them out of here,* he thought.

"My dear Paul." It was the chef, who approached their table. "I thought that was you. Who are these stunning ladies with you today?"

Paul stood and shook the chef's hand. "Good to see you, Peter. This is my cousin Margaret and my friend Emily."

"Your resemblance to the royal family is amazing," Peter said, shaking Margaret's hand. "One of Paul's aunts looks almost like the queen, and I went to school with her. Emily, it's a pleasure. Any friend of Paul's is a friend of mine. When did you get back, Paul?"

"Just before Christmas," Paul said. "This is the first chance I've had to come to town. I met Emily over there. I hope to join her in California come April."

"Most excellent," Peter said. "Are your mother and grandmother fine?"

"Yes, they send their greetings," Paul said. "As soon as it gets warmer, you can probably expect a visit."

"If your grandmother is still driving that old Ford, God help us all," Peter said, laughing. "She terrorises all the Calgary drivers with that thing. Enjoy your meal, and say hello from me to the family." As Peter headed back to the kitchen, he stopped at a few tables on the way, bypassing the one the executive's wife had come from. Emily looked at Paul and raised her eyebrows.

"I believe, my dear," Margaret said, "you will find that Katherine owns this fine eatery and the hotel it is connected to. I also believe the service we are receiving from our waiter is about to get much, much better and that a certain pipeline manager will most likely be transferred to the frozen north shortly."

"Don't be so catty," Paul said. "I won't hold what a man's wife does against him...yet. I'll be checking into his expenses and performance though. If he was a decent guy, Peter would have stopped and talked to him. You might be right, cousin."

"Just what kind of family are you?" Emily asked. "I'm confused."

"All in good time, dear." Margaret patted Emily's arm. "I am sure you haven't told Paul everything your family does either. It is only the smart thing to do. Tatiana seems to like you, so I am prepared to like you too. That is almost all that matters."

"Almost all?" Emily asked. "Is there more?"

"Well," Margaret said, nodding at Paul, "it all depends on what he thinks. So far he seems quite taken by you, dear. If you are interested, I can give you some tips on how to snare an elusive rabbit like him."

"If you don't watch it, this rabbit might turn into a wolf," Paul said, smiling. "With all the 'help' Emily is getting, she might just mess it up, and then the rabbit would not be pleased...not pleased at all."

As Margaret predicted, the service picked up substantially, and the trio had an enjoyable meal that was over all too soon. As the ladies made their way to the powder room, Paul tried to settle up the bill. "No, no," Peter said. "This is on me. It would not do to charge the owner's son for a meal."

"Peter," Paul said, forcing a roll of bills into the man's hands, "if my mother finds out you are comping guests without her permission, she will be pissed. There is enough there to cover the meals and the booze. Thank you anyway, Peter. You work hard, and I cannot expect you to pay for our meals. I know how many dinners you would have to make to pay for ours. You impressed my cousin, so I expect your business will pick up some because of it. Give this to the waiter." Paul handed Peter a couple twenties. "Tell him not to judge people by their clothing next time. He might have gotten more."

The trio headed out into the now-dark streets, bundled up against the subzero temperatures and the wind coming off the tops and around the tall buildings. Margaret had a bottle of vodka under her jacket, and Emily had a large can of Mott's Clamato juice under hers. When they reached the truck, Paul started the engine to let it warm up. He tied down the packages in the back of the pickup and put a tarp around them to keep them dry and secure.

As they hit the highway, the heater blasted hot air that defrosted the windshield so Paul could see without ducking his head. They left the lighted streets of Calgary behind for the pitch-dark highway, which was lit only by the dim headlights of the truck.

Margaret and Emily happily chatted away, and Paul took his right hand off the steering wheel to hold Emily's left with it. She gave his hand a squeeze and laid her head on his shoulder. Margaret, who did not miss any of this, looked out the passenger door window and smiled. They reached the main house before eight o'clock, and Paul, with some help from Emily, carried the packages into the warm kitchen. While his mother helped Emily and Margaret with the packages, Paul went to the barn to saddle the two horses.

"You let me worry 'bout that," the ranch hand on duty said. "Go get something to eat. I'll have them ready for you."

Paul thanked the man and went back to the house, where he found his father and Margaret's husband grabbing a couple beers from the fridge. He shook hands with both men and then poured a cup of steaming coffee. Sitting down, he undid his jacket and stretched his feet out before him. Emily traipsed back into the kitchen and saw he still had his jacket on. "I've got a two-hour ride home," Paul said, "so I will just finish my coffee and be off."

They sat quietly while he drank the coffee, and then he rose, closed his jacket back up, and pulled on his thick gloves. Emily followed him to the porch, shutting the kitchen door behind her. She took Paul's arm and turned him toward her, putting her hand behind his head and pulling it down. She held him close and kissed him, and he pulled her even closer.

"I'll be back in the morning," he said. She nodded, kissing him again before letting him loose and watching him until he disappeared in the darkness of the yard. She walked back into the kitchen, closing the door and leaning against it, running her finger over her lips. Looking up, she saw Margaret and Katherine watching her from the kitchen table. "I think I am very much in love with your son, Mrs. Bekenbaum," Emily said. "I am not sure that is a good thing."

"All of us must make important decisions at certain points in our lives, Emily," Katherine said. "I was afraid too. I was afraid Nicolas would reject me because of George, and I was so in love with him I thought I might die. I was so afraid of being hurt again that I wouldn't tell him. But these men and this family are not like others you have met. Paul would not have asked you home if he thought you were unworthy. He has shown you he loves you. Now you must wait and make up your mind whether you want him. These men are loyal to a fault, and he will never stray, but you have to share him. His first love is the regiment and always will be."

Paul was feeding the last quarter bale of hay to a horse when, one by one, the horses backed out of their feeding stalls and looked past the corral to the road, their ears forward and nostrils flaring. Listening for a moment himself, Paul gathered up the oats and baling twine and placed them in their spots on the inside wall of the feeding station. He walked down the narrow aisle until he reached the door that led outside. He opened it and slid through, closing and latching it behind him. He was now outside the combination feeding station, tack room, and feed room, and he walked around the corral toward the one-room cabin, where smoke came out of its single chimney. The day was calm and sunny, slightly warmer than the day before, but it was still cold enough to justify insulated clothing and boots. Today he wore a fur hat with earflaps instead of the Stetson. The roar of Chevrolet engines became louder, and two crew-cab pickups jounced into the yard, stopping in front of the corral. Three men piled out of the front and rear seats of the first truck, and three men came out of the front of the second, while Emily, Katherine, and Nicolas emerged from its rear doors. Immediately the men unloaded riding and pack saddles from the trucks' beds, along with rifle scabbards and saddlebags. "You'll have to wait a bit," Paul said. "I just gave the horses their feed. They should finish it before you load them up."

"No problem," Nicolas said. "Gives me a few more minutes with my lady." He pulled Katherine close and kissed her.

"Get a room," Paul said, until he saw his father eyeing the cabin. "Not that one! I just put on clean sheets, my last ones."

"You just want it for yourself. I know I would if I was you. *Oof,*" he said as Katherine poked him hard in the ribs.

"When you were his age, you hardly had the courage to say hello to me," Katherine said. During the good-natured kidding, the older couple kept their arms around each other, looking into each other's eyes, oblivious to their surroundings.

"Are you joining them?" Emily asked Paul.

"I wanted to," he answered, "but two things happened in the last couple of days." He took her hand and led her into his cabin. "First my girlfriend showed up," he continued. "Then I received a letter from Caltech telling me I have to go early if I want to take a certain course, which I do."

"Your girlfriend?" Emily asked quietly.

"Unless you have an objection to that," Paul said. "You are a girl, and you are my friend, no?"

"Um, yes...well, I guess so," Emily replied, confused. Paul bent down and kissed her.

"Do they call it something different in the States?" Paul asked.

"No, *girlfriend* is just fine," Emily said, smiling and kissing him back. *For now,* she thought.

"What's this about leaving early for Caltech?" Katherine asked from the doorway.

"Yes, Mom," Paul replied, "the professor teaching one of the courses I really need is leaving the school at the end of next term, so if I want to take the course, I have to go this term."

"When will that be?" his mother asked.

"The sooner I can get a flight the better," Paul said, "and not in a bloody cold and noisy Hercules either."

"But Emily just got here," his mother protested.

"Come on, Mom," Paul said. "It's no fun around here for outsiders in the winter time, and you know it. Besides, I should meet my girlfriend's family. We can catch the soonest flight out of Calgary together. I better go supervise those idiots out there before they wreck my horses."

Katherine looked at Emily and held out her arms. Emily rushed into them, smiling like a schoolgirl. "He called me his girlfriend," she said.

"You've got it made now." Katherine smiled and kissed the top of Emily's head. "These Bekenbaum men never know what hits them."

CHAPTER 10

Two days later Paul and Emily were filing through customs in Denver, where they had a four-hour layover before the flight to LA. Paul stood in line behind Emily, who passed through readily, but the customs agent eyed Paul and his duffel bag with suspicion. Paul handed the man his passport and dug into his jacket pocket for his student visa and military ID. "Hold it right there," the customs man said, waving to his supervisor, who hurried over. Both men poured over Paul's Canadian passport, leafing through its pages and checking the stamps entered in it.

"You have been to Russia, Yemen, and Angola recently," the supervisor said. "Those are all communist countries, so your entrance into the United States of America is denied."

"Really, just like that?" Paul asked. "A couple of low-ranking civil servants can unilaterally deny entrance into the United States on their own volition? Perhaps you want to rethink that decision, and before you consider arresting me, I have not crossed that nice little yellow line on the ground there, so technically I'm not on American soil yet."

Emily, not expecting trouble, had already exited the customs area. Realizing Paul was not behind her, she stuck her head back in to see the two agents harassing Paul. Paul waved his hand at her to take off, giving the OK signal.

"Do you think so, commie?" the first agent said. "We can deny entry to anyone we think is inappropriate or poses a danger to our country, and we can arrest anyone we choose."

"OK, make your day," Paul said. "Who am I to tell you that you are making bad career choices? It's going to take more than you two out-of-shape morons to arrest me though. Maybe you'd better call for some FBI backup or something. If you take that pistol out of its holster, I might have to shove it up your ass."

The supervisor had second thoughts and put his hand on the agent's gun hand, stopping him from pulling out the pistol. He nodded at the other passengers, who were scrambling out of harm's way. A couple of muscular men, seeing trouble brewing, headed over.

"Got a commie Canuck here causing all kinds of trouble and threatening bodily harm," the first agent said.

"Marshals or FBI?" Paul asked.

"Both," one of the men said, flashing a US marshal badge.

"Well, sir," Paul said, "this gentleman has decided that World Court and Congress be damned—he is unilaterally denying me entry into the United States based on some stamps in my passport. I have other documentation that would explain all of this, but he refuses to see it."

"He has other documentation, and you didn't look at it?" Now the supervisor was clearly worried. Paul handed the marshal his papers, and he looked at them one by one. He passed them over to the FBI man, who looked at them and handed them back to Paul before speaking into his handheld radio. A few minutes later, a delegation of officials appeared, both federal and state.

"We are sincerely sorry for the misunderstanding, Mr. Bekenbaum," a gray-haired senior State Department man said. "We had been briefed that you were coming and were on hand for such a scenario. Welcome to the United States of America, Mr. Bekenbaum. We will do everything in our power to make sure your stay is enjoyable and profitable."

Paul was gracious. "Thank you, sir. It's not a problem at all, sir. Just a stressed-out customs agent having a bad day, sir. It's not a big deal. Oh, by the way," Paul said to the customs agent, "I really would have shoved that pistol up your ass if you had drawn it."

"That man's family is one of the most powerful in North America, you fool," the State Department man said. "He is a war hero in his own right, from an elite fighting force that trains our elite forces. He could have killed all four of you without breaking a sweat. Jesus! What morons."

"What was that all about?" Emily asked when Paul finally joined her.

"I dunno," Paul answered. "Something about being the ten thousandth person through the gate or something. Not a big deal. Where can we get some coffee? We have four hours to kill."

"No, we don't." Emily pointed to a man holding a sign with her name on it. "Pop sent his own plane to pick us up."

"Oh shit," the State Department man said, watching Paul and Emily walk to the man with the sign. "We just dodged a big bullet. Do you know who that girl is?"

"No shit," the marshal said. "That idiot almost pissed off two very powerful families."

"A transfer to the Aleutian Islands to inspect fishing boats might be in his future," the State Department man said.

In a twin turboprop executive airplane with eight comfortable seats, Paul and Emily were soon winging their way over the Rockies en route to Emily's family's private airstrip. Emily informed Paul the landing strip was on what he would call a "farm" but what they called a "ranch." The Hershmire ranch sat on one square mile of land with an airstrip and hangar, a large garage, servants' quarters, and a huge main house. No California estate was complete without tennis courts and a swimming pool, and it also had what looked like a ten-stall equestrian center with indoor and outdoor riding arenas.

"Do you have horses?" Paul asked as the airplane turned to line up with the airstrip for landing.

"My mother likes to dabble a bit," Emily answered. "We have a couple Palominos and four Arabians. Mother is thinking about trying to establish some Appaloosas as well."

"Arabians and Appies are flighty and a little goofy, but at least they are not thoroughbred race horses," Paul said. "But what do I know? We just have cow ponies."

The airplane landed and taxied to the hangar. A Buick station waggon was waiting, and the driver put Emily's bags and Paul's duffel in the rear. He spoke in Spanish to Emily, and she responded in the same language. The man was all smiles as she hugged him, and then he narrowed his eyes and looked Paul up and down as Emily introduced them.

The drive was a short distance to the house, where a number of people awaited their arrival. Most were short and had the dark skin of people from northern Mexico. Paul's assumptions about their origin were confirmed when they greeted Emily in Spanish. All smiled and gave her hugs, but most eyed Paul with noncommittal or hostile looks. A tall older man strode out the front door and hugged Emily, picking her up off the ground and swinging her around. She squealed in mock outrage. "Papa, I am hardly twelve anymore," she protested, "and we have a guest."

She kissed him on the cheek, and he put her down. He strode up to Paul, his right hand outstretched, giving Paul the once-over as he approached. "Aaron Hershmire," he said.

"Paul Bekenbaum, sir. It's a pleasure to finally meet you, sir." The man's strong grip tried to crush Paul's hand, but Paul kept a smile on his face and his voice calm. "Emily has told me so much about you, sir. It is an honour."

Emily took Paul by the arm, breaking her father's grip and giving him a look that had daggers in it. "Be nice, Papa," she said. "His family bent over backward to make me feel at home."

"Oh my God!" said a woman with a slight accent, from the doorway. "What on earth are you wearing? You didn't go out in public like that, did you?"

Emily had on a thick cotton plaid shirt over a white turtleneck sweater, and both were tucked into Levi's riding jeans. Tall, insulated boots covered the legs of her jeans. Paul wore an insulated Levi's jacket over a down-filled vest. His heavy canvas Levi's shirt was tucked into the same type of pants Emily was wearing, except his pants legs went down over the tops of his cowboy boots.

"Mother," Emily said, crossing to the older, dressier version of herself and kissing her on the cheek. "It's so nice to be home again. It was below zero and snowing when we left, Mother, and I had no chance to change. Mother, this is the man I told you about—Paul Bekenbaum. Paul, this is my mother Harriet."

Paul nodded his head and noticed the older lady did not extend her hand. In keeping with protocol, he did not extend his either. "A pleasure, ma'am," he said, smiling. "The picture your daughter showed me of you does not do you justice by half."

"Humph," Harriet said, nodding her head at him. "Come, Emily. You must change for dinner." She took her daughter by the hand. Emily gave Paul a look and a shrug of her shoulders, walking into the house with her mother leading.

"I suppose we should go in as well," Aaron said. "We will have a drink before dinner, young man. Give your jacket to Consuela there."

Paul stripped off the jacket, handed it to the portly older woman, and smiled to her as she took it. She was taken by surprise when he thanked her by name. He followed Emily's father into the large Spanish-style home and down a richly appointed hallway to a library and billiards room, which had a large bar running down one side of it. "Name your poison, son," Aaron said.

"A bottle of beer would be fine, if you have one," Paul said.

"Sure, we have a few," Aaron replied. "Is Budweiser OK? Glass or bottle?"

"Just the bottle, Mr. Hershmire. Thank you," Paul said.

Aaron pulled four bottles out of a large fridge and popped the tops off all of them. He handed two to Paul and beckoned him to follow. They walked through the house to the back, where a large patio surrounded the full-size pool. Aaron directed Paul to a patio set beneath a plant-covered trellis and motioned him to sit on a beautiful leather chair. Aaron took its twin on the other side of the patio table and placed his beer on an immaculate solid-wood end table with a leather insert. Paul put his second beer on a coaster on the table and held the first.

"Mud in your eye," Aaron said, lifting his beer. Paul returned the gesture. "So, Emily tells us you are attending Caltech."

"Yes, sir," Paul said. "They have some interesting research going on in their electronics and radio departments, and they allowed me to enroll in the electronics program."

"But your family is mostly involved in the oil patch, I believe," Aaron asked.

"Just the pipeline service industry, sir," Paul said. "I hope to integrate radio and electronic technology into pipeline monitoring, to enable us to spot potential problems before they become big ones."

"A noble goal," Aaron said. *He is not just an academic with good looks*, he thought. "Haven't you just finished a peacekeeping tour?"

"Yes, sir," Paul replied. "It is mandatory for people in my community to spend the first five years after high school in military service, sir."

"I wasn't aware Canada had mandatory military service," Aaron said.

"No, sir," Paul said. "Canada does not, but our community does, sir. It is a little complicated, but it goes back to our original charter with the Dominion of Canada and the crown, sir. We also do a lot of testing and evaluations of equipment for the DND and tactics evaluations, as well as training for NATO and US troops."

"Wow," Aaron said. "That's impressive."

"Our community's families have been involved in the military for hundreds of years, sir," Paul said. "It was the primary reason the dominion wanted us to come from Russia. I believe your government made a similar offer, but it wasn't good enough."

"You are that group?" Aaron asked. "You are related to the Rosenthals out of Texas, are you not?"

"I believe my great-grandfather's brother married a Rosenthal, sir," Paul said. "His first daughter, Susan, is still alive. She is the last of the original colonists who is still living."

"What a small world this is becoming," Aaron said. "The Rosenthals are neighbors to my family back in Texas. I think we came over from the old country in the same boat. Honey," Aaron said as Harriet and Emily came into view. "Paul's family is related to the Rosenthals."

"Really?" She looked with new interest at Paul. "Emily dear, you did not tell me that."

"I probably wouldn't have even if I had known," Emily said. "The Rosenthals and our family are quite close, Paul. But how would you have known that?"

"Yes, Paul tells me his great-uncle married a Rosenthal," Aaron said. "The man's oldest daughter is still alive. She's the last of the original settlers. Imagine that."

"Susan is a Rosenthal?" Emily asked Paul, looking directly at him with accusing eyes. Emily had met Susan briefly at a family dinner in Didsbury.

"Only by marriage, Emily. Her mother was killed in Afghanistan before my family came to Canada. Her stepmother was a Rosenthal—Wilhelmina Rosenthal—but Susan did not ever let that get between them. My great-grandmother Elizabeth and Wilhelmina were the best of friends, and Wilhelmina mentored Tatiana when my grandfather married her. My grandmother is Russian, sir, ma'am," Paul said. "At the end of the first war, my grandfather rescued her from the Bolsheviks. She came from the aristocracy and then had nothing. She had a lot of adjusting to do."

"Your grandmother is Russian aristocracy?" Harriet asked, a look of keen interest now on her face.

"Mother," Emily said, "we are in America now, not Ireland."

"Yes, ma'am, but she doesn't talk about it, and we don't ask," Paul said. "It doesn't matter now anyway. The Bolsheviks have destroyed all the land and titles and most of the people. We are in Canada now and have no wish to return."

"Emily tells me you breed horses," Aaron said, changing the subject.

"Yes, sir," Paul said. "I am trying to keep my great-grandfather's horse line alive. I have added American quarter horses to the bloodline, improving it from its already impressive quality. I noticed you have a pair of palominos, ma'am."

"They were a gift from a neighbor," Harriet said. "I like their looks and traded my thoroughbreds for them. I like my Arabians, though, and am thinking of trying to breed Appaloosas."

"Yes, Emily told me as much," Paul said. "If you are interested, I could put you in touch with some of my people who have a pure bloodline of painted horses. They originated from Red Cloud's Cheyenne band in Wyoming."

"Real painted horses?" Harriet asked.

"Yes, ma'am," Paul replied. "The breeders' association has traced the bloodline all the way back to when my great-grandfather allowed his stallion to breed one of their mares. This line comes from that breeding."

"Could you do that for me?" Harriet asked. "And my name is Harriet, not *ma'am*."

Well, that didn't take long, Aaron thought.

Emily was smiling from ear to ear. "I told you," Emily whispered to Aaron. Paul and Harriet continued talking about horses. "And not once has Paul asked me how much money we have or what our family background is, nor did anyone in his family."

"I could use another beer," Aaron said. "Emily, come with me, and you can get your mother a bottle of wine." Emily kissed Paul on the cheek and accompanied her father to the bar, knowing there was more to the request than simply getting some booze.

"Are you sure about this, Em?" Aaron asked. "We can't find out too much about them."

"Thank you for trying to look out for me, Papa," Emily said, "but, yes, I am sure. From what I can see, Paul could make a very good living breeding and selling horses alone. This thing he is working on at Caltech...well, MIT wanted him badly for it. I'm pretty sure the only reason he chose Caltech was to be near me."

"Texas was after him too," Aaron said. "They offered him more than Caltech or MIT, so you could be right. If it works out, his percentage of the royalties on the projects he works on at Caltech alone will make him very wealthy."

"Papa!" Emily said sternly. "Now you sound like Mamma. If your parents had thought like that, you never would have married her."

"My parents did think like that," Aaron said. "I married her anyway, and that is why I was banished out here. But you are right, and I am sorry. I just don't want you to fall for somebody who is after your money and not you."

"Papa, I had him the second day I was in Yemen," Emily said. "That was before he knew who we were and when he thought I was a poor freelance reporter. I didn't know I cared about him yet, and he didn't admit it to me until Tatiana gave the OK. But I think he would have defied her anyway."

"She has that much power over the family?" Aaron asked.

"It's more like they respect her and seek her advice," Emily said. "I get the feeling that in affairs of the heart, the Bekenbaums leave well enough alone. They seem to be very open minded, and class and money rarely have anything to do with marriage or love matters."

"Well, they hold their affairs tightly," Aaron said, "but the Rosenthals speak highly of them, as do the Olynicks. It is your affair, my daughter, and I will keep out of it, but I shall be keeping an eye on him just the same."

"Tatiana and Katherine will keep their eyes on me as well, I am sure," Emily said, laughing. "I am taking their little prince away from them, after all."

The next morning, Paul was up and by the corral as the sun came over the eastern horizon. The station-waggon driver from the day before was feeding the horses, and Paul noticed the type and amount of food he gave each animal. When the man was finished, he walked over to Paul. "Can I help you with something, sir?" the man asked with a slight Spanish accent.

"Are you expecting to work those animals some?" Paul asked.

"No, sir," he answered. "I don't think the missus is riding today."

"Ah. Do you feed grain to them daily?" Paul asked. "Doesn't that make them a little hard to handle?"

"Arabians are a little high-strung all the time, sir," the man said. He gathered up his things and walked toward another corral, where horses were milling about.

"Now, this is more like it," Paul said. "Cow ponies—do they work for a living, or are they only for show?" Seeing what the man was doing, Paul grabbed a bale of hay and spread it in the empty feeder.

"They work for a living," the man replied, nodding thanks to Paul. "We are a working ranch and have about three hundred head of cattle here."

"Really?" Paul said. "We have about three hundred Angus back home. They're pains in the ass for us this time of year. We have to hunt 'em out of the bush and bring them to feeding stations, or they will starve or freeze to death in the snow. Need a hand?"

"Can you ride?" the man asked.

"Been on a horse a time or two," Paul answered.

"OK, you can come along," the man said. "We are going to go check on the cows this morning. Follow me, and I will find some tack for you."

Paul followed the man into a large tack room and was pointed to an old worn but well-cared-for saddle and bridle. Paul hoisted the saddle onto a shoulder, looped the reins of the bridle around the other arm, and followed the man back out to the corral. Three other men of Mexican descent joined them. They talked in Spanish to one another for a moment, and the first man nodded his head in Paul's direction.

After the horses finished eating, the three newcomers climbed into the corral and, using lariats, roped three horses. They brought them back to the corral and tied them to the top rail, and two of the men walked back to the milling herd. They targeted a specific horse and lassoed another at random, and then they brought both horses back to the others tied to the corral.

"That one's yours," the leader of the group said to Paul, nodding his head at the horse that had been targeted.

Paul saw the other men smiling as they climbed through the fence rails and saddled their mounts. He tucked his pants legs into his riding boots and, like the other men, climbed through the fence and then grabbed the saddle blanket and saddle. He expected the mare to explode on him at any second, but she just stood there and cocked an ear back as he placed the saddle on her back and did up the cinch. The saddle was an ornate version of the western saddles he was used to, with a rear cinch but no breast strap. He adjusted the stirrups to fit himself, and by the time he had placed the bridle on the mare, the rest of the group had mounted, ridden out of the corral, and turned to face him.

One man rode back and closed the corral gate, thinking Paul hadn't seen him.

Paul's reins were tied together, as were the rest of the men's, and Paul took a second to untie them. Holding tight to the reins with one hand, he untied the lariat from the fence and from the horse's neck, looping it and tying it on the saddle. The whole time, the mare stood calmly, once in a while turning her head to look at him. Paul now took hold of the main cinch, punched her belly with his knee, waited for her to exhale a breath, and pulled the cinch tight. Holding the reins tightly, he mounted, and she exploded into motion the second his right foot hit the stirrup. First she reared back to her full height on her hind legs, and then she bucked as high as she could, spinning while she did so. She did this for thirty seconds before finally giving up and halting.

Paul nudged her with a heel and headed her to the corral gate, reaching over and pulling the latch as he got there to let the mare push it open with her chest. He rode through, turned her sideways, closed the gate, and latched it again. "You don't ride her much, eh?" Paul asked the foreman. "She is well trained. Somebody spent a lot of time on her. Wonder who spoiled her?"

The yard was full of servants and ranch hands who came out to see Emily's latest boyfriend be humiliated. Instead they watched with their mouths open.

"Where are the cows, gents, or are we gonna sit here all day gabbing?" Paul asked.

The five men rode out of the yard and down a trail, coming to the pasture the cows were grazing in. The cattle, a Hereford mix, were scattered about the pasture in small groups of ten or twenty, grazing or lying down. Paul gazed around the pasture, gauging the animals' condition and saw a two-year-old steer that did not look right. The steer was limping on a back leg, and Paul turned the mare to head in the steer's direction. As he moved toward the cattle at a slow walk, the cows watched Paul angle in to intercept the injured steer. The slow pace and Paul's relaxed demeanor convinced the cattle that he was no threat. The cows, including the steer, went back to their grazing. Paul maneuvered the mare so she was between the steer and the rest of the small herd. As they approached, the steer moved away from them. After he was ten yards away from the herd, he tried to head back to it but was blocked by the mare. He swung the other way, and again, the mare blocked his way and pushed him farther away. Now the steer got concerned and moved faster—to the left, to the right, away—and then circled around again, trying to get past Paul and the horse. Each time, the mare was there to block him and push him farther away from the rest of the cattle.

Paul dug into his jacket pocket and found a spare bootlace about eighteen inches long. He stuck the lace in his mouth and clenched it with his teeth. He then unhooked the lariat from the saddle, shook out its loop, and slowly swung the free end back and forth on the right side, away from the steer's sight. The steer had stopped and was looking for a way around them. Paul had the mare standing still and looking straight on at the steer. One ear was turned back in Paul's direction, and the other faced forward. Paul nudged her forward with his right heel and tightened both knees on her barrel in anticipation. As he had anticipated, the steer exploded into a gallop to the right in an attempt to get by them. The mare took off after him, and Paul swung the lariat around his head. Judging the moment, he let his hand fly forward and the rope's loop left his hand and hit the ground in front of the steer. Pulling it tight, he captured both hind legs in the loop, wrapped the rope's free end around the saddle horn with two fast half hitches, and braced himself for impact, as did the mare, who braced her front legs and squatted on her rears as the steer came to the end of the rope's free play and skidded to a stop. The rope pulled both hind legs out from under it, and the steer hit the ground. The mare took the impact and backed up, keeping tension on the rope and preventing the steer from rising.

Once Paul saw that the steer was secure on the ground and that the rope was not coming off the saddle, he jumped off the mare and ran to the steer, pulling the bootlace from his mouth as he went. Paul reached the steer and used the rope as leverage to flop the steer on its side. Paul grabbed a front leg, pulled it back to the two captured rear legs, and tied all three legs together under the lariat. Once he did that, he gave two sharp tugs on the rope, and the mare moved forward two steps, giving him enough slack to release the lariat. He gathered it up as he walked back to the mare and untied it from the saddle horn before once again fastening it back on the saddle.

The steer had struggled to get up for a while but was now just lying there, looking at Paul with big eyes as he came nearer again. Paul pulled out the clasp knife he always carried and extracted the larger blade out from its handle. Bending down, he used his left hand to grab the steer's right rear leg just below the hoof, and with his right hand, he stuck the knife into the cleft of the hoof, prying it apart to remove the stone that was lodged there. Paul looked at the hoof to see that there was only some bruising—no open sores or bleeding—and he put the knife back in his pocket. With a flick of the wrist, he undid the knot he had used to secure the steer's hind legs and stepped back as the steer surged to its feet. With a shake of its head, it ran off to join the rest of the herd.

All that time, the mare just observed with her ears forward, while the reins dangled on the ground. As Paul came up to her and gathered the reins, she rubbed her head on his shoulder.

"Yes, girl," Paul said, rubbing her between the ears and patting her neck, "you did a fine job."

Mounting her once again and settling himself back in the saddle, he noticed he had an audience—not only the ranch hands but also Emily, her mother, and her father, who were mounted on Arabians. Putting pressure on his right knee, Paul headed the mare over to where everyone was and came to a stop beside Emily. "Nice herd you have here, Mr. Hershmire," Paul said. "You should have some nice calves in a couple months."

"Nobody has done that on that horse," Harriet said. "Nobody has even ridden her for a couple of years."

"She has been well trained," Paul said. "I wouldn't be surprised if she has been in a rodeo or two."

"That's my brother-in-law's horse," Emily said. "He bought her after he married my sister, but he got bored and hasn't ridden her since."

"That was good work, son," Aaron said. "Do you do that kind of thing often?"

"I hate to see a good steer go lame for no reason," Paul said. "It could mean the difference between breaking even and losing money in a bad year."

"Paul's family raises some kind of big black cattle, Papa," Emily said. "They have to use horses to work them because of the terrain."

"How far away is the university from here?" Paul asked.

"About half an hour," Emily answered.

"Do you think your brother-in-law would sell me this mare?" Paul asked. "If she's not too expensive and your father will let me board her here, it would be nice to come out and help the boys with the cows on weekends."

"Son, if you have a dollar, you can have the horse," Aaron said. "My son-in-law never paid for her in the first place. Never mind the boarding fee. You'll work it off on the weekends. Looks like you might be able to teach my lads a few things. Come on, ladies. Let's finish the ride and go for breakfast. See you back at the house, Paul."

"I haven't seen anybody that good with a rope since my papa," the ranch foreman said. "We usually rope the neck."

"It's easier on the cow if you can get the hind legs," Paul said. "Looks like you guys do things as a group, so it should be easier for you. I'm usually out on my own. You need a good reliable horse and need to know what you're doing, or you'll end up walking home with bruised legs and a battered ego."

After the morning's work, Paul headed for his guest cabin to wash up and change. He found Aaron waiting for him on the porch. "Sit for a bit," Aaron said, handing Paul a beer from a bucket of ice. "Isn't the first time I've smelled horse and man sweat, and it probably won't be the last." Paul took the beer and sat down, taking three big swallows to quench his thirst. "OK, son," Aaron said. "Cut the bullshit, and get down to it. What are your intentions with my daughter?"

"Well, sir," Paul said without hesitation, "if she'll have me, in two years after I finish at Caltech, I'd like to marry her, sir."

"Have you asked her yet?"

"No, sir," Paul said. "Two years is a long time, especially for a girl like Emily. I am going to be pretty busy at school, and I imagine she has a lot of guys hanging around. I'll just play it by ear until then."

"Your family will not have a problem with you marrying Emily?" Aaron asked.

"No, sir. It's none of their business, sir," Paul said. "Their only stipulation is that I have to be able to support a family before I get married, and that will be no problem after I am finished with school. Speaking of money, sir…" Paul dug into his pocket and gave Aaron a dollar. "That's the price for the mare, correct? If I may, I have a proposition for you. I would like to bring one of my mares and a stallion here. In return for the boarding, Mrs. Hershmire could breed my stallion with her mare and her stallion with my mare. I would give her both colts the first year and one the second."

"That sounds good to me, Paul," Aaron said, "but you better run it by Harriet first. As for Emily, you should ask her before the weekend is over, Paul. You don't want to keep a prime filly waiting, do you?"

"Do you think so, sir?" Paul asked. "I mean, I don't have a whole lot to offer. What I have at home doesn't come close to what she has here."

"Where's Papa, Mamma?" Emily asked, coming into the kitchen to pour a cup of coffee.

"He's having a heart-to-heart with Paul, dear," Harriet said.

Emily kept pouring the coffee into her cup, even though it was overflowing and going down the sink. "Oh God, no, Mamma," she cried, spinning around to look at her mother. "He will ruin everything and scare him off. Do you know how hard it was for me to get him to come here? He has this stupid honour thing, and I don't want to push him too far."

"It will be just fine, dear," Harriet said. Emily spun back to the sink and looked anxiously out the window. Harriet came quickly to her daughter and put her arms around her. She could feel her shaking and holding the tears at bay. They saw the two men walking together up the driveway to the house. Aaron was talking and gesturing. Paul had his head down, nodding, and his hands in his pockets. The ranch foreman walked to Aaron, who pointed at Paul and then at the garage. The foreman nodded and trotted toward the garage. Aaron came on toward the house, leaving Paul in the driveway.

Emily pushed her mother away and ran to the door, flinging it open before her astonished father could reach for the handle. "Daddy, how could you?" she yelled at him, pushing him in the chest with both palms. "I told you how I felt about him." She rushed past him and ran to Paul, who barely had time to turn around before she had hold of his shoulders. "Where are you going? Please don't leave," she said. "I don't care what he told you or said to you. I love you and want to be with you—"

Paul put his finger against her lips. She took his hand away and started to talk again, but he put the finger from his other hand on her lips. She took that hand away too, and he kissed her. She let go of his hands and felt his arms pull her close, and she kissed him back, holding him hard against herself. He broke from her and looked into her eyes. "I thought it was a cardinal sin for a girl to say she loves a guy before he tells her the same," Paul said, his eyes laughing.

"I don't care," Emily said. "I love you, and I don't care who knows. If my father has told you to leave, I am leaving with you. I am over twenty-one and can do what I please."

"I am not going anywhere." Paul kissed her again. "Your father has agreed to rent me that guesthouse while I go to school, and I have agreed to do some ranch work on the weekends to pay for boarding the mare I just bought. I have to go to the university now and register so I can spend the next week here with you. Your foreman, Manuel, is going to drive me in."

"I'm coming along," Emily said.

"No, Love," Paul said. "I have a lot of things to accomplish in a short amount of time. I'll be back for supper. You would just distract me, and I wouldn't be able to get everything done. This way, it will all get done, and you can distract me for the rest of the week." Manuel pulled up in the Buick station waggon and honked the horn. Paul kissed Emily and ran to the car.

Emily slowly walked back into the kitchen, with a dreamy faraway look in her eyes. "He called me *Love*, Mamma," she said and ran to her bedroom, screaming at the top of her lungs. "He called me *Love!*"

"Jesus," Aaron said. "She wasn't that bad with her high-school boyfriend."

"She wasn't in love," Harriet said. "What did the boy say?"

"He loves her," Aaron said.

"Where is he going?" Harriet asked.

"He is going to town to register at the university, open a bank account, and buy a vehicle," Aaron said. "He also has a proposition for you, which I think you should take. But talk to Emily first about the quality of his horses. He wants to bring a stallion and a mare here. You can breed your palomino mare with the stallion and have your stallion breed his mare, and he'll give you the first year's colts. He wants the second colt from his mare, and he wants both horses back."

"Emily!" Harriet shouted. "You get back down here this instant. You are an adult, not still in high school."

Emily came dancing back to the kitchen from her room. "Yes, Mommy?" She batted her eyelashes.

"Oh, Jesus, Mary, and Joseph," Harriet said, her Irish brogue thick. "Now can ya concentrate enough to answer a question not related to God Almighty, Paul the first?"

"Yeah, Mommy. He is such a dreamboat though." Emily was laying it on thick now, pouting.

"Your young lad wants to make me a business proposition, and I need some facts," Harriet said. "What kind of horses does he have? Are they any good?"

"Oh that," Emily said. "I am no expert, but yes, they are good horses. The bloodline is over a hundred years old. It is an off-shoot breed of the Cossack horses that his great-grandfather started back in Russia. The horses are well sought after there and will fetch top dollar if Paul ever decides to sell one. He gave the Saudi crown prince four of them this summer, and I thought the man would die from a heart attack. You would be wise to take him up on it, Mother."

"You gonna marry Miss Em?" Manuel asked Paul as they sped down the two-lane highway.

"If she'll have me," Paul said. "I'm kinda from a different class than she is."

"Miss Em and Mr. A—they not care about those things," Manuel said. "Consuela, she says Miss Em thinks highly of you, and so does Mr. A. Even the missus seems to like you, and she don't like nobody."

"I have to finish school first, Manuel. I don't think it will be fair to Emily to make her wait that long."

"You kidding me, man?" Manuel said. "She's hot to trot for you, bro. You better tie her down quick before she changes her mind. You are way better than the other yahoos she has brought here. You're better than that no-good lawyer her sister married."

"Manuel, first things first," Paul said. "I need to find a bank, my friend, and I need you to come with me to provide the mailing address and telephone number for the ranch."

"Sure thing, Mr. Paul," Manuel said, pulling into a small shopping mall. "There is the bank we all use. They know me there. It will all be good."

Paul, with Manuel beside him, walked up to a teller and asked to see the manager. They were ushered into the man's office, and Paul produced his passport and immigration papers to prove he was allowed to be in the United States. He gave the man a bank draft from his family's bank. Seeing the number of zeros on the check, the manager's eyes went wide.

"Do you mind if I make a few calls to verify this check?" the manager asked. "You do understand you will not be able to withdraw any of it until the check clears."

"Yes, sir," Paul said. "I have some cash to tide me over."

Paul sat in the manager's office, waiting for him to return, while Manuel found a payphone out in the mall and telephoned his cousin at a car dealership. The manager came back to Paul, and he had a large friendly grin on his face. "Well, Mr. Bekenbaum," the man said cheerfully, "there is no problem at all with the check, and you may immediately withdraw any funds you need."

"I wonder, sir," Paul said, "if you could help me out. I will be purchasing a vehicle today, and I wonder if the dealership could call you directly to arrange the transfer of funds."

"Certainly, Mr. Bekenbaum," the manager said, handing Paul his business card. "Anything you need, sir."

Paul left the bank and jumped back into the Buick. "Manuel, find me a nice jewelry store. That is the next stop."

"I thought you had to go to the university," Manuel asked. "You are not going to make it if you go to a jewelry store and buy a car too."

"I have found in my tender years, Manuel," Paul said, "that keeping things from a woman is sometimes difficult. Women tend to stick their noses into things, even if it means ruining a surprise."

"Oh yes," Manuel agreed. "I too have seen this with my Consuela."

"If Emily was to ask you after we get home—" Paul asked.

"I would tell her how bored I was waiting in the parking lot of the university for you and how we had to rush from there to make it to the car dealership in time."

"Very good, my friend," Paul said. "Is this the place?" They pulled into another strip mall and parked in front of a small jewelry shop.

Manuel followed Paul inside and spoke Spanish to the woman behind the counter. "My cousin Manuel tells me you are looking for some jewelry for Miss Emily," the clerk said. "Perhaps a nice locket or bracelet or some nice earrings?"

"No," Paul replied, walking over to the rings. "Do you know Emily?"

"Oh yes," the woman said. "We were in grade school together, and she still drops by and we go for coffee when she can."

"Good, then you can help me pick out a wedding band and engagement ring," Paul said to the woman, shocking Manuel. "I don't have a lot of money, but I would like something nice." Paul settled on a single diamond engagement ring and matching wedding band. The sales clerk said the engagement ring would most likely be too large to fit her finger, but Emily could bring it in and have it and the wedding band properly sized at any time.

"How would you like to pay for it?" the woman asked. "You can put some money down and pay the rest in installments. The interest rate is low, and Manuel tells me you are going to school and working part time, so that may help."

Paul pulled a roll of bills out of his front pocket and counted out thirty-one hundred-dollar bills onto the counter. "Keep the extra twenty," Paul said. "You were very patient with me, and I am bribing you for your silence as well. I want to surprise her tonight after supper, so please don't tell her."

"My lips are sealed, Mr. Bekenbaum," she said, putting the engagement ring in a small ring box, which Paul shoved into his jean jacket.

"You're going to make her happy, sir," Manuel said, grinning as they walked to the car.

"I hope so, Manuel," Paul said, looking at the floor of the car. "I hope so."

They pulled into a car dealership, and Manuel introduced Paul to yet another cousin, who steered Paul over to where a Camaro and Mustang were sitting. He expected Paul to be like any other twenty-three-year-old male, figuring he would end up selling him a four-door sedan because that would be all he could afford. "Nice cars," Paul said. "Not my style though. Let's have a look at those trucks over there. This Chevy is the same year as that Chevy and the same model. Why is it cheaper?" Paul asked.

"It's a four-wheel drive, and nobody wants four-wheel drives out here," the salesman said. "We took it as a trade-in because the customer has been with us for years."

Paul took it for a quick test drive and found it had reasonable mileage for its age and that it drove all right. The price was decent, so he offered five hundred dollars less than the asking price and was surprised the salesman took it.

"Look, Paul," the salesman said, "trucks are not big sellers here, especially four-wheel drives. That thing has been on the lot for three months, so the boss said to take any decent offer. Do you want to put a down payment on it and pay it out over a couple of years? It's no problem. We'll just get the paperwork started and get you some registration papers and license plates."

Paul, Manuel, and the salesman went into the man's office. Paul handed him the bank manager's card. "I have made arrangements with the bank to transfer whatever funds are needed into your account," Paul said. The salesman picked up his telephone, punched an internal number, spoke quickly into it, and then hung up again and looked strangely at Paul.

An older man rushed into the office excitedly. "Mr. Bekenbaum, are you sure you want that used truck? I could easily set you up with a new one."

"No, this one will suit me fine," Paul said, smiling. "Thanks anyway. I take it there was no problem with the bank. Thank you then, gentlemen. If Manuel and I do not leave soon, we will be late for supper." Paul shook both salesmen's hands. "I want to fuel this baby up," Paul said to Manuel. "If it's been sitting here for three months, the fuel is bad. These big-block Chevys are picky."

"You noticed the 427 engine?" Manuel said. "I wasn't sure you had seen it."

"My mamma never raised no dummies," Paul said. "This truck is a special order and has all kinds of neat goodies on it. Even if it gets wrecked, I can fix it up and resell it for a major profit. Your cousin and his boss are not too bright."

"They don't do trucks," Manuel said. "If you had gone for the Camaro, you would have had a fight on your hands."

To Paul, dinner was a subdued affair. He was used to large gatherings with a lot of joking and conversation. Here, the meal was low-key, and the talk was of Paul's idea to breed Harriet's horses with his.

"I know you wanted to play with paints," Paul said, "but I believe with my horses, you will have a superior breed that will be able to do ranch work but also be pleasurable to just ride and enjoy."

Dinner was done and the sun was setting. Harriet suggested Emily take Paul to see the sunset. The couple left the house and walked down the lane, holding hands. They ended up by the corrals, looking at the western sky as the sun began its descent on the horizon.

"I don't know how this is done in America," Paul began. He held both Emily's hands in his as he gazed into her deep-green eyes. "To tell the truth, I don't know how it's done back home either. Emily Hershmire," Paul said softly, "I have never felt this way before, ever. I love you with all my heart and all my life, and I ask you if you will spend the rest of your life with me as my wife."

Her mouth dropped open, and Paul felt her pulse hammering through her hands. "Oh God, yes," she whispered, releasing her left hand and pulling his head down to hers so she could kiss him. She kissed him on the mouth and the cheeks and the mouth again. "The custom here is for the boy to go down on one knee and ask while holding an engagement-ring box open in front of him," Emily said, "but I understand if you don't have a ring." Paul dug in his pocket, pulled out the box, and opened it. He went down on one knee and held the box out to her. "Oh my God!" she yelled before putting her hand to her mouth. "Can you afford this, Paul?"

"It's my back pay from the army," Paul said. "It was more than I expected."

She put the ring on her figure and held it up to see it shine in the dimming daylight. She dropped to her knees in front of him. "Paul Bekenbaum, I love you with all my heart and will spend the rest of my life with you as your wife," she said strongly, looking into his deep-blue eyes.

"So say I, in front of God and my new wife," Paul said, "what is done to her and hers is done to me and mine, and what is said in front of God cannot be undone."

"We are not married yet, my love," Emily said.

"If that is what you say." Paul smiled.

Suddenly several screaming women surrounded them, pulling Emily up and holding up her ring hand for everyone to see. One was Harriet, who beamed almost as much as her daughter did.

CHAPTER 11

"OK, BOYS, THAT'S ENOUGH FOR the week," Paul said to the group of college men at the foot of the climbing wall. "Next week, we'll start rappelling the wall with weapons and packs. I've got midterms this week, so I need to study, and I am sure you guys do too."

"Jeez, Warrant," one young man said, "you just had to bring that up, didn't you?"

"Well, I can tell you one thing for sure, Walawitz," Paul said. "You flunk out of college, and you are for sure going to Vietnam as a rifleman."

"Got news for you, Warrant," Walawitz said. "We're all going to Vietnam. No rich boys in this group."

Deciding to forgo a shower and change of clothing in the locker room, Paul walked out of the gym that held the climbing wall and walked to his truck in the parking lot. He was still getting used to having to lock it, but soon enough he had the engine running and the air conditioning turned on. He wasn't used to the high temperatures in California this early in the year, so he had taken to running the air conditioning to cool off the truck's cab. Luckily for him, the cab's windows were deeply tinted because as he drove off campus, an antiwar demonstration was under way, and he was still in uniform. As a Canadian, he was generally exempt from the harassment anyone of military age with a short haircut received. The student body just thought it was a Canadian thing. But being spotted in uniform would result in at least being yelled at and at most being severely beaten.

A half hour later, he pulled up in front of his guesthouse and climbed out of the truck's cab. He didn't notice the young man with long, stylish hair sitting under the veranda of the guesthouse next to his, and he headed for the shower and a change of clothing. Emily's sister and her husband were coming for the weekend, and he hoped to find some time to study.

After coming out of the shower, he slipped on a pair of blue jeans, a T-shirt, some sneakers and headed for the main house. Along the way, he greeted several ranch hands, who were heading for their suppers, and asked after their families and laughed at their jokes. He took the steps to the back door two at a time and greeted the kitchen staff in his joking way before one escorted him to the formal dining room.

A younger version of Emily was seated next to her, holding her hand and admiring the ring on it, while Harriet sat on Emily's other side. A man with a polo shirt, casual pants, expensive deck shoes, and expensive long haircut was talking with Aaron. Paul took in the scene, marveling at how Emily beamed in the light of the room. He thought he could stand there forever and be content just watching her.

At first the dinner was pleasant. Emily's sister, Sarah, was nice if a little boring. She didn't appear to go out much, and if she did, it was to the country club or shopping mall. Her husband, Burt, was a corporate lawyer who had just been made partner. He was conscious of his standing as an up-and-coming go-getter who knew people, and he didn't have a problem letting others know it.

Paul ate quietly, taking in the social interactions between the family members, but he couldn't help noticing the cold shoulder Burt gave him. Paul had plenty of relatives back home he didn't talk to, so one more wouldn't matter. Then Burt turned his attention to Paul, and things changed rapidly. "When you came home, I noticed you were in an army uniform," Burt said. "Do you think it is appropriate to wear a uniform off the base?"

"I usually don't," Paul said, "but the ROTC class I was instructing ran a little late. I know how important this dinner is for Emily, so I came straight home."

"Will you be going into the army full time after college?" Burt asked.

"No, sir," Paul said. He did not like where this was going. "I have already served my five years and am now in inactive reserve until I graduate. Then I will be placed back on active reserve for another ten years."

"You have already served five years?" Burt asked. "You must be a captain at least by now or maybe a major. I couldn't recognise your rank badges."

"I have been privileged to be promoted to master warrant officer, sir," Paul replied, "but my duties are mostly administrative."

"You won't be going to Vietnam then?" Burt asked.

"My country is not involved in the Vietnam conflict, sir," Paul replied. "My regiment has a few members over there as observers, but we have no reason to be there other than that."

"Aren't you training the next generation of American officers who will be going over there?" Burt asked. "I think it is an immoral war, and your training of those young boys to be killers is abhorrent."

"Of course you are allowed to think and say as you wish, sir. This is, after all, a free and democratic country," Paul said. "I am not in a position to debate for or against your feelings in regard to Vietnam, as I am not an American and am not in possession of all the facts."

"All the troops who go there should be treated as war criminals," Burt said.

"Yes, did you see how they bombed that poor village last night on the television?" Sarah said, supporting her husband. "The one woman was holding her dead child. It was so sad."

"This man here is training new men to go over there and do the same things," Burt said, now warming to his subject.

A large photo album plunked onto the table in front of Burt, startling him. Emily had slipped out of the room unnoticed and had now returned with a grim look on her face. "These are the photographs I took the first day I met Paul," she said. "It was just outside the border of Yemen, and a village had been hit by a Yemeni warlord's band of toughs. Open it up, Burt. That first picture is Paul holding and consoling an eight-year-old girl who will be scarred forever from the battery acid thrown in her face. In the background, you can see Paul's men digging graves. The next pictures are of dead girls lying in a row. Not one is older than twelve. The next is of a line of girls being treated for injuries such as battery-acid burns or bullet wounds. What you don't see are their female teachers, who were raped and had their throats and bellies cut open.

"These girls' crime was being taught to read and write and do arithmetic. Being able to read their holy book and being able to count money to help their families—for this, they were killed and raped and tortured. Paul's regiment saved whomever they could, but they arrived too late to save them all. Now, Burt, who do you think gave these hoodlums the money to buy their arms so they could terrorise innocent preteen girls?" Emily was almost yelling now. "You did, Burt. You negotiated with that warlord so the company you represent could drill for oil unmolested in Yemen. And you have the balls to accuse my fiancé of being a war criminal."

Paul got up and took Emily by the shoulders. "Easy, Em," Paul said. She buried her head in his shoulder and cried. "He didn't know. How could he? He was just protecting the oil company's workers." Paul steered Emily to the door and saw that, to his credit, Burt was paging through the photo album and reading Emily's notes about the pictures. Paul walked Emily over to the corrals, and she stood with her head on his shoulder for a while.

She turned and kissed him. "I get so upset when you just sit there and take it," she said. "I know the good you have done and the hardships you have faced."

"Look, Em," Paul said, "my people and I do those things so others do not have to, so they can sleep safe and know no one will come to kill them in the night. We fight so you and your sister can live your lives freely, can read and write and take your proper places in society. My people have been doing this for as long as time itself, Emily. We are used to the hardship and the killing. We know it is sometimes necessary to kill a person so others may live. This is not something regular citizens can understand or stomach in some cases. When people like Burt have made up their minds, anything—and I mean anything—I say will only inflame them more. In some ways, that is good. If they are angry enough, they can influence policymakers of their countries to change their policies and bring their boys home. I don't agree with making soldiers pay for mistakes their governments make.

A lot of boys over there come from poor backgrounds and have no choice but to serve."

"You served in Yemen?" Aaron asked. The whole family had come out of the house and approached the couple.

"Yes, sir," Paul said. "I served two years in Yemen and two years in Cyprus before that."

"Canada is sought after for peacekeeping missions," Emily said, "and Paul's regiment is the one they call on for tough jobs."

"My cousin was in Yemen for a while," Harriet said. "He was on bodyguard detail for the Prince of Wales when he was stationed there."

"We didn't see much of the Brits, Harriet," Paul said. "We were in the buffer zone between Yemen and Saudi Arabia."

"I am sorry, Paul," Burt said, holding his hand out.

"Look, sir," Paul said, accepting the handshake, "we all have personal feelings and opinions. You are basing a lot of decisions on what you see on TV. One of the biggest and best strategies the Bolsheviks use is to terrorise the local population and make it look like government forces did it. Your media is falling for it. I am not saying you should stop disagreeing with your country's policy, but get all the facts. Support your troopers. A lot of them come from the poorer sections of your society and feel it is their only way to get ahead."

"Get involved politically, Burt," Emily said. "Use your influence to change policy. I, like you, do not agree with America being in Vietnam, but I don't take it out on the men fighting there. I am taking it out on my politicians, who sent them there in the first place."

CHAPTER 12

"OK, BOYS," PAUL SAID. "TODAY, we go up in the helicopter and do this for real." His class of twenty was at the National Guard base, standing on a helipad and waiting for their helicopters to arrive. "The first trip will be at ten feet," Paul continued. "You won't have any equipment, just yourselves. We will do that twice, and then we will do that twice again but in full combat gear. If none of you are killed, we will go to the final phase—full combat-insertion drill from twenty feet. Those of you who are not killed doing that drill will be qualified to continue training for combat insertion with an emphasis on urban environments and hostage rescues."

The whole year of instruction had been aimed at this one point, and the troopers were now ready to begin real-life training—jumping out of helicopters and rappelling down ropes to the ground. On cue two helicopters arrived, and the troopers broke into groups of five to board the idling machines, which took off as soon as the last troopers were seated. At the end of the day, there were no fatalities, and the ROTC class was pumped and excited to take part in real-life training instead of make-believe drills at the university.

At six o'clock the next morning, the class was back on base, this time with full combat loads and weapons. Everyone, Paul included, piled into the helicopters, and they flew for an hour into the desert to a training facility that had a number of mock buildings. The helicopters landed and waited for the last troopers to be clear before taking off again to refuel for the coming training exercises.

"Gentlemen," Paul began, "today you will take part in live-fire operations. The ammunition you will fire is paint bullets instead of lead bullets, but they will injure you badly if you get hit at close range. We will engage a number of targets in this urban-training facility. There will be good guys and bad guys here. The bad guys have black targets, and the blue guys are good. Shoot the bad guys, not the good guys. You will operate in groups of five, and you will be timed. Later you will rappel onto the top of that building over there and clear it of bad guys from the top down. Any questions?"

"Yeah, Warrant," Walawitz said. "Where are we ever going to use this?"

"That's what my people said before Sicily," Paul said. "The German and Italian soldiers would hole up in the houses and buildings of the towns. We had to learn the hard way what you are going to learn here today."

The training cadre walked the ROTC men through the course, showing them what to expect and how to enter the buildings, and then they had them run through the courses. Paul kept moving around, taking notes, and encouraging them as he went. Finally when they broke for lunch, he sat on a step and took a bite of the sandwich he had made himself.

"Your boys are doing very well, Warrant." A man sat beside Paul on the step. "They're better than all the other ROTC groups we get in here. They all seem gung ho and eager to get on with it." Paul saw the man had a major's insignia on his green beret, the Army Rangers' flash on one shoulder, and Special Forces' on the other. His parachute wings and expert combat infantry badges were prominent, and he had two stars above the parachute wings.

"I have found that being honest with troopers pays dividends, sir," Paul said. "These boys know they are going to Vietnam after college and that what I am teaching them may save their lives and those of the troopers under them."

"If you're half as good an instructor as the one I had for my three months of frozen hell up in the Great White North, these boys are getting one hell of an education," the major said.

The rest of the training cadre appeared, gathering around Paul and the major. They were all experienced Special Forces men—Green Berets. Paul enjoyed their company. It had been a long two years, and this was the first time since he had come to America that he was interacting with real professional soldiers. When lunch was over, his trainees hung outside the circle of professionals, listening with big eyes to the stories the experienced men told.

Finally the major stood, ending the conversations. "The army is finding itself increasingly involved in hostage-taking situations," the major began, calling the ROTC group in to join the training cadre. "This means we have had to adapt our training to deal with these situations. Today you men will be trained in just that situation. A group of bad guys has taken control of that building, threatening to kill all the hostages if we don't meet certain demands. They have no intention of letting anyone go and are going to blow themselves and the building up, so you have to go in there and clear them out. Save as many hostages as you can, but the main priority is to clear the bad guys out before they blow up the building. You have fifteen minutes to clear it before it explodes. You will be inserted on the roof. We have no intel on how many bad guys are there or where they are. Good luck, gentlemen."

Paul accompanied his men to the helipad, giving them some last-minute advice. "Expect the unexpected. These bad guys are usually very motivated, and a lot of them are quite intelligent. They will not play by the rules, so don't expect them to. Be smart, be aware, and come back alive."

The helicopter arrived to pick up the first group. Most of the trainees died before they got halfway down the building, and the rest died when the building blew up in smoke belching simulated explosions. The next group did not fare much better.

The Special Forces major and his team gathered up the dejected ROTC men for a pep talk. "You did very well for your first time out," the major said. "The first time this team did this exercise in the Great White North, we got our asses handed to us worse than you guys did today. We were overconfident, and our opponents took advantage of that. You men did better than we did because of your trainer. He has been there and done that more than once. The regiment he belongs to is very good. Here, we call them the EBB. They developed this technique and kicked our asses training us. They also trained the SAS that week and kicked their asses too. So, Warrant, to pay you back for all the niceties you heaped on us, it is your turn to run the gauntlet instead of walking around here with your fancy clipboard and stopwatch."

"Sure, no problem," Paul said. "You have any forty-five ammo? And I will need six clips for my C7. I will pass on the grenades for the launcher, but I want six hand grenades as well." Paul walked over to his duffel bag to pull out his weapons harness and combat rifle. The Green Berets had already loaded the magazines for his rifle and pistol, and Paul shoved them into his ammo pouches and hung the grenades in their designated places.

He removed his outer jacket, revealing the combat shirt underneath, which showed his regimental and qualification badges. He shrugged on the weapons harness and buckled it up, making sure everything was secure but loose and that the pistol was butt forward and high on the left. He reached back into the duffel bag for his dark-blue, almost black, Canadian Forces beret with its brass regimental crest in the middle. He jammed it on his head, cocking it to the right and rear.

"Aren't you going to wear your blue bonnet?" the major asked.

"Nope, I'm a member of the regiment, sir," Paul replied.

"We in the American army," the major explained to all who were present, "are allowed to keep a regimental flash on one shoulder from a regiment we have served with in the past. In the Canadian Army, they are allowed to wear the headgear of that regiment. The master warrant here has the right to wear a blue beret, signifying he has served with the United Nations. He chooses not to. The class will also notice his weapon is different than the ones you are using. It is not your standard American government-issued M16. It is a modified version of that weapon, built to Canadian Army specifications, and has a grenade launcher mounted underneath. If I were to guess, I would bet it has other modifications the EBB specifies for its own use. It is also standard for every trooper in the EBB to be issued a 1911 forty-five-calibre Colt automatic pistol. You will see that he has it mounted high—within easy reach but out of the way. Also notice his weapons harness is of a different design. It is from Finland

and is much better than ours. So now, Master Warrant, it is time to put up or shut up."

The helicopter flew in, coming to a hover two feet off the ground and five yards in front of the gathered class, with its engines running just below takeoff speed. Paul ran to the helicopter and jumped through the open door, fastening his rifle across his chest with its barrel down. The second he hit the seat, the Huey was airborne again. Beating to the west, it flew away from the mock buildings, gaining speed and altitude for the insertion. Paul stuck his head out the door and saw ten Green Berets sprinting toward the buildings, holding weapons, and putting on black armbands.

"So it's going to be like that, eh?" he said to himself as he took the rappelling rope on the helicopter's floor. He attached it to the rails embedded in the helicopter floor and tugged hard to make sure it was fastened. He pulled out his specially made rappelling device, hooked it onto the rope, and made sure it was fastened tightly. Paul had spent many hours perfecting this device on the university's climbing wall and in Emily's ranch workshop. This would be the first time using it for a real drill out of a helicopter. It was designed to allow him to drop quickly to the ground while still being in control of the descent and even able to stop if he had to.

With a shout into Paul's ear, the crew chief told him they were on the final approach. Paul stood and tossed the loose end of the rope out the door. He then tucked the rope under his butt and held it tightly against his hip with his right hand. He engaged the brake on the device, turned to face the door, leaned out, placed all his weight on the rope, and stepped onto the skids. The wind and rotor blast hammered at him. The helicopter flared, entering its hover, and the second its forward motion stopped, Paul kicked loose from the skids and released the device's brake. He plummeted twenty feet down the rope in less than three seconds and was on the ground before the crew chief turned to tell him to go. The second he felt his feet hit the ground, he flung the rope away from him with his right hand. With a flick of his thumb, the braking device fell off the rope. He sprinted away from the rope to the edge of the roof and peered quickly over the edge. He had put his aviator sunglasses on before entering the helicopter, and they helped cut the sun's glare. He jacked a round into the chamber and sighted down the street at two black-banded Green Berets who were not going fast enough to have reached concealment. He fired a single shot into the middle of each man's back, taking both out of the fight before they even knew it had started. He ran to the door heading from the roof to the interior stairwell and flung it open. He tossed a practice grenade down the stairs and ducked back out to wait for it to detonate.

"Shit!" he heard, just before the grenade went off. After it detonated, he jumped into the stairwell and shot the trooper waiting there. He pulled his sunglasses off and shoved them into a pocket. Paul took a clip of ammo and two more grenades from the "dead" trooper's belt. Noticing the small earphone in the man's ear, Paul pulled it out and followed the wire. He found a pocketed portable radio attached to the other end of it, and he relieved the trooper of that as well. He put the earbuds into his ear and clipped the radio to the back of his weapons belt. He was just in time to hear the passwords and find out where everyone else was located. One step at a time, he moved downstairs.

"Shit," the Green Beret major said. "Three down in less than a minute." He was standing with his second-in-command and a civilian, who was dressed in a dark suit, white shirt, and black tie. Paul's ROTC class was standing not far away.

"Maybe your boys will take this seriously now," the civilian said.

"I told my people these guys were good," the major said. "I trained with them."

The civilian had to wait to respond, as another grenade and two single shots went off in the building's top floor. "That will be two more," the civilian said.

"Stay awake, Black Team!" the major yelled into his radio. "This guy isn't playing around."

"Bravo," the speaker said.

"X-ray," another voice said, followed by another gunshot. This one came from the second floor.

"He must have missed the one on the third floor," the major said. Suddenly an explosion went off in the third-floor room where his man was hiding. "Shit! Now he's playing with us."

"X-ray, Bravo," came a voice. The words were barely out of the radio before there were three rifle shots—a single and a double tap—on the main floor.

Several silent seconds ticked by. "Tango," came across the radio.

"Alpha," came another voice. A trooper on the roof across from the main building stood up, and two more soldiers in separate windows came into view in the window openings. The people observing heard a plunk and saw a dark object heading for the right window. There was another plunk, and an object headed for the left window. A double tap followed a single shot, and the trooper on the roof took two steps back as red blotches appeared on his chest. This was followed in rapid succession by

Bears Maul

two explosions producing red smoke from the windows as Paul's launched grenades went off.

"Bang, bang." A voice came on the radio. "You're all dead."

Paul walked out of the front door of the building, putting his sunglasses on and holding his rifle barrel down. His right finger was beside the trigger.

"Six minutes," the major said. "Close enough anyway." He walked toward Paul, holding his pistol behind his back.

"You got us good," the major said, smiling as he approached Paul.

"I did now," Paul said, raising the rifle and pulling the trigger once.

The major looked down, saw a red blotch on his chest, and frowned. "That's not very sporting," he said.

"Drop the act," Paul said. "I saw your black armband as I came out of the helicopter, Major. My granddad fell for that one in World War I. It almost killed him."

"Jesus," the major said, shaking his head. He brought the pistol out from behind his back and holstered it. The rest of the troopers came out of the building. All had red blotches on their bodies in the kill zone, except for those who had fallen victim to grenades—they were fully covered in red dye. "I thought you weren't going to use the grenade launcher," the major said.

"I lied," Paul replied, smiling. "I figured you guys would pull something like this."

Everyone gathered around Paul. His ROTC lads pummeled him on the back, and the Green Berets shook his hand.

The major touched the bear on Paul's right collar. "How come you don't have an eagle?" the major asked. "It damn well looks to me like you qualify for one."

"Oh no, sir," Paul replied. "I'm just a part-time soldier. The eagles are for the real soldiers."

"Shit," the major mumbled, walking over to where the civilian still stood.

"That is what we are looking for," the civilian said. "CIA needs that type of capability, and he says he is only a part-time soldier." The man walked toward Paul, who was still listening to his ROTC students laughing and telling him what a great day this had been—to finally experience some real soldier work instead of pretending to jump out of helicopters. "Morning, Master Warrant," the civilian said, showing Paul his ID. "Did you perfect that technique in Cyprus or in Yemen?"

"Neither," Paul said. "The boys and I have been playing around on this equipment at the university, pretending to jump out of Hueys, for about a year now. They did pretty good for pretend soldiers, eh?"

"Could they do it for real?" the CIA man asked.

"It's been my experience that the body remembers the training, sir," Paul said. "The mind may rebel, but the body just takes over. Isn't that right, Major?"

"Do you think you could train a group of highly motivated professional soldiers to do what you have shown these kids?" the man asked, ignoring the major.

"Only if they are very quick learners," Paul said. "In three weeks I graduate, and then I'm getting married and going back to the Great White North, sir, for good."

"I think we can prevail on your government to let you stay for another year or two," the man said.

"Maybe so," Paul said, "but my term is up. I am done, so I don't think so, but thanks for the offer anyway. I am sure some of the major's people are more than capable of doing some training. If you will excuse me, my ride home is here."

The two helicopters were back, and Paul joined his trainees for the ride back to Caltech. The usual group of disgruntled students waved placards and fists as the helicopters came over the fence and deposited the troopers on the helipad. The men filed over to the armoury building to turn in their weapons and unused practice ammunition. Paul handed in his ammunition, but he put his weapons into his office's locker. His weapons, highly modified versions of what the Canadian Forces used, were not US issue. Since it was Thursday—the trainees' last day on campus for the week—Paul congratulated them once more on their day's performance and told them all to report to him at 1400 on Tuesday.

All classes were pretty much done for the year, and Paul's exams were finished. All he had to do now were final evaluations of his trainees, hand in the paperwork, get his marks, collect his data, get married, and live happily ever after with Emily back home in boring Didsbury, Alberta.

He had to stop in at the neighbors' on his way back to his guesthouse to set up some things for the wedding. He had briefly made it home for Easter while Emily was on assignment in Lebanon, and his family had made plans to attend the nuptials. The wedding wouldn't be a traditional Canadian family affair—that would have to wait until Paul and Emily got back to Canada—but the family would bring a little tradition with them to America.

Paul pulled into the driveway and slowly drove to the guesthouse he now shared with Emily. She had moved in a month after he took up residence, deciding it was foolish to stay apart since they were getting married anyway. If not for Paul's stubborn insistence on finishing school first, they would have been married already. Paul's mother shook her finger at him, and Tatiana pulled on his ear when he told them of the delay, but a series of phone calls and telegrams between the two families had seen everything straightened out. Paul took the advice of his father and grandfather, letting the women of the family handle wedding details.

"The man just shows up to the wedding and does what he is told," Nicolas had said. "It wouldn't matter if you bitched about it anyway. The ladies will do what they want."

Paul just nodded his head and agreed with everything he was told to do for the wedding. Both his and Emily's families were Catholic, so the nonsense the church forced a nonmember to go through was unnecessary. Paul's cousin used his influence to expedite Emily's landed immigrant status so she could enter Canada without any problems after the wedding. Even though another cousin, an ordained priest, was coming to help with the wedding, Paul and Emily would go through the marriage ceremony again once they got back to Canada. Paul did not understand why, but Nicolas and John, rather than his mother and grandmother, had insisted on it. The look Paul received from his grandmother told him he had better go along with it.

Emily was in New York to wind things down and hand in her final stories, and he didn't expect her back until Tuesday morning at the earliest, so he had the weekend to himself. Not that he would be lounging around—the wedding was next Saturday, and his family was arriving Thursday afternoon. He had to arrange everything for them. He and the ranch hands had cleaned up and fenced off five acres of pasture closest to the yard, and they had set up cisterns and run water lines to two large tents to serve as shower and washroom facilities. Plumbers worked ten-hour days to get boilers, as well as fresh- and waste-water tanks, hooked up and functioning properly.

Paul and the ranch hands moved the horses out of the barn and cleaned it out, removing straw and manure, pulling down stall walls, and scrubbing concrete floors before laying down a temporary plywood floor for an improvised banquet hall. Electricians were busy as well, getting everything ready, and the caterer supervised the construction of a temporary kitchen, which would be used to prepare the wedding meal.

It was late Sunday night when Paul got to the guesthouse and later still when he got to bed. He was exhausted not only from the military exercises on Friday, but also the work he had done wiring speakers for the sound system in the barn.

Paul had just gotten off the telephone in his tiny ROTC office, which was located in the back corner of the armoury. The airline confirmed that Emily's flight from New York was on time, so he was anxious to see her when he arrived home later that afternoon. There was no way he could get out of duty today to pick her up from the airport, and Emily assured him she was a big girl and could take a cab home. His mind wandered to the delights he would share with her tonight when the telephone rang and brought him back to reality.

"Caltech ROTC ready room, Master Warrant Bekenbaum speaking. How may I direct your call, sir?" Paul said into the handset.

"Paul, this is Colonel Williamson," said the commander of the National Guard battalion the ROTC was attached to. "How soon can you have your people ready for a mission?" he asked.

"It depends on the mission, sir," Paul replied. "A couple of hours to a couple of days."

"Have you been watching the news, son?" the colonel asked. "The governor is advised of your counterinsurgent capabilities and is requesting our assistance. The situation is grave, and local authorities are unable to handle it. You and your platoon are hereby placed on active duty and authorised to use deadly force to rectify the situation. Once again, how soon can you and your people be ready?"

"Two hours, sir," Paul replied, deadly serious now. "I need to get the lads out of class and over to the armoury, and we need to kit up. I need authorization for full ammo loads, sir. I will also not allow deployment until I assess the situation and the terrain and make a plan, sir."

"Yeah, I told the governor's people the earliest we could get out there was after lunch," the colonel said. "Two Hueys will pick you up around oh-ten fifteen. Does that give you enough time? Your authorization for weapons and ammo has already been telexed to your quartermaster, so that is not an issue."

"We should be OK, sir," Paul said. "I'll get the ball rolling on our end."

"Right. Good luck, Mr. Bekenbaum." The colonel hung up.

Paul consulted his binder, which contained his platoon's lesson schedules. He telephoned various department offices to inform them of the emergency call-out and then headed to the weapons lockers. "Full combat loads, Sergeant," he said to the man behind the meshed-in counter. "I guess this is the real deal. I want eight grenades for my launcher and four clips each for my rifle and sidearm. Get the same loads for the rest of my troop. Do you have any flash bangs? I want two for each trooper and four for me. We also need flak jackets but not helmets. I want balaclavas for everyone. Can you handle all that?"

"Yes, sir," said the sergeant, a Korean War vet. "I've got the lads working on some of it right now. That's a nasty deal you've gotten yourself into there, Mr. Bekenbaum."

"So they tell me, Sergeant," Paul said. "OK, I'm going to get my gear and come back here. If the lads show up, give them their gear and tell 'em to wait by the front door. Oh, and I'm going to need ten rappelling ropes, each twenty-five feet long. Don't worry about connectors, since we've got our own."

Paul walked back into his office and pulled his weapons from the duffel bag that was stuffed into the tall safe. He quickly stripped off the workday US Army uniform he normally wore and put on his regimental battle dress. Looping his weapons belt over his left shoulder, he put the rifle over his right and walked back down to the main building. About half his troopers were milling about on the parade floor. Seeing how he was dressed, they quieted down. "Get your asses out of those civvies and into combat dress!" he yelled at them. "Then get to the sergeant and draw your gear. We've got less than two hours, so move it!"

The other five troopers jogged into the hall and, seeing the activity and Paul loading cartridges into clips, ran for the locker room to change without being told. Paul put two loaded clips in the cargo pockets of his battle trousers and the other two in pouches on his weapons belt. The four clips for his pistol were on the pistol belt beside the holster. He loaded three grenades into the launcher under his rifle's barrel and put the other two into a pouch on his belt. Then he hung four grenades on the upright straps of the battle harness, two to a side. He pulled the cleaning kit from the butt of his rifle and started the ritual of cleaning his primary weapon.

    His troopers had never seen him this serious, nor had they seen him in his regimental uniform before. His high-top boots reached just under his calves, and his trousers were tucked into and evenly bloused over their tops. A large knife in a scabbard was sewn to the outside of his right boot, and all his shoulder badges were small and dull—even the ones on his epaulets that designated him as an officer. His beret was well worn, and the regimental crest was not brass but cloth, as was the bear on his right collar. *Canada* was embroidered over both shoulders—a green version of the new Canadian maple-leaf flag under it on his left and his regimental colours on his right.

    As his troopers gathered, they followed his lead, quietly loading clips with live ammunition and cleaning weapons. Whatever they were getting into was the real deal, and they knew it. "OK, boys, gather around," Paul said. The men from the armoury watched from the periphery, as did the base's officers and men from other platoons. No one interfered or commented as Paul gave his briefing. "The governor of California has requested our services," Paul began. "There is a hostage crisis somewhere, and we are apparently the only ones capable of handling it. Local authorities are losing control of the situation, so we are it, gentlemen. I don't know any more than that at this time, nor do I want any speculation based on what you have heard on the radio about the situation. My experience is that the media often gets it all wrong, so it's best not to pay attention to news reports. Choppers will be here in ten minutes to transport us to where we have to deploy. We will be briefed on the situation at that time. I don't want to see your name tags or the words *US Army* on your chests. You will wear the balaclavas pulled down so only your eyes can be seen, from the second we walk out that door until we get back after the mission. Is that clear?"

He looked at each man, getting confirmation that they had heard him. "There is going to be a media frenzy at the site, and I don't want any of us to be recognised," Paul continued. "These bad guys are nasty types. They will go after you, your families, and your friends. If they don't know who you are, they can't retaliate. I have equipment to neutralise live television cameras, but we can't stop print cameras, so make sure your face is covered at all times. That goes for all of you people too." Paul turned to the onlookers. "They will kill you and your families and friends as well. America has been isolated from this kind of thing, but it is normal in the Middle East. Are there questions?"

"Any idea about how many weapons we will face or what types they will be, Mr. Bekenbaum?" Walawitz asked.

"Not at this time, Wal," Paul answered. "Prepare for the worst, and pray for the best. Anything else? OK, grab your gear, and let's go."

Each man put on his flak jacket and zippered it shut and then put on the heavy shoulder harness, which carried all the spare ammunition, pistols, and grenades. They each grabbed coiled climbing ropes and placed them around their shoulders. Finally they each grabbed an M16 by its carry handle and then walked out the door to the helipad. Each man pulled down his balaclava to cover his face, except Paul, who waited until he arrived at the pad. Only then did he remove his beret, roll it up, and place it under his left epaulet before pulling the balaclava down over his mouth and nose.

They reached the helipad and heard the unmistakable thump of an approaching Huey, so the men arranged themselves five on each side of the pad. The machine barely touched down and they rapidly boarded, taking off within a minute of its landing. Paul motioned for the doors to be closed, and they were sealed off from any onlookers' view. It became slightly quieter inside the helicopter. It was a different copter crew this time, as the crew they had used a couple of days earlier had been from the regular army, and this group was from the California National Guard.

The helicopter landed at a small airport outside LA proper, and Paul saw no evidence of television crews or other news media. In fact, the area was effectively cordoned off. The crew chief leaned over and spoke into Paul's ear as soon as the skids hit the ground and the rotors spun down. "Stay in the chopper," the crew chief yelled. "We are shoving the chopper into the hangar, and then you guys can get out."

It took about ten minutes for the rotor blades to slow down and stop, and then the pilot, copilot, and both crewmen jumped out of the chopper. Leaving their helmets on and visors down, they pushed the Huey into the hangar. As soon as the hangar doors were shut, they opened the Huey's doors for the platoon to dismount. Looking quickly around and seeing nothing but uniformed policemen—both state and city—and FBI and army uniforms, Paul pulled off his balaclava, stuck it into his right pants pocket, and put his beret back on. Other members of the platoon rolled theirs up as well, so they were covering only the top halves of their heads. They trooped over to a table, where an aerial map and building plans were taped to a wall behind it.

"Master Warrant Bekenbaum and party of nine, reporting as ordered, sir!" Paul barked out. He and his platoon stood at attention and saluted in the American fashion in front of the US Special Forces lieutenant colonel, who was the highest-ranking officer in the room.

The colonel returned their salutes, told them to be at ease, and then introduced the head of the FBI contingent who started the briefing. He explained that a group of black militants had taken control of a bank in suburban LA and had about twenty hostages. The building was a ten-storey midrise, with the bank located on the ground and second floors. The whole building was evacuated, except for the bank. After the militants cleaned out the bank's vault and tellers' drawers, they moved everyone to the bank's second-floor rear offices. Negotiations affected the release of five hostages, who informed police that eight people were involved in the heist. All were black—six men and two women—and all were armed with automatic weapons of Soviet manufacture, including grenades and pistols. One hostage had been in the military during World War II, and he was sure they had what looked like a couple bricks of C4 and detonators. They took the building late on a Friday, and negotiations were going nowhere. "The governor doesn't want the regular army involved," the FBI man said. "None of the rest of us are capable of assaulting the building without causing a lot of casualties among our people and the hostages. Somebody told us you guys are the best bet, so here you are. The ball is now in your court."

Paul looked at the building's layout to ascertain the location of the hostages and militants on the second floor. An internal stairwell led from the bank to the second floor in the middle of the building. Two more stairwells were at each end, and two elevators serviced the building. The FBI explained that the building's power was shut off, so the elevators were not working. "OK, leave things with me for a few minutes so I can figure out a way to do this without everyone dying. Send the Huey crew over, would you?" Paul said to the pilot, "All right, Captain, I am going to need you to come in fast and hard. Then come to a completely motionless hover, no more than twenty feet off the roof, for no less than thirty seconds. Will that be a problem, or do I need another pilot?"

"No, Warrant," the captain deferred. "I did a number of insertions like that in Vietnam, so I should be OK with it. The winds will be a little tricky, but at least nobody will be shooting at us."

"You hope," Paul said, laughing. He looked at a television that was set up in one corner. Every news outlet and station in LA, as well as some national and foreign ones, surveilled the bank building from every vantage point. "We have to assume the bad guys are watching all that," Paul said, pointing at the TV. "I'm pretty sure I can knock out the live signals as we come in, but we should assume we didn't."

"Excuse me, sir," Paul said to the FBI man. "Can we get one of those helicopters over here?" Paul pointed at the helicopters circling around the building. "Not the police ones—the news network ones."

"Should be no problem," the FBI man said. "The media might bitch, but we can federalise them for temporary duty. Will the captain be able to fly it?"

"A Bell Ranger is a Huey with nicer options," Paul said. "Right, Captain?"

"Yeah, most of them are easier to fly," he agreed. "You get it here, and I'll fly it."

"I assume people on the scene are in contact with the militants? I'll need the telephone number the negotiators are using and the number the militants are using. I would like to talk to a negotiator right now please. Oh, Captain," Paul said to the pilot, "you and your crew work on your flight plan. I want to hit that roof and have you gone in less than a minute. Once we're on the roof and disconnected from the ropes, get out of there. Am I clear?"

"Roger, Warrant." The captain took out a notebook and called his crew over to the maps and photos.

"Walawitz, you're second in command today," Paul said. "We'll divide into two groups—one for each stairwell. I imagine they are locked, and they might be wired with C4, so we need two sets of keys for the doors and a couple mechanic's or dentist's mirrors. I prefer the mechanic's ones because they telescope. I've got a set of wire cutters on me. Make sure your group has at least one pair. We'll get the doors open, disarm the trip wires, and make the C4 safe. Then we'll hit them and hit them hard. Make no bones about it—these guys will kill the hostages, so we need to kill them first. Work on your order of entry. I'll be going in first in my group."

"Warrant, we have the on-scene captain on the line." The FBI man held up a telephone receiver.

"Good morning, Captain, this is Sierra One," Paul said. "In two hours my people and I will enter your hostage scene and take control. Once I tell you I have arrived, I will have complete control of the scene, and your people are to stand down. You will hear explosions and gunfire, no doubt. Do not react unless I tell you to. Is that clear?"

"How are you coming in, and how will we know you are here?" the captain asked.

"You won't be able to miss us," Paul said. "You let me worry about that. If nobody but us knows our plan, nobody but us knows our plan. I'll let you handle the media, OK?" Paul hung up, walked back to where his men were, and verified everything was in order. Then he went to where he had left his gear, pulled out a small box the size of two rifle clips tied together, flipped up its antennas, and switched on the power. Immediate yells from those watching the TV told him the device was working properly, and he switched it back off again.

"Handy gadget," said the major Paul had trained with on Friday. "Your government has all kinds of handy gadgets."

"It's not government issue," Paul said, smiling. "It's something I cooked up in the lab. The rights are available for lease, if you're interested. I've already got a patent."

"Caltech doesn't waste any time, do they?" the major said.

"I didn't use Caltech's lab for this project," Paul said. "I used my own Mickey Mouse lab for this design. DND is already licencing it, and so are the Brits and the Germans. The French are going in with the Belgians and the Dutch for a licence, and your people are evaluating it."

"You amaze me to no end, Bekenbaum," the major said. "If this thing works, I can bet there will be a deal by the end of the day. You can tune it to different radio frequencies, right?"

"Nope, it blocks out the whole radio spectrum," Paul said. "If you want to block a different frequency band, you'll need a different device. I'm working on a tunable version, but with current technology, it's just too bulky to be portable. Ah, it sounds like my chariot is here."

A helicopter could be heard approaching and then setting down outside the hangar. Minutes later, a protesting pilot was led away from the hangar by policemen, while other policemen opened the hangar doors wide enough for it to be pushed inside. Once it was in the hangar and the hangar doors were closed, National Guard men flung open the helicopter's doors. To lighten the load, the seats were quickly unbolted from the passenger compartment and discarded along with the camera mounts and anything else not necessary for the mission. The rail mounted to the floor on each side of the military helicopter was unbolted and transferred to the civilian model, and the National Guard crewmen assured Paul the mounting points were exactly the same for both vehicles, so there was nothing to worry about as far as safety.

Paul led the platoon to the news helicopter, and they mounted the skids on both sides of the helicopter. They stepped off, practicing with small pieces of rappelling rope and the device Paul had invented for faster descent. Once all the troopers were comfortable that they could deploy successfully, Paul gathered them all around him. "This is for real, boys," he said. "You are used to the noise and the kick from the rifles, so just let your training kick in. Do the job as you were trained. Keep your eyes moving. These bad guys are using real bullets, so if you get hit, it's going to hurt really bad. So, hurt them first, just like we planned. They will be tired and not expecting us. They are likely not trained as well as we are on how to use weapons, but they are highly motivated and will kill us if they get the chance. We go silent, we go fast, and we go deadly. We all know where to be and where everyone else should be. Don't piss around. If the target has a gun, the target is dead—even if the gun is not pointed at you. To make my point as clearly as I possibly can, know that my grandmother killed ten German soldiers while they stood and watched her do it in World War I. And one of my female cousins killed some more in World War II and Korea. A woman can and will shoot you dead if she can. Now repeat after me: if a target has a gun, the target is dead." He had the platoon repeat the statement three times, and then he told them to hit the washroom since they would be leaving soon.

"They'll be all right," the Green Beret major said. "You trained them well, better than my bunch trained their kids."

"They're a good group of kids," Paul said. "I hope they learned well. I would hate to lose any of them." The major, the helicopter crew, and Paul went quiet for a few seconds, remembering other times in other places. "What the fuck?" Paul said, looking around. "It's what we're paid for."

"What's that saying you guys have?" the major asked. "If you can't take a joke, you shouldn't have joined."

"Too right," the crew chief said. "I'm going to miss my door gun. I almost feel naked without it."

"Sure, Sarge," the copilot said. "The way I heard the story, you damn near shit yourself every time you landed in a hot landing zone."

"Goddamn right I did," the door gunner said, laughing. "Wasn't *damn near* a couple of times neither."

All the veterans had a laugh at that. The young troopers came back to see the veterans laughing so hard some were crying. The troopers looked at one another. "Can't be all that bad," Walawitz said. "Mr. Bekenbaum looks like he's gonna piss himself from laughing so hard."

"All right, mount up, lads," Paul ordered. The platoon members took their places, sitting on the floor of the copter with their feet on the skids. Their ropes were tight, with the device locked in place. Their rifles were slung across their chests, barrels pointed down. As the helicopter wheeled out of the hangar, all the troopers, Paul included, pulled their balaclavas in place to leave only their eyes visible. Paul pulled a clip from his pants pocket and banged it on the side of the helicopter to get everyone's attention. He waved it around and loaded it in his rifle. He pulled the arming bolt back to chamber a round and put the safety on. He did the same with his Colt automatic pistol and then holstered it. The rest of the troop followed suit, and before they were airborne, everyone's weapons were loaded and ready.

It was a nice day, and Paul enjoyed the ride. As he looked out over the city, the wind blew through the doors around him. The helicopter was five hundred feet above the ground.

"Five minutes, Warrant," the crew chief yelled in Paul's ear. Paul started singing the Beach Boys' "Fun, Fun, Fun," raising his hands and swaying as if he were on a dance floor. The rest of the platoon did the same thing, and two crewmen joined them. Since they were standing and strapped in, they actually danced. The copilot looked back and shook his head before shrugging his shoulders and joining the chorus, followed by the pilot.

The crew chief touched Paul's right shoulder to signal that it was time to deploy. Paul stood up and turned around, as did the rest of his men. They put all their weight on the ropes, leaning back. Paul reached into his right pocket and flicked the switch on his blocking device to block any TV-signal transmissions within a half-mile radius. The news helicopter hovered twenty-five feet above the building, and five heavily armed men jumped out of each side and slid down ropes. In less than a minute, the helicopter was gone, trailing the ropes.

"Did you get that shot?" A CBS man ran up to Emily on the ground. "All our equipment is down. I've never seen anything like that, have you?"

"Yes, I got the shot," Emily said. "And no, I have never seen anything like that."

Emily's boss had asked her to cover this situation as her farewell story. "As a combat reporter, you will have a better perspective than most local journalists," her boss had said. "It will probably be a colossal bore, but you have a knack for being in the right place at the right time. I want you there in case something happens."

It certainly seems as though something big is going to happen, Emily thought. *Those guys are not policemen. They look like military.*

"The cops won't tell us anything," a radio reporter said. "They say they don't know what that was. Are any of you guys able to get through to your stations?" No one from TV or radio was able to get through, and no one wanted to leave to find a pay phone. They knew they would not be let back in once they crossed the police barrier. Emily and other print-media personnel furiously wrote their observations in the notebooks they always carried. Emily was the only one to capture the helicopter and its load of men on film.

Paul dropped his frequency jammer on the center of the rooftop as he stepped away from the ropes. He unslung his rifle, putting it against his shoulder and releasing the safety as he pivoted around the roof to make sure it was clear of targets. Seeing that it was, he put the safety back on and headed to the rooftop door. Two troopers, rifles ready, crouched down at each side of the door. Paul gingerly pushed the latch and pulled the door open a crack. Just as he had suspected, a trip wire was attached to it. He closed it again and pulled the mechanic's mirror from his pants pocket, extended it fully, and cracked the door open again. The other end of the trip wire was attached to a block of C4. Paul verified that cutting the wire would not set it off, and he proceeded to cut it.

He opened the door fully and quietly crept down the stairs to where the block of explosives was placed. He cut the rest of the trip wire off the detonator, as well as the duct tape holding the explosives to the stairwell's handrail, and put the block of C4 in his pants pocket. Followed by four troopers, he crept down the stairwell until he reached the eighth floor of the ten-floor building. The other five troopers would take the other stairwell and meet Paul and his team. He gently pushed open the fire door leading to the lobby. The building was dark, since the power was off. Paul walked down the hall until he found an unlocked office door and entered. Paul's nine men followed him in, and they made sure they were alone. Paul picked up a telephone and called the LAPD captain. "We are in," he said. "When was the last time you talked to the bad guys?"

"About five minutes ago," the captain answered. "Nothing has changed."

"OK, stand down. Everything is in my hands now." Paul dialed another number and put the phone on speaker as it rang.

"Yes," an African-accented voice said.

"Is this Mustafa?" Paul asked.

"Yes, who is this?" the voice demanded.

"May the blessing of the prophet be upon you, Mustafa," Paul said. "Allah be praised. My name is Ricky Ricardo, and Allah has seen fit to make me your new negotiator."

"There will be no more negotiating," Mustafa said. "You have been given our demands and our timetable. We will not deviate from this course."

"I see," Paul said. "Then as Allah wills it, the new plan is this, my friend. You have ten minutes to release all the hostages. Then you have another five minutes to throw all your weapons into the street and come out with your hands on your heads. Do I make myself clear, Mustafa?"

"You are a fool, Ricky Ricardo. I will kill all of the hostages. On this, I am firm! Are you clear on that?" Mustafa yelled into the phone.

"After the ten minutes is up, Mustafa, you will be explaining yourself to Allah. It is your choice, my friend," Paul said calmly.

"What do I care about the lives of some unbelievers?" Mustafa yelled into the phone. "If you come, you will be explaining yourself to Allah—not I!"

"We are all Allah's children, Mustafa," Paul said. "It saddens me to hear you are taking this course of action, but you leave me no choice. Allah be with you, my friend." Paul cut the connection.

"Shit, I didn't know you're a Muslim," Walawitz said.

"I'm not," Paul said, "and neither is he. We'll go now. You take the south stairwell, and I'll take the north." Paul led his four troopers quickly and quietly down to the second landing and put his ear to the fire door. He didn't expect to hear anything, and he was not disappointed. He motioned the trooper with the key to approach. Paul squatted down beside the door, while the trooper freed the lock and silently opened the door slightly. Again there was a trip wire, and again, Paul cut the wire. The troopers entered the corridor, in a single-file line, and duck-walked down the hall. Paul had them stop a quarter of the way along. He went down on his belly and crawled to the large central area opposite the elevators. He pushed his mirror around the corner and saw seated hostages, guarded by two armed men. He crawled in reverse to his men and motioned them to try a side door, which turned out to be unlocked. Paul peered inside, and the room was empty. Just as Paul's men were about to enter the room, his other five troopers entered the hallway from the south stairwell. Paul used hand signals to point out the targets he had seen and motioned them forward to assault by the elevator corridor.

Paul and his four men entered the empty office and duck-walked toward the central stairwell. The hostages were being held in a large central atrium-like area, where they could be spread out but still observed. A row of windows at head height lined the office the troopers were in, overlooking the atrium. Paul took advantage of his position to locate the militants, but he spotted only five of the eight militants guarding the hostages. A tall man stood by a desk, vainly trying to make a phone call. Nobody would be answering now that the assault was under way. Paul had each of his men quickly poke his head up to see the targets while he made up an on-the-spot assault plan. Noticing that the windows opened like doors, he had his men slowly and quietly open three. He motioned for three men to be shooters at the windows and chose another to accompany him through the door. Paul motioned for the three men to toss flash bangs at the opposite wall, and he used his fingers to count down from three to one. As he made a fist, the men tossed the flash bangs out the windows. Paul's trooper kicked in the door as the bangs went off, and Paul went in and shot the man at the telephone.

Paul's men fired from the windows behind him, and Paul pivoted. He was screaming, "Get down! Get down!" at the top of his lungs. Spotting a woman leveling a pistol at a hostage, he shot the militant in the forehead and searched for another target. He heard a report from a heavier-calibre rifle on full automatic, spun in that direction, and pulled his trigger as he zeroed in on the target. Six bullets, almost simultaneously from six different directions, hit the man. Two hostages were down, screaming. Paul put them out of his mind and scanned the surroundings. Six targets were down, and the other two had to be downstairs. He sprinted to the head of the stairwell and in rapid succession tossed two flash bangs down the stairs. He followed them down, hitting the floor just as they went off. He scanned the area, saw a target by the front door, and shot her as she held her head—the flash bang had gone off right at her feet. Seeing movement to his right, he spun in that direction and saw Walawitz's two shots hit the last man and put him out of the picture. Walawitz was about to congratulate himself when Paul fired his rifle twice at a blond white woman holding an automatic pistol behind Walawitz. Both men spun around but saw no more targets. The screaming penetrated Paul's brain, and he went back upstairs.

One of Paul's troopers wrapped a bandage around the arm of a man sitting on the floor. A small girl of about nine writhed on the ground, screaming. She was hit in the shoulder, and Paul took charge of her right away. He put a compression bandage on the front of her shoulder, and feeling around, he discovered it was a through shot. The bullet had gone out the back of her shoulder but was more of a graze and not all that serious. He quickly put another compression bandage on the back of her shoulder and tied both together, all the while talking soothingly to the youngster. She finally saw his kind eyes and stopped screaming.

Once the girl was quiet, Paul picked her up and placed her on his hip. He held her there with his left hand while he walked to the table with the telephone. "This is Sierra One," he said. "We have neutralised all the targets and have two casualties. We will send out the hostages shortly. Do not—I repeat, *do not*—shoot anyone. All—I repeat, *all*—the targets are down. One casualty is ambulatory, and a trooper will walk out with the other, so please don't shoot my trooper. Please call the chopper back in fifteen minutes, and don't let anybody enter the building until we are gone. Clear?"

Paul hung up and pulled a whistle from his shirt pocket. He held it up to the little girl.

"Could you help me out, love, by blowing this whistle as hard as you can?" he asked. She nodded and blew the whistle long and loud, bringing silence to the room. "Ladies and gentlemen, you are now free. Please follow me. Authorities are waiting to meet you outside. Lads, help us out a bit, would you?" Paul asked his troopers. "I need two of you to escort the hostages down and open the doors. The rest of you, police up the C4 and head for the roof. The chopper should be here in fifteen." Paul looked at the little girl on his hip. "Where's your mom, sweetheart?"

"She had to work, and Grandma took me to the bank. The bad people came, but they let Grandma go," the little girl said, still holding his whistle.

"I will take you outside, and someone will take you to your grandma, OK?" Paul said.

"Sure, mister," the little girl said. Paul walked her down the stairs and to the door. Paul watched hostages walk out of the bank and then sprint to paramedics, firemen, and police officers on the other side of the street. Many were breaking into tears.

"Mister," the little girl said as Paul walked out the door. He stood for a minute, catching his bearings and letting his eyes adjust to the sunlight. "Why do you have a bear on your collar?"

"He's my family's mascot," Paul said. "He looks out for us so we can help little girls like you."

"When I grow up, I'm going to help little girls, like you do," she said.

They hadn't gotten halfway across the road before the girl's mother broke free from the crowd and rushed to Paul. "Easy, ma'am. She's got a shoulder wound." Paul passed the girl to her crying mother.

Paul turned away and started back across the road, but the little girl stopped him. "Mister, you forgot your whistle!" she yelled, holding it out to him.

"You keep it, sweetheart," Paul said. "You earned it for being so brave." With tears in his eyes, he turned and walked into the bank.

Walawitz was waiting for Paul when he entered, and they climbed the stairs to the roof together. "No casualties for us, and we all used less than a clip of ammo," Walawitz reported. "I'm amazed there were only two minor injuries when that target let go on full auto."

"Not as amazed as I was seeing that blond militant pointing a Magnum at the back of your head," Paul said. "I don't get it. These extremists hate us and our ways, yet she still joined them. They would have killed her as soon as they got tired of her."

"Hey, boss, when's the bus coming?" one trooper hollered at Paul as he reached the roof. "I've got a hot date tonight, and I don't want to be late."

"Do you have a hot date tonight, Shultzie?" Walawitz asked. "I didn't know any women who were that desperate."

Paul smiled to himself as he listened to his men relieve their pent-up stress, as soldiers everywhere did, by making jokes. "Put the safeties on, boys," Paul said. "I hear our limo approaching."

Paul released the clip on his rifle and ejected the cartridge in the chamber. He placed the cartridge back in the clip before putting it into his pants pocket. He did the same with his pistol and watched as the rest of his men did the same. The news helicopter came into sight and slowed down as it approached the rooftop. The men crouched as it flared and came to a hover two feet off the roof. The men ran inside it, once again placing their feet on the skids. Looking over his shoulder at Walawitz, Paul sang "Fun, Fun, Fun" again, and the whole group joined in. People on the ground who happened to be looking up saw the troopers bouncing their arms to the beat of the song as the chopper left the area.

Emily snapped her last shots as the helicopter left the roof. She sat on the curb, writing her thoughts down and making an outline of a story. As soon as the helicopter left, the police ran into the building. Looking at her watch, Emily found it had been a half hour from the time the men exited the helicopter until it picked them up again.

"We've got communications again," a TV engineer hollered at his reporter. The whole radio-television crowd sprinted toward their vehicles to get the breaking story out.

"Excuse me, Captain," Emily said to a police officer. "Could you tell me who those people were?"

"All I know is that the man on the telephone called himself Sierra One to me and Ricky Ricardo to the militants," the captain said. "I don't think they were feds or army personnel. Sorry, I just don't know."

Emily took notes on details of the dead and injured, and when she felt she had enough information, she walked back to her rental car and headed to the LA office of the *American Press*. She sent her roll of film to be processed and put her thoughts in order for the story.

It took hours, but once she got her pictures, she started writing. She led with the men rappelling out of the helicopter and finished with the picture of the trooper and the little girl. The girl held a whistle in her hand, and her shirt and the trooper's were red with her blood. The trooper's face was covered with a balaclava. Tears streamed from his eyes as he handed the child to her mother. Then she saw the bear on the trooper's collar, and looking closer, she saw the maple leaf on his shoulder and the beret rolled under his epaulet. She knew who the trooper was.

The helicopter came to a stop in front of the hangar, and the troopers and helicopter crew disembarked. They walked directly into the hangar, where clapping and cheering greeted them.

Paul stripped off his balaclava, tucked it into his left pants pocket, put his beret back on, and unbuckled the weapons harness. He walked over to the military Huey, placed his now-unloaded weapon against a seat, and dropped the weapons harness on it, with his flak jacket on top of the harness. He felt cooler now as his sweat-stained shirt was exposed to the air. He was about fifteen pounds lighter, having gotten rid of all his gear.

His troopers and the chopper crew were reliving the drop and pickup, as they mimicked the song and dance they did on their way in and out. The pilot ran his hand through his hair and walked up to Paul. Paul offered the man his hand. "Excellent job," Paul said. "Thank you. That was difficult in an urban environment."

"No problem, Warrant, all part of a day's work," the pilot said, shaking Paul's hand. "If you would put a good word in for me with any Canadian oil-services companies looking for chopper pilots, it would be greatly appreciated."

"Your partner, too?" Paul asked.

"Yeah, if you could," the captain said. "There is a shortage of flying jobs in the States."

"Names and contact info, Cap," Paul said. "The boss is coming to town at the end of the week. I'll let him know then. Start packing. What about your National Guard commitment?"

"We can pack that in at any time," the man said. "It's not as if there is a shortage of chopper pilots anymore."

The brass was coming, so Paul straightened up as well as he could and hollered, "Officer on deck!" to get the troopers' attention. All the men, aircrew included, came to attention and saluted. The same lieutenant colonel returned the salute and put them at ease.

"Master Warrant Bekenbaum," the head FBI man said. "You killed nine militants and are responsible for wounding two civilians, one of them a child. You also recklessly endangered more civilians and property with your actions in regard to the helicopter. And you put your own people at risk and could have damaged or destroyed that helicopter. That is totally unacceptable."

Paul looked at the man to see whether he was being funny, which he was not, and then at the lieutenant colonel to see whether he would get any backup, which he did not.

"We will be drafting an official letter of protest to the Canadian government about your behaviour in this matter," the FBI man continued. "What do you have to say for yourself?"

"First, you asked me to help. I didn't volunteer," Paul said. "Second, I am attached to and under orders from the State of California. Finally, the next time you fucking Yanks need some help, I can fucking guarantee my regiment will tell you to go fuck yourselves. Now what do you have to say about that, Mr. High-and-mighty Asshole? You, Colonel, can kiss your nice easy pencil-pushing job good-bye," Paul said, pointing his finger at the lieutenant colonel. Then he gave a look that could kill at the Green Beret major. "And as far as providing any more training for American army personnel, I can pretty much guarantee that is finished."

Paul turned to the helicopter pilot. "Captain, as commander of this mission, I order you to prepare your helicopter to fly me and my troopers back to our base. My job here is done." Paul worked hard to keep his temper under control, and the whole hangar was deathly quiet as he walked over to the chopper and flung himself in. His troopers followed and pushed the helicopter toward the hangar doors as the aircrew opened the doors.

Five minutes later the chopper was airborne, heading back to Paul's team's drop-off point.

By the time they landed, Paul had calmed down a lot. He handed his weapons and gear to a trooper to carry into the armoury, and he turned to speak with the crew chief of the Huey. "Are you an aircraft mechanic?" Paul asked. After the man acknowledged he was, Paul asked, "What about your assistant? I just offered your pilot and copilot jobs. If you're interested, we need experienced mechanics almost more than we need pilots. Talk it over with your people, and let me know by next Tuesday at the latest."

"Shit, no problem, Warrant. I'm in. I got nothing holding me here," the crew chief said. "Cory has a wife and kids, but I'll ask him."

"Our company pays top scale and offer pension and medical benefits," Paul said.

"Like I said, count me in," the crew chief said. "I'll talk with Cory and have the captain let you know if he is in or not."

The captain pilot and his copilot came to attention when Paul approached them and saluted. An astonished Paul returned the salute. "Master Warrant, you did an excellent job back there," the captain said. "My report will reflect that, as will the rest of the crew's reports. It has been an honour, sir. I was wondering if you could see fit to provide us with some regimental patches, sir, for our uniforms, sir."

"Sure, no problem, Cap. Come on. I'll take you to the armoury, and you can make your reports there," Paul said.

As the men wrote their after-action reports, Paul went to his office and ripped the regimental patches off all his uniform shirts and jackets. He dropped them on his desk and wrote out his own report, praising those who deserved praise and condemning those who needed it. Finally he recommended that all further joint missions, for training purposes or in the field, between the regiment and American armed forces be discontinued immediately. He said future training should be confined to NATO and Commonwealth countries, because they were old friends of the regiment and appreciated its cooperation. His report to his family would be much more scathing, including the recommendation to sever ties completely or cut loose the American companies they owned.

Picking up his report and the patches, he walked back into the general area of the armoury. As he collected each man's report, he handed him a regimental patch and shook his hand. His final act was to call them all to attention, and he rendered them the regiment's hand salute. "It has been an honour, gentlemen," Paul said. "No matter what anyone says, you did outstanding work today and should be commended for it. All the targets were taken out quickly and cleanly, as you have been trained. The hostages suffered two minor injuries, and we suffered none. The quartermaster will be happy we used a minimum amount of ammunition. I am getting married in three days and will be out of your lives forever. That means tonight I'm buying!"

CHAPTER 13

EMILY SAT UP AND WAITED for Paul all night. She finally fell asleep on the living room couch but woke when she heard two vehicles pull up at high speed. Their doors flew open, and she heard very drunken voices singing "Fun, Fun, Fun" at the tops of their lungs. Emily ran to the front door to see the sun coming out. Fourteen very drunk men stood beside Paul's truck, a military deuce, and a half Dodge truck with canvas sides over its bed. One man reached into the bed of Paul's truck and handed him two duffel bags. One had a rifle barrel sticking out of it, and the other had clothing poking through its undone zipper.

"Whoa! Shit, Warrant," said a man with captain's bars on his epaulets and pilot's wings on his chest. "Is that where you live? Who's the babe? You better hope your fiancée doesn't catch you with her, man. Those rich broads will have your nuts for breakfast if they ever find out you're horsing around on them." The rest of Paul's friends generally accepted the sentiment.

"Boys, what kinda guy do you think I am?" Paul stood as straight as only a drunk can. "That, boys, is my dear Emily. She can have my nuts for breakfast, lunch, and dinner."

"OK, boys, I'll take him from here," Emily said, putting a shoulder under Paul's arm to help steady him. As he reached the door, his men came to attention at the captain's order and saluted as well as totally drunken men could. Then they piled back into the deuce and a half, once again singing the Beach Boys song, which made absolutely no sense at all to Emily. "Did you have fun?" Emily asked.

"Oh yes," Paul answered with a sly grin. "We had our final training exercise, and then we went out to celebrate our graduation and my impending nuptials. Now I should find someplace to fall down before this spinning room spits me out into the yard." Paul staggered over to the couch, collapsed in a heap, and passed out completely.

Emily picked up his feet and moved him around so he was more or less on the couch, and then she saw the dark stains on the left shoulder of his shirt and on the tops of his boots. She picked up a blanket, draped it around his sleeping body, and kissed his lips. She sat in the chair opposite him and was about to fall asleep. However, she was kept awake by his reliving the assault in his sleep. He issued orders and talked through his decisions to shoot or not. He talked about his anguish over the little girl being hurt, anger at the American government, and pride in his men. Finally, he said how much he loved and had missed her.

Emily woke up to a crick in her neck, the sun in her eyes, and the sound of a truck horn. Paul was no longer on the couch. He slammed a closet door shut and walked across the floor. "Good, you're awake," Paul said, picking her up out of the chair, pulling her close, and kissing her long and tenderly.

"I have to go, but I will hopefully be back by tonight or tomorrow morning for sure," he said, kissing her again.

"But I just got back from New York. Where are you going?" Emily asked, confused.

"I have to meet my parents and family. They should be in town by now," Paul said, walking out the front door.

"Wait, I'm coming with you," Emily said, grabbing her purse.

"No, love," Paul said in German. "You cannot."

"What the hell do you mean I cannot?" Emily was getting angry. "I haven't seen you for two weeks, and now you are leaving to meet your parents, who I haven't seen for six months, and you say, '*Ich can nicht*'?"

"No, love, you cannot." Paul tried to give her a hug, but she pushed him away and became angrier by the minute.

"Emily, my little one," her father said in German. He was now standing beside her, his arm around her shoulder. "You must stay."

She shoved her father away and was about to lambaste him as well, but her mother took her by the arm and turned Emily toward her. Emily's sister stood beside their mother. "My lovely lass," her mother said, laying the Irish brogue on thickly. "You must let him go. He must go and come back. That is the way it is, the way it has always been, and the way it will always be."

"What are you talking about?" Emily yelled. "Are you all insane? I have to meet Katherine and Tatiana to plan things!"

"The planning is all done, my little one," Harriet said. "We must prepare to meet the family."

"I still don't understand," Emily said. She spun around, looking for support from Paul, and noticed he was in uniform. It was a uniform she had never seen before. It was dark blue, almost black, and the trousers had a wide red stripe down them. The double-breasted tunic had six red cartridge loops on each side of its gleaming brass buttons. Instead of the single crowns he wore on the epaulets of his regular uniform, his sleeves had three large gold-colour V's topped by crowns and single gold-colour slashes below each elbow. Both shoulders had the regimental flash, but the Canadian flash was missing. Brown boots came to just below the knee and laced up the front, and topping his head was an old-style campaign hat with a brass maple-leaf dead center. A brass bear shone brightly on his right collar. He held an old-style leather pistol belt and curved scabbarded sword.

Paul kissed Emily quickly and jumped into the passenger seat of his truck. Manuel put the truck in gear and turned it around. Emily saw Paul's rifle and saddle in the truck's bed, and a pole stuck out of the tailgate by two feet. "What the hell is going on?" Emily demanded, all patience finally gone. "Sarah didn't have to go through all this nonsense."

"I was not the eldest child of a prominent family marrying the heir of an old and even more prominent family," Sarah said. "There are traditions at work here that are older than our country, sister."

"Come, lass, we have much to do." Emily's mother dragged her to the main house, where the servants had a bath drawn for Emily and scented candles burning. They made her get in the bathtub, and her sister and mother washed her hair while she relaxed. Then they helped her out of the tub and wrapped her in plush towels, bundling her into her mother's dressing room, where several women waited.

The women trimmed her hair and painted her nails. The Mexican women stood back and watched, as Harriet and Sarah braided Emily's long black tresses into two braids, wrapped them around her head, and pinned them with wildflowers and white daisies. The servants took over and did Emily's makeup, putting eyeliner and blush on her but nothing too heavy. Harriet and Sarah went off to do their own preparations. By the time

Emily's beauty routine was done, Harriet and Sarah were back, and the Mexican women left the Hershmire women alone. Sarah wore a traditional German dress—all green with gold hems and linings—and high black boots that shone. Harriet was dressed in traditional Irish garb. Both women held garments, and they bid Emily to rise and get dressed.

First Emily put on a pure-white linen shift, and then came a sky-blue dress with a thick red border and gold-braided lace in the shapes of branches and leaves. Next was an apron of dark green with the same gold lace. The final touch was a pure-white lace veil arranged to flow gracefully around Emily's shoulders and to her waist. When Harriet and Sarah stood back to admire their handiwork, they all heard faint pistol shots in the distance. Consuela rushed into the room, dressed in highly colourful traditional Mexican clothing.

"They are coming," she said. "We must go."

Harriet pulled the veil down over Emily's face and shoulders. She took one of her arms, while Sarah took the other. They guided Emily out to the front porch. Emily looked around and saw all the ranch hands dressed in their ancestral finery with silver coins sewn into the seams of their black jeans. They had brushed their horses so their coats were shining, and the silver borders of their fancy saddles shone so brightly it almost hurt to look at them. The ranch hands pulled their large black sombreros over their eyes, and each had a Winchester rifle braced on one knee. They looked out at the hillside that bordered the ranch. Emily gazed at the hilltop in time to see fifty mounted troopers crest the hill. They rode in line abreast, and lance pennants and flags flew in the breeze. It was a sight that had not been seen for a hundred years. The regiment had arrived.

Manuel stayed with Paul until the mixed passenger and freight train reached the small local depot. He then shook Paul's hand and drove back to the ranch. Paul sat on the edge of the platform, his saddle and tack beside him, and put on his weapons. First he belted the pistol holster on his left, and then he slung his sword across his back with the hilt over his left shoulder. The train came to a stop, and people immediately poured from the passenger coaches and headed to the freight cars to unload luggage.

"Well, brother, long time no see." George held out both hands as he approached Paul.

Paul rose, and the brothers gave each other a long hug. "Holy shit, you made major," Paul said, seeing the insignia below the eagle on his brother's collar. Other than George's officer's insignia and a second slash on each sleeve, the men were dressed identically.

"And you still won't take an eagle," George said, tapping the bear on Paul's collar. "When will you become a real officer? You are more than qualified."

"Ah, don't start, George," Paul said. "Not this weekend. I am an officer, by the way, just not a gentleman. Did Jill come with you? I haven't seen her for a long time."

Jill was George's wife. He had married last year, when he returned from Vietnam. She was not a member of the regiment or a born citizen of their community, but she was welcomed as Paul hoped Emily would be. "She's here," George said. "She'll be in one of the waggons, dressed in period costume."

"Where is my grandson?" Tatiana hit the ground from her coach. "Ah, there you are, both of you." She hugged Paul and kissed him on the cheek.

"Don't you just look smashing?" Paul held her at arm's length. She wore the same uniform as everyone else.

"Do you think this is odd?" she said.

"Where's my damn horse?" Susan bellowed as she came out of the coach. "If we had run our operation like this in South Africa, the Boers would have chewed us all up. Paul, you look handsome in that uniform."

Paul gave her a hug and kiss. "Auntie, surely you will ride in a carriage," Paul asked his ninety-year-old great-aunt.

"Young man, I was riding a horse the day I was born. I'll be damned if I'll ride in a carriage when the regiment is on the move," she said, drawing herself up straight. She, too, was in uniform with a pistol on her left side, a sword across her back, and a single brass star on her collar below the eagle.

They all became too busy to chat, as uniformed troopers brought horses out of cars. The horses were saddled or placed into harnesses. Waggons were rolled out of other cars, and harnessed horses were backed into the waggons. Male and female troopers boarded the waggons, and civilians dressed in late-nineteenth-century American clothing loaded into them as well. A trooper brought one of Paul's horses. Paul quickly saddled him, placed his lance in its boot at the rear of the saddle, slung his rifle across his back, and joined the other riders. One handed Paul a coiled whip. There were ten waggons and fifty riders.

After a signal from Nicolas, other train cars opened, and fifty Black Angus cattle bolted out of the cars. Whip-wielding riders surrounded them so they would bunch up and stay in one place. At another signal, twenty-five horses bolted out to the same reception. Fifteen painted horses and ten of Paul's horses were in the small herd. Paul's horses quickly got control of the painted horses, and all stood, waiting.

John rode to the front of the troopers and waggons, and the elder members of the regiment joined him. Susan had a Mauser on her back, John and Tatiana had Lee-Enfields, and Nicolas and Katherine had M1 Garands. All had lances couched behind them. The colour party joined the group, making fifteen people. Two guards of the colour party were armed like Paul, having C7s with grenade-launcher attachments. The standard-bearers had Garands. As the groom, Paul was called forward to join the main party. He and George moved to the front of the column.

The large assembly of armed cavalry drew a large group of spectators, who lined the street across from the regiment. Two police cars with flashing lights stood ready, and more police cars waited in the distance. John looked over the assembly and, being satisfied, waved his arm. The regiment moved to the sounds of whips cracking over the cattle's heads. The advance party moved into a column of four and trotted to position themselves a hundred yards ahead of the cattle-and-horse herd. The waggons fell in behind the herd, and the ten-man rear guard came last. By the time everyone was on the move, the column was a mile long. People lined the streets to watch the parade. A TV news crew stationed itself along the route and filmed as the regiment went by. Once they had left the town proper and were on the gravel road leading to the Hershmire ranch, John ordered the trot. Hooves hitting the ground filled the air with a sound that rivaled thunder.

Nicolas dropped back to ride alongside Paul. He dug into his saddlebag, pulled out a newspaper, and handed it to Paul. "Does that look like anyone you know?" Nicolas asked.

Paul unfolded the newspaper and saw a picture of himself handing the little girl hostage to her mother. It took up the whole front page. Looking farther down the page, he saw the photographer's name. "Shit!" Paul said.

"What? Are you pissed off about the picture?" George asked. "Nobody but us knows it's you. By all accounts, you did a fabulous job."

"I didn't know Emily was there," Paul said. "I should have known better. Now she's going to be even more pissed than she already is." He showed George that Emily's name was credited under the photograph.

"Oh, it gets better, Paul," Nicolas said. "Inside is a series of pictures taken with a speed winder of you lads deploying onto the rooftop. It's impressive stuff. She also writes as well as she takes pictures. She calls you *the unknown Special Forces group* and says you should be treated as heroes for saving all those people."

"Ah, come on, Pop," Paul said. "It's all in a day's work. You know that. My jammer worked perfectly, though, and so did the C7. The tactics were sound and worked as we had hoped they would. If we followed the American assault model instead of ours, it would have taken much longer to deploy. We would have lost our advantage. You saw my report, right? That son of a bitch wants to charge me, and that SOB colonel stood there and let him threaten it."

"Yes, Paul, I read it. Your grandmother is furious. We sent a strongly worded letter to the State Department, expressing our concern at your treatment over here and also the treatment our boys got in Vietnam from the Seventh Cavalry. We informed the State Department and US Army that there won't be any more joint training or deployment missions. It wasn't just that, Paul," his father continued. "The way the Seventh Cavalry treated our regiment in Vietnam is not what we expect from a wartime ally. America's current administration is hostile toward Canada, and the feeling is mutual with our current administration. Unfortunately you were also caught up in it. We will expand our interests elsewhere. West Germany, in particular, is very interested in what we have to offer. Our family will make out OK without the Americans."

"What's with Aunt Susan?" Paul asked.

"She was coming anyway," Nicolas said, "but when she heard what we were planning, there was no way we could keep her from riding in. It might kill the old girl, but she'll die happy."

"I heard that, Naj," Susan said from up front. "I might be old, but my ears still work. I was born on a saddle, lived in a saddle, and if I die in the saddle, I will be complete."

"No dying allowed at my wedding, Auntie," Paul said. "It might put a damper on things."

"Are you kidding me?" Susan said. "Have you ever been to one of our funerals? This party would last a week instead of just three days."

"Whose idea was this big shindig anyway?" Paul asked.

"Your mother's actually," Nicolas said. "She said big-shot American society weddings are generally boring. They have a church ceremony, the bride and groom get married, and then they walk outside. Everyone throws rice, the bride tosses her bouquet, and the couple takes off. Everyone has a sandwich and a glass of champagne, and they leave. Your mother suggested we spice it up a bit and pay for our kind of party. Your grandmother thought it would be nice to commemorate the family's arrival in America a hundred years ago, and then all this nonsense with the government started, and we said, 'What the heck? Let's show these people who they are messing with.'"

"The whole colony wanted to come," George said, "but we limited it to close extended family. The Americans would have thought we were invading otherwise."

"Vietnam was a bust then?" Paul asked.

"They wanted our bodies all right," George said, "but American command wanted cannon fodder in the jungle and not recon men. The officers and I accompanied them on a few raids, but I would not allow our troopers to be used just so they could have bigger body counts. They have no goals or end in sight. We received an offer from the US Marines that suited our needs. They liked what they saw and copied our methods. And we learned what works and, most importantly, what doesn't work. I think you are on to something, Paul—small-scale inserts for scouting and recon and antiterrorism missions. The rest of the time, we operate in our normal mode as mechanised infantry."

"Not having the cost of operating a large fleet of helicopters is a big bonus," Paul said. "That reminds me—I have two experienced pilots and two technicians coming to the firm."

"The firm?" Nicolas said. "Why not the regiment?"

"They are ex-military," Paul said. "We can use them for training our people but not in the regiment itself. They were the helicopter crew at the bank."

"OK then," Nicolas said. "Did the trials go well with the pipeline x-ray device?"

"Yes, and our company was able to find good manufacturing means as well," Paul answered. "I traded some work on other things for exclusive rights to the patent. Caltech doesn't know or understand the oil business, so it was no big deal. I've got a few more ideas, but those can wait until I get home."

A news helicopter flew by, making the horses and cattle nervous. A trooper fired a flare gun directly at the pilot's window and kept firing until the helicopter was at a safe distance. That pilot was clearly in communication with somebody, because when two more helicopters showed up, they stayed far enough away not to cause trouble.

"We're about a half hour out," Paul said. "Is somebody going to clue me in as to what's going to happen?"

"You follow orders, Warrant," Nicolas said, smiling. "Just like I told you before, when the command party approaches the main house, you, as the ranking noncommissioned officer, will of course accompany it." Nicolas sang the regimental song in Russian, and the hillsides echoed rich and haunting a cappella voices of over three hundred males and females. It was the regimental song that had seen the regiment through suffering and victory since the regiment's inception long ago in a land far away.

The regiment climbed the last hill before the ranch proper. Paul relayed the order to close up ranks, and other sergeants passed it back down the line with a series of lance-pennant signals. The advance party slowed down, while the other troops sped up. The advance party shifted into columns of eight, and the waggons became a double column sandwiched between the advance and rearguard formations.

The horse herd automatically moved to the right of the waggons in a maneuver the horses had been well trained to do. The cattle herd moved to the left, although reluctantly. Riders coaxed them with a lot of loud whip cracks above their heads. The standard-bearers removed the leather cases protecting the new national and old regimental banners. The banners were shaken out and temporarily secured to the banner shafts. They would be allowed to fly free when the advance-to-contact call was given.

As the leading riders reached the crest of the hill, the lance pennants again signaled the order, and the leading columns spread left and right. Susan spurred five yards to the front, with Nicolas on her right and Paul on her left. The colour party was in the middle of the single line of troopers, who sat on their horses at the crest of the hill. A thunder of hooves could be heard as the rear guard cantered to each side of the formation to protect the wings.

A bugle signal was given, and all the troopers removed their lances from the scabbards behind their right legs. They placed the lances between their right knees and their horses. They held them with their right hands, gripping the shafts through their loops.

Another bugle call was given, and the waggons formed circles. The waggon drivers unhitched the horses and moved them to the centers of the circles. Rifles were unslung and defensive positions taken up. Two waggons—each protected by four troopers, who had their rifles ready on their right knees—pulled forward and advanced with the mounted troopers. At another bugle call, the troopers broke into a trot, and the standard-bearers let the banners fly free. It was not long before the well-trained horses were in perfect alignment, their heads bobbing in synchronicity. As the advancing troopers made out the line of mounted and armed cavaliers in their highly decorated costumes and horse tack, Susan made another arm gesture. The line of advancing cavalry broke into a canter, and some of the troopers were a little slow.

Again the horses lined up perfectly, but now their excitement got the best of them, and here and there, a horse whinnied or shook its head. The sound of fifty horses cantering was like dull thunder on the prairie, and it grew louder as the bugled charge was sounded. The troopers lowered their lances, and as their song was at its apex, they yelled a challenge at the people waiting in front of the house. Many of those people looked startled. The banners were flying so the designs were visible. The red-and-white Canadian flag contrasted the yellow, blue, and red regimental colours, which had yellow battle-honour streamers flowing down both sides.

At fifty yards from the house, without a bugle signal, the line came to a complete stop. The dust from their passage came over the riders' backs. They held their lances level, pointing at the house and people in front of it. "Regiment, at ease!" Susan yelled in Russian. The lances were pulled up in a ripple that looked like a wave of steel points. Each trooper in turn placed his or her lance back in its holster before turning forward to sit straight in the saddle. The horses stayed completely still. "Regiment, prepare to salute," she yelled, again in Russian.

The troopers withdrew their swords from the scabbards at their backs and held them vertically in front of their noses. "Salute!" The swords flashed down and to the side, while the regimental colours were lowered to horizontal.

The only people in uniform at the house were Paul's ROTC class in their dress uniforms, and they stepped smartly forward. Walawitz, the most senior of them, barked an order, and they returned the regiment's salute.

"Regiment, at ease," Susan barked, and they returned their swords to their scabbards. The troopers faced forward once again, expressionless.

"Command, forward," Susan barked slightly less loudly. She, Nicolas, and Paul rode to stop five yards from the fifty or so people standing on the front porch. The servants were dressed in brightly coloured traditional Mexican garb. Harriet wore what appeared to be a traditional Irish dress. Aaron wore long Bavarian leather shorts, a white shirt, a small leather vest, and a small cap with a feather in its crown. Sarah, Emily's sister, was in a beautiful traditional German dress. Her husband was in a nineteenth-century formal suit, complete with a top hat. The rest of the crowd were similarly dressed in nineteenth-century American clothing, except for one, who stood shielded from view behind her family. "The regiment has come to negotiate the bride price between our son Paul and your daughter Emily," Susan said in English.

"We will hear your offer," Aaron said. He and Harriet moved forward.

"The regiment offers fifty bags of flour," Susan said, waving her hand over her head. The two waggons trundled forward, their tarps thrown back to show the huge bags in their beds. Aaron motioned with his hand, and a rider examined both waggons and nodded his head at Aaron after his inspection was complete.

"Not enough," Harriet said, her head held high.

"The regiment also offers fifty head of cattle," Nicolas said, waving his hand. To the sounds of whips cracking, the pure Black Angus cattle came over the top of the hill. Two cavaliers went to the cattle at a gallop. They counted and surveyed the animals, galloped back, and nodded to Aaron again.

"Not enough!" Sarah said, stepping beside her mother.

"Paul Bekenbaum offers twenty-five of his own horses!" Paul yelled. He raised his hand over his head, made a fist, and pumped it up and down three times. Again whips cracked, and hooves thundered as twenty-five horses alongside their outriders streamed over the hill. Ten yards to the side of the troopers' line, the outriders cracked their whips again. The horses milled in a circle, showing off ten copper-colour Cossack mounts and fifteen painted ponies. Three cavaliers ran over to a corral and opened the gate, and the outriders herded the horses into it.

"Not enough!" This came from a heavily veiled woman in a traditional German costume yelled. "I would see this man who presumes to marry me!" she demanded. This was obviously not part of the script, and Susan and Harriet looked dumbfounded.

"With your permission, ma'am?" Paul asked, and Susan nodded her head. Paul dismounted and handed his reins to Nicolas. He marched ten yards to the porch, his arms swinging high in the Canadian way. He stopped with his right knee raised high and stomped his right foot to the ground. He raised his right hand in the Canadian salute.

"Master Warrant Officer Paul Bekenbaum, prepared for inspection, ma'am!" he yelled out, snapping his arm back to his side and coming to rigid attention.

Emily took her father by the arm and pulled him down the porch stairs to stand in front of Paul. She looked Paul up and down and then walked completely around him. "Where have you been hiding that uniform?" she whispered. "I can't wait to rip it off you." She took her father back to the porch and turned to face the regiment, sticking her nose in the air.

"He will do," she said. She then turned her back and started to walk back into the house. She stopped at the doorway, put her left hand on the frame, looked back, flung her head, hitched her right hip, and walked into the house in a swirl of skirts.

"Jesus," Nicolas said. "Do you women teach each other that?"

"We'll never tell," Susan said, laughing, as Paul walked back and mounted his horse.

"OK, show's over," she said. "Where do we camp?"

The cattle were herded into a fenced pasture and let loose. The colourful ranch hands showed the waggon drivers and the riders where to make camp and pasture their horses, and the regiment began the process of setting up camp. The waggons dispersed to various parts of the field, and people unloaded tents and kits from some. Others went to the mess tents to unload kitchen supplies. Every fourth trooper took four mounts to the temporary corrals, while his troop mates stacked weapons and gear near tents. Then all the troopers unsaddled and groomed their mounts before turning them loose and walking back to the tents with their tack. They erected the tents and changed into jeans, T-shirts, and other casual civilian attire.

In groups of five, the troopers converged on the huge mess tent and found seats after filling plates high with fresh food. Much laughter ensued as they recounted the day's events. Most had never been part of a mass mounted movement like this, and many troopers had made stupid mistakes along the way. Their companions were having fun reminding them of their missteps.

Paul's ROTC class showed up just as the vodka and beer were breaking out. The boys surrounded Paul, shaking his hand and slapping him on the back. They, too, had changed into casual clothing, and they accepted large glasses of the clear fire but with looks of concern.

"You can't wear the patches on your shoulders until you have toasted them properly," Paul said, banging the table with his fist to get everyone's attention.

"To our new honorary members!" He held his glass high. "Anyone stupid enough to follow me out of a perfectly functioning helicopter to a rooftop twenty-five feet below and into a building full of armed bad guys—and who can walk out the other side of it in one piece—is good enough to wear the patch and have a drink with us. So say I!"

"So say all of us!" the rest of the mess hall yelled. They drained their glasses and slammed them down on the tables.

"Holy shit!" Walawitz exclaimed after a few seconds of coughing. "That shit goes down nice and smooth but bites you in the ass after."

"I can tell your ancestors weren't from Russia," Paul said, laughing.

"I never said we were." Walawitz held his glass out for a refill. "We're Polish."

"That explains it," Paul said. "Polish vodka isn't as good as ours."

"Damn straight," Walawitz said. "I almost shit myself when you guys charged the house. Christ, that was impressive."

"Even I, Manuel, had trouble keeping myself and my mount from running away." Manuel, with his wife, Consuela, by his side, was dressed like the others in blue jeans and T-shirt. "Only my determination to protect my Consuela and the patrón strengthened my nerve."

"Only the shit that was running out of yours and your horse's arses," Consuela said, laughing. "You couldn't have run if you'd wanted to."

"This also is true," Manuel said. "My God, Paul, I never knew how terrifying fifty horses coming at a full gallop and fifty lances pointed at your heart could be."

"Now you know how Napoleon felt when we decimated his ranks," Paul said, "but enough of this kind of talk. It is time to celebrate the joining of two families…in anticipation of tomorrow."

"Manuel," Nicolas said, extending a glass of vodka to him, "a Cossack will use any excuse to have a party."

"Sounds like a Mexican to me," Consuela said. She grabbed the glass out of Nicolas's hand and slammed it back without batting an eye. "You go get your own, Manuel, and get me another."

"That sounds like a Cossack woman," Nicolas said. He was smiling until Katherine punched him in the arm.

"And don't you forget it," Katherine said. The party was officially on now that the wives had joined in.

Mexicans, Americans, and Canadians mixed well. The beer, vodka, and tequila flowed freely, and as the liquor took effect, the inevitable happened. Some of the ROTC lads sang a popular folk song titled "Where Have All the Flowers Gone?" Very soon all of the young people joined in. While the hippie peace movement had adopted the song as an unofficial anthem, the soldiers really understood what the song was about. They sang it slowly, emphasising its meaning.

One ranch hand had a guitar, and he played a Mexican ballad, which was also slow. The other ranch hands and their wives joined in the singing, some with tears in their eyes. A woman yelled something in Spanish, and the guitar player stopped, nodded his head, and played a different, more upbeat tune. The woman danced the flamenco, and the other women joined her. The men danced in a circle around them, clapping to the beat. The women danced faster and faster, slamming their heels so the ground trembled. The regiment gathered around and cheered them on, clapping in time to the beat and whooping at times to encourage them. At the final strum of the guitar, the dancers froze. Each had one hand in the air and the other on a hip, chest rising and sucking air from the exertion. The mess tent erupted in applause and cheers. The regiment always appreciated a good show. They looked at one another and shrugged. They knew what was coming next, but nobody wanted to be first.

Before anyone could do anything, a fiddle started a jig, and soon another joined it. The Hershmire clan had stealthily entered. The female members of Harriet's family came into the center and danced to a lively Irish beat. The Bekenbaum clan clapped their hands and stomped their feet, adding distinctive whoops and hollers. The Irishmen launched into a second tune right after the first, and some of the regiment's people slipped out of the tent but returned before the song ended.

The ever-vigilant Tatiana noticed them and nodded her head. She poked John, who walked over to the man with the guitar and asked to borrow it for a moment. Tatiana walked proudly to the center of the room and slowly turned in a circle. Susan and Katherine joined her, and the three women walked in a circle, facing inward toward one another. They walked slowly, and John strummed a few chords on the guitar to get a feel for the instrument. One of the regiment's men by the door played his accordion, using random notes. Another man by the door plucked the strings of his balalaika, turning a peg to tune it. The three musicians met just outside the circle the three women were pacing, and a few other older men joined them. Some grabbed spoons from the tables, and others slapped their hands to their thighs. They slowly came together to make a tentative beat, and then John nodded. The music stopped, and the women stopped in midstride. Each slowly raised one hand above her head and pointed her head away from the center. The members of the regiment knew what was coming, and they rapidly moved tables and chairs to the sides of the tent.

Nicolas sang in English, his voice strong:

A young Cossack was far from home and afraid,
Standing in line with his brothers, so far from home, in a land far away;
Shoulder to shoulder, their horses stood, so close they could not sway;
Each man thinking of home, and sweethearts so far away,
Their hearts beating hard, the enemy fierce, coming their way.

The three women in the center slowly danced with their arms outstretched. More women joined the group, and the circle soon filled and expanded as the empty center space grew larger.

All in a line they came, the enemy so fierce, so many;
They outnumbered us by ten or maybe twenty;
Our hands were clammy, our foreheads sweaty;
Our oh so few against their so many.

Paul entered the center of the circle and danced the same steps as the women in the ring, and the beat became faster.

We sat thinking of home and should we run;
Then Andreas to the front he did come.
Riding up and down, looking up at the sun,
Laughing, he pointed and said, "Let them come;
Come on, boys, do you want to live forever?
Let's show the enemy that they can never
Break these lines that will be strong forever."

The beat went up again, now matching the rhythm of a horse at a fast walk. George and another trooper joined Paul. Their feet moved faster, and their hips swayed to the right and left as they moved about the circle. They moved away and back together and then broke away once again.

The men, their hearts uplifted,
Sat straight, and at the order, their rifles they lifted;
The enemy to a trot and leveling their lances came on;
Our rifles to chests, we sighted upon.

The beat swiftly changed to a gallop, and the singing now changed to Russian. The whole regiment joined in, clapping to the beat, and the three men formed a line, put their arms on one another's shoulders, and danced in a circle. They squatted down and back up, faster and faster. Then they broke apart and moved around the circle, squatting down to kick one leg out and then another. The beat went faster, and the three men alternated opposite hands and feet on the ground, almost lying on their backs. They flipped over onto their chests and did the same motions. First Paul and then the others did back flips before coming to their feet, dancing to the edges of the circle, and beckoning to the crowd. Two women joined in. They and the men circled one another as the crowd cheered and whooped.

A veiled figure entered the circle as the beat slowed once again. Emily was still in her dress, the white veil covering her head and shoulders. She danced slowly toward Paul, almost touched his hand, and then circled away. The singing stopped as the two lovers played their parts in the song, flirting with each other, circling around and around, almost but never quite touching, breaking away, and turning their heads at the last moment. As the music slowed to a sad lament, the older women came and spirited Emily away, making a small circle within the larger circle. They curtsied to Emily, and she looked over their heads and stretched her hand gracefully toward Paul, who stopped, clutched his heart, and looked sadly around. The music stopped. Then with a crash, it began again, and Paul leaped as high as he could with his legs outstretched. He grabbed his toes and let go to jump again. The other two men joined him, and the beat was frantic as they swirled around, one bouncing after the next. Faster and faster the beat went, until first one, then the next missed a step, and they collapsed in a heap, laughing hard.

The music stopped, and the tent went crazy, with everyone laughing and cheering and hugging each other. Walawitz pounded on a table until the room went quiet. "What happened to the troopers in the song?" he asked. "We never heard the end."

"Shit, Walawitz," Paul yelled out, "we all died! Somebody give me a drink. All that dancing dried me out." The room erupted in laughter, and someone shoved a glass into Paul's hand. He made a big show of draining it before accepting a bottle of beer.

Walawitz went up to Paul, who was now looking around the crowd for Emily. "Was that the same song you guys were singing when you came over the hill today?" Walawitz asked.

"Yeah," Paul said. "It used to be the Don Cossacks song, but after Afghanistan, somebody changed the words. It's what we sing when we are happy or when we are sad. It was sung before each of those yellow streamers you see on the standard, except the first one. More than one enemy has run after hearing that song."

"You guys were at Falaise, weren't you?" Walawitz asked.

"Why do you ask?"

"My father was there," Walawitz answered. "He said you guys sang a song he would never forget. He heard it even over the engine noise and gunfire. The sight of you guys roaring over a hill with guns blazing and that yellow-and-blue flag flying put the life back into my dad and his buddies."

"Yo, Pop!" Paul yelled out. "Walawitz's dad was with the Poles at Falaise."

Nicolas ran over and picked up Walawitz in a big bear hug. "Are you Ivan's son?" he asked. "How is he? Is he still alive?"

"Yeah, sure, he's alive and cranky as ever," Walawitz said. "You know him?"

"Know him? Shit, we fought side by side for more than a year," Nicolas said. "I thought the reds got him after the war. Our regiment was sent to Austria, and your father's regiment stayed on in France."

"No, he immigrated here and married my mom. They live not far from here."

"Well, son," Nicolas said, "you take Paul's truck, and go get your folks right now. Tell your pop that Naj said to get his ass up here. Remember that—Naj."

"Yes, sir!" Walawitz looked at Paul, who dug into his pants pocket and gave him his truck keys. "Holy shit," he said. "I can't believe your dad's Naj. He's a goddamned god to my old man and his buddies. He's larger than life. I thought he was a mythical figure. But I have served with you, and, holy shit, it must all be true." He hurried away.

Katherine came up and put her arm around Nicolas, as he had a faraway look in his eyes. It was the look soldiers have when they relive events from far away and long ago. Katherine said nothing. She just kissed Nicolas on the cheek and laid her head on his shoulder.

An arm came around Paul's waist, and a warm mouth kissed his neck. He turned to see Emily was now in blue jeans and a tight alpaca sweater. "Hey, are you supposed to be here?" Paul asked. "I thought it was bad luck for the groom to see the bride the night before the wedding."

"You've already seen me in my birthday suit," Emily said. "Why should this day be any different?"

"I said as much to John at our wedding," Tatiana said. "These Bekenbaums can be such pains in the ass sometimes."

"They are cute pains in the ass," Katherine said.

"Come," Tatiana said, taking Emily on one arm and Paul on the other. "We have something else to discuss. Let the others enjoy themselves for a moment without us." She nodded at John, who hastened over to the Hershmires. She walked out of the mess tent with the young couple, and Nicolas and Katherine trailed behind. They walked to the end of the camping area, away from everyone and everything else. The moon was full, and it was a cloudless night, so it was easy to move around.

Tatiana talked about what a nice night it was and how wonderful it was to get away for even just a short time. When John and the Hershmires joined them, she got to business. "Our regimental song was made on the way back from Afghanistan to the regiment's home in Russia. Normally it is sung as it was intended in Russian, but I had John translate the first few verses and sing them in English tonight. It loses a bit in translation, but not too much. Our people were sent to Afghanistan to help the British with a problem they had with Islamic extremists in what is now Pakistan. That was the official story.

"The real reason we were sent was because the czar wanted to expand his influence in the region and possibly resettle the area for Mother Russia. Taking control and settling lands was a role traditionally performed by the Cossacks. We were becoming too powerful and had too many friends, so the czar thought to kill three birds with one stone. First the czar would help the British, and they would look the other way on some things he was doing in Iran. Second, Russia would gain prestige by helping the Afghans, and third, the regiment would experience massive losses and cease to exist...or so the czar hoped.

"The regiment was two thousand in all, bears and eagles combined. Eight hundred British infantry were garrisoned in a town called Kandahar, and another eight hundred British cavalry, who were actually Germans under British rule, met us in Iran and stayed with us. Ten thousand Islamic cavalry invaded the region, and British command told us to hold them off as long as we could.

"Andreas Bekenbaum, our commander and Paul's ancestor, was a master tactician. Anyone who met him would do anything for him. He had a knack for providing the best weapons and military hardware available, and he changed tactics to suit those weapons—something the regiment still does to this day. On the day of the battle, the regiment lined up, but unlike the song says, they were not on horseback. They deployed in two lines, wearing red coats and appearing to be British infantry.

"Andreas wanted the invading Muslim army to think they were facing only regular British infantrymen, not the regiment, because they avoided us like the plague. He wanted to provoke a battle, and he got it. The enemy formed up as old cavalry forces did—in a large mass, with their horses shoulder to shoulder—and Andreas calmly walked his horse up and down in front of his troopers, who were for all the world looking and acting like British regulars. As the enemy came within three hundred yards of our lines, Andreas rode to the rear, and at two hundred yards, the regiment opened fire. After the first volley, the enemy spurred to the charge, expecting to hit the regiment's line before they could reload. But we had Winchesters, and the closest the enemy got was fifty yards away.

"The bears were positioned along and behind hills on both sides of the small plain, and at the first sound of contact, they climbed the hill and opened fire from both flanks, also with Winchesters. The combined fire devastated the enemy, and they fled however they could. We suffered two casualties, as a few enemy riders broke through the bears' lines in desperation. The Germans and, even worse, the mounted Afghans the regiment had trained hunted down those few who'd gotten away.

"We killed around eight thousand enemy troopers that day. John was stationed there in World War I and saw the battlefield. John told me the expended rifle cartridges and bones of horses were still clear to be seen. Susan was born on that battlefield. Her mother gave birth after being ridden down by an escapee. Susan is the last of the original Canadian settlers, and her mother and two other men killed in the battle are buried there. The song we sing is in commemoration of that battle and has been sung before every major engagement the regiment has fought in since then. It is sad and happy, like a Russian soul.

"Harriet and Aaron, at the end of the ceremony tomorrow after everyone leaves, including your priest, my family and the regiment have our own ceremony to perform. We will stay along with our priest. No one who is not a member of the regiment, including family members, will be allowed to attend."

"The ceremony and words are an old tradition originated in Germany many generations ago," John added. "It is part of the feudal system, and it is honoured to this day. Emily, for all intents and purposes, you and Paul are already married, and as such, you are part of our family. Paul told me he said the words when he proposed to you and that you accepted them. After the ceremony he will repeat the words, as will you." John took Emily's head between his hands and kissed her on both cheeks. He walked behind her and placed both hands on her shoulders, speaking softly in German. "I am John, son of Andreas, son of Helmut, family Bekenbaum. This is Emily. What is done to her and hers is done to me and mine. So say I in front of God and man."

"I am Nicolas, son of John, son of Andreas, son of Helmut, Bekenbaums all," said Nicolas, kissing Emily on both cheeks and standing behind her with his hands on her shoulders. "This is my daughter Emily. What is done to her and hers is done to me and mine. So say I in front of God and man."

Katherine came forward, kissed Emily on the lips, and went down on her knees before her. "I am Katherine, daughter of Tatiana, daughter of Elizabeth. This is my daughter Emily. What is done to her and hers is done to me and mine." Katherine rose and joined the men standing behind Emily.

Tatiana stood and gracefully walked to Emily, embracing her and kissing her. She held her at arm's length and looked into her eyes. "I am Tatiana, adopted daughter of Elizabeth, daughter of Nicolas of house Romanov. This is my granddaughter Emily. What is done to her and hers is done to me and mine. Kneel, child." Emily knelt down in front of Tatiana, who placed both hands on Emily's shoulders. "The members of our branch of the Bekenbaum family are not earls of the British Empire, child," she said softly in English so only Emily could hear. "They are grand dukes and duchesses of Russia. Paul does not know this, nor does he know he is heir to the Russian Empire. This is why the ceremony we just performed is important. I am the czar's only living child—a secret we keep from the whole world. Can you keep this secret? Our lives and the lives of all our people depend on it."

Emily was having trouble breathing. She knew the family had some very deep and important connections, but she hadn't known they were this important or this deep. She looked at Tatiana and then at her mother. "No, dear, you can't even tell your parents," Tatiana whispered. "Can you keep this secret?"

"Yes," Emily gasped out.

"Then rise, Grand Duchess Emily, and speak our words," Tatiana said. "Go to Paul, kiss him on both cheeks, stand behind him with your hands on his shoulders, and speak the words. They will bind your family and ours together."

Emily stood, with Tatiana's help, and walked to Paul. She embraced him and kissed him on both cheeks. She walked behind him, placed both hands on his shoulders, and with her head held high, spoke in a clear loud voice. "I am Emily, daughter of Harriet, member of house Hershmire. This is Paul, my husband. What is done to him and his is done to me and mine. So say I in front of God and man."

The impact of what was witnessed dawned on Aaron, who took off his hat and made the sign of the cross. He handed his hat to a confused Harriet. He walked up to Paul, grasped him by both shoulders, and kissed him on both cheeks. Then he joined Emily behind Paul and took him by the shoulders. "I am Aaron, son of Isaac, son of Albert, son of Heinrich von und zu Hershmire, Graf of Munster," he said in formal German. "This is Paul, my daughter's husband. What is done to him and his is done to me and mine. So say I in front of God and all of you." Aaron made the sign of the cross again, went to each Bekenbaum, and kissed them on both cheeks. They kissed him back.

Aaron moved to his wife and put his arms on her shoulders, looking deep into her eyes. "This is an old ceremony," he said. "It's older than the British Empire and the Holy Roman Empire. Emily is our oldest child, dear. Paul is the Bekenbaums' oldest heir. Before the Hershmires came to America, we were what you would call earls in Germany, Harriet. This ceremony has just bound our two houses together in mutual support."

"Is that a good thing?" Harriet asked. "It doesn't really matter, as long as Emily and Paul are happy."

"Oh yes, dear, it is a good thing," Aaron said. "You see, the old noble families are still influential. They just operate in the background these days. How do you like being related to the house of Windsor?"

"What are you talking about?" Harriet asked. "I'm an Irish Catholic. My family was minor nobility in the old days, but there is no way we were related to the house of Windsor."

"But I am, dear," Aaron said. "We're distant cousins, and the Bekenbaums are closer, I think."

"What?" Emily looked at Paul. "Is Margaret Windsor—Princess Margaret, the queen's sister—your cousin? And is Charles Windsor the Prince of Wales?" Paul nodded and shrugged his shoulders. "My God!" Emily exclaimed. "The bloody queen of England is your cousin!"

"Yes," Tatiana said, "that's all true, and sometimes Liz gets off her high horse and cavorts with us lowlifes."

"All of us will deny it all if you should spill the beans," Aaron said.

"Now I know why that State Department guy was at the airport waiting for us that day," Emily said. "Between our two families, we are more powerful than the Kennedys."

"Probably," Nicolas said.

"Who checks on things of that nature anyway?" John asked. "Our family minds our own business, and the Windsors mind theirs. We all get along that way."

"If you are cousins to the British royals, and we are cousins to the British royals, is it legal for us to get married?" Emily asked.

"People had very big families back in the nineteenth century, Emily," her father said. "Queen Victoria had eight children or so."

"My family had five children," Tatiana said.

"Nobility married nobility, Em," Paul said. "It's much like rural families today. After a few generations, everybody is married to everybody, and you're related to everyone somehow. If we are cousins, it's very far down the line. It's like Charles and me. We are cousins, but what…fourth or fifth cousins or something? We're not really related anymore."

"I was trying to pry into your backgrounds," Harriet said. "No wonder I didn't get anywhere."

"My nephews put a stop to much of your investigation," John said. "They inherited our earldom, but only the name and original family businesses. The regiment is the true holder of the earldom, and my nephews chose not to serve. So the regiment and earldom passed down to me and my descendants as next in line. It's a little complicated, and there is no real guarantee Paul will be accepted as the new leader of our Cossack host, but I don't believe there will be a problem."

"OK, young lady," Tatiana said, "tomorrow is a long day, and it is getting late. Say good night to Paul, and we will leave the men be." After one last hug and a quick kiss, Emily reluctantly went with the three older women. All four looked back over their shoulders, flipped their hair, hitched their hips, laughed, and walked into the darkness toward the main house.

"OK, that's it," John said. "I finally figured it out. They teach each other that move."

"Nope, I don't think so," Aaron said. "Harriet's from Ireland, and she was doing it when I courted her."

"Damn!" John said. "So it can't be a German thing either. Or does Harriet have a German background?"

"Ah, that could be it," Aaron said. "I'll have to check. That reminds me. Are you related to the von Bekenbaums in Cologne?"

"Yes, in more ways than one," John said. "My grandfather gave up the *von* in his name, but my oldest uncle retained it and the family's titles and lands. Nicolas and I fought against our cousins in World Wars I and II. The von Bekenbaum that Nicolas fought came over here, married my niece, and served with Nicolas in Korea. Hans and Ingrid don't live too far from us back home."

"Ah, well then, Hans's older brother married my aunt," Aaron said. "Cousins."

"Ah jeez!" Paul said. "Does that mean I can't marry Em?"

"No, have no fear of that, son," Nicolas said, laughing. "She would be your third cousin twice removed. She's what we call an outlaw, in our family. She's your third cousin but only by marriage. If you thought Ingrid was hard to manage before, wait till she finds out this one—related to the Windsors."

"Who's Ingrid?" Aaron asked.

"She was my gunner in World War II and Korea," Nicolas said. "When she puts on her dress uniform, you can hardly see her for all the medals on it. She has the ego to go with them."

"Yeah, you should see her put the SAS and Green Beret tough guys in their places," Paul said. "They don't like a five-foot-four woman telling them what to do. She's the commander of the joint training we provide for NATO. To stop any possible crap she might get, she usually picks the biggest guy in the formation on the first day and kicks the crap out of him."

"She pairs the tough guy up with a female probationary trooper the first week of training," Nicolas continued. "That usually clues the rest of the Special Forces people into the fact that they really don't know too much."

"Our people begin training at age thirteen," John explained. "After graduating grade twelve, the regiment lets them have a break until the first workday in January. Then they start their five years of full-time military service. Their six-month training period begins the same time as the NATO Special Forces' training, and the new members of the regiment train alongside NATO teams. Our kids are highly motivated and already generally better trained than the NATO people when training starts."

"During the last month of training, they break into their own units by country again," Nicolas said. "That's when the fun begins. They compete against each other for that whole month. It's very rare our kids don't come in first, and they're never below second."

"Impressive," Aaron said. "Are all your people frontline troops then? Who does the service requirements for you?"

"Our kids complete another month after the initial training," Paul said. "It's optional. Those who want to be combat troops take that training and then must pass final qualification exams. Those who do not want to participate or don't pass are slotted into trade or service positions. Take me as an example. I am in the service battalion. You can tell what branch a member is in by the bear or eagle on their collars. To keep our status and privileges in the colony, we must serve for five years full time. And in order to serve, we must meet minimum standards."

"What about those who are not physically capable of meeting the minimum standards?" Aaron asked. "Do they lose their ability to be citizens of the colony?"

"Everyone serves," John said. "Those who are disabled are tested for aptitude and placed in clerical or administrative positions. They are not allowed to leave the colony to serve, unless it is for training purposes. Even then, they receive and must maintain minimal firearms training. Only those with severe physical or mental disabilities are exempt."

"Historically, Aaron," Nicolas said, "our regiment has been and continues to be sent to remote locations on our own, with little or no support. All members of our regiment must be able to defend themselves. On more than one occasion, including right from the beginning in Afghanistan, our service people were required to fight."

"Sounds like your regiment is like our Marine Corps," Aaron said. "I served with them in World War II as a supply officer because I have bad knees. Every marine had to qualify as a rifleman. My men and I had to man the bunkers more than once to fend off Japanese counterattacks."

"*Semper fi,*" Nicolas said.

"Hurrah," Aaron said, smiling. "Once a marine, always a marine. Were you guys in Korea?"

"Yeah," Paul said, "Pop commanded and was damn-near killed at Kapyong."

"I thought that was the PPCLI," Aaron said after whistling.

"Fourth Battalion, Princess Patricia's Canadian Light Infantry at your service," Nicolas said with a smile. "During the first part of World War II, we were known as Third Battalion SAS, and then we were the First Special Services Division for a while. Then at the end, we were the First Canadian Parachute Brigade for Normandy and Calgary Tanks."

"I was attached to Far East Command, British Expeditionary Force in World War I," John said. "Then Lord Strathcona Horse, Canadian Expeditionary Force in France. During the Boer War, we were Lord Strathcona Horse."

"Now we are usually referred to as the Fourth Battalion, PPCLI," Paul said. "The Canadian government puts us with whoever needs us, and we like the anonymity."

"Just like your participation in the hostage situation at the bank?" Aaron asked. "No, Emily did not tell me. I saw the uniform, as she did, and figured it out from there."

"Emily knows?" Paul asked. "Shit, I was hoping she missed it was me."

"She is not stupid, Paul," Aaron said. "She took the pictures that are plastered all over the world. The one of you handing the injured little girl to her mother is on front pages worldwide."

"Ah shit!" Paul said. "Note to self: don't wear identifying uniforms in the future."

"We don't want any bad guys coming after our families," Nicolas said. "There is a new kind of war we are waging, Aaron. These extremist types target the weak. They will go after our families to try to influence us. That's why we wear balaclavas to cover our faces. Paul forgot he had Canadian flashes on his shoulders. He made sure his troopers took the words *US Army* and their name tags off their uniforms, but he forgot his own."

"OK, I think it is time to rejoin the party," John said. "I can tell you categorically, Aaron, that the regiment has absolutely no official knowledge of who participated in that hostage action. We were not asked to contribute, nor were we consulted on any possible actions."

"Fair enough," Aaron said. "Unofficially, thank you for your service, Paul. All the families of the hostages are trying to find out who those troopers were to thank them. Most feel you guys should be awarded medals, including the old guy who was wounded and the little girl's family."

"I am sure the troopers involved know it, Aaron," Paul said. "Let's go back to the party. I have a beer or two with my name on them."

CHAPTER 14

"Christ, my head hasn't felt this bad since the day I got married," George said, coming out of Paul's shower, which was turned to cold.

"Here, suck on this." Paul handed a small bottle of oxygen to George. "It works like a damn."

"It pays to have relatives in the upper echelons of the medical profession," George said, smiling. "I've used this trick before."

Paul laced his high-top cavalry boots and made both pants legs even and bloused perfectly around the tops. Looking in the mirror, he made sure his old-style shirt collar was done up completely before putting on a dark-blue, almost black, tunic. He had spent a lot of time polishing all the uniform's brass, so after he buttoned up all the buttons, he ran a rag over the brass to eliminate any fingerprints. The .45-calibre pistol rounds in the six red loops on each side of his buttons shone brightly, as did the bear on his right collar and maple leaf on his left. He had brass Canada badges on both shoulders, above the three sergeant's stripes. Topping those were a crown on his left shoulder and a blue-and-yellow regiment patch with a red maple leaf in the center on the right. His two UN medals—one for Cyprus and one for Yemen—sat above his left-breast pocket. His parachute wings and American expert-combat-infantry badge were on the right. He buckled his red belt over his tunic, making sure the highly polished buckle with the maple leaf was centered, and again rubbed off any fingerprints with a rag. Today the regiment would wear black lambskin hats with the tops folded up to reveal a red inner lining. Large brass maple-leaf badges with beavers on top gleamed brightly in the centers of the black hats, and the regiment's eagles and bears were pinned on either side of those. Paul picked up his sword and contemplated what to do with it. "Do we wear this stupid thing on our left sides or what?" he asked.

"Nope," George answered. "It goes across your back, with the hilt on the left. Here, I'll help you. All you enlisted men are hopeless."

Other than the major's crowns on his epaulets, the eagle on his collar, and a bronze star instead of a Yemen medal on his chest, George's uniform was identical to Paul's. He took Paul's sword, putting it over Paul's head and onto his back. He adjusted it so the hilt was above his left shoulder and the straps were tight enough to keep it from flapping about. Finally he checked that they were all straight and centered properly.

"Thank God old Andreas hated wearing spurs," George said. "Can you imagine the pain in the ass they would be walking up and down stairs?"

After last checks in the mirror and of each other to for nonexistent dirt or dishevelment, Paul opened the door and motioned for George to precede him. "Ah, good of you to remember the courtesy required of an officer and gentleman," George said.

"Nah," said Paul, "it's more about age before beauty."

Harriet and Sarah fussed over Emily's hair and gown one last time. Harriet then joined the bride's family's grand procession into the barn that was now a church and reception hall. Nodding her head to friends, neighbors, and dignitaries she knew and recognised, she took her place in the front row and smiled at Paul's parents and grandparents and the groom himself, who stood tall and proud at parade rest with his brother at his side.

Emily tapped her right toe nervously, while her sister arranged her trailing veil behind her so she wouldn't trip on it. The dress was pure-white silk, simple but elegant, and cut to emphasise her slim build without restricting movement. Her ebony hair was draped behind her shoulders and lay midway down her back. A simple single braid was wound around the crown of her head and had yellow roses woven into it. Her father came to her, wearing his Marine Corps officer's dress uniform, complete with his medals, ribbons, and ceremonial sword. Six of his old troopers, also dressed in stunning blue Marine Corps dress uniforms, arranged themselves three to each side of Emily and her father. Sarah carefully draped the front of the veil over her face and down to her shoulders. Sarah gave Emily a quick hug and walked to the front of the line. She nodded her head at the ushers, who opened the door, and the bridal party began a slow measured march.

"*Achtung!*" someone inside yelled. "*Fass links!*" All of the regiment's uniformed people snapped to attention and turned left in one smooth motion. The barn's interior thundered as three hundred pairs of boots and shoes hit the floor in unison. Emily had never before seen the regiment massed in full dress uniforms, and she marveled at the impressive sight. The women wore long elegant evening gowns that matched the regiment's dark-blue and red colours, with crimson sashes draped over their left shoulders and falling to their right hips. Their medals, badges, and eagles were pinned to the sashes.

Emily saw that only Paul was wearing a bear. Every other trooper in the assembly had an eagle. Tatiana's sash had a number of medals on it, with a Victoria Cross at the very top. Nicolas also had one, as well as several other medals, one of which looked like the Congressional Medal of Honor. John had both of those and a few more. Six people, one of them female, were dressed in red Welsh Guards uniforms. Emily smiled to herself and thought her mother would most likely have a fit when she saw who they were. Emily's eyes fell on Paul, who smiled at her from the front. Everything else moved to the back of her consciousness as he took all of her attention. Two priests came in front of the couple and began the mass. The regiment's priest was also in uniform, a cross instead of an eagle or bear on his collar.

The mass was conducted in English, and the couple knelt only when they took communion. Sarah and George helped Emily with her dress and veil as she stood once again. The wedding ceremony began, and Emily's heart threatened to break out of her chest. At the point when Emily and Paul exchanged vows, Sarah expertly peeled back Emily's veil and quickly pinned it in place to reveal Emily's full face for the first time since the ceremony had commenced. Emily saw the love in Paul's eyes and hoped it reflected back to him in hers. Her priest recited the vows, and she repeated them, handing her bouquet to Sarah before she placed on Paul's ring finger the simple gold band he had chosen. He repeated the same vows and placed a beautiful and expensive diamond ring on hers. He was deadly serious the whole time, but then his eyes smiled. "I'm going to have to work for a hundred years to pay that thing off," he said under his breath.

"Yes, and you're going to love every second of it," Emily replied under hers.

The priest pronounced them man and wife. He led them to one side of the altar area to sign all the forms, with Sarah and George as witnesses. In addition to the Californian and Catholic Church forms and licenses, there was a Province of Alberta marriage license and the Canadian landed immigrant status form Emily had to sign and Paul was required to sign as her sponsor. Once all that was done, Emily's priest escorted her and Paul back to the front of the assembled regiment. The priest joined the crowd of nonregiment people outside, shutting the doors behind him.

The only people left inside were members of the regiment. Susan, as the eldest member, called them to attention. She nodded at Emily, who turned to Paul, knelt on one knee, and took his hand. Katherine stood by her right side, and Tatiana stood by her left. "I am Emily Grafin von Hershmire, daughter of Katherine, daughter of Tatiana," Emily said loudly in German. "This is my husband, Paul. What is done to him and his is done to me and mine. So say I in front of God and man." The regiment's priest brought a crucifix forward for her to kiss after she made the sign of the cross. He then stepped back, and Katherine helped Emily stand.

Tatiana and Katherine rejoined the regiment, and Paul turned Emily so she was facing them. He stood behind her, his hands on her shoulders. The standard-bearer brought the flag forward and lowered it. Paul took one corner in his right hand. As he did so, the regiment knelt in one smooth motion. "I am Paul, son of Nicolas, son of John, son of Andreas, family of Bekenbaum, Canadians all," he barked out in German. "This is my wife, Emily. What is done to her and hers is done to me and mine. So say I!"

"So say all of us!" the regiment yelled back in unison. In that moment Emily finally realised what she was just made a part of, and her heart skipped a beat as she gazed at the flag. It was the original flag, faded slightly, with patched bullet holes and yellow streamers hanging from the standards point. Some of its ribbons were ragged at the edges and showing their ages. The standard-bearer slowly raised the colour to its full height and placed it on his belt.

Paul came to attention, raising his right foot high and stomping loudly on the floor.

"Regiment, attention!" Paul yelled out in his best parade-ground Russian, and the regiment came to attention. Continuing to speak in Russian, he had them form columns of two before holding his arm out for Emily. The couple marched to the front of the column, where troopers with an accordion and a balalaika waited. Without orders, the musicians played the traditional Cossack tribute-to-the-bride song, and the regiment sang.

After the first verse, the door swung open. Paul and Emily, followed by the standard-bearer and the regiment, walked out the door to join the other guests, who broke out in applause as they came into view. The regiment, still singing, formed a two-line crescent behind Paul and Emily. When they finished, a hush fell in the yard as the two priests walked forward.

"Ladies and gentlemen, I give you Mr. and Mrs. Bekenbaum!" the regiment's priest yelled out. He raised his right hand over his head and pointed at the couple with his left, and the crowd hurrahed, hooted, and hollered.

After the formal wedding dinner, Walawitz and the eight other members of Paul's ROTC class walked up to the standards behind the head table. They were decked out in their blue US

Army officers' dress uniforms, which were unfamiliar to them since they rarely wore those. The stars-and-stripes was on the left of the regimental colour, and the maple-leaf flag was on the right. Walawitz and the other men looked at the regimental colours and the battle-honour streamers arranged around it.

"Impressive, isn't it?" said the Special Forces major who had given the ROTC class their anti-insurgent training. He, too, was in a blue dress uniform. "That is one of the most decorated regiments in the world, gentlemen, and they don't even show their parent regiment's honours from Waterloo, Crimea, and long before those actions, the Cossack Life Guard honours. Look over there at those two Native American troopers. What do you see?"

Both men wore regiment uniforms, but most of their decorations were American. The Native Americans had the same master-warrant-officer stripes Paul had, but the hash stripes on their sleeves indicated they each had twenty-five years' service. In addition to the Congressional Medal of Honor both men wore around their necks, their right shoulders bore Purple Hearts, bronze and silver stars, VE medals, medals from Sicily and Italy, three-star parachute wings, and red patches shaped like arrowheads. Looking around, Walawitz noticed about half the regiment's people had that same patch. It was the patch his father wore on his old World War II uniform. Walawitz saw his father hug the two Native Americans and then Nicolas, who had thumped him on his back to get his attention.

"That red patch is from the First Special Services Regiment," the major continued. "A third of that regiment were Canadian, and half the Canadians were from the EBBs. Take a good hard look, boys. Rarely, if ever, do the EBB wear their medals in full view. Today it is to honour your teacher. You might not see it here, but I saw it in Yemen. Warrant Bekenbaum doesn't wear an eagle—just his warrant-officer badge—but in fact, he is usually the one in charge. Only his father and grandfather are more highly ranked than he is. You were trained by the best, boys." The major shook his head. "That stupid FBI asshole and chair-warming colonel fucked it for us all. The regiment will no longer train any US Army personnel."

After the meal and obligatory speeches from the politicians, the party began. Paul and Emily worked the room, never straying far from each other. Two red-coated British officers finally cornered them. Emily's mother took notice and headed over as Margaret began to speak.

"Thought you could get away without inviting us, eh?" Margaret said, laughing and wagging her finger accusingly at Paul.

"On behalf of my mother, I congratulate you, Bekenbaum," Charles said. "Mother said you *are* going to stop by on your trip to Europe."

"Oh, Charles, you are such a bore sometimes," Margaret said. "Liz said to make sure you get your butts over to see her, and she said, 'Welcome to the family,' cousin." She grabbed Emily in a big hug and kissed her on the cheek. Emily eyed the brass eagle on her collar.

"Yes, I earned this the hard way," Margaret said. "Your husband's cousin had me freezing my ass off all over Alberta for six months to get it. They don't just give these away, you know. Charles doesn't have one, nor does Liz. Not only that, but Katherine was in my group, and she made her work just as hard as the rest of us. Her own aunt—can you imagine?"

"Emily!" Harriet said. "Where are your manners! Excuse my daughter, Your Majesties. She is American and has not been taught the proper etiquette." Harriet dropped her head and curtsied.

"Oh, poo, poo," Margaret said. "As you can see, I am Colonel Windsor, and I am here with my nephew, Captain Windsor. There is no royalty here, cousin. We know who you are, and we are here to celebrate our cousin Paul's marriage to our new cousin Emily. My, what a strange family we have."

Margaret took Harriet by the arm and walked away with her, leaving Charles with Paul and Emily. "It's a fine line you have to walk, Captain," Emily said. "I don't envy you in the least."

"You get used it after a while," the Prince of Wales said. "It helps when we have people like the Bekenbaums, who understand and occasionally allow us to pretend we are normal."

"What's your cover story, in case somebody spills the beans?" Paul asked.

"Why, my dear aunt is the colonel-in-chief of the regiment, or something like that, and she simply had to attend the marriage of its commander's son." Charles smiled. "Of course I had to come along to be her chaperone and to learn how to do these types of things."

"It's more like she's the chaperone," Paul said. "Have you been able to see any sights?"

"Yes, we have been here about a week now," Charles replied. "Auntie has spent a lot of money shopping, and I have been to a few clubs. But Mommy insists we return home now, so we are leaving tonight." Margaret returned with the governor of California in tow and took Charles off Emily and Paul's hands, momentarily leaving the newly married couple on their own.

"Now's our chance," Paul said. He quickly looked around and noted no one was paying attention to them. "Let's go!" Emily took Paul's arm, and the couple nonchalantly walked to a side door, opened it, and left without looking back. Emily wrapped the long veil around her right arm and hitched up her dress with her left hand. They both hurried across the yard to Paul's guesthouse, where Emily rushed into the bedroom and took off her wedding garments. She looked in Paul's direction, watching him watching her, and smiled, blew him a kiss, and then slammed the bedroom door on him.

His dream of enjoying the night alone was shattered minutes later as he was removing his boots and prepared to change into a T-shirt and jeans. A loud knock came at the door, and Paul opened it to see a telecommunications clerk holding a piece of paper.

"Sorry, Mr. Bekenbaum," the clerk said. "Priority message from DND."

Paul took the message from the clerk and read the information. He looked at the closed bedroom door and sighed. "OK," Paul said quietly, "tell them we need a Hercules aircraft at the nearest air-force base as soon as possible. All we have are personal small arms and very little ammo, so we will have to equip in Germany when we arrive. We will depart with one hundred fifty troopers from this location. Notify the regiment to load the rest of the battalion and go to Calgary or Red Deer, whatever is easiest for DND and the air force. Full weapons loads and combat vehicles. Got all that?"

"Yes, Mr. Bekenbaum," the clerk said. "Should I inform the generals, sir?"

"No, I'll handle that," Paul replied. "Thanks though. Just transmit all that, and after I have informed the regiment, go have a beer or two. We won't be leaving until sometime tomorrow anyway."

Paul walked to a wardrobe and opened it up to reveal normal and battle military uniforms. He chose the battle dress and laid it on the couch. He glanced at the bedroom door and began to take off his dress uniform. He carefully hung it up and donned the battle dress. Walking to the desk, he picked up his sword and hung it on a peg on the side of the wardrobe. Then he strapped on his pistol belt. Removing his Colt from the holster, he grabbed a clip from a pouch. He made sure it was full, shoved it into the butt of the pistol, and then put the gun back in its holster. He was reaching for his rifle when Emily spoke from the now-open bedroom door.

"That's not exactly what I was expecting to see when I opened this door," she said.

Paul took the C7 from the wardrobe and propped it against the desk. He picked up the message, and handed it to Emily. She was in the doorway, wearing blue jeans, a polo shirt, and running shoes. Her hair was pulled back in a ponytail, and a large luggage bag was at her feet. Paul tugged on his combat boots and laced them as she read the two pages. He stood and waited for the inevitable storm he figured Emily would unleash.

"Change of plans then," she said, handing the message to Paul and shoving the bag into the bedroom with a foot. "I guess the government will pay for our honeymoon then."

"What?" Paul said. Emily dumped the contents of her bag onto the bed. "You can't come. It's a hot zone," he explained.

Emily sorted through the clothing, placing only the most comfortable and casual items back in. She then pulled her cameras and many boxes of film from the closet, loading film into both cameras. She placed one camera and the fresh rolls of film in the bag and closed it, and she hung the other camera around her neck. "I've been in hot zones before, Paul," she said, wrapping her arms around him. "If the DND thinks this is going to keep me from my new husband, they are mistaken."

She pulled him close and kissed him, forcing her tongue between his closed lips. She felt him relax and respond to the kiss. Emily broke the kiss and pushed away from Paul. Grabbing his beret from the desktop, she placed it on his head at the normal cocky slant and then patted him on the crotch. "That will have to wait, love," she said, looking into his eyes and smiling. "We have work to do. The rifle will be a bit much I think. Leave it here."

Paul nodded, and they walked back to the noisy barn. Anyone looking would have seen a pistoled combat trooper walking hand in hand with a beautiful woman. Several uniformed people saw them, stopped what they were doing, and made their way back to the barn. Emily stopped and stood in front of Paul, making sure all his buttons were done up and laces tied. She opened the big barn door, and the two walked in, with Emily a step behind Paul.

"Oh no!" Tatiana said from the dance floor as she spotted Paul and Emily walking in.

The room became silent, slowly at first and then rapidly, as people saw how Paul was dressed. He walked purposefully to his grandfather, stopped directly in front of him, and stomped his right foot down. "A message from DND for the general, sir!" He handed the message to John. Emily stood to one side with her camera to her eye, and she snapped the exchange and waited as John read the message.

John passed it to Nicolas, who nodded and passed it to Susan. "Right, Mr. Bekenbaum," Nicolas said. "Inform the regiment, if you please."

Paul marched up to the head table, where the colours were displayed. He raised his right leg and stomped it to the floor. Then he spun around to face the crowd, coming to rigid attention. "Orders on deck!" he yelled. "Fall in!" Quickly the dark-blue-uniformed men and women fell in, arranging themselves in their sections, platoons, and companies. The regiment was in two lines at full attention in seconds.

"The ready detachment of the regiment will prepare for immediate departure to the Golan Heights!" Paul barked out. "Battle dress and personal weapons and ammo only. You will be issued further equipment at a later time and place! The mission is hot—I repeat, *hot*—and we expect a warm reception. The rest of the battalion will join us en route, with vehicles and equipment. Unready force members are to return home at their earliest convenience. Regiment dismissed!" Paul walked away from the head table and back to his parents and grandparents, and Emily stood to his side.

"Don't worry," Katherine said. "We will take care of Emily when you leave and handle whatever needs doing. You two go and enjoy what little time you have left tonight."

"You won't have to look out for me, Mother." Emily put her hand through Paul's right arm. "I'm going along."

"I know you are an accredited journalist, Emily," John said, "but the regiment has strict rules about noncombatants entering hot war zones. Sorry."

Tatiana was displeased, and everyone knew she was about to explode. "Is that weapon functional and loaded?" Tatiana asked, pointing at Paul's pistol.

"Yes, ma'am," Paul replied.

"Do you have a functioning rifle and ammunition close by?" she asked.

"Yes, ma'am. They're in my barracks, ma'am," Paul replied.

"Is there a place nearby where we can shoot?" she asked.

"Yes, ma'am. On the property, ma'am," Paul replied.

"Good. You go get your rifle, and bring it and that pistol there immediately," Tatiana ordered. She pointed her finger at Emily. "Young lady, do you know where this firing range is?"

"Yes, Grandmother, I do," Emily replied. "Paul has let me use his rifle and pistol there."

"We walk there can or must drivink." She was getting excited now, and her Russian accent came through.

"It's very close. We could walk there in five minutes," Emily answered.

"Good." Tatiana took Emily's arm. "We go! You show way. You three, you come!" She was pointing at John, Nicolas, and Katherine.

"Mother, what are you doing?" Nicolas asked. "It is the dead of night and dark. Surely this could wait until morning."

"No wait—do now," Tatiana said. Becoming frustrated, she switched to Russian. "Night maneuver and qualification, you dummies! Do I have to spell it out for you?"

"Oh, I see," Nicolas said, not really understanding. Then he saw the Windsors approach in their red uniforms, and he slowed to let them catch up. John, Katherine, and Tatiana carried on.

"What's going on, Naj?" Margaret asked.

"The Syrians and Egyptians have gone after Israel again," Nicolas said. "The UN wants us there to monitor the border between Israel and Syria once a ceasefire is agreed on. DND has decided to send us now."

"What's that about?" Margaret asked, nodding toward the little group that hurried off into the darkness.

"Emily wants to go, but the regiment's regulations won't allow it," Nicolas said. "All of us know she'll end up there on her own if we forbid it. Tatiana thinks she has a way around the minimum qualifications."

"Ah yes," Margaret said, "the night maneuver and firing exercises are a minimum standard that trump most of the other qualification exams. She looks capable of the minimum physical parts."

"Yeah, she jogs two miles a day," Nicolas said.

"Charles, do you have time to try too?" Margaret asked her nephew. "You always say you would like a closer relationship with the regiment."

"Do you think it would be all right?" Charles asked. "Would anyone complain about favoritism?"

"The test won't be as easy as you think, Charles," Nicolas said. "If your guards have the required weapons and you are familiar with them, you might pass. Notice I said *might* pass. I personally don't think Emily will."

Margaret waved at an SAS man, and he jogged over. She explained to him what was required. The man surrendered his pistol to Charles and waved over another man, who pulled from his overcoat a scaled-down version of the C7 with a folding stock and gave it to the prince.

"You are going dressed like that?" Nicolas asked.

"Why not?" the prince asked. "Adding a little colour to the test won't hurt."

Trailed by the SAS men, Nicolas and the Windsors walked out to the ranch's firing range, where they found Paul field-stripping his C7 and his Colt pistol and laying the pieces neatly on a table.

"Tatiana dear," Margaret said, "Naj has agreed for my young nephew to be tested at the same time as Emily. I can vouch for his required physical capabilities, as can the sergeant there. Right, Sergeant?"

"Yes, ma'am," the sergeant said. He saluted and introduced himself to Tatiana. "Sergeant Macintosh, Special Air Services colonel. I had the pleasure of attending the colonel's training course two years ago, ma'am. Captain Windsor completed and passed pilot survival and evasion classes, ma'am. He has also completed and passed airborne-infantry-officer training, ma'am. He easily passed the minimum standards, ma'am."

"Very well, Sergeant," Tatiana said. "Mr. Bekenbaum, set up two sets of targets down range please. Captain, strip your weapons on that table."

Katherine waved an aide to her side and spoke into his ear. Saluting, the aide jogged back toward the ranch.

Even on a cloudless full-moon night, it was difficult to see the farthest target. Emily was not sure she would be able to hit it. She and Paul had spent many hours practicing taking down and reassembling weapons and firing rounds at paper targets, but they'd never done it at night and never in front of spectators. The little clearing was filling up with quiet groups, who arranged themselves to watch. One was the ROTC group and the Green Beret major. Another group contained Emily's father and his marine buddies, and still another had red-arrow flashes on their berets. The last group stood with the very large and intimidating master warrant officers, who had the same flashes on their shoulders. The Green Beret major introduced his group of college men to the men with the arrowhead flashes.

"Do this just like you did it with Paul," Tatiana said to Emily. "In a night shoot, you only have to hit the target with three shots. Just focus, and block out your surroundings."

"How am I supposed to put the guns together in the dark?" Emily said. "I'll never be able to do it, and then I will have to call the State Department for clearance to go. I refuse to be away from my new husband."

"Yes, dear, we know." Tatiana switched to German. "Mother Elizabeth felt the same way when Andreas was sent to Afghanistan. They had just been married, and women were not allowed to serve in the Russian army at all back then. She got the selection committee to agree to allow women to try out to be medical personnel during that campaign. Elizabeth, her sister Katia, and four others not only qualified but also did it on horseback well under the time limit and with expert status. They won their eagles, not bears, that day."

"I sat waiting five years for Naj to come home," Katherine said. "Every time I saw a Western Union man coming down the street, I feared the worst. I was in the radio room when Naj was cut down in Korea. I felt so helpless, so useless. I made Tatiana qualify me the next Friday, and then I took advanced training classes and received my eagle."

"Both of you have medical training and skills," Emily said. "I have none of that."

"You're a combat reporter and photographer," Tatiana said. "Canada has been at the forefront of that area since South Africa. Do you want to go with Paul or not? That is the only question. If you want him badly enough, you will pass."

"Colonel, the targets are ready, ma'am," Paul said, coming to attention before Tatiana.

"Carry on, Mr. Bekenbaum," Tatiana said.

"Candidates, front and center!" Paul barked. Both candidates marched up to him, came to attention, and saluted. Emily's salute was almost as good as that of the Prince of Wales, who was still in his dress uniform with jangling medals and all. Paul worked hard to not laugh at the contrast between Charles and Emily, who was in a polo shirt, blue jeans, and running shoes.

"Candidates will reassemble their weapons and fire at the appropriate target," Paul said briskly. "Candidates have five minutes to complete the task and will fire five rounds—and five rounds only—from each weapon. Begin!"

Emily's lack of knowledge about military things showed itself. At the word *begin*, Charles flew into action, running to his table to assemble his pistol and rifle. Emily stood for a second before it dawned on her that Paul had hit the start button on his wristwatch. She swung into action and ran to her table. Her hands flew through the motions of putting all the weapons' pieces together. She slapped a clip into the pistol's butt, pulled the slide back, extended both arms before her, sighted down the barrel, and fired five times. She ejected the clip and cartridge from the chamber, placed the live cartridge back into the clip, and picked up the C7. She inserted its clip and charged the rifle. Wrapping the sling around her left arm as Paul had shown her, she leaned her elbows on the firing table and put the iron sights on the center of the target, which was one hundred yards away and dimly lit in the moonlight. Using her right hand, she flipped the selection lever to single shot, removed the safety, and squeezed the trigger to fire her five shots. She unloaded the rifle, reengaged the safety, placed it back on the table, and came to attention. Charles finished right after she did, putting the safety on his weapon and slamming it down on his table. Paul hit the stop button and noted the time.

"At ease," he said and then walked down to the targets.

Again Emily's lack of formal military training showed as she nervously tapped her foot on the ground while waiting for the accuracy report. "You only had to hit the target three times, love," Margaret said from behind Emily. "It will be all right."

Paul returned with the targets and showed them to Tatiana and the command group. Charles was as nervous as Emily while awaiting the results of the test. "Candidates, attention!" Paul barked.

"Candidate Windsor, you have passed," Tatiana said. "Because of this night exercise and your past training accomplishments, you are now a certified combat-infantry rifleman. Congratulations, Captain." The aide, who had just returned, passed the bear to her. Tatiana approached the Prince of Wales and pinned it on his right collar. Charles saluted, and Tatiana returned the salute. "Welcome to the regiment, Your Highness," Tatiana said. She turned to Emily. "Candidate Bekenbaum, you have also qualified as a rifleman. Congratulations, Ensign."

Tatiana gave Paul a stern look and jerked her head toward Emily. Paul was thinking of something else and had missed Tatiana's comment, but now he saluted Emily. "Congratulations, Ensign Bekenbaum," Paul said. "Welcome to the regiment."

Emily stood looking at her husband, who was still at attention and holding his salute.

"Even the lowest of the lowest ensign is an officer, dear," Margaret whispered into her ear. "You have to return the salute of a subordinate, or he will hold that salute until you walk away."

Emily gave something of a return salute, and Paul winked at her. He unpinned his bear and pinned it onto the right collar of her polo shirt. Smiling, he lifted her off the ground and kissed her. "You can come with the regiment, Em," he whispered into her ear. "For the record, you shot two bull's-eyes and hit the target with all five rifle shots, and you hit the bull's-eye with all your pistol shots. Those are eagle scores, love."

"That's a tough test, even for elite troops who are in practice," the Special Forces major said.

"Shit," Master Warrant Officer Red Cloud said. "Naj popped Kraut and Italian sentries at twice that distance under the same conditions. Emily did good—don't get me wrong—but it is nothing special for us."

CHAPTER 15

THE SUN WAS JUST BEGINNING to light the horizon when Emily rolled off Paul. She took some deep breaths to slow her heart. She looked over at her husband, who absently stroked her bare shoulder. He gazed at the ceiling, also trying to control his breathing and racing heartbeat.

"Is it true that I am your superior officer?" Emily linked the fingers of her right hand into his much larger ones.

"Technically, you are a commissioned officer," Paul said, "but you're probationary at this point. Your rank is ensign, which is the lowest grade of officer, but you are superior to any noncommissioned officers. If you were to try to exercise that right, everyone but the lowliest of new recruits would ignore you. They will provide you every courtesy due an officer and will couch their orders as requests, but if you do not comply, they will do what they want anyway, and you will have lost any respect you could ever hope to get from them. In addition, bears are technically in the service branch and subservient to those in the combat branch. So you might get seniority over an eagle, but he or she may not listen to you."

"But you are a bear and noncommissioned officer, yet a lot of people defer to you and accept your orders," Emily said.

"I am the top noncommissioned officer in the regiment, Em," Paul said. "I am similar to the colonel, but I'm an enlisted man. That is by choice, and everyone in the regiment knows it and my reason for it. I usually make requests rather than orders, unless we are in combat or under duress. In that case I issue direct orders out of necessity. God forbid it, but if you are ever in a combat situation, you may very well see corporals issue orders to lieutenants. We have a loose command structure, much like the Israelis use. A twenty-year combat vet is not going to wait around for a wet-behind-the-ears officer to make a decision."

"This is a whole new world for me," Emily pondered aloud. "I have much to learn and little time to learn it in."

"Don't worry," Paul said. "I will team you up with a decent section commander, and she will try to teach you. Notice I said *try*. You are a little stubborn, you know." Paul received a not-so-gentle punch in the belly for that comment.

"While what you say is most likely true," Emily said, pecking him on the lips, "I am sure it is against regulations to badmouth a superior officer, and it is never good to say such things to a lady. I order you to join me in the shower in five minutes." She jumped off the bed. "Should you disobey that order, you will be cut off for two months."

"Yeah, like you could go that long without some action," Paul said. Emily pranced to the bathroom and stuck her tongue out at him. He tossed a pillow at her, and she disappeared behind the door.

"Good morning, Mr. Bekenbaum, Ensign," Nicolas said as the newlyweds came up to his desk, which had been a banquet table during the previous night's festivities. "Ensign, why don't you round up some breakfast for the master warrant? The caterers should be almost ready to serve. Then Colonel Bekenbaum wishes to see you. She is over by the hayloft."

"Sir!" Emily said, saluting and marching to the food-service line.

"Early days, Paul," Nicolas said, smiling. "She is trying. Mother was and still is much more difficult. Now let's get to business. DND says the fastest they can get a Hercules down here is a week from today. The rest of the battalion will be in Germany by then. See if you can round up a commercial plane for us, will you?"

"Who's paying, and will we be reimbursed if we front payment?" Paul asked.

"Pay it out of regimental funds," Nicolas said. "Let the pencil pushers figure it out later."

"Thank you, Ensign," Paul said to Emily, who came back with a large cup of coffee and a plate heaping with pancakes, back bacon, and eggs.

"Anytime, Master Warrant." She smiled seductively, posing with her hands on her hips and her chest out and running her tongue over her lips. She skipped away to Tatiana, who was about to give Emily a lighthearted lecture on the proper behaviour of a female officer.

"It shouldn't be too bad," Paul said. "Grandma is smiling, and she really likes Emily. I'm going to team her up with Helga's section."

"Good, that's a veteran crew on their last deployment," Nicolas said. "Helga has a good head on her shoulders and a lot of patience. The latest word I have is that no agreement for a ceasefire has been reached yet. The Egyptians have suffered badly and are ready to quit, but the Syrians think they can still win. The Egyptians have agreed to the terms, including letting

UN troops observe. The Syrians, however, are balking at a line of demarcation and demilitarization and especially at us being the UN's peacekeepers for the region. Regardless, we are going. The Egyptians welcome our participation."

"So we are going, but the final destination is unclear," Paul said. "I suppose we'll follow standard UN rules of engagement and the usual small-calibre weapon systems?"

"As usual I defer to your judgment, Paul," Nicolas said. "See if you can pressure the Syrians into complying. The Saudis still control the show over there. Nothing happens without their OK. We could save a lot of lives on both sides of the conflict."

Tatiana was still speaking to Emily, who had respectfully saluted her. "I know this is a steep learning curve for you, Em. But we don't salute indoors, for one, and we don't flirt while on duty. You have to separate your personal life from regimental and company business, dear. I am sure your father taught you that, and really the regiment is just like a big company in operation but with more immediate, and often deadly, consequences.

"Pack enough personal clothing only for two days. Once we arrive in Germany, you will be outfitted with the proper battle gear and weapons. You will be with a veteran armoured-vehicle section. The troopers are mostly male, but the commander is female. You will be in confined spaces almost all the time. Captain Hoenadle will inform you of what kind of perfume or antiperspirant to use, if any, and what other feminine-hygiene products you may require. I haven't been in a combat zone for thirty years. Things change, so talk to the captain.

"Officially you are the regiment's historian and photographer. The regiment has no noncombatants, and you may be required to defend yourself, your section mates, or civilians. You will become proficient in all aspects of modern warfare and our weapon systems. These books will help you out." Emily looked at the stack of binders Tatiana plunked on the table in front of her.

"You will most likely have a lot of time on your hands," Tatiana continued. "We say, 'Hurry up, and wait.' All militaries are like that. The government wants us to do something and get to where it is supposed to happen in a hurry, and then we sit around and wait for something to happen. When it does, it happens fast—very, very fast. The colonel will find you once we arrive in Germany."

"Thank you, Colonel. Are you coming with us?" Emily asked.

"No, love, I stay home these days. My role is mostly ceremonial, but I occasionally mentor a lost young puppy I take under my wing. Paul loves you very much, my granddaughter, and so do I. Helga is a good person, and she and her crew are very good. She will teach you what you need to know as an officer. The rest of the crew will help you become a soldier. When you come back from deployment, you can make a choice of staying in the service or not. By the time you return, you will have completed almost two years of full-time service. Your deployment history requirements for the regiment will most likely take another three years, so your permanent-colonist status is assured. Once you have that, your Canadian citizenship is guaranteed should you want it. Please, love," Tatiana said, taking Emily's face in both her hands and looking deep into her eyes, "do avoid getting pregnant. I know you are young and in love, but if you have to leave to have a baby, it will make things more complicated."

"I'll try, Grandmother," Emily said, "but your Paul is very, very hard to resist."

"So was his grandfather," Tatiana said, her eyes looking far away and long ago. "As a matter of fact, he still is. From now on, between you and me, we'll call each other Tat and Em, yes? You already know about the difference on how to act when family is about, and now you know about the military aspect of behaviour. There are a few other things, but we will talk of that when you return. Do you have any questions, Ensign Bekenbaum?"

"No, Colonel," Emily said. "Thank you for all your advice and for giving me such a wonderful man, Tat."

"You just make sure you give me some wonderful great-grandchildren, Em," Tatiana said, "just not right away. If that is all, Ensign, you are dismissed until we send for you."

A trooper gave Emily a C7, a Colt pistol with a web belt and holster, ammo pouches, spare clips, and several boxes of ammunition. She spent the afternoon sighting in the two weapons to suit herself before cleaning and oiling them. She loaded each spare clip as she had seen Paul do, put them into their pouches on the weapons harness, and adjusted it so it felt comfortable. She took apart her cameras to clean and service them with as much care as she had her weapons, making sure she had her cleaning and repair kits in the camera bag as well as the telephoto and wide-angle lenses. Next she put in about fifty rolls of thirty-five-millimetre colour film. She hoped she would have enough time in Germany to pick up some more film and notepads, too.

Paul got back to the guesthouse just as the sun was going down. He showed Emily how to pack her duffel bag by demonstrating with his. Both collapsed into bed, almost too tired to do anything else…almost.

The regiment exited the packed school buses Paul had found to transport them to the airport just after lunchtime. A man in a commissary truck handed out sandwiches to the troopers as they filed up the portable stairwell into the Boeing 707 that would take them from LA to Germany. It would be a nine-hour flight, and they wouldn't have any food until they landed.

"Those are a new type of uniform you guys are wearing," said the African American man operating the commissary truck. "Are you National Guard marines off to Vietnam?"

"Something like that," Paul said, watching his troopers file by.

"I was there with the Vietnamese army as an adviser in '62," the man said. "Good luck, Gunny. Your people look pretty good."

"Thank you, sir," Paul said.

"Golan Heights—never heard of that place when I was over in 'Nam," the man continued. "They don't tell us sergeants any more than they need to, eh, Gunny?"

"Too right, Sergeant, too right," Paul said. "You take care now, Sergeant."

"You too, Gunny," the man said. Paul caught up to the last trooper and put his arm around her waist. When her hat fell off, he stooped to pick it up and received a kiss from the black-haired beauty. "Goddamn," the black ex-sergeant said. "If I'd had one like her in my unit, I wouldn't have retired."

"If we had more like them in the service, Vietnam would be over by now," a Green Beret major said, pouring himself a coffee.

"Are they Force Recon?" the ex-sergeant asked. "I'm class of '62, sir."

"No, Sergeant, those are the people who trained the people who trained you," the major said. "They're highly motivated and operate under the radar. We would be lucky to have them. They're Canadians."

CHAPTER 16

EMILY'S EARS POPPED AS THE jet lost altitude. They were landing at the air base in Gander, Newfoundland, to refuel and let everyone stretch before the final leg across the ocean to Germany. She had spent the five hours since takeoff from California reading one of the manuals Tatiana had given her. Not large, it was on officer etiquette, what each rank was responsible for, and how to identify each rank by badge. It was really not all that different from a large business venture, as far as distribution of power, so she did not have much difficulty with that aspect. She said as much to Paul as the seat-belt sign came on for the approaching landing.

"Good, you caught on to that quickly," Paul said. "I want you to read about basic tactics next. You might find yourself in a bad spot one day, and that little tactics book could save your life. As an ensign, you are responsible for twenty troopers. Master Corporal Klausman has been running the section himself, so I'm assigning you to him until we link with the regiment's people at the base in Lahr. Basically you are a babysitter. Make sure the troopers get off the plane, stay together, and get back on." Paul then yelled to a man across the aisle and two rows up. "Hey, Kurt, the ensign here is going to give you a hand! Try not to fuck it up too much, won't you?"

"No problem, Warrant," Klausman said, grinning. "What would my day be without a wet-behind-the-ears ensign hanging on my every word? Think the base exchange will be open, Warrant?"

"It should be, Klausman," Paul said.

"Good. Tell the ensign to bring some cash with her." Kurt tapped a finger on his epaulet.

"Shit, thanks, Kurt. I forgot about that," Paul said.

"Emily, do you have any cash?" Paul asked. "If not, I'll give you some. Never mind. I'll give you fifty anyway. After you supervise the unloading of your troopers, Master Corporal Klausman will escort you to our military store. You need to pick up a few officer-type things, and they come out of your own pocket. You will need to produce that ID card and the orders Tatiana gave you."

By then, the plane was rumbling down the runway, slowing down, and taxiing. It came to a stop in front of a military air terminal instead of a regular one. The troopers walked out of the airplane, stretching, and lined up in their sections and platoons. Master corporals, sergeants, and second lieutenants counted heads and reported to lieutenants and captains, who reported to majors, who reported to Paul and the colonel.

After that was done, Master Corporal Klausman suggested to Emily that the troopers be told to report at the gate in an hour—sober and in uniform. Emily agreed, and Klausman issued the order. "Now, Ensign, let's at least get you kitted out for the uniform you are wearing," Kurt said. "Once we get to Lahr, the provost—especially the Yanks' provost—doesn't like service people out of uniform. Being without rank badges is classified as being out of uniform."

"Provost?" Emily asked.

"Provosts are called MPs, or military police, in the States," Klausman said. "They are all over us in Germany for lots of chicken-shit stuff. I figure they must get paid for every offence they write up or something." Kurt turned his attention to the pretty clerk at the order desk. "Hi there. How are you today?"

"Just fine, love," she answered with a weird accent that sounded like a combination of Irish and Scotch. Emily later learned it was a Newfoundlander's accent. "Now, ya know ya can't buy anything at ta officers' store, love. Or are ya here to tell me how lovely I am and ta ask me ta marry ya and take me ta Alberta with ya when ya goes home once again?" She batted her long eyelashes at Kurt and winked at Emily.

"If I was ten years younger and not married with two kids, I would take you up on that offer, love," Klausman said. "The brand-new ensign here needs some rank badges before she gets thrown in jail in Germany."

"I woulda tolds ya I couldn't go with ya anyway. Me husband and three li'l ones would suffer without me, don'tcha know?" The clerk said to Emily, "OK, love, let's see yer orders and ID then." The clerk rummaged around in some bins and came up with two brass crowns, two Canada brass badges, and two miniature red maple-leaf Canadian-flag pins. "These and yer orders should getcher by, ma'am. Twenty-two fifty, ma'am. Oh shit, wait a bit. Here, this is a Pixly beret badge, but it will do ya until ya gets yer own. I can't help ya with yer regiment's stuff. You guys keep that to yourselves. Now it comes to an even twenty-nine, ma'am."

"You guys have to buy your own decorations?" Emily asked. "American soldiers don't."

"We enlisted men and noncommissioned officers don't, ma'am," the corporal said. "It's just the officers who do, ma'am. You won't need cash for most of this stuff, ma'am. Once we get to Lahr, you will be issued a pay book. The regiment will deduct all that stuff from your pay. The regiment pays a certain amount for battle and fatigue uniforms for officers, but you are responsible for badges and accoutrements. You will also be measured up for normal dress and formal dress, which you will have to purchase, as well as an officer's sword and—because you're a woman—an officer's sash. You will also have to pay a monthly officers' mess bill, whether you use it or not, and any booze or food bills over the maximum allowed per month."

"I am beginning to understand why the master warrant is still a master warrant," Emily said.

"Ha, that's a good one," Klausman said. "I never even thought of that. Mr. Cheapy. No, ma'am, that is not the reason your husband is still a warrant. We only have so many officer slots and eagle slots. He knows—and we know—that he is really in charge of this battalion. Believe me, he can definitely afford to be an officer, even before he met 'your moneyness.' By staying a bear and a noncom, he allows someone else a slot—maybe someone who needs the money or a leg up. Paul doesn't have much of an ego, and like I said, he is the one in charge. You will see the colonel going to him, not the other way around."

"He said something like that when we first met at some kind of race he was in with the Saudis," Emily said. "Your regiment won, but Paul gave back the horses they won and gave the Saudis his troopers' horses in return."

"Feisal and his bunch of thieves are still trying to beat us, eh?" Klausman asked. "They haven't beaten us yet. They try once each generation. Those were Paul's horses, not the troopers', and he paid the troopers for the Arabians he gave back. The horse thing is a cultural thing with the Saudis, and the Bekenbaums gain much prestige by being generous. Honestly Paul did not miss the money—believe me. Ah, is there more to the man than you imagined?" Klausman laughed. "He makes more money in a year selling his horses than a normal man makes in ten. And your grandchildren won't be able to spend the royalties he is going to get from that invention of his. It's too bad we got called up. Paul had a wonderful six-month honeymoon planned for you."

"I'll get a two-year one this way," Emily said, smiling, "and I'll get paid for it too."

"That's the spirit, ma'am," Klausman said, and they both enjoyed a laugh.

"Are there rules against a lowly ensign buying an exalted master corporal a beer?" Emily asked.

"Why no, ma'am," Klausman said. "The ensign is *expected* to buy the exalted master corporal a beer after he tells the ensign the facts of life."

"Good, I really would hate to give Mr. Cheapy any of his money back," Emily said.

As they drank their beers, Klausman showed Emily where on her jacket and beret to pin her new badges. "You are supposed to have badges on your blouse, too," Klausman said. "Don't take your jacket off in Germany until you get your new uniforms and they are all badged up, OK?"

Emily shrugged on her jacket, buttoned it up in the right way, and placed her beret squarely on her head. She and Klausman walked out to the tarmac area and waited for their troopers. Once everyone was lined up and counted, reports passed up the chain of command, and they all went back to their places on the airplane for the last four hours to Germany. "Paul, will we be able to stay together once we get on base?" Emily asked once they were airborne.

"Yes, love," Paul said. "We aren't the only officer-noncom marriage. There are even a few officer-enlisted marriages. The Canadian Regular Force lets us manage our own affairs in that regard, Em. It's easier that way."

"Thank God," Emily said. "Being this close to you but not sharing your bed for two years would have driven me to distraction."

"During the Boer War, the Brits tried to make an issue of our women serving in the field alongside men," Paul said. "They could not forbid women from coming, but they forbade them from entering the camp at night. So we made our own camp half a mile away in a more defensible position. Because we had a smaller camp, the Boers hit us at daybreak and suffered a lot of casualties. The Brits, as usual, were too scared to march that day, so we stayed put. The Boers hit the Brits the next morning, and we had to go to their rescue. We had no problems with women entering camp after that."

"Is that where Susan got her Victoria Cross?" Emily asked.

"No, my grandfather's brother, Stephan, got his there. Susan got the Distinguished Service Cross in South Africa," Paul said. "In World War I, Susan was commander of a hospital in France. The Germans purposely bombed it, and Susan got the VC for repeatedly going in and rescuing patients. My great-aunt was killed, along with two other nurses and a couple troopers. The Germans succeeded only in pissing us off more. Grandfather was on his way from Palestine to Afghanistan at the time, and he told me he had a hard time holding the troopers back from shooting all the prisoners they were taking."

"When were you going to tell me how much money you had?" Emily asked Paul, changing the subject.

"Does it matter? I love you, and I am pretty sure you love me. Otherwise you wouldn't have married me."

"Knowing you are wealthy would have made it easier to convince my mother you weren't after my money," Emily said.

"It could also have made it worse," Paul said. "Our family competes directly with your father in some areas. Not to worry—I told him about it. He's good with it."

"Were you going to tell me about the hostage situation at the bank?" Emily said. "My husband is a big hero, plastered on front pages all over the world."

"Em, I am sorry." Paul took her hand and looked into her green eyes. "There will be times when I cannot tell you where I am going or what I am doing. That is for your safety as well as mine. That operation could still turn nasty. When religion is involved, people lose all reason. They commit terrible atrocities, even against their own people. They would not hesitate to kill you or our children, our grandchildren, or our friends' children. I mistakenly wore my own uniform, and something as simple as that could have made our wedding a disaster."

"So that's why most of your wedding guests were armed," Emily said. "I wondered about that but just thought it was ceremonial."

"Usually, it is," Paul said. "This time the weapons were loaded, and all of us were careful not to get drunk. One of the books Grandmother gave you outlines our regimental history and our role in things. We are supposedly a light-armoured reconnaissance battalion, but we occasionally operate as an assault battalion. Increasingly we are doing special operations behind battle lines. That is something my father specialised in during World War II, before and after you Yanks got involved."

"What about those two Indians at the wedding?" Emily asked. "What is their story? That Green Beret major spent a lot of time with them."

"Both are Cherokee," Paul replied. "My father trained them and eight other Cherokee, and he led them on their first mission. At their graduation ceremony before they left Montana, we adopted them into our Cossack host—Andreas's host—and gave them eagles. They were the only Americans we did that with. After their graduation, the Americans all went on leave. So did most of the regiment, except my father. He stayed to be with my mother and stepbrother. The regiment came back from leave back home in Didsbury, and we boarded the train in Montana and headed east. The first stop was Wyoming to pick up the Cherokee. One of our old-timers saw the large group of Cherokee at the platform, recognised what was going on, and told my father. It turns out Andreas—my dad's grandfather and founder of the regiment—had given Red Cloud, the Cherokee chief, an eagle for all his help when our people came across the American west in the 1870s. Red Cloud was the grandfather of a trooper we had given an eagle to, and his family adopted Red Cloud's last name. After the war the two men who had survived asked if they could join us in Alberta, as the American government treated them shabbily. Now the two men and their families, as well as the families of the eight Cherokee troopers who were killed in the war, are members of our colony."

"Why do you keep all of this a secret?" Emily asked. "The world should hear what you and all your family have done, what your colony has done."

"The Crown and Canadian government gave us special privileges, Em," Paul said, "privileges other groups were not and never have been given. Thirty miles from our colony, other Germans from Russia founded colonies, but they do not enjoy the same privileges we do. They are nonviolent religious groups who see that, for some reason, all of us feel compelled to serve in the military. They don't understand we are more Cossack than German in our thinking and upbringing and that being in the military is a requirement for membership in the colony. We don't pay taxes—personal, corporate, provincial, federal, school, Medicare—none of them, Emily. We train and initially equip our own troops. The Canadian government resupplies us when we go active, like we are now, and pays our salaries and expenses. We fund the regiment at all other times, and we pay our nonactive members. We build and maintain our own schools and hospitals. We pay for any university programs our people are qualified to enter and want to attend. We provide start-up funds for those who want to start their own businesses. Most people who want to be farmers or ranchers already are, and each family has its own land or otherwise leases or sells it to others to farm for them. The colony owns the land and takes ten percent of any crops or animals, as it does the profits from any business it funds. Those are the only taxes we pay, and everyone pays the same amount. No matter how much or how little you make, you pay ten percent."

"Your poor people don't complain about that?" Emily asked.

"Nobody is forcing them to stay, Emily," Paul said. "They are free Canadian citizens and can leave anytime they choose. Once they leave, they lose all their privileges and perks. We let them return up to five years later with no questions asked. Beyond that, if they come back, they are not full members and are not allowed the perks. Some, not many, we have expelled."

"What about your personal wealth?" Emily asked. "The Canadian government doesn't come after you, even if your company operates outside the colony?"

"As long as a company is registered in the colony, the Canadians have no jurisdiction," Paul said. "Not so in the United States or other countries—we pay their taxes. In fact, most of our companies are outside the colony and are subject to Canadian taxation, just not our portions of any dividends or wages we receive. The system is a win-win for all of us. Once in a while, a politician tries to change the rules, like this new prime minister. Unfortunately for the Canadian government, only the queen can rescind our charter. I don't think she can either, though, unless we fail to live up to our end of the agreement." Paul raised his hand. "Before you ask any more questions, a lot of that information is in the books Grandmother gave you. You have many years ahead of you to learn all this. It's not that hard. My mother is American, and she learned it."

"That is another thing I have to find out about," Emily said. "I think I still have to pay American taxes, and I am not sure how serving in a foreign army works."

"Helga's husband is American," Paul said. "Ask her or my mother about that stuff. I was born in Canada, so I don't worry about it. Come to think of it, I don't know about George either. He was born in the States. Look, love, we should really get some sleep."

A flight attendant woke Paul up with a touch on the shoulder, and Paul felt the plane bank gently. The flight attendant handed him a message and went down the aisle. The airplane was quiet, as most of the troopers were asleep. Those who were awake, like Emily, were reading. Emily had drawn her sunshade, and the overhead reading light obscured her face as it shone on the text in which she was absorbed.

Paul read the message and grunted to himself. He leveraged himself up out of his seat and walked to the lavatory. On his way back, he tapped each company commander on the shoulder and said there would be a meeting at the front of the plane in twenty minutes. He also passed Emily on his way to what would normally be the first-class cabin, where he told the majors and the colonel about the meeting. He handed the message to the colonel, who read it and passed it to his clerk. The clerk gathered the headquarter staff for a meeting briefing before the meeting.

"Klausman," Paul said, coming back to the coach section and waking him up. "There's a meeting up front in ten. Take Ensign Bekenbaum with you, and try to keep her quiet during the briefing."

Emily had opened the sunshade in Paul's absence. He sat down and saw the streetlights of the cities and towns passing underneath. They would land in Lahr in the dark, since the time in Germany was eight hours ahead. "Meet up front in ten minutes, Ensign," Paul told Emily. "Bring a notepad and pencil. Klausman will be there, so stand beside him. Don't ask any questions this time, OK? Let Klausman handle that. He knows what is relevant and what isn't. We should be landing in half an hour, and you will have to stick with your platoon until we reach the barracks and the troopers get settled in. I am going to be extremely busy for the next few hours, and so are you. I will link up with you wherever our billet ends up."

Emily nodded, putting her books and things in order. Paul stopped her to gently kiss her, and then he put his arm around her and held her. She kept her head on his shoulder for the whole ten minutes. He stood and made his way forward, the rest of the platoon commanders following.

"Right then," the colonel said. "We land in twenty minutes, and three buses are waiting for us. We'll muster by platoon. HQ will take the first bus. By the time we hit the base, it will be morning, so those of you who need other equipment, which is almost all of us, will be able to make that happen. I am told base guides will be assigned to help us out and show us to our barracks. At this point I am not informed whether the rest of the battalion has arrived or about the status of our combat vehicles. We have a few days to acclimatize, but don't count on too many. The UN wants us in place as soon as the situation allows it. Are there any questions?"

"Will we be able to badge up at base, Colonel?" a captain asked.

"Yes," the colonel answered. "The regiment maintains a depot at the base, and a supply of uniforms and weapons is on hand for this type of operation. Is there anything else? OK, back to your troopers then."

Paul stayed up front. He was part of the HQ element for the time being. He had a lot of staff work to accomplish until the rest of the battalion showed up and the specialists took over. The last he saw Emily, she was sitting in her seat next to Klausman. The seat-belt sign came on, and they made their final descent into Frankfurt.

It was ten in the morning by the time they got off the buses and assembled at the Canadian Forces base in Lahr. As promised there was a guide for each section, and the noncoms took charge, leaving the officers to gather with their own guides. A female captain approached Emily and extended her right hand. "Hi, I'm Sharon, and you are Emily. I am going to escort the poor lost ensign on her amazing journey to transform from a somewhat-normal but beautiful woman into a fierce warrior ready to take on all comers." Like many of the regiment's members, she was blond and blue eyed with a figure to kill for. She was about five foot eleven—three inches taller than Emily—and didn't have an ounce of fat on her.

"Captain Chimilovitch, if you are ready, I can escort you to the officers' quarters first, then show you the mess and finally the stores," said a female corporal in the Service Corps.

"Lead on, my good lady, lead on," Sharon said. "At the moment, the ensign and I are the only two women here, so your life just got a lot easier."

"Chimilovitch—that's not German, is it?" Emily asked.

"The ensign is not as dumb as a typical ensign. Did you hear that, Corporal?" Sharon said. "No, it's Ukrainian. My people were Cossacks, and they immigrated to the States in the 1850s. My great-granddad joined the Marine Corps during the Civil War, made gunnery sergeant, and was about to retire after the war when he got an offer to attend a trade mission to Russia because he spoke Russian. Once there, he met up with a fellow named Andreas, who convinced him to join his host of happy-go-lucky foolish young Cossacks. The rest is history."

"Cossacks? I thought the regiment were all German cavalry troopers," Emily said.

"It's a long story," Sharon said. "Something happened in Germany, so the whole regiment, including their families, deserted and went to Russia as a group. The Cossacks were an autonomous group of people the Russians used to conquer and then colonise new lands, and the Cossacks were more than happy to accept a fully armed and trained veteran lancer regiment into their midst. They eventually adopted them. Yes, technically, they are German, but they are Cossacks by blood as well. A German will call them *Swatz See Deutch*, or Black Sea Germans, because our people come from the Odesa region of what is now called Ukraine. It's a whole lot easier just to say we are Canadian and not worry about it. This is nice, Corporal." Sharon opened a door and tossed her duffel onto the bed. "I'll take this one, and the ensign will want to see the master warrant's quarters, which I hope are far away from me. It's hard to sleep next to newlyweds."

The women's next stop was the officers' mess, where Sharon showed Emily how to present her ID card. The mess sergeant noted it and started an account for her. They went from there to the officers' store for uniforms. "Hold it right there, you two," a voice called out behind them. The three women turned around to see two men in air-force uniforms—a sergeant and an officer. The sergeant had a provost's band on his arm and looked uncomfortable. The officer had both hands on his hips and looked disgusted. His uniform was impeccable, his trousers bloused perfectly over his shiny parachute boots. Instead of a tie, a yellow ascot was tucked stylishly around his neck. Emily did not see any wings on his uniform, so she guessed he was not a pilot.

"What is this reservist doing on my base?" the air-force captain demanded. Sharon stopped Emily from saluting the captain by holding onto her right arm.

"The ensign is with me, Captain. What business is it of yours that she is on a Canadian Forces base?" Sharon asked.

"Both of you are out of uniform and subject to charge," the captain barked. "Reservists are not allowed on this part of the base, and I am adding insubordination to the ensign's charges for not saluting a superior officer."

"I suppose you and the sergeant should escort us to the brig to process the paperwork," Sharon said. "Corporal, thank you for your time. Would you be good enough to stop by HQ to let them know we will be detained for a while?"

"Good," the air-force captain said. "Sergeant, escort these females to the office. I will drive the vehicle and meet you there."

"I am sorry, Captain, ma'am," the sergeant said, as the air-force captain jumped in his jeep and drove away. "He is the officer of the day."

"It's not a problem, Sergeant," Sharon said. "Your captain will obtain an interesting education today."

Sharon and Emily were filling out the forms at a counter in the police station's front office when the door banged open and slammed noisily shut. "Who the fuck is the stupid asshole who arrested my people?" Paul yelled, stomping into the room.

"Um…it would be the OOD, Master Warrant," the sergeant said.

"Get that dumb son of a bitch the hell out here, right the fuck now!" Paul yelled.

"Yes, Master Warrant." The sergeant ran to the door marked *Officer of the Day* but before he could knock on it, the door flew open. A red-faced captain rushed out, ready to confront Paul.

"Are you the stupid fuck who thinks he can charge and arrest my people without talking to me first?" Paul demanded. "A Mickey Mouse zoomy captain who ain't seen a minute's real duty. What the fuck are you—an admin clerk in a fancy fucking uniform? Fuck, you're not even a fucking Mickey Mouse policeman! This fucking captain has seen duty in Cyprus twice and just came back from Vietnam. Where the fuck have you been—stuck up some colonel's butthole in Ottawa? Sergeant, get your fucking commander on the phone, right the fuck now!"

"Already done, Master Warrant," the harried sergeant said. "He's on his way, Master Warrant."

"Since when does a captain take orders from a warrant officer?" the air-force captain demanded. "Sergeant, arrest that man for insubordination and disrespecting a superior officer!"

"At ease, Sergeant!" An air-force colonel with pilot and parachute wings on his uniform had come in. "When a master warrant talks, a captain listens, Captain. What the hell is going on here?"

"Sir, the OOD took it upon himself to arrest two of my officers without ascertaining the facts or consulting me or my staff, sir!" Paul said. He stood at attention, looking two inches above the colonel's head.

"That was a very bad move, Captain, very bad," said the colonel, shaking his head. "I am sorry, Master Warrant. The captain is new here and obviously had not read the order of the day, which orders everyone on the base to be as accommodating as possible to your people because of the circumstances. There will be no charges, and I assure you, Master Warrant, that the captain shall be duly disciplined. Captain, I would have a word with you in private. Please wait for me in your office."

"I am sorry, Mr. Bekenbaum, Captain, Ensign," the colonel said. "He's a keener. He just joined us from advanced training and thinks he's hot shit."

"Is he Air Commando?" Paul asked. "He has no jump wings."

"He will try to qualify tomorrow," the colonel said.

"Good, the ensign will be joining him, as will the captain. I will be the load master," Paul said. "If he somehow does not kill himself and passes, I will assume he has passed the minimum firearms standards and assign him as air-support controller for the regiment."

"Oh shit," the colonel said.

"He collects the pay, wears the fancy uniform, and talks the fancy talk, and now he'll pay the piper," Paul said, an evil grin on his face. "All right, you two slackers, the sergeant is taking you to get your kit before I charge your asses myself and make him join the regiment as well."

"I'd join you guys anytime, Master Warrant," the sergeant said. "I qualified as an expert on the firing range and am a certified jump instructor. I was in the top ten in my Air Commando training class and have an expert rating in com operating and repair. I am also rated expert in air-to-ground target controlling, Master Warrant."

"He's the best man I have, Paul," the colonel said. "Unfortunately, no wars are being fought, so the poor sergeant has no job to do. Being a policeman is less boring than sitting in a radio shack all day. I was going to assign him to you people anyway."

Paul looked the sergeant up and down a few seconds and then looked at Sharon, who shrugged her shoulders. "Captain, Ensign, would you please mind waiting for the sergeant outside?" Paul asked. After they left, he said, "OK, Sergeant, I need good people like you. Can you handle that dumb son of a bitch?" He pointed at the OOD's office.

"Not a problem, Master Warrant," the sergeant said.

"OK, on one condition," Paul said. "That ensign has never even put on a parachute before. Your task is to ensure she does not die tomorrow nor get seriously injured, *capisce*? I will be unhappy if my new wife comes back in more than one piece."

"No problem, sir," the sergeant said. "The colonel and I have done that type of thing in the past."

"Sergeant, escort the ladies to the officers' store, and come back here. Get your orders, grab your shit, and move into the enlisted barracks. See me at HQ after six. The colonel and I have some catching up to do over beers at the officers' mess."

"OK, Ensign," the air-force sergeant said to Emily, "this is standard procedure. You observe a parachute jump first, and then you'll take the training. As a safety precaution, I am going to strap a parachute on you, but it is nothing to be alarmed about. The chute will be hooked up to a line, and in case of emergency, the chute will deploy, saving your life. You will observe from the back of the Herc, and the rear door will be open, so there is an extremely small chance you might get sucked out of the airplane—hence the parachute. In the unlikely event you are sucked out of the airplane, do not panic. I have inspected that parachute and packed it myself. It will work perfectly. Once the line comes to an end, it opens the parachute, and you will experience a rapid slowdown from your uncontrolled descent. We will be no higher than two thousand feet, so it should take a couple of minutes to hit the ground. Enjoy the ride, and always look forward, not down. When you feel your toes hit the ground, relax your knees, and roll. Roll over, try to stand, and gather up the lines and silk. One of us should be close by to help you. Got it?"

"It's clear as mud," Emily said.

She and the sergeant were standing beside a Hercules transport plane with its rear doors open. As soon as the sergeant had fastened all her buckles and made sure she was safe, he nodded at Paul, who waved his finger in a circle in the air. The left engine turned over, and the assembled troopers jogged into the belly of the plane. Ten of them were qualifying for their parachute wings today. As the last one entered, the sergeant motioned for Emily and Sharon to precede him. Paul hit the button to close the door as they passed him, and the big rear doors closed as the left engine caught and then the right spun up.

There were no seats in the aircraft, so the troopers sat on the floor with their backs against the fuselage. Emily followed their lead, sitting on the cold deck. Paul gave her a pat on the shoulder and a wink, checking on each trooper and counting them while the Herc taxied to the runway. He entered the flight deck and closed the door. The aircraft went to full power and rumbled down the runway, lifted off at a high bank, and climbed steadily before leveling off and making a gut-wrenching turn.

Paul came back to the troopers, had Emily and the air-force sergeant stand, and then opened the rear doors. The noise was incredible, and the wind whipped around their legs. Emily felt two sets of arms grab her under the armpits, lift her up, and run with her out the rear of the aircraft. Paul flared his parachute expertly just before hitting the ground, running two steps before collapsing the shroud and hitting the release button. He had instructed the pilots to make two passes, tossing Emily out on the first and then the regular troopers on the second. He had just finished gathering up the loose silk of his parachute when he was shoved off balance and onto the ground.

A furious Emily straddled him and threw punches into his chest. "You asshole!" she yelled. "You could have killed me! That was not funny!" Paul had expected something like that, so he just took it. She didn't hit him all that hard, just enough to let him know she was upset. After a few seconds, she stopped and smiled. "Besides, I'm free-fall qualified already, you numskull. I've made more than twenty jumps, so the joke's on you."

"Why didn't you say so?"

"You never asked. Where are my wings?" Paul dug them out of his breast pocket and gave them to her. "You make sure you mark down that I'm jump qualified and have completed a jump. I want my jump pay. I have my eye on a nice little car I want to buy."

"Your wife is an amazing lady," the sergeant said to Paul back at the plane. "She made that crappy round chute dance. How long has she been in the regiment?"

"Including today, three days. Before you say anything more, don't ask. It's a long story, and I haven't slept in two days. Everybody get into the trucks," he said to the other troopers who had just finished their jumps. "You people are buying the beer."

"Attention on deck!" a trooper yelled out as the command group marched to the head table in the dining hall.

"At ease!" the colonel ordered. "At oh five hundred tomorrow, we will board Hercules transports to Israel. Vehicles and drivers will meet us at the airport. We will then proceed to our positions on the Golan Heights, and I want every weapon loaded and ready for bear. The situation is still tense, and anything could happen. We will take no crap from either side, and punish or reward impartially. If anybody—I don't care from which side—takes a shot at us, we will nuke his or her ass. We have to build our own positions, so we go fifty percent on duty and fifty percent off duty until that is done. Until we are positive the situation has settled down, we will continue that stance. Any questions?"

"Any artillery and air support, sir?" a second lieutenant asked.

"Dutch artillery and US Navy Air," Paul said. "We will have com frequencies for you as soon as we land."

"Remember, people," the colonel said, "right now, we are peacemaking, not peacekeeping. Dismissed. Paul, go to your wife. We can handle everything tonight. This is likely the last night you will have together for a bit."

That night Paul and Emily lay on their sides with their legs intertwined. Paul absently ran his finger over and around Emily's right breast. "Did you meet with Helga and get everything squared away?" Paul asked. "She's a good commander, and she has a top-notch crew. You will mostly be in the rear, so you will be all right."

"Paul dear," Emily said, taking his hand from her breast and holding it. "Number one, this is not the first time I have been in a war zone, and I usually don't have nine other people with guns and armour around me. Number two, you are more worried about this than I am. And number three, if you are not planning to do anything else tonight, will you please quit teasing my breast? You are making me extremely horny."

CHAPTER 17

———◆———

"Did you get any sleep last night, Warrant?" the air-force sergeant asked Paul, sitting beside him in the cramped and filled-to-capacity Hercules transport plane.

"Hey, I've been married a week now and have been with my extremely sexy wife for all of three nights," Paul said. "What the hell do you think?"

"Whoa, touchy, touchy," the sergeant said. "Sorry I asked."

"No, I'm the one apologizing, Sergeant," Paul yelled as the airplane engines picked up to takeoff speed. "I plan on sleeping all the way to the airport. Night-night." Paul pulled his beret over his eyes and was asleep in less than a minute. Pretty much everyone on the airplane followed his example.

The bus ride from the airport to the port was uneventful, and it was now late enough in the day to hint at the heat the afternoon would bring. The vehicles were parked and ready to go when the troops walked off their buses. Paul had no trouble finding his Cougar armoured troop carrier modified for electronic surveillance and driver. All the vehicles were painted white, with large UN logos on their sides and hoods.

"Are you ready to go, Corporal?" Paul asked, throwing his gear in the back and stowing his rifle in gun rack.

"Yeah, Paul, it's all good," the driver said. "We've got full tanks and ammo lockers. There's food for two weeks and water for three days. I haven't had a chance to check out the electronics yet, but that is your baby."

Paul climbed up to the commander's position and turned on a number of switches before opening the top hatch and sticking his head out. He looked around and saw Emily joining the Bison, an older armoured troop carrier, whose crew would act as his security. He made a very loud wolf whistle, which garnered a bunch of angry looks from the crew, until they saw it was Paul. Emily put a hand on her hip and moved to the Bison with an exaggerated hip-swinging walk, blowing a kiss at Paul before climbing in to the laughter of her crewmates. Paul laughed as well, adjusting his headset over his beret.

Paul's crewmates entered the Cougar, made themselves comfortable, turned on electronic equipment, and adjusted their headphones. "Crank it up, Corporal," Paul told the driver. "Tango Four...Tango Two, over," Paul said into the microphone. "Ready to move out, Tango Four?" he asked, making contact with the Bison. "Let's get this show on the road," he announced over both the radio and intercom. His driver revved up their vehicle, and they headed down the road with the hatches open. Paul pulled his goggles over his eyes as they hit the street and sped up.

They reached the bottom of a hill a couple hours later. The area was dotted with burned Soviet and American tanks and armoured vehicles. Some were still smoldering. Paul ordered his driver to pull up to the Israeli's position and stop. He pulled himself out of the top hatch and walked toward the group of Israeli officers and men manning the barricades.

"Goddamned Germans," an Israeli major said in Russian to his comrades. "Too bad we didn't get them all after the war."

"If you do not have your people and equipment off this hill and beyond the demilitarised zone by six this evening, Major," Paul said in Russian. "I am prepared to open fire on you. From that remark you just made, it will be my pleasure to do it. You and Uncle Joe's people killed a lot of mine before we could get them out of Russia."

Another officer in a different uniform walked up with a few of his own officers, and all of them smiled after overhearing what Paul had said. "I am the Syrian commander of this sector," the officer said to Paul. "It is good to see that not all the world believes the bullshit the Israelis are spouting."

"Well, Mr. Syrian Commander, I am going to tell you the same thing," Paul said. "I am not here to take sides or make friends. Get your people down your side of the hill and out of the demilitarised zone, or I will blow your asses off as well."

"You dare to challenge me with those puny vehicles?" The Syrian laughed. "A lot of good they will do against a frontline Soviet tank."

Four Phantom jets with American markings flew overhead at low altitude, the missiles on their wings in plain view. "I have zoomy friends, Tank Man," Paul said. "Now get the hell off my hill." Paul went back to the Cougar and yelled down as he climbed back aboard. "Hey, Sergeant Macleod, will the zoomies have any CF104s here?"

"No," Macleod answered, "the Canadian government doesn't want to put dents in them. We have Phantoms from the US carrier group and some tactical bombers should we need them."

"Right," Paul said. "Is your Arty group set up yet, Klugman?"

"Should be here by nightfall, Warrant," the Dutch artillery officer answered.

"We should have a few sensors deployed by then," Paul said. "The first couple nights are going to be interesting, I think. Both sides are probably going to play some games." The Cougar stopped at the top of the hill and turned broadside. Paul looked around and appreciated why both sides wanted this hill. He could see deep inside both countries from its top. "Can you lend me a few troopers to mount some sensor arrays, Helga?" Paul asked as the Bison came to a stop beside him. "I'm moving the Cougar to the Israeli side of the hill. I trust them a little more than the Syrians...but not much more."

"We'll dig in on this side for now," Helga said. "I'll set out some pickets and roving patrols for tonight." She and her crew had been together for almost twenty years, and this would be their last deployment.

Paul received reports from the other units, and soon two more Cougars and five Bisons were on the hill. He made a plan to cover the hill on the fly. By nightfall the Dutch had set up their artillery pieces at the bottom of the hill on the Israeli side, and Paul had issued the Dutch sufficient security forces to protect them in case of attack. Everyone worked frantically to get as much done as possible before darkness set in.

As Paul had predicted, as soon as the sun went down, the Syrians opened fire on their positions. The Syrians were immediately met by a barrage of 7.62- and 20.00-millimetre fire from the Cougars and Bisons, as well as a number of portable antitank rockets. As soon as target coordinates were sent, 105 artillery shells impacted all along the Syrian line.

The rest of the night was quiet.

Emily had no official duties this morning, so she photographed still-burning tanks on the Syrian slope and the blackened barrels of the Cougars' and Bisons' armaments. The hills that made up the Golan Heights were a beehive of activity as the regiment deployed throughout the region, digging in and planning command posts and communication centers. Already recovery vehicles were pulling destroyed tanks—both Syrian and Israeli—out of the way to the bottom of the hill and edge of the demilitarised zone. A bulldozer made a road, and watch- and radio towers were being erected all along the heights.

"Where are your helmet and flak jacket, Em?" Paul came up behind her. "The Syrians have a number of tanks and mortar positions pointing at us. They will mortar us next, and after that, they will lob a few rockets and sniper rounds at us for a few days. After they find out we don't scare easily and fight back hard, they will stop. Until then, you wear your flak jacket and helmet, got it?"

Suddenly tank shells randomly exploded all along the ridge. Paul grabbed Emily under the arm and almost carried her to the nearest Bison. They both flung themselves under it as mortar shells added destruction to the tank rounds. All along the ridge, Canadian vehicles opened fire. The Dutch joined in a short time later, sending artillery rounds buzzing overhead. Emily and Paul's position under the Bison was such that Emily was able to see a lot of the shell impacts on the Syrian positions. As she took pictures, two flights of Phantoms flew overhead. Some shot missiles, and others dropped bombs and napalm on the Syrian tanks. The battle was over in less than fifteen minutes. Paul and Emily crawled out from under the Bison, and Paul called out to the Bison's commander for an action report.

"Two minor casualties, sir," the commander reported a short time later. In contrast, judging from the columns of smoke rising into the air along the Syrian's lines, they had suffered badly.

"Why do they keep doing this?" Emily asked. "There is supposed to be a ceasefire agreement."

"It's an honour thing with the Syrians," Paul said. "It doesn't matter to their president how many of his people get killed. He can't be perceived as being weak. He doesn't understand that we don't think the same way and let him kill a few of us to satisfy his honour."

"He kills hundreds of his own people just so he doesn't look bad?" Emily said. "That is asinine."

"Get used to it," Paul said. "The Syrians don't understand how we think. After this they will target civilians—and not just here. The West, on the other hand, underestimates their resolve and willingness to die for what they believe in. We want to open dialogue with them and try to work things out. They think we are weak for doing that. We come from a culture that stresses cooperation. We have to cooperate in an unforgiving climate. These people have been fighting for thousands of years. The thought of cooperating is alien to them. Wear all of your gear for the next little while, Em. Soon we will have our own barracks complex, and once the Syrians figure out we are not intimidated, they will leave us alone. We'll revert to observer status, and if the situation stays cool, we'll go home when somebody else takes over."

As Paul had said, the incidents occurred farther apart as diplomatic efforts paid off and the regiment took a toll on the Syrians' equipment and soldiers. The regiment fired warning shots at any armed individual or vehicle in the demilitarised zone. If offenders did not leave, they were shot at—which usually disabled vehicles and sometimes killed people. Soon enough, incursions from the Syrian side stopped. None came from the Israeli side. Rocket, mortar, and artillery fire coming at the regiment soon stopped as well, as retaliation was swift and deadly. Now the Syrians fired over the DMZ and into Israel proper. If the Syrians thought that would be safer for them, they were mistaken. The regiment responded to such instances just as swiftly and with as much deadly force. The Syrians stationed across from the regiment stopped attacking completely. There were still rocket and mortar attacks, but nowhere near the regiment's area of responsibility.

As days went by, with local help from both Israelis and Palestinians, the regiment built barracks and roads. They set up power, water, and sewer lines and even planted trees and grass. Overtures from the UN to Syrians to hire some of their people went unanswered, so Palestinians worked the areas claimed by Syria. UN agencies also worked to build medical clinics and schools in the Palestinian areas. Again regimental personnel were very visible members of the construction processes, getting dirty right alongside the Palestinians.

The UN made good on the regiment's vehicle and material losses, and the regiment's medical staff treated the few injuries. Injured troopers were back on duty within days. In fact, more construction-related injuries occurred than combat injuries.

CHAPTER 18

EMILY SURPRISED PAUL WITH THE news that she was three months pregnant, and she absolutely refused to be sent home. She had passed her qualification exams for not only first lieutenant but second as well, and she was now in charge of her own platoon, commanding a Bison crew. When not on patrol duty, she and her section went out among local people on the Israeli side to do public-relation meet-and-greets, take pictures, and write stories about the local population and historic surroundings. The international press picked up many of her stories and photographs, and Emily was gaining a reputation as a fair and unbiased reporter who was respected by both sides.

At eight months pregnant, it became difficult for her to get around, so after today's trip, she would take a flight back to Canada to be among friends and family when the baby came. Emily's bright-white Bison with UN markings slowly made its way down the main street of the small town she and her crew were visiting. All the hatches were open to get as much fresh air as possible into the vehicle, and the troopers were halfway out of the hatches, waving and joking with civilians. Everyone in the town knew the crew was working on the school, and the whole town was jubilant and in a party mood. Out of the corner of her

291

left eye, Emily saw movement that didn't fit. She looked fully in that direction to see a man aiming a rocket-propelled grenade at them.

"Contact left! Contact left!" she yelled, grabbing the C9 machine gun mounted by her hatch. As she swung it to bear, she chambered a round. Just as she was about to squeeze the trigger, her world disappeared in a flash and a boom, and darkness descended.

"Master Warrant, a word if you please," the colonel said.

Paul was on top of the communication shack, realigning antennae. He looked down to see a solemn colonel and his staff accompanied by the regiment's priest. Paul tossed his wrenches at the trooper who was helping him and started down the ladder to the street. "Morning, Colonel, Father," Paul said, saluting. "What can I do for you this morning?"

"Paul, Emily's Bison was hit by an RPG this morning," the colonel said, not mincing his words. "Two troopers were killed, and all others were wounded. Emily and the other wounded have been sent to the hospital. You are to report to the hospital immediately with Father Holztman."

Paul was stunned. There had been no attacks at all, let alone on the regiment, for months, and now Emily was wounded. The colonel and the priest bundled Paul into a Cougar, which raced out of the base to the Israeli hospital and slid to a stop in front of the emergency room. A nurse from the regiment greeted them as they entered. "We've had two amputations and multiple shrapnel wounds and fractures, as well as concussions and blood loss," the nurse said. "The amputees are being prepped for evacuation to Germany. The others will be OK here. Emily will be fine in time, Paul." The nurse took his arm. "She was blown clear of the Bison, and she has a broken arm, concussion, and lots of minor shrapnel injuries and bruising. The baby is premature but healthy so far, and we are keeping a close watch on both your ladies. They should be fine in a few months, Paul."

"Good, good," Paul said. "Can I see them now please?" The nurse steered him toward the maternity ward, but he pulled away. "No, I want to see my wounded troopers first, especially the ones going to Germany. You told me my wife and daughter are fine, but these two troopers are severely injured. I must see them before they leave."

The nurse led Paul to the ward, and he went to both men, who were heavily sedated. Paul knelt, made the sign of the cross, and prayed for them. He stood, put on his beret, and saluted each man, tears running down his cheeks. He had grown up with both of them and knew their families. As he left, his eyes were dry and becoming hard. Those around him knew a firestorm was coming.

Emily was talking on a telephone in her room, so Paul stayed outside for a minute. He pointed at the colonel and his staff and waved them over. "Get hold of Arafat, and tell him to meet with me at eighteen hundred hours today," Paul ordered. "He had better have a good reason for this attack, and he better have names or bodies for me by the time we meet. I want my platoon ready to go on short notice and the rest of the anti-insurgent company in the country ASAP. We need another chopper, and have mine on call by the time I leave here. Has the regiment been informed of the attack?"

"Yes," the colonel said, "the regiment has been informed, and people from external affairs are on their way here. The regiment has contacted the Saudis already to express our concern and to ready the Arab League for repercussions."

"Good enough. Now go handle that stuff, and then come back," Paul said. "I need to see my new daughter and wife."

"No, Daddy, I insist," Emily was saying into the telephone. "If you send an airplane for me, the only way your granddaughter and I will get on it is if you also transport my two wounded troopers and their medical staff to Calgary International. No, Daddy, her name is Elizabeth after her great-great-grandmother, and I will not hear otherwise. I don't care what Paul says. That is her name, and that is the end of it. Tell the pilot to configure the plane for two stretchers. I love you, Daddy. Good-bye." She put the telephone down and lay back on a raised pillow, with her eyes closed and her daughter in the crook of her left arm.

She was soon asleep, and the nurse gently took her daughter from her hands and raised her eyebrows at Paul, who held out his arms. He took the small blanket-wrapped package, placed it against his chest, and looked into his newborn daughter's face. The child snuggled deeper into his arms and was content, and Paul quietly sat holding his daughter in the chair beside Emily's bed. "I am Paul, son of Nicolas, son of John, son of Andreas, clan of Bekenbaum, Canadians all. This is Elizabeth, my daughter. What is done to her and hers is done to me and mine. So say I in front of God," Paul said in German. He made the sign of the cross on Elizabeth's lips.

"So say we all," the two nurses in the room replied, also in German, making the sign of the cross.

"Elizabeth Susan Bekenbaum, Graffin und zu Hershmire," Emily said, taking Paul's hand. "You picked a bad time to be born but a strong and powerful family to be born into. We're a large, free, and loving family who will support you and defend you, console you when you are hurt, and celebrate you when you achieve. We're a family that will allow you to be who you wish to be, not what society wants you to be. Welcome to the regiment, my daughter."

"Well said, Lieutenant," Paul said. "I see my daughter has all her fingers and toes, although she is a bit quiet. How is my wife doing?"

"My arm is broken, and I just gave birth, dummy. How am I supposed to feel?" Emily said, but she was smiling. "I am fine, my husband, my love, my life. Unfortunately the Bison is a write-off, and my driver and loader have lost a leg each. That pisses me off. Three civilians were killed and twenty wounded, pissing me off even more."

"I have a meeting with Arafat," Paul said. "I intend to express my disappointment in his organization."

"The poor man really did not know what he was about to stir up, did he?" Emily said.

"Elizabeth Susan, born on the battlefield like her great-great-aunt," Paul said, looking at his daughter's face. "Are you sure you are OK, Em? Do you need anything?"

"I am very tired, and even with all the painkillers, I'm a little sore, but it's nothing compared to what others are enduring. I miss my husband and suspect I will be missing him much more before too long. You make sure to be careful," she said, holding his arm tightly. "I cannot and will not stop you, but be careful."

Elizabeth fussed, and the nurse took her from Paul and headed for the nursery. "Sir, your wife should really get some rest," another nurse scolded Paul, looking at his dusty boots and uniform.

Outnumbered and outranked, Paul kissed Emily good-bye, collected his bodyguard trooper and sidearm, and headed out of the hospital. Israeli police cars were parked in front and behind the Cougar, and an armoured army vehicle was parked beside it. The major who had given Paul such a hard time the day they arrived in Israel leaned against the Cougar. He stood straight when he saw Paul, and the master corporal assigned as his driver and bodyguard walking toward him. "Good afternoon, Major," Paul said, and he and the master corporal saluted. "Sorry to drag you out here for nothing."

"Not for nothing, Mr. Bekenbaum, I assure you," the major said, returning the salute. "Our people are leaving no stone unturned as they look for the perpetrators of this crime. They will be severely punished. If your people require anything, you have but to ask."

"My people are fine and well cared for, thank you," Paul said. "I would like to inquire into the health of the injured civilians and about the families of the dead. Perhaps we can assist them somehow. I would also like my Bison back. I want to assess the damage to see if we can do anything different to protect them in the future."

"The civilians are in this very hospital and receiving the best care we can give them," the major said. "I will supply the names of the dead and injured to you. The Bison is already on its way to your camp."

"Warrant, the Saudis and Arafat will meet us at eighteen hundred at the Jordanian palace," Paul's radio operator said from the Cougar. "The External Affairs people are not sure they can make it on time."

"I don't care about whether External Affairs can make it or not. This is regimental business." Paul turned to the major. "Major, I will require open air-space clearance from your people on short notice. Also, eight more of my armed people will be here in twelve hours. I would like a Huey if you have one, with at least the ID numbers painted out or the whole chopper painted black. I might have a name or location or both for you shortly. I will want surveillance. We will exact our own retribution, if you please. If you say no, we will do it anyway, and you will be completely out of the loop."

Israeli and Jordanian border guards were ready for the Cougar, waving it through the border's crossing point without stopping it. The Jordanian military police took up positions ahead of and behind the Cougar, and motorcycle police blocked the roads to allow the procession to proceed without delay to the large complex that housed the royal family. After stepping out of the vehicle, Paul and his section master corporal pulled down their blouses, straightened their belt buckles, and adjusted their berets to rest just over their eyebrows before allowing their escort to guide them into the building. In the waiting room, both men declined refreshments and assumed the parade rest position with both feet shoulder width apart and hands clasped in the smalls of their backs.

The door to the reception room opened, and both men were invited in. The Canadians marched into the room, stopped at attention in front of the Jordanian king, and stomped their feet in unison. "Master Warrant Officer Bekenbaum, Canadian Armed Forces and party, Your Highness!" Paul said sharply.

King Hussein rose, smiling, and extended his right hand. "Paul, it's so good to see you once again. Master Corporal, it's a pleasure. Have you met everyone before?" the king said, indicating the four other men in the room.

Paul shook hands with the Saudi prince and Arafat, ignoring the two functionaries with them. "Are you treating my horses well?" Paul asked the prince. "Hopefully you can give us a better race next time."

"Ah, they have settled in nicely," the prince answered. "The colts they produce are superior to both parents. It will not be so easy for you next time. Is your father well?"

"Last time I spoke with him, all was well. He always asks after you," Paul said. "You two should meet up. You were close during the war."

"For a long time after as well," the prince said, "but life gets busy, my son, as you are finding out."

"Are your wife and new child doing well?" Arafat asked.

"Yes, I just left them," Paul said. "They are both resting. I trust your family is doing well."

Arafat said, "Are any teenagers ever happy? But things go well, thank you."

"What can we do for you, Paul?" the Jordanian king asked. He knew the Westerners would not long tolerate the Arab custom of a long chat before business. "All of us here express our condolences to your injured comrades and their families."

"That was unacceptable," Paul said. "What is being done for the injured and killed civilians?"

"During a struggle for freedom, sometimes sacrifices must be made," Arafat said smugly.

The Saudi prince did not like what he saw on Paul's face and interjected quickly. "Of course we will supply nothing but the best treatment, Paul. We will pay for it all and offer job training, schooling, or whatever is necessary to provide a better life for them and their descendants."

"The regiment does not take sides in a case like this," Paul said, after a moment of reflection. "We were sent here to first make peace and then keep the peace. Our regiment, on behalf of our people, took it upon ourselves to provide medical facilities and basic schools for the people in the West Bank. The UN,

Israelis, your organization, and the Saudi people supported this, Mr. Arafat. I take offence to your comment, Mr. Arafat. We have no quarrel with the Palestinians and are not involved in any way in your ongoing issues with the Israelis. We have done whatever we could to help your people, even giving them well-paying jobs and technical training. We have, in fact, also funded and supervised a number of your people in starting their own businesses and bettering their neighborhoods. Now you tell me that killing my people and your own is acceptable because of the struggle." Arafat tried to reply. "I will not let you speak until I am finished, sir. You will supply us with the names of the individuals—or the people themselves—who are responsible for this attack, Mr. Arafat." Paul had steel in his voice. "This is not a request, and this is not a debate. Do you understand?"

"How can I be expected to know that?" Arafat asked.

"This attack was well planned, and with modern and expensive weapons," Paul said. "The attackers knew many civilians were in the crowd as well as a large press presence. Members of your organization did this, Mr. Arafat. You know it, and I know it. In addition the funding for all these activities comes from Saudi Arabia. You have until sunup tomorrow morning, gentlemen. After that the regiment will exact punishment as allowed and demanded under Islamic and Shari'a laws. We will hunt down all those responsible and punish them. Two will be killed, two will have legs amputated, and ten will be whipped with twenty lashes. Nor will you be left untouched, Prince, Mr. Arafat." Paul looked each man in the eyes. "I will punish one of each of your wives and one of each of your children, just as you have punished mine."

He let them ponder that for a time.

"You think you can do what you like because no one will say anything," Paul continued. "I do not care about world opinion or what my country's government says. You have made this a personal matter, not business. I hold you personally responsible. Prince, think long and hard about this and your response to it. Our families have long held mutual respect for each other, which was not always the case. Both families benefit from our association, but I know my family will survive without it. This situation has the risk of becoming a blood feud. We are both deeply religious families, which in itself could cause further issues. Both our families are proud, have long histories of helping the underdog, and are fiercely resistant to oppressors. Ask yourself and the rest of your family whether you want to continue down this road you have started on."

Paul now addressed Arafat. "Mr. Arafat, I am not an Israeli or an American. I don't want to sell your people anything, nor do I want to exploit your land or people for any purpose. Our only goal was to give your citizens a fighting chance at normal lives. You attacked us; we did not attack you. How you approach this is how I will respond, in the press and in the field. You have badly underestimated our resolve. Your people repeatedly asked us to intervene against you on their behalf. If we come in, we will come in hard and fast. If you and your supporters survive, we will send you to the World Court to be tried as war criminals. If you think the Israelis are bad, just wait. You will be begging them to help you once we start. You have woken the bear, sir, and the bear is angry. Unlike the bear, the eagle is swift and strong and sees far. The beaver works hard and is protective of its family. This is what you have woken, sir. The maple tree is strong and tall. It provides sweet nectar to its friends. It sinks its roots deep and takes over the land if not controlled. You think about that, sir, and if you still can't figure out what I am talking about, we are happy to provide a demonstration like the one we gave the prince's ancestors a hundred years ago. Good day, gentlemen." Paul abruptly left the room.

"He is blowing smoke, hoping to scare us," Arafat said. "Westerners are all the same. I will give him the one who pulled the trigger. That will make him happy, and he will go away. They will charge him, put him in jail for a year, and he will be back with us once again."

The Jordanian king stood, and the Saudi prince followed. "If Paul is only half the man his father and grandfather are," the king said to Arafat, "you and I are in a lot of trouble, but his father tells me Paul is twice the man he is. That young man will cause us all a lot of problems. Get your people under control, or he will get them under control for you. You have gone too far this time." The two royals left the Palestinian leader sitting in an empty room.

The briefing room was filled to capacity with officers and senior noncoms.

"The Israelis have given us intel on the attacker and his buddies," the colonel told Paul. "They are monitoring the situation and have provided us with maps of the area. As long as we give them notice, they will clear us for whatever air space we require."

"Do we have a person to liaise with?" Paul asked. "Get a hold of that guy, and keep your eyes on the scene. Major, come up with an attack plan. I want a Cougar and two Bisons for follow-up. No rookies please. We'll hit that place at daybreak. If anybody wants me, I will be with my wife for the next few hours."

"Good morning, my love," Paul said, walking into Emily's room and kissing her on the forehead. "The doctor tells me you are giving him a bad time."

"I am fine," Emily said, a little perturbed. "Women have been giving birth for thousands of years. This is nothing new. I have a broken arm and some bruises, so other than a little discomfort, I am fine."

"Do you have any headaches?" Paul asked.

"I do not have a concussion," Emily said. "And Elizabeth would do better if she were with me and not in that nursery."

Paul looked at his own doctor, not the Israeli doctor. She nodded in agreement with Emily. "As soon as the paperwork is done, you'll be out of here," Paul told her, "but you'll only go to camp. You will not be in command of a Bison or Cougar at this point." Paul directed orders to the doctors. "Doctors, please set in motion the release of the lieutenant and her daughter." He turned back to Emily. "My love, work out the details with the docs here. I have to go."

They kissed, and Emily had trouble letting him go. Reluctantly she let him loose and watched him walk out of the room. He went without his usual swagger. He pulled in his neck and squared his shoulders, walking with purpose. The regiment's doctor stopped him in the hallway.

"I will be returning to our base with our people," the regiment's doctor said to Paul. "I assume I can expect more casualties shortly."

"Expect the worst, and hope for the best," Paul said. "As soon as we have better intel, we can plan operations, Doc. I'll let you know."

"Morning, Paul," his sergeant said. "Mossad just dropped off new intel on the people they're watching, and the Saudis dropped a street map and some more intel about another group on the other side of town. I'm working up more detailed maps for that area and sent a couple lads to check it out."

"Do you have any numbers of bad guys?" Paul asked.

"The Saudis think there are about fifteen or so," the sergeant answered. "They also said nobody suspects the bad guys are where they are and that security in their compound is lax."

"Arafat has given us nothing?" Paul asked.

"No, nothing but BS about looking hard and not finding anything out," said the sergeant.

"I thought as much." Paul looked at the street map with the location marked on it.

"Task three Bisons and a Cougar for that location," Paul said. "Pick some good crews for me, and get them ready to go. I want to hit both targets at the same time. When will the rest of the team be here?"

"In a couple hours, Paul," the sergeant replied. "The Israelis gave us a flat-black Huey and want to know if we need pilots. I told them no, and our ground crew is going over it with a fine-tooth comb as we speak."

"Send all the groups here for a meeting at twenty-two hundred," Paul ordered. "I want to hit the bad guys at daybreak."

"Jeez, Paul, I can't leave you alone for two minutes without you getting into trouble," George said the next day, hugging Paul tightly. "Is Emily OK? You're a new papa! Congrats. Aunt Susan is pleased."

"I wish this reunion were under better circumstances," Paul said. "We have the group responsible located and isolated. I want you to command the air assault, and I'll take the other target on the ground. You have two Hueys, two Bisons, and a Cougar. The sergeant here will run you over to your target for a quick look, and then I want you to brief your people and be ready to brief the rest of us at twenty-two hundred local time. If it all works out, our assault teams will hit the bad guys at daybreak tomorrow."

"Right, Sergeant, off we go then," George said.

"External Affairs is on line three, Paul," said the corporal minding the phone.

"Look, Paul," said the consular person on the other end of the line, "a rapid-response team is being dispatched to handle this situation. We are working hard with Hammas and the Israelis to locate the people responsible for the attack on your people. The Israelis gave us permission to join them once they find them."

The rapid-response team was made up of Royal Canadian Mounted Police antiterrorism people, who were more similar to police than soldiers and operated like it. "When will the Mounties arrive?" Paul asked.

"The soonest they can get here is next Wednesday," the diplomat said. "External Affairs had to get clearance from the Israelis and our own minister, plus we had to requisition a Hercules for them and arrange passports, visas, and the like."

"Thanks, keep me posted." Paul hung up and shook his head. "Sending me some Mounties next bloody Wednesday. Yo, Corporal, coffee would be good."

"Major Bekenbaum will tell us his air-assault plan," Paul said to the assembled group. "George, if you please."

"Once the Bisons and Cougar have blocked the streets at each end of the targets' locations, they will radio us." George pointed to the map on the wall. "We will rotate no more than one minute away. Once we receive the go, we will assault the open courtyard here. The first group will set up a safe perimeter for the second Huey. Once the ground-assault people see us, they are to proceed directly to the house holding the bad guys, with the Cougar right in front of the house and the Bisons to either side of the house. Half of those who dismount from the Bisons are to take up positions on each side of the street. The rest will follow the Cougar's dismounts, who will hopefully blow the gates to the courtyard. Anything that moves or shows a weapon is to be taken out. Once my air people are inside, they will search out targets of opportunity, destroy radio equipment, and put explosive charges on any ammunition and weapons we find. We want a prisoner or two, if possible, but not if it puts us in jeopardy. Gather up any papers, documents, or pictures—anything that even remotely looks important. We'll sort it all out later. Paul?"

"My people," Paul said, "will be in position three blocks away from our target. Once George's group is given the go, we'll go too. I want one Bison to block the ends of each street and the others to park in the front and rear of the target house, with heavy weapons ready to give support and half the dismounts providing security. One Cougar will smash the front gate, and one will smash the rear. We also will take out any target that shows itself at any point. This is a punishment raid, not a police raid. Our information is that these people are the upper echelon of the leadership for this insurgent cell. Prisoners will be nice but not necessary. The important thing is to get in, hit them extremely hard, grab any papers you find, and get the hell out with few, if any, casualties. Captain, will our mortars be sighted in if we need them?"

"Yes, Master Warrant," the air-force captain said, his holier-than-thou attitude drastically changed from ten months earlier. "I have it on good authority that some Israeli gunships and Mirages may come by to check out the firefight if asked."

"Make sure you hear from us first," Paul said. "Nothing will ruin your day more than having a two-hundred-pound bomb or three-point-five rocket hit you in the ass. Everybody will wear black battle dress without name badges or markings. Let the press figure out who we are if they can. The choppers are black, but what about ground vehicles?"

"The vehicles are all painted black, Mr. Bekenbaum," assured the maintenance warrant officer. "They don't have any numbers or ID marks showing, inside or out. We have modified a wash bay to repaint them white once you get back."

"Good job," said Paul. "I didn't think about repainting them. Pilots, I want one Huey to circle and provide air cover over each target for as long as it can. Once both assault teams break off, head back to base. George, split your people among the ground vehicles to exit." Paul made the sign of the cross and went to one knee. "In the name of the Father, the Son, and the Holy Ghost, please watch over my troopers tomorrow. If it is your will, allow us all to reach home without harm. Amen. OK, dismissed. Get some sleep, and we'll assemble at oh four hundred."

The vehicle park was a hub of activity. Troopers in black uniforms loaded weapons onto vehicles and performed radio checks. Some smoked last cigarettes and conversed with troopers from other sections, while others sat in hatches or inside the vehicles. Paul waved an arm over his head, and vehicles throughout the lot started their engines. Troopers tossed cigarettes and loaded into them. Paul stepped into his Cougar and made his way to the commander's position, seeing the vehicle's electronics come alive as he passed. This would be a dark-com mission until all the vehicles were ready. Once Paul's team was in place, he would radio the helicopters to signal the air assault. All would become dark again until extraction time.

Paul resumed the loose-knee sway he had perfected after hundreds of hours inside an armoured vehicle and fed a fresh magazine into the C9 mounted outside his open hatch, while the gunner fed the twenty-millimetre and then the C9 mounted coaxially to it in the turret. The dismounts charged their C7s and grenade launchers, and Paul made sure his were loaded as well. As the force commander, he would not enter the target building. He would direct and supervise the assault. His team had the farthest to go before splitting up, going down separate streets as they drew near the target until finally coming to a stop two blocks away.

Paul picked up his microphone and said, "Tango One."

"Tango Two," came a quiet voice over his headphones.

"Tango Three," George said, with chopper noise in the background. "Tallyho, good hunting, boys. Target in site…engaging."

"Go, go, go," Paul yelled, kicking his driver on the shoulder. The Cougar leaped into action, flying down the street and coming to a screeching halt in front of the target building. As the dismounts ran out of the vehicle, its turret swung, and the twenty-millimetre cannon roared into life, smashing the courtyard's gate to splinters before the Bisons fully stopped.

Paul started his stopwatch and charged his machine gun, slowly swinging it up and down and left and right, matching his eye movements. The turret and twenty-millimetre cannon did the same. Seconds later, gunfire erupted inside the building as Paul's troopers eliminated targets. A short time later, a Huey thundered around and over the building, adding a blinding searchlight and thunderous noise to the neighborhood. The firing stopped, and soon troopers escorted—or dragged—two prisoners to the waiting Bisons. They tossed them inside, none too gently. Men with heavy bags stuffed full of papers followed the men with the prisoners. The officer in charge ran out and signaled to Paul that he was the last to leave.

"Tango One, disengaging," Paul said as the officer drove into his Bison. All the troopers on perimeter duty charged back into their vehicles and secured their loading ramps. The vehicles took off, with spinning tires and roaring engines. Their lights lit up the road as if it were daylight.

"Air Two, engaging," a voice said over Paul's headphones. The machine gun mounted on the Huey's left door opened up, and an explosion and ball of fire let everyone know the target had been eliminated.

"Tango Two and Three, RTB," George's team said, instructing them to return to base.

Paul looked at his stopwatch. It had only been twenty minutes, and the regiment took out two cells of the insurgents' best trained and armed people and their leadership. The vehicles were back at the base and going through the high-pressure car wash to remove the black paint before the sun was over the horizon.

"Just in time for the nightly news," Emily said, kissing Paul on the cheek as he entered the operations room. "The phones are already ringing from the BBC and *American Press*. The UN called and wants us to send two sections to have a look at the buildings. Your father is on his way from the airport."

"Schedule a press conference for an hour from now," Paul ordered. "As you seem to insist on being at the center of things, you can handle it. 'The regiment has no knowledge of what just happened. We are appalled at the destruction and saddened at the loss of life...blah, blah.'"

"Can I talk about our casualties from a couple days ago?" Emily asked.

"It's up to you," Paul said. "The families back home have been informed. Be on that plane my father came in on when it leaves, and I want it out of here ASAP. Go and write your PR material. I have to debrief my people."

Paul waited until all the troopers were seated and had their balaclavas pushed back, leaving their faces clear. They all had steaming-hot cups of coffee and glowed with satisfaction of completing a successful mission.

"OK, settle down," Paul said. "The international press will be here in an hour. I want all of you out of those uniforms and far away by the time they get here. Major Bekenbaum, please start."

"Yes, Master Warrant," George said, standing and pulling a notebook from his breast pocket. "At my target, thirty-two people are dead, and we have one wounded prisoner. We found a large cache of small arms and ammunition, as well as RPGs similar to the one from the attack. There was a large amount of explosives and bomb-making materials but little in the way of documentation or paper. We grabbed some RPGs and a few other weapons and torched the building to destroy it and the rest of the weapons and explosives. The prisoner is female, as were about a quarter of the dead, and they were definitely ready to take part in the fighting. We have no KIA or wounded on our side."

"Thank you, Major," Paul said. "Captain?"

"Yes, Master Warrant," said the captain who had led Paul's assault. "We have eighteen dead and two prisoners, about evenly matched female to male. We found normal small arms for defence—no explosives but a large number of files and paperwork. We believe this was the leadership of this group of insurgents. No one was KIA, and there aren't any casualties in our assault team, Master Warrant."

"Speak for yourself," joked a female trooper halfway back in the crowd. "Do you know how hard it is going to be to get my hair to its normal glamorous self? And how about my nails? Why, it will take weeks to get them back in shape."

"You're just like your mother, Heidi," Nicolas said from the doorway. "Always bitchin' about how hard done by you are."

"I was going to report this horrible treatment to the colonel," Heidi said, grinning, "but now that the general is here, I don't have to."

Nicolas walked up and stood beside Paul in front of the troopers. "Sounds like this was a successful raid, as is our tradition," Nicolas said. "We have dealt out punishment to those who have done us harm, and we have dealt them a serious setback. Well done, everyone."

"As far as the prisoners are concerned," Paul added, "keep the lights on in their cells twenty-four seven. Keep them in isolation. No one talk to them, and handle them in black uniform with your faces covered. Give them food and water every four hours. When we think it is time, we will have a chat with them. All rise." Paul made the sign of the cross and thanked God for allowing them to return from the mission unharmed, and then he dismissed the troops.

"Good job, Paul." Nicolas shook his and George's hands. "You too, George. Who's handling the press conference?"

"Emily," Paul said. "It is her job, after all. Before you give me any static, I almost had to tie her down to keep her from coming on the raid."

"Yeah, the doctor briefed me on the way down here," Nicolas said. "Emily will be on that plane with me when I leave this afternoon?"

"Yes, sir, along with your new granddaughter," Paul said.

"Your mother is anxious about that," Nicolas said, "but not as anxious as my mother."

"I'll bet Tatiana wanted to grab a rifle and head down here," George said, and they all laughed, mostly because it was true.

"We got lucky, Pop," Paul said. "We never thought about fighting with the Cougars and Bisons in an urban environment. We should experiment with some better lightweight armour."

"It's always been a trade-off," Nicolas said. "We are a scout regiment, not an armoured regiment. We need speed and maneuverability, which come at the expense of armour, but go ahead and investigate. We were wondering whether the Syrians or someone else would hit us soon. You are due to rotate out of here in two months, and they would like to tell their followers we are leaving because we are scared. Now they have to rebuild. Turn the papers and prisoners over to the Israelis once we have what we need from them. George, you owe me a beer. Then I want to see my granddaughter, and then I want a bed. I meet with King Hussein tomorrow morning."

Paul watched Nicolas and George leave the operations room for the barracks. He went into his office and stripped off his weapons and black uniform, replacing them with his normal base uniform. He glanced at his watch, walked over to the briefing area, and leaned against the back wall as Emily began the briefing. "Two weeks ago, while en route to conduct a humanitarian medical mission, some of our regiment's troops were ambushed in a cowardly attack that killed two unarmed civilians and wounded thirty others. Six troopers, including myself, were wounded—two severely, with loss of limbs—and our vehicle was totaled," Emily announced. "At this point we are waiting for the Israelis and Palestinians to finish their investigations as to the identities of these people who carried out this cowardly attack and decide how they are going to apprehend them. That is all we know at this point. Are there any questions?"

"Do you have any idea who was responsible for the attacks this morning?" an American asked.

"We are just as mystified as you are," Emily answered.

"Surely you must know something, if you weren't involved yourselves," a British reporter commented.

"While I can say the regiment and Canadian government are displeased by the attack on our troopers, you all know we are here operating as UN peacekeepers on the Golan Heights. Other than providing voluntary humanitarian efforts in town, we have no mandate to pursue operations outside the Golan Heights area," Emily answered.

"What about reports we are hearing about the deployment of the RCMP rapid-response team to the area?" asked a man with a CBC logo on his jacket.

"As far as I know, External Affairs has told us that if they come, it will be in a week's time, and they will be here only to assist the local authorities," Emily said.

"You keep referring to the attackers as cowards," said another American. "Are they not trying to free themselves from the Israeli overlords, and therefore, shouldn't they be called *freedom fighters?*"

"I know this is your first war assignment, Chuck," Emily said, "but surely you can't be naïve enough to call these cowards *freedom fighters*. They could have hit us anywhere along the route to the town. There are plenty of places to make an attack from cover, but they chose to do it in the center of town to maximise damage to civilians. These are the same people who burn down schools and medical clinics, who throw acid in little girls' faces for daring to go to school. No, they are not freedom fighters. They are cowards and bullies who prey on the weak. Maybe if you were not too scared, you would actually go down to the villages and talk to the people instead of relying on Israeli and Hammas propaganda."

"Congratulations on your baby," a female Australian reporter said. "Did you name her Elizabeth after the queen?"

"Thank you," Emily said, her smile returning. "No, Elizabeth Susan is named after her great-great-grandmother, who gave birth on a battlefield, and her great-great-aunt, who was born on a battlefield, as my baby was."

"We have reports that playing cards with the regiment's crest on them were found on the dead bodies in the attacked buildings this morning," the Australian said. "Do you care to comment?"

"I don't know what to tell you," Emily said. "We hand out a lot of card decks to a lot of people. If, as all of you are hinting, this was a raid on those who attacked us, I congratulate those who conducted the raid. Would we have liked to conduct an operation of that type on those who attacked us? Certainly. But as I said, neither the UN nor the Canadian government authorised us to carry out operations outside the Golan region."

"What about reports of vehicles leaving and returning to your base before and after the attacks occurred?" the BBC man asked.

"Are you kidding me?" Emily asked. "We send out and retrieve patrols from this base all the time. We have to monitor the DMZ. That's what we are here for. If this is where this conference is headed, I'm calling it a day. I'm tired, hungry, and sore, and my daughter needs me. Good day, everyone."

The next day, as Emily expected, the headlines were about her and her daughter and the innocent civilians in the line of fire. Two months later, Paul and the remaining members of the regiment boarded the last Hercules after supervising the loading of their equipment onto freight aircraft. Paul found a seat up front in the packed aircraft. Most of the troops were goofing around, glad to be going home and he joked back as he made his way up the aisle. They would only be stopping in Greenland to change pilots; the plane would refuel in the air for most of the trip. Even so, it was going to be a long, noisy twenty-hour trip.

It was not until they had reached European airspace that Paul began to relax. The last few days had been hectic. Showing his replacement form the Royal Twenty-Second battalion that was replacing them the ropes. Handling all the paper work for turning over vehicles, heavy equipment, and radio equipment to their replacements. New equipment from the Department of National Defense would replace the ones left behind which had been from the EBBs' own equipment stocks. Paul soon found the dull thrumming of the engines making him drowsy, and it was not until the aircraft loadmaster tapped him on the shoulder just before landing in Greenland that he woke up.

They had to wait two hours in Greenland while the Hercules was refueled and maintained. None of them were ready for the cold temperature at the airport, even though it was summer. All of them were laughing at themselves, buttoning up jackets, and rolling down sleeves. If they were cold now, wait until January when it really was cold.

Airborne once again, most everyone, including Paul, fell back asleep again. Even in the uncomfortable and noisy airplane, this was the first time in a year that most of them felt almost completely safe. Nobody would be shooting at them at least.

His internal clock woke Paul up before the loadmaster came up to him. He was looking out one of the windows and watched a large city pass beneath them.

"We've got about half an hour," the loadmaster said. "They've lengthened the runway at Olds long enough for us to fit. We'll start descending shortly."

"Wakey, Wakey, sleeping beauties, this is your pilot speaking," bellowed out of the intercom speaker just forward of Paul. "We have just flown over Edmonton and should be arriving at your destination in half an hour. Local time is sixteen thirty-five. It's a nice sunny day and a balmy twenty-five degrees. I can almost smell the barbeque beef already. We thank you for flying DND Air and hope not to see you anytime soon."

The noise level increased as excited troopers started talking and checking the duffle bags stashed so long ago under their seats. Paul kept his emotions in check. He still had to supervise the unloading and dismissal of the troops and then go to the base, check in and drop off the paperwork. It would probably be dark by the time he finally reached home.

Hydraulic whining told of the flaps engaging, then thumps on the floor as the landing gear came down. They might have lengthened the runway, but the steep angle they were coming in at suggested it was still short. The pilot touched down hard and then kicked in the reverse thrust of the engines immediately, causing all of them to fall forward to the limit of the seat-belt travel. Slowed enough, the engines note lowered as the reverse thrust was removed and the engines throttled back. The left engine cut out completely as they swung onto the taxiway leading to the hangar area.

Then cheers as they stopped moving, troopers hugging and patting shoulders. They had once again returned safe at home. Paul grabbed his duffle bag and briefcase from under his seat and made his way past the cheering and laughing troopers to the rear loading ramp as did all of the officers. Then he grabbed the mic at the rear.

"All right you bums! Settle down! I have been told we have people waiting for us out there. You come out of this aircraft in order and acting like soldiers! Is the clear!" Paul let the bedlam subside. "Form up in your sections and companies to right and left of the loading ramp behind your officers! Everybody up!"

The troopers stood, straightened out their uniforms as good as they could, and had duffle bags ready to hoist on a shoulder. Then Paul hit the button that opened the large rear door and loading ramp. The officers came out first and deployed to the rear and both sides of the airplane. Then the troops jogged down the ramp and joined their formation positions. Paul looked out at the large crowd of friends and relatives waiting for them, hoping the troops would keep it together for just a little longer. As the last trooper passed him, he turned to the load master.

"Thanks, Master Sergeant," Paul said shaking the man's hand. "Hope we didn't cause you too much trouble."

"Hell, no, Master Warrant," he replied. "You guys slept most of the way. Easy duty this trip. Nobody shooting at us for once."

Paul walked out of the aircraft with his duffle over his left shoulder, briefcase on top and made his way across the formation receiving reports from each company commander as he passed them. He crashed to a halt in front of the colonel and saluted.

"Sir! Battalion all present or accounted for, Sir!"

"Carry on, Master Warrant," the colonel said a little louder than normal conversation. He was just as anxious as the troops to get gone.

"Get ready to duck and cover, Colonel," Paul said in a stage whisper with a small grin on his face.

Then he took two steps back, saluted again, and came to attention.

"'Tallion! 'Tension! 'Tallion! Dismissed!" Paul bellowed and bedlam erupted.

Ordered lines of troopers disappeared as troopers rushed the bystanders, many of whom were rushing them as well. Wives and kids hugging fathers or mothers, husbands or wives who they had not seen for a year. Now alone where the formation had just stood, Paul waved back at the aircrew that had come out to watch, shrugged his duffle to get a better grip, and started walking toward the parking lot, hoping somebody would give him a lift. He made his way through the crowd, receiving handshakes and thumps on the back as he passed people he knew, and then he was in the parking lot looking around.

A young woman holding a child turned her back to him and reached in the open driver's window of a red Mustang and laid on the horn. Then reached in further and cranked up the radio. Paul dropped his gear and started sprinting as soon as he heard "Fun, Fun, Fun" blasting out of the car. Emily had just enough time to turn around, and he had his arms around her.

"Maybe now we can go on a proper honeymoon," she said breathlessly, as they came up for air. "And you're paying, Mr. Cheap."

AUTHOR'S NOTES

My father was a ham-radio operator, and few people know that these amateurs can and will be called on to provide communication services during emergency situations. One such instance for my father was during the Cuban Missile Crisis in 1962. Beginning in August of that year, my father and his buddies spent every weekend on a remote military base in the woods of Alberta. For two weeks in October, my mother and I didn't see him at all. So for us, the crisis was all very, very real.

Canada was at the forefront of UN peacekeeping efforts right from the start of those efforts. My mother's brother was a member of 2PPCLI and did his first tour during the Suez Crisis and then a number of tours in Cyprus. Unlike the policies of our neighbors to the south, if the Canadian government does not wish something to be published or made public knowledge, it will not be. While I have no proof Canada was involved in Yemen or Chad, that does not mean Canadian troops were absent. Canada also sends members of its military to train with other countries. A second cousin of mine, while serving with 1PPCLI, was attached to the US Marines and awarded the Bronze Star Medal and two Purple Hearts while serving in Vietnam.

For purposes of brevity, I have combined the Yom Kippur and Seven-Day Wars into one fictional conflict. Canada did and still does send peacekeepers and observers to the Golan Heights.

As part of its NATO commitment, Canada provides military training facilities for other NATO members. Three are in Alberta. Suffield Weapons Range, in the eastern part of the province, is in the heart of the dry desert like prairie and is used by armoured regiments to train, as the terrain is similar to that found on the steppes of Russia. Camp Weinright is located in northern central Alberta. This area is favoured by the German Army, as it is heavily forested. On Alberta's northeastern edge, Cold Lake Air Weapons Range is the largest area in North America reserved exclusively for air-combat training. The American cruise-missile program used this range to test its devices, and two large air-combat training exercises that involve every nation in NATO are conducted there annually.

I have even witnessed vehicles of Russian manufacture with Georgian national markings on them transiting from Weinright to Suffield. Residents of Medicine Hat are no strangers to British soldiers as the UK has a full battalion of armoured troops stationed at Suffield at all times for training.

The countries, troops, and aircrews who use these bases love them. Because of their remote locations and lack of civilians around, the troops can experience the thrills of actual combat conditions and firing live ammunition without complaints from local inhabitants. Deer and bears don't complain much.

It has been said that behind every story is a kernel of truth. This one is no different. I began writing this edition of the Bears and Eagles saga in spring 2013 at my home in a small community just east of Calgary, Canada, where I lived with my wife, Marg. In May, Marg and I decided for a number of reasons that it was time to move, and we put up for sale the place we had spent the last twenty-five years of our lives. Except for a few stolen moments at work each day, my writing came to a halt. By the end of July, we had sold our old house, found and bought our new home just east of Didsbury, and moved in. It was a hectic, stressful time for all.

That winter I resumed writing, and by March I was almost finished. Then my dear lady and her cousin shanghaied me off to Las Vegas. It was the first time my wife and I had been to Vegas. Like many long-married couples, we had experienced many ups and downs, but none were more frustrating than our recent move to our new home, which at several times came to the brink of ending our relationship. The trip put a new vigor back into our lives, and for the first time in many years, my wife and I held hands once again when we walked down the street.

I started the editing phase of the Bears and Eagles series while in Vegas. All the books' contents were scattered and broken up into many different files. It was more than a year since I had looked at the first book's files. My lady and her cousin gave me input on the female elements, such as what kind of clothing a character might wear to a party (I really am kind of a guys' guy), and I spent my spare time putting the first book together.

While writing this series, I thought back to when my wife and I had first met forty years earlier and allowed myself to experience the feelings I had back then. This is the basis for all of my male hero's feelings in these stories. My lady and I became closer on that trip to Vegas, and things changed for the better. But at the end of March, Marg became very ill. By the end of October, the love of my life and reason for being for over forty years was gone. Up until the last day, she was coherent, and her bubbly personality, fierce love for her family, and concern for us were ever evident. Unlike most people in this day and age, she chose to have quality of life instead of extending her life. She forewent chemotherapy, which at best would have prolonged her life by only six months. She also chose to spend her last days at home instead of in a hospice or hospital, and she was right about both decisions. At times during the last months of her life, it felt as if we were dating again.

Marg always wanted to ride horseback after I brought Barney to our acreage many years ago. At that time, Barney was five. He was a registered standardbred I had rescued. He had been "rough broke" and had worked herding cattle at a local feed lot. He was somewhat easily spooked and definitely not a beginner's horse. Marg, at five foot one, barely cleared the top of his back when she stood beside him. I found another standardbred for her. Buster was well over twenty years old and very docile, but I still could not teach Marg to ride. I have been around horses most of my life, and my mom tells me I was bucked off my first horse when I was two. I just get on a horse and ride. I couldn't teach her how.

Slowly Marg overcame her fear of this large beast—Buster was over sixteen hands tall—and she was doing well. She and I were even able to gallop the quarter mile down the side of our property without any wrecks, but one day the inevitable happened. We were walking home, and a partridge exploded from right under the nose of Marg's horse, who then exploded in the opposite direction and threw poor Marg to the ground. So there I was, trying to control Barney, grabbing hold of Buster and calming him down, and attempting to ascertain whether Marg's screaming meant she was actually hurt or just scared. After a few minutes, the horses and Marg settled down. Even though the last thing she wanted was to get back on old Buster, I convinced her.

Our oldest son took a photo when she came back into the corral. In the photograph she has a bloodstain down the middle of her shirt from a bloody nose, but she is sitting square in the saddle, both hands on the rein and fierce determination on her face.

At times Marg had to be coaxed to confront her fears, but eventually she always faced them head-on and laughed about them later. Most people she met liked her. She was bubbly, friendly, and an excellent listener (unless she was listening to me). She loved her boys and me to distraction, and we miss her deeply. She is the basis of all the love interests in this series.

Margarete Maria Belenczuk Wollbaum
January 1955–October 2014
Have I told you lately how much I love you?

ALSO BY R.P. WOLLBAUM

Bears and Eagles
Eagles Claw
Eagles Talon
As Eagles Swarm   *A historically astute and powerful account of a world fractured by war.* Kircus Reviews

Made in the USA
Columbia, SC
15 June 2017